Mother Earth:
And Other Stories

Isaac Asimov was born in Russia near Smolensk in 1920. He was brought to the United States by his parents three years later and grew up in Brooklyn. He graduated from Columbia University in chemistry and after a short spell in the Army, gained his doctorate in 1949 and qualified as an instructor in biochemistry at Boston University School of Medicine, where he became Associate Professor in 1955. He retired to full-time authorship in 1958 while retaining his connection with the University. His first story 'Marooned Off Vesta' appeared in 1939 in *Amazing Stories*. Asimov became a regular contributor to the leading SF magazines of the day including Astounding, *Astonishing Stories*, *Super Science Stories* and *Galaxy*. He won the Hugo Award four times and the Nebula Award once. With nearly five hundred books to his credit and several hundred articles, Asimov's output was prolific by any standards.

Isaac Asimov died in 1992 at the age of 72.

BY THE SAME AUTHOR

ROBOT STORIES AND NOVELS
I, Robot
The Rest of the Robots
The Complete Robot
The Caves of Steel
The Naked Sun
The Robots of Dawn
Robots and Empire

THE GALACTIC EMPIRE NOVELS
The Currents of Space
The Stars, Like Dust
Pebble in the Sky

The End of Eternity

THE FOUNDATION SAGA
Prelude to Foundation
Forward the Foundation
Foundation
Foundation and Empire
Second Foundation
Foundation's Edge
Foundation and Earth

SHORT STORY COLLECTIONS
The Complete Stories:
Living Space: And Other Stories
Nightfall: And Other Stories
The Martian Way: And Other Stories
The Bicentennial Man: And Other Stories
Ring Around the Sun: And Other Stories
Gold: The Final Science Fiction Collection
Magic: The Final Fantasy Collection

ISAAC ASIMOV

Mother Earth: And Other Stories

THE COMPLETE STORIES

HARPER
Voyager

Harper*Voyager*
An imprint of HarperCollins*Publishers* Ltd
1 London Bridge Street
London SE1 9GF

www.harpercollins.co.uk

HarperCollins*Publishers*
Macken House, 39/40 Mayor Street Upper
Dublin 1, D01 C9W8, Ireland

This paperback edition 2024
1

Copyright © Asimov Holdings, LLC 2024
Individual story copyright details appear on page 369

Isaac Asimov asserts the moral right to
be identified as the author of this work.

A catalogue record for this book is available from the British Library.

ISBN: 978-0-00-867247-8

This collection is entirely a work of fiction. It is presented in its original form and may depict ethnic, racial and sexual prejudices that were commonplace at the time it was written. The names, characters and incidents portrayed are the work of the author's imagination, and any resemblance to actual persons, living or dead, events or localities is entirely coincidental.

This book is set in Janson Text LT Std by HarperCollins*Publishers* India

Printed and bound in the UK using 100% Renewable
Electricity at CPI Group (UK) Ltd

All rights reserved. No part of this publication may be reproduced, transmitted, downloaded, decompiled, reverse engineered, or stored in or introduced into any information storage and retrieval system, in any form or by any means, whether electronic or mechanical, without the express written permission of the publishers

This book contains FSC™ certified paper and other controlled
sources to ensure responsible forest management.

For more information visit: www.harpercollins.co.uk/green

Contents

The Prime of Life	1
Mother Earth	3
Darwinian Pool Room	47
Shah Guido G.	55
Button, Button	67
Everest	83
The Pause	89
Let's Not	103
Youth	107
Sucker Bait	139
What's in a Name?	211
The Dust of Death	231
Blank!	245
Silly Asses	251
Buy Jupiter	253
Author! Author!	259
The Proper Study	291
Waterclap	299
2430 AD	335
Thiotimoline to the Stars	345

The Winnowing	355
Birth of a Notion	363
Copyright information	369

The Prime of Life

It was, in truth, an eager youth
    Who halted me one day.
He gazed in bliss at me, and this
    Is what he had to say:

'Why, mazel tov, it's Asimov,
    A blessing on your head!
For many a year, I've lived in fear
    That you were long since dead.

Or if alive, one fifty-five
    Cold years had passed you by,
And left you weak, with poor physique,
    Thin hair and rheumy eye.

For sure enough, I've read your stuff
    Since I was but a lad
And couldn't spell or hardly tell
    The good yarns from the bad.

My father, too, was reading you
    Before he met my Ma.
For you he yearned, once he had learned
    About you from *his* Pa.

Since time began, you wondrous man,
    My ancestors did love
That s.f. dean and writing machine
    The aged Asimov.'

I'd had my fill. I said, 'Be still!
    I've kept my old-time spark.
My step is light, my eye is bright,
    My hair is thick and dark.'

His smile, in brief, spelled disbelief,
    So this is what I did;
I scowled, you know, and with one blow,
    I killed that rotten kid.

Mother Earth

'But can you be certain? Are you sure that even a professional historian can always distinguish between victory and defeat?'

Gustav Stein, who delivered himself of that mocking question with a whiskered smile and a gentle wipe at the gray mustache from the neighborhood of which he had just removed an empty glass, was not an historian. He was a physiologist.

But his companion *was* an historian, and he accepted the gentle thrust with a smile of his own.

Stein's apartment was, for Earth, quite luxurious. It lacked the empty privacy of the Outer Worlds, of course, since from its window there stretched outward a phenomenon that belonged only to the home planet – a city. A large city, full of people, rubbing shoulders, mingling sweat—

Nor was Stein's apartment fitted with its own power and its own utility supply. It lacked even the most elementary quota of positronic robots. In short, it lacked the dignity of self-sufficiency, and like all things on Earth, it was merely part of a community, a pendant unit of a cluster, a portion of a mob.

But Stein was an Earthman by birth and used to it. And after all, by Earth standards the apartment was still luxurious.

It was just that looking outward through the same windows before which lay the city, one could see the stars and among them the Outer Worlds, where there were no cities but only gardens; where the lawns were streaks of emerald, where all human beings were kings, and where all good Earthmen earnestly and vainly hoped to go some day.

Except for a few who knew better – like Gustav Stein.

The Friday evenings with Edward Field belonged to that class of ritual which comes with age and quiet life. It broke the week pleasantly for two elderly bachelors, and gave them an innocuous reason to linger over the sherry and the stars. It took them away from the crudities of life, and, most of all, it let them talk.

Field, especially, as a lecturer, scholar and man of modest means quoted chapter and verse from his still uncompleted history of Terrestrian Empire.

'I wait for the last act,' he explained. 'Then I can call it the "Decline and Fall of Empire" and publish it.'

'You must expect the last act to come soon, then.'

'In a sense, it has come already. It is just that it is best to wait for all to recognize that fact. You see, there are three times when an Empire or an Economic System or a Social Institution falls, you skeptic—'

Field paused for effect and waited patiently for Stein to say, 'And those times are?'

'First,' Field ticked off a right forefinger, 'there is the time when just a little nub shows up that points an inexorable way to finality. It can't be seen or recognized until the finality arrives, when the original nub becomes visible to hindsight.'

'And you can tell what that little nub is?'

'I think so, since I already have the advantage of a century and a half of hindsight. It came when the Sirian sector colony, Aurora, first obtained permission of the Central Government at Earth to introduce positronic robots into their community life. Obviously, looking back at it, the road was clear for the development of a thoroughly mechanized society based upon robot labor and not human labor. And it is this mechanization that has been and will yet be the deciding factor in the struggle between the Outer Worlds and Earth.'

'It is?' murmured the physiologist. 'How infernally clever you historians are. What and where is the second time the Empire fell?'

'The second point in time,' and Field gently bent his right middle finger backward, 'arrives when a signpost is raised for the expert so large and plain that it can be seen even without the aid of perspective. And that point has been passed, too, with the first establishment of an immigration quota against Earth by the Outer Worlds. The fact that Earth found itself unable to prevent an action so obviously detrimental to itself was a shout for all to hear, and that was fifty years ago.'

'Better and better. And the third point?'

'The third point?' Down went the ring finger. 'That is the least important. That is when the signpost becomes a wall with a huge "The End" scrawled upon it. The only requirement for knowing that the end has come, then, is neither perspective nor training, but merely the ability to listen to the video.'

'I take it that the third point in time has not yet come.'

'Obviously not, or you would not need to ask. Yet it may come soon; for instance, if there is war.'

'Do you think there will be?'

Field avoided commitment. 'Times are unsettled, and a good deal of futile emotion is sweeping Earth on the immigration question. And if there should be a war, Earth would be defeated quickly and lastingly, and the wall would be erected.'

'Can you be certain? Are you sure that even a professional historian can always distinguish between victory and defeat?'

Field smiled. He said: 'You may know something I do not. For instance, they talk about something called the "Pacific Project".'

'I never heard of it.' Stein refilled the two glasses, 'Let us speak of other things.'

He held up his glass to the broad window so that the far stars flickered rosily in the clear liquid and said: 'To a happy ending to Earth's troubles.'

Field held up his own, 'To the Pacific Project.'

Stein sipped gently and said: 'But we drink to two different things.'

'Do we?'

It is quite difficult to describe any of the Outer Worlds to a native Earthman, since it is not so much a description of a world that is required as a description of a state of mind. The Outer Worlds – some fifty of them, orginally colonies, later dominions, later nations – differ extremely among themselves in a physical sense. But the state of mind is somewhat the same throughout.

It is something that grows out of a world not originally congenial to mankind, yet populated by the cream of the difficult, the different, the daring, the deviant.

If it is to be expressed in a word, that word is 'individuality.'

There is the world of Aurora, for instance, three parsecs from Earth. It was the first planet settled outside the Solar System, and represented the dawn of interstellar travel. Hence its name.

It had air and water to start with, perhaps, but on Earthly standards it was rocky and infertile. The plant life that did exist, sustained by a yellow-green pigment completely umelated to chlorophyll and not as efficient, gave the comparatively fertile regions a decidedly bilious and unpleasant appearance to unaccustomed eyes. No animal life higher than unicellular, and the equivalent of bacteria as well, were present. Nothing dangerous, naturally, since the two biological systems, of Earth and Aurora, were chemically unrelated.

Aurora became, quite gradually, a patchwork. Grains and fruit trees came first; shrubs, flowers, and grass afterward. Herds of livestock followed. And, as if it were necessary to prevent too close a copy of the mother planet, positronic robots also came to build the mansions, carve the landscapes, lay the power units. In short, to do the work, and turn the planet green and human.

There was the luxury of a new world and unlimited mineral resources. There was the splendid excess of atomic power laid out on new foundations with merely thousands, or, at most, millions, not billions, to service. There was the vast flowering of physical science, in worlds where there was room for it.

Take the home of Franklin Maynard, for instance, who, with his wife, three children, and twenty-seven robots, lived on an estate more than forty miles away, in distance, from the nearest neighbor. Yet by community-wave he could, if he wished, share the living room of any of the seventy-five million on Aurora – with each singly; with all simultaneously.

Maynard knew every inch of his valley. He knew just where it ended, sharply, and gave way to the alien crags, along whose undesirable slopes the angular, sharp leaves of the native furze clung sullenly – as if in hatred of the softer matter that had usurped its place in the sun.

Maynard did not have to leave that valley. He was a deputy in the Gathering, and a member of the Foreign Agents Committee, but he could transact all business but the most extremely essential, by community-wave, without ever sacrificing that precious privacy he had to have in a way no Earthman could understand.

Even the present business could be performed by community-wave. The man, for instance, who sat with him in his living room, was Charles Hijkman, and he, actually, was sitting in his own living room on an island in an artificial lake stocked with fifty varieties of fish, which happened to be twenty-five hundred miles distant, in space.

The connection was an illusion, of course. If Maynard were to reach out a hand, he could feel the invisible wall.

Even the robots were quite accustomed to the paradox, and when Hijkman raised a hand for a cigarette, Maynard's robot made no move to satisfy the desire, though a half-minute passed before Hijkman's own robot could do so.

The two men spoke like Outer Worlders, that is, stiffly and in syllables too clipped to be friendly, and yet certainly not hostile. Merely undefinably lacking in the cream – however sour and thin at times – of human sociability which is so forced upon the inhabitants of Earth's ant heaps.

Maynard said: 'I have long wanted a private communion, Hijkman. My duties in the Gathering, this year—'

'Quite. That is understood. You are welcome now, of course. In fact, especially so, since I have heard of the superior nature of your grounds and landscaping. Is it true that your cattle are fed on imported grass?'

'I'm afraid that is a slight exaggeration. Actually, certain of my best milkers feed on Terrestrial imports during calving time, but such a procedure would be prohibitively expensive, I'm afraid, if made general. It yields quite extraordinary milk, however. May I have the privilege of sending you a day's output?'

'It would be most kind of you.' Hijkman bent his head, gravely. 'You must receive some of my salmon in return.'

To a Terrestrial eye, the two men might have appeared much alike. Both were tall, though not unusually so for Aurora, where the average height of the adult male is six feet one and one half inches. Both were blond and hard-muscled, with sharp and pronounced features. Though neither was younger than forty, middle-age as yet sat lightly upon them.

So much for amenities. Without a change in tone, Maynard proceeded to the serious purpose of his call.

He said: 'The Committee, you know, is now largely engaged with Moreanu and his Conservatives. We would like to deal with them firmly, we of the Independents, that is. But before we can do so with the requisite calm and certainty, I would like to ask you certain questions.'

'Why me?'

'Because you are Aurora's most important physicist.'

Modesty is an unnatural attitude, and one which is only with difficulty taught to children. In an individualistic society it is useless and Hijkman was, therefore, unencumbered with it. He simply nodded objectively at Maynard's last words.

'And,' continued Maynard, 'as one of us. You are an Independent.'

'I am a member of the Party. Dues-paying, but not very active.'

'Nevertheless safe. Now, tell me, have you heard of the Pacific Project.'

'The Pacific Project?' There was a polite inquiry in his words. 'It is something which is taking place on Earth. The Pacific is a Terrestrial ocean, but the name itself probably has no significance.'

'I have never heard of it.'

'I am not surprised. Few have, even on Earth. Our communion, by the way, is via tight-beam and nothing must go further.'

'I understand.'

'Whatever the Pacific Project is – and our agents are extremely vague – it might conceivably be a menace. Many of those who on Earth pass for scientists seem to be connected with it. Also, some of Earth's more radical and foolish politicians.'

'Hm-m-m. There was once something called the Manhattan Project.'

'Yes,' urged Maynard, 'what about it?'

'Oh, it's an ancient thing. It merely occurred to me because of the analogy in names. The Manhattan Project was before the time of extra-terrestrial travel. Some petty war in the dark ages occurred, and it was the name given to a group of scientists who developed atomic power.'

'Ah,' Maynard's hand became a fist, 'and what do you think the Pacific Project can do, then?'

Hijkman considered. Then, softly: 'Do you think Earth is planning war?'

On Maynard's face there was a sudden expression of distaste. 'Six billion people. Six billion half-apes, rather, jammed into one system to a near-explosion point, facing only some millions of us, total. Don't you think it is a dangerous situation?'

'Oh, numbers!'

'All right. Are we safe despite the numbers? Tell me. I'm only an administrator, and you're a physicist. *Can* Earth win a war in any way?'

Hijkman sat solemnly in his chair and thought carefully and slowly. Then he said: 'Let us reason. There are three broad classes of methods whereby an individual or group can gain his ends against opposition. On an increasing level of subtlety, those three classes can be termed the physical, the biological, and the psychological.

'Now, the physical can be easily eliminated. Earth does not have an industrial background. It does not have a technical know-how. It has very limited resources. It lacks even a single outstanding physical scientist. So it is as impossible as anything in the Galaxy can be that they can develop any form of physico-chemical application that is not already known to the Outer Worlds. Provided, of course, that the conditions of the problem imply single-handed opposition on the part of Earth against any or all of the Outer Worlds. I take it that none of the Outer Worlds intends leaguing with Earth against us.'

Maynard indicated violent opposition even to the suggestion, 'No, no, no. There is no question of that. Put it out of your mind.'

'Then, ordinary physical surprise weapons are inconceivable. It is useless to discuss it further.'

'Then, what about your second class, the biological?'

Slowly, Hijkman lifted his eyebrows: 'Now, that is less certain. Some Terrestrial biologists are quite competent, I am told. Naturally, since I am myself a physicist, I am not entirely qualified to judge this. Yet I believe that in certain restricted fields, they are still expert. In agricultural science, of course, to give an obvious example. And in bacteriology. Um-m-m—'

'Yes, what about bacteriological warfare?'

'A thought! But no, no, quite inconceivable. A teeming, constricted world such as Earth cannot afford to fight an open latticework of fifty sparse worlds with germs. They are infinitely more subject to epidemics, that is, to retaliation in kind. In fact, I would say that given our living conditions here on Aurora and on the other Outer Worlds, no contagious disease could really take hold. No, Maynard. You can check with a bacteriologist, but I think he'll tell you the same.'

Maynard said: 'And the third class?'

'The psychological? Now, that is unpredictable. And yet the Outer Worlds are intelligent and healthy communities and not amenable to ordinary propaganda, or for that matter to any form of unhealthy emotionalism. Now, I wonder—'

'Yes?'

'What if the Pacific Project is just that? I mean, a huge device to keep us off balance. Something top-secret, but meant to leak out in just the right fashion, so that the Outer Worlds yield a little to Earth, simply in order to play safe.'

There was a longish silence. 'Impossible,' burst out Maynard, angrily.

'*You* react properly. *You* hesitate. But I don't seriously press the interpretation. It is merely a thought.'

A longer silence, then Hijkman spoke again: 'Are there any other questions?'

Maynard started out of a reverie, 'No . . . no—'

The wave broke off and a wall appeared where space had been a moment before.

Slowly, with stubborn disbelief, Franklin Maynard shook his head.

Ernest Keilin mounted the stairs with a feeling for all the past centuries. The building was old, cobwebbed with history. It once housed the Parliament of Man, and from it words went out that clanged throughout the stars.

It was a tall building. It soared – stretched – strained. Out and up to the stars, it reached; to the stars that had now turned away. It no longer even housed the Parliament of Earth. That had now been switched to a newer, neoclassical building, one that imperfectly aped the architectural stylisms of the ancient pre-Atomic age.

Yet the older building still held its great name. Officially, it was still Stellar House, but it only housed the functionaries of a shriveled bureaucracy now.

Keilin got out at the twelfth floor, and the lift dropped quickly down behind him. The radiant sign said smoothly and quietly:

Bureau of Information. He handed a letter to the receptionist. He waited. And eventually, he passed through the door which said, 'L. Z. Cellioni – Secretary of Information.'

Cellioni was little and dark. His hair was thick and black, his mustache thin and black. His teeth, when he smiled, were startlingly white and even – so he smiled often.

He was smiling now, as he rose and held out his hand. Keilin took it, then an offered seat, then an offered cigar.

Cellioni said: 'I am very happy to see you, Mr Keilin. It is kind of you to fly here from New York on such short notice.'

Keilin curved the corners of his lips down and made a tiny gesture with one hand, deprecating the whole business.

'And now,' continued Cellioni, 'I presume you would like an explanation of all this.'

'I wouldn't refuse one,' said Keilin.

'Unfortunately, it is difficult to know exactly how to explain. As Secretary of Information, my position is difficult. I must safeguard the security and well-being of Earth and, at the same time, observe our traditional freedom of the press. Naturally, and fortunately, we have no censorship, but just as naturally, there are times when we could almost wish we did have.'

'Is this,' asked Keilin, 'with reference to me? About censorship, I mean?'

Cellioni did not answer directly. Instead, he smiled again, slowly, and with a remarkable absence of joviality.

He said: 'You, Mr Keilin, have one of the most widely heard and influential talecasts on the video. Therefore, you are of peculiar interest to the government.'

'The time is mine,' said Keilin, stubbornly. 'I pay for it. I pay taxes on the income I derive from it. I adhere to all the common-law rulings on taboos. So I don't quite see of what interest I can be to the government.'

'Oh, you misunderstand me. It's my fault, I suppose, for not being clearer. You have committed no crime, broken no laws. I have only admiration for your journalistic ability. What I refer to is your editorial attitude at times.'

'With respect to what?'

'With respect,' said Cellioni, with a sudden harshness about his thin lips, 'to our policy toward the Outer Worlds.'

'My editorial attitude represents what I feel and think, Mr Secretary.'

'I allow this. You have your right to your feelings and your thoughts. Yet it is injudicious to spread them about nightly to an audience of half a billion.'

'Injudicious, according to you, perhaps. But legal, according to anybody.'

'It is sometimes necessary to place good of country above a strict and selfish interpretation of legality.'

Keilin tapped his foot twice and frowned blackly. 'Look,' he said, 'put this frankly. What is it you want?'

The Secretary of Information spread his hands out before him. 'In a word – co-operation! Really, Mr Keilin, we can't have you weakening the will of the people. Do you appreciate the position of Earth? Six billions, and a declining food supply! It is insupportable! And emigration is the only solution. No patriotic Earthman can fail to see the justice of our position. No reasonable human being anywhere can fail to see the justice of it.'

Keilin said: 'I agree with your premise that the population problem is serious, but emigration is not the only solution. In fact, emigration is the one sure way of hastening destruction.'

'Really? And why do you say that?'

'Because the Outer Worlds will not permit emigration, and you can force their hand by war only. *And we cannot win a war.*'

'Tell me,' said Cellioni softly, 'have *you* ever tried emigrating? It seems to me you could qualify. You are quite tall, rather light-haired, intelligent—'

The video-man flushed. He said, curtly: 'I have hay fever.'

'Well,' and the secretary smiled, 'then you must have good reason for disapproving their arbitrary genetic and racist policies.'

Keilin replied with heat: 'I won't be influenced by personal motives. I would disapprove their policies, if I qualified perfectly for emigration. But my disapproval would alter nothing. Their policies *are* their policies, and they can enforce them. Moreover, their policies have some reason even if wrong. Mankind is starting again on the Outer Worlds, and they – the ones who got there first – would like to eliminate some of the flaws of the human mechanism that have become obvious with time. A hay fever sufferer *is* a bad egg – genetically. A cancer prone even more so. Their prejudices against skin and hair colors are, of course, senseless, but I can grant that they are interested in uniformity and homogeneity. And as for Earth, we can do much even without the help of the Outer Worlds.'

'For instance, what?'

'Positronic robots and hydroponic farming should be introduced, and – most of all – birth control must be instituted. An intelligent birth control, that is, based on firm psychiatric principles intended to eliminate the psychotic trends, congenital infirmities—'

'As they do in the Outer Worlds—'

'Not at all. I have mentioned no racist principles. I talk only of mental and physical infirmities that are held in common by all ethnic and racial groups. And most of all, births must be held below deaths until a healthful equilibrium is reached.'

Cellioni said, grimly: 'We lack the industrial techniques and the resources to introduce a robot-hydroponic technology in anything less than five centuries. Furthermore, the traditions of Earth, as well as current ethical beliefs, forbid robot labor and false foods. Most of all, they forbid the slaughter of unborn children. Now, come,

Keilin, we can't have you pouring this out over video. It won't work; it distracts the attention; it weakens the will.'

Keilin broke in, impatiently: 'Mr Secretary, do you want war?'

'Do I *want* war? That is an impudent question.'

'Then, who are the policy-makers in the government who *do* want war? For instance, who is responsible for the calculated rumor of the Pacific Project?'

'The Pacific Project? And where did you hear of that?'

'My sources are my secret.'

'Then, I'll tell you. You heard of this Pacific Project from Moreanu of Aurora on his recent trip to Earth. We know more about you than you suppose, Mr Keilin.'

'I believe that, but I do not admit that I received information from Moreanu. Why do you think I could get information from him? Is it because he was deliberately allowed to learn of this piece of trumpery?'

'Trumpery?'

'Yes. I think Pacific Project is a fake. A fake meant to inspire confidence. I think the government plans to let the so-called secret leak out in order to strengthen its war policy. It is part of a war of nerves on Earth's own people, and it will be the ruin of Earth in the end. And I will take this theory of mine to the people.'

'You will not, Mr Keilin,' said Cellioni, quietly.

'I will.'

'Mr Keilin, your friend, Ion Moreanu is having his troubles on Aurora, perhaps for being too friendly with you. Take care that you do not have equal trouble for being too friendly with him.'

'I'm not worried.' The video man laughed shortly, lunged to his feet and strode to the door.

Keilin smiled very gently when he found the door blocked by two large men: 'You mean, I am under arrest right now.'

'Exactly,' said Cellioni.

'On what charge?'

'We'll think of some later.'

Keilin left – under escort.

On Aurora, the mirror image of the afore-described events was taking place, and on a larger scale.

The Foreign Agents Committee of the Gathering had been meeting now for days – ever since the session of the Gathering in which Ion Moreanu and his Conservative Party made their great bid to force a vote of no confidence. That it had failed was in part due to the superior political generalship of the Independents, and in some part due to the activity of this same Foreign Agents Committee.

For months now, the evidence had been accumulating, and when the vote of confidence turned out to be sizably in favor of the Independents, the Committee was able to strike in its own way.

Moreanu was subpoenaed in his own home, and placed under house arrest. Although this procedure of house arrest was not, under the circumstances, legal – a fact emphatically pointed out by Moreanu – it was nevertheless successfully accomplished.

For three days Moreanu was cross-examined thoroughly, in polite, even tones that scarcely ever veered from unemotional curiosity. The seven inquisitors of the Committee took turns in questioning, but Moreanu had respite only for ten-minute intervals during the hours in which the Committee sat.

After three days, he showed the effects. He was hoarse with demanding that he be faced with his accusers; weary with insisting that he be informed of the exact nature of the charges; throat-broken with shouting against the illegality of the procedure.

The Committee finally read statements at him—

'Is this true or not? Is this true or not?'

Moreanu could merely shake his head wearily as the structure spidered about him.

He challenged the competency of the evidence and was smoothly informed that the proceedings constituted a Committee Investigation and not a trial—

The chairman clapped his gavel, finally. He was a broad man of tremendous purpose. He spoke for an hour in his final summing up of the results of the inquiry, but only a relatively short portion of it need be quoted.

He said: 'If you had merely conspired with others on Aurora, we could understand you, even forgive you. Such a fault would have been held in common with many ambitious men in history. It is not that at all. What horrifies us and removes all pity is your eagerness to consort with the disease-ridden, ignorant and subhuman remnants of Earth.

'You, the accused, stand here under a heavy weight of evidence showing you to have conspired with the worst elements of Earth's mongrel population—'

The chairman was interrupted by an agonized cry from Moreanu, 'But the motive! What motive can you possibly attribute—'

The accused was pulled back into his seat. The chairman pursed his lips and departed from the slow gravity of his prepared speech to improvise a bit.

'It is not,' he said, 'for this Committee to go into your motives. We have shown the facts of the case. The Committee *does* have evidence—' He paused, and looked along the line of the members to the right and the left, then continued. 'I think I may say that the Committee has evidence that points to your intentions to use Earth man power to engineer a coup that would leave you dictator over Aurora. But since the evidence has not been used, I will go no further into that, except to say that such a consummation is not inconsistent with your character as displayed at these hearings.'

He went back to his speech. 'Those of us who sit here have heard, I think, of something termed the "Pacific Project", which, according to rumors, represents an attempt on the part of Earth to retrieve its lost dominions.

'It is needless to emphasize here that any such attempt must be doomed to failure. And yet defeat for us is not entirely inconceivable. One thing can cause us to stumble, and that one thing is an unsuspected internal weakness. Genetics is, after all, still an imperfect science. Even with twenty generations behind us, undesirable traits may crop up at scattered points, and each represents a flaw in the steel shield of Aurora's strength.

'*That* is the Pacific Project – the use of our own criminals and traitors against us; and if they can find such in our inner councils, the Earthmen might even succeed.

'The Foreign Agents Committee exists to combat that threat. In the accused, we touch the fringes of the web. We must go on—'

The speech did, at any rate.

When it was concluded, Moreanu, pale, wide-eyed, pounded his fist, 'I demand my say—'

'The accused may speak,' said the chairman.

Moreanu rose and looked about him for a long moment. The room, fitted for an audience of seventy-five million by Community Wave, was unattended. There were the inquisitors, legal staff, official recorders— And with him, in the actual flesh, his guards.

He would have done better with an audience. To whom could he otherwise appeal? His glance fled hopelessly from each face it touched, but could find nothing better.

'First,' he said, 'I deny the legality of this meeting. My constitutional rights of privacy and individuality have been denied. I have been tried by a group without standing as a court, by individuals convinced, in advance, of my guilt. I have been denied adequate opportunity to defend myself. In fact, I have been treated throughout as an already convicted criminal requiring only sentence.

'I deny, completely and without reservation, that I have been engaged in any activity detrimental to the state or tending to subvert any of its fundamental institutions.

'I accuse, vigorously and unreservedly, this Committee of deliberately using its powers to win political battles. I am guilty not of treason, but of disagreement. I disagree with a policy dedicated to the destruction of the larger part of the human race for reasons that are trivial and inhumane.

'Rather than destruction, we owe assistance to these men who are condemned to a harsh, unhappy life solely because it was our ancestors and not theirs who happened to reach the Outer Worlds first. With our technology and resources, they can yet re-create and redevelop—'

The chairman's voice rose above the intense near-whisper of Moreanu, 'You are out of order. The Committee is quite prepared to hear any remarks you make in your own defense, but a sermon on the rights of Earthmen is outside the legitimate realm of the discussion.'

The hearings were formally closed. It was a great political victory for the Independents; all would agree to that. Of the members of the Committee, only Franklin Maynard was not completely satisfied. A small, nagging doubt remained.

He wondered—

Should he try, one last time? Should he speak once more and then no more to that queer little monkey ambassador from Earth? He made his decision quickly and acted upon it instantly. Only a pause to arrange a witness, since even for himself an unwitnessed private communion with an Earthman might be dangerous.

Luiz Moreno, Ambassador to Aurora from Earth, was, to put not too fine a point on it, a miserable figure of a man. And that wasn't exactly an accident. On the whole, the foreign diplomats of Earth tended to be dark, short, wizen, or weakly – or all four.

That was only self-protection, since the Outer Worlds exerted strong attraction for any Earthman. Diplomats exposed to the allure of Aurora, for instance, could not but be exceedingly reluctant to return to Earth. Worse, and more dangerous, exposure meant a growing sympathy with the demigods of the stars and a growing alienation from the slum-dwellers of Earth.

Unless, of course, the ambassador found himself rejected. Unless he found himself somewhat despised. And then, no more faithful servant of Earth could be imagined, no man less subject to corruption.

The Ambassador to Earth was only five foot two, with a bald head and receding forehead, a pinkish affectation of beard and redrimmed eyes. He was suffering from a slight cold, the occasional results whereof he smothered in a handkerchief. And yet, withal, he was a man of intellect.

To Franklin Maynard, the sight and sound of the Earthman was distressing. He grew queasy at each cough and shuddered when the ambassador wiped his nose.

Maynard said: 'Your excellency, we commune at my request because I wish to inform you that the Gathering has decided to ask your recall by your government.'

'That is kind of you, councilor. I had an inkling of this. And for what reason?'

'The reason is not within the bounds of discussion. I believe it is the prerogative of a sovereign state to decide for itself whether a foreign representative shall be *persona grata* or not. Nor do I think you really need enlightenment on this matter.'

'Very well, then.' The ambassador paused to wield his handkerchief and murmur an apology. 'Is that all?'

Maynard said: 'Not quite. There are matters I would like to mention. Remain!'

The ambassador's reddened nostrils flared a bit, but he smiled, and said: 'An honor.'

'Your world, excellency,' said Maynard, superciliously, 'displays a certain belligerence of late that we on Aurora find most annoying and unnecessary. I trust that you will find your return to Earth at this point a convenient opportunity to use your influence against further displays such as recently occurred in New York, where two Aurorans were manhandled by a mob. The payment of an indemnity may not be enough the next time.'

'But that is emotional overflow, Councilor Maynard. Surely, you cannot consider youngsters shouting in the streets to be adequate representations of belligerence.'

'It is backed by your government's actions in many ways. The recent arrest of Mr Ernest Keilin, for instance.'

'Which is a purely domestic affair,' said the ambassador, quietly.

'But not one to demonstrate a reasonable spirit toward the Outer Worlds. Keilin was one of the few Earthmen who until recently could yet make their voices heard. He was intelligent enough to realize that no divine right protects the inferior man simply because he is inferior.'

The ambassador arose: 'I am not interested in Auroran theories on racial differences.'

'A moment. Your government may realize that much of their plans have gone awry with the arrest of your agent, Moreanu. Stress the fact that we of Aurora are much wiser than we have been prior to this arrest. It may serve to give them pause.'

'Is Moreanu *my* agent? Really, councilor, if I am disaccredited, I shall leave. But surely the loss of diplomatic immunity does not affect my personal immunity as an honest man from charges of espionage.'

'Isn't that your job?'

'Do Aurorans take it for granted that espionage and diplomacy are identical? My government will be glad to hear it. We shall take appropriate precautions.'

'Then, you defend Moreanu? You deny that he has been working for Earth?'

'I defend only myself. As to Moreanu, I am not stupid enough to say anything.'

'Why stupid?'

'Wouldn't a defense by myself be but another indictment against him? I neither accuse nor defend him. Your government's quarrel with Moreanu, like my government's with Keilin – whom you, by the way, are most suspiciously eager to defend – is an internal affair. I will leave now.'

The communion broke, and almost instantly the wall faded again. Hijkman was looking thoughtfully at Maynard.

'What do you think of him?' asked Maynard, grimly. 'Disgraceful that such a travesty of humanity should walk Aurora, I think.'

'I agree with you, and yet . . . and yet—'

'Well?'

'And yet I can almost find myself able to think that he is the master and that we dance to his piping. You know of Moreanu?'

'Of course.'

'Well, he will be convicted, sent to an asteroid. His party will be broken. Offhand, anyone would say that such actions represent a horrible defeat for Earth.'

'Is there doubt in your mind that such is the case?'

'I'm not sure. Committee Chairman Hond insisted on airing his theory that Pacific Project was the name Earth gave to a device for using internal traitors on the Outer Worlds. But I don't think so. I'm not sure the facts fit that. For instance, where did we get our evidence against Moreanu?'

'I certainly can't say.'

'Our agents, in the first place. But how did they get it? The evidence was a little *too* convincing. Moreanu could have guarded himself better—'

Maynard hesitated. He seemed to be attempting a blush, and failing. 'Well, to put it quickly, I think it was the Terrestrian Ambassador who somehow presented us with the most evidence. I think that he played on Moreanu's sympathy for Earth first to befriend him and then to betray him.'

'Why?'

'I don't know. To insure war, perhaps – with this Pacific Project waiting for us.'

'I don't believe it.'

'I know. I have no proof. Nothing but suspicion. The Committee wouldn't believe me either. It seemed to me, perhaps, that a last talk with the ambassador might reveal something, but his mere appearance antagonizes me, and I find I spend most of my time trying to remove him from my sight.'

'Well, you are becoming emotional, my friend. It is a disgusting weakness. I hear that you have been appointed a delegate to the Interplanetary Gathering at Hesperus. I congratulate you.'

'Thanks,' said Maynard, absently.

Luiz Moreno, ex-Ambassador to Aurora, had been glad to return to Earth. He was away from the artificial landscapes that seemed to have no life of their own, but to exist only by virtue of the strong will of their possessors. Away from the too-beautiful men and women and from their ubiquitous, brooding robots.

He was back to the hum of life and the shuffle of feet; the brushing of shoulders and the feeling of breath in the face.

Not that he was able to enjoy these sensations entirely. The first days had been spent in lively conferences with the heads of Earth's government.

In fact, it was not till nearly a week had passed, that an hour came in which he could consider himself truly relaxed.

He was in the rarest of all appurtenances of Terrestrial Luxury – a roof garden. With him was Gustav Stein, the quite obscure physiologist, who was, nevertheless, one of the prime movers of the Plan, known to rumor as the Pacific Project.

'The confirmatory tests,' said Moreno, with an almost dreadful satisfaction, 'all check so far, do they not?'

'So far. *Only* so far. We have miles to go.'

'Yet they will continue to go well. To one who has lived on Aurora for nearly a year, as I have, there can be no doubt but that we're on the right track.'

'Um-m-m. Nevertheless, I will go only by the laboratory reports.'

'And quite rightly.' His little body was almost stiff with gloating. 'Some day, it will be different. Stein, you have not met these men, these Outer Worlders. You may have come across the tourists, perhaps, in their special hotels, or riding through the streets in inclosed cars, equipped with the purest of private, air-conditioned atmospheres for their well-bred nostrils; observing the sights through a movable periscope and shuddering away from the touch of an Earthman.

'But you have not met them on their own world, secure in their own sickly, rotting greatness. Go, Stein, and be despised a while. Go, and find how well you can compete with their own trained lawns as something to be gently trod upon.

'And yet, when I pulled the proper cords, Ion Moreanu fell – Ion Moreanu, the only man among them with the capacity to understand the workings of another's mind. It is the crisis that we have passed now. We front a smooth path now.'

Satisfaction! Satisfaction!

'As for Keilin,' he said suddenly, more to himself than to Stein, 'he can be turned loose now. There's little he can say, hereafter, that can endanger anything. In fact, I have an idea. The Interplanetary Conference opens on Hesperus within the month. He can be sent to report the meeting. It will be an earnest of our friendliness – and keep him away for the summer. I think it can be arranged.'

It was.

Of all the Outer Worlds, Hesperus was the smallest, the latest settled, the furthest from Earth. Hence the name. In a physical sense, it was not best suited to a great diplomatic gathering, since its facilities were small. For instance, the available community-wave network could not possibly be stretched to cover all the delegates, secretarial staff, and administrators necessary in a convocation of fifty planets. So meetings in person were arranged in buildings impressed for the purpose.

Yet there was a symbolism in the choice of meeting place that escaped practically nobody. Hesperus, of all the Worlds, was furthest removed from Earth. But the spatial distance – one hundred parsecs or more – was the least of it. The important point was that Hesperus had been colonized not by Earthmen, but by men from the Outer World of Faunus.

It was therefore of the second generation, and so it had no 'Mother Earth'. Earth to it was but a vague grandmother, lost in the stars.

As is usual in all such gatherings, little work is actually done on the session floors. That space is reserved for the official soundings of whatever is primarily intended for home ears. The actual swapping and horse-trading takes place in the lobbies and at the lunch-tables and many an irresolvable conflict has softened over the soup and vanished over the nuts.

And yet particular difficulties were present in this particular case. Not in all worlds was the community-wave as paramount and all-pervading as it was on Aurora, but it was prominent in all. It was, therefore, with a certain sense of outrage and loss that the tall, dignified men found it necessary to approach one another in the flesh, without the comforting privacy of the invisible wall between, without the warm knowledge of the breakswitch at their fingertips.

They faced one another in uneasy semi-embarrassment and tried not to watch one another eat; tried not to shrink at the unmeant touch. Even robot service was rationed.

Ernest Keilin, the only accredited video-representative from Earth, was aware of some of these matters only in the vague way they are described here. A more precise insight he could not have. Nor could anyone brought up in a society where human beings exist only in the plural, and where a house need only be deserted to be feared.

So it was that certain of the most subtle tensions escaped him at the formal dinner party given by the Hesperian government during the third week of the conference. Other tensions, however, did not pass him by.

The gathering after the dinner naturally fell apart into little groups. Keilin joined the one that contained Franklin Maynard of Aurora. As the delegate of the largest of the Worlds, he was naturally the most newsworthy.

Maynard was speaking casually between sips at the tawny Hesperian cocktail in his hand. If his flesh crawled slightly at the closeness of the others, he masked the feeling masterfully.

'Earth,' he said, 'is, in essence, helpless against us if we avoid unpredictable military adventures. Economic unity is actually a necessity, if we intend to avoid such adventures. Let Earth realize to how great an extent her economy depends upon us, on the things that we alone can supply her, and there will be no more talk of living space. And if we are united, Earth would never dare attack. She will exchange her barren longings for atomic motors – or not, as she pleases.'

And he turned to regard Keilin with a certain hauteur as the other found himself stung to comment:

'But your manufactured goods, councilor – I mean those you ship to Earth – they are not *given* us. They are exchanged for agricultural products.'

Maynard smiled silkily. 'Yes, I believe the delegate from Tethys has mentioned that fact at length. There is a delusion prevalent among some of us that only Terrestrial seeds grow properly—'

He was interrupted calmly by another, who said: 'Now, I am not from Tethys, but what you mention is not a delusion. I grow rye on Rhea, and I have never yet been able to duplicate Terrestrial bread. It just hasn't got the same taste.' He addressed the audience in general, 'In fact, I imported half a dozen Terrestrians five years back on agricultural laborer visas so they could oversee the robots. Now, they can do wonders with the land, you know. Where they spit, corn grows fifteen feet high. Well, that helped a little. And using Terrestrian seed helped. But even if you grow Terrestrian grain, its seed won't hold the next year.'

'Has your soil been tested by your government's agricultural department?' asked Maynard.

The Rhean grew haughty in his turn: 'No better soil in the sector. And the rye is top-grade. I even sent a hundredweight down to Earth for nutritional clearance, and it came back with full marks.' He rubbed one side of his chin, thoughtfully: 'It's flavor I'm talking about. Doesn't seem to have the right—'

Maynard made an effort to dismiss him: 'Flavor is dispensable temporarily. They'll be coming to us on our terms, these little-menhordes of Earth, when they feel the pinch. We give up only this mysterious flavor, but they will have to give up atom-powered engines, farm machinery, and ground cars. It wouldn't be a bad idea, in fact, to attempt to get along without the Terrestrian flavors you are so concerned about. Let us appreciate the flavor of our home-grown products instead – which could stand comparison if we gave it a chance.'

'That so?' the Rhean smiled. 'I notice you're smoking Earth-grown tobacco.'

'A habit I can break if I have to.'

'Probably by giving up smoking. I wouldn't use Outer World tobacco for anything but killing mosquitoes.'

He laughed a trifle too boisterously, and left the group. Maynard stared after him, a little pinch-nosed.

To Keilin, the little byplay over rye and tobacco brought a certain satisfaction. He regarded such personalities as the tiny reflection of certain Galactopolitical realities. Tethys and Rhea were the largest planets in the Galactic south, as Aurora was the largest in the Galactic north. All three planets were identically racist, identically exclusivist. Their views on Earth were similar and completely compatible. Ordinarily, one would think that there was no room to quarrel. But Aurora was the oldest of the Outer Worlds, the most advanced, the strongest militarily – and, therefore, aspired to a sort of moral leadership of all the Worlds. That was sufficient in itself to arouse opposition, and Rhea and Tethys served as focal points for those who did not recognize Auroran leadership.

Keilin was somberly grateful for that situation. If Earth could but lean her weight properly, first in one direction, then in the other, an ultimate split, or even fragmentation—

He eyed Maynard cautiously, almost furtively, and wondered what effect this would have on the next day's debate. Already, the Auroran was more silent than was quite polite.

And then some under-secretary or sub-official threaded his way through the clusters of guests in finicking fashion, and beckoned to Maynard.

Keilin's following eyes watched the Auroran retreat with the newcomer, watched him listen closely, mouth a startled 'What!' that was quite visible to the eye, though too far off to be heard, and then reach for a paper that the other handed him.

And as a result, the next day's session of the conference went entirely differently than Keilin would have predicted.

Keilin discovered the details in the evening video-casts. The Terrestrian government, it seemed, had sent a note to all the governments attending the conference. It warned each one bluntly that any agreement among them in military or economic affairs would be considered an unfriendly act against Earth and that it would be met with appropriate countermeasures. The note denounced Aurora, Tethys, and Rhea all equally. It accused them of being engaged in an imperialist conspiracy against Earth, and so on – and on – and on.

'Fools!' gritted Keilin, all but butting his head against the wall out of sheer chagrin. 'Fools! Fools! Fools!' And his voice died away still muttering that same, one word.

The next session of the conference was well and early attended by a set of angry delegates who were only too eager to grind into nothingness the disagreements still outstanding. When it ended, all matters concerning trade between Earth and the Outer Worlds had been placed in the hands of a commission with plenary powers.

Not even Aurora could have expected so complete and easy a victory, and Keilin, on his way back to Earth, longed for his voice to reach the video, so that it could be to others, and not to himself only, that he could shout his disgust.

Yet, on Earth, some men smiled.

Once back on Earth, the voice of Keilin slowly swirled under and down – lost in the noisier clamor that shouted for action.

His popularity sank in proportion as trade restrictions grew. Slowly, the Outer Worlds drew the noose tighter. First, they instituted a strict application of a new system of export licensing. Secondly, they banned the export to Earth of all materials capable of being 'used in a war effort'. And finally they applied a very broad interpretation indeed of what could be considered usable in such a connection.

Imported luxuries – and imported necessities, too, for that matter – vanished or priced themselves upwards out of the reach of all but the very few.

So the people marched, and the voices shouted and the banners swung about in the sunlight, and the stones flew at the consulates—

Keilin shouted hoarsely and felt as if he were going mad.

Until, suddenly, Luiz Moreno, quite of his own accord, offered to appear on Keilin's program and submit to unrestricted questioning in his capacity as ex-Ambassador to Aurora and present Secretary without Portfolio.

To Keilin it had had all the possibilities of a rebirth. He knew Moreno – no fool, he. With Moreno on his program, he was assured an audience as great as his greatest. With Moreno answering questions, certain misapprehensions might be removed, certain confusions might be straightened. The mere fact that Moreno wished to use his – *his* – program as sounding board might well mean that already a more pliant and sensible foreign policy might have been decided upon. Perhaps Maynard was correct, and the pinch was being felt and was working as predicted.

The list of questions had, of course, been submitted to Moreno in advance, but the ex-Ambassador had indicated that he would answer all of them, and any follow-up questions that might seem necessary.

It seemed quite ideal. Too ideal, perhaps, but only a criminal fool could worry over minutiae at this point.

There was an adequate ballyhoo – and when they faced one another across the little table, the red needle that indicated the number of video sets drawing power on that channel hovered well over the two hundred million mark. And there was an average of 2.7 listeners per video set. Now the theme; the official introduction.

Keilin rubbed his cheek slowly, as he waited for the signal. Then, he began:

Q. Secretary Moreno, the question which interests all Earth at the moment, concerns the possibility of war. Suppose we start with that. Do you think there will be war?

A. If Earth is the only planet to be considered, I say: No, definitely not. In its history, Earth has had too much war, and has learned many times over how little can be gained by it.

Q. You say, 'If Earth is the only planet to be considered—' Do you imply that factors outside our control will bring war?

A. I do not say 'will'; but I could say 'may'. I cannot, of course speak for the Outer Worlds. I cannot pretend to know their motivations and intentions at this critical moment in Galactic history. They *may* choose war. I hope not. If so be that they do, however, we will defend ourselves. But in any case, *we* will never attack; *we* will not strike the first blow.

Q. Am I right in saying, then, that in your opinion there are no basic differences between Earth and the Outer Worlds, which cannot be solved by negotiation?

A. You certainly are. If the Outer Worlds were sincerely desirous of a solution, no disagreement between them and us could long exist.

Q. Does that include the question of immigration?

A. Definitely. Our own role in the matter is clear and beyond reproach. As matters stand, two hundred million human beings now occupy ninety-five percent of the available land in the universe. Six billions – that is, ninety-seven percent of all mankind – are squeezed into the other five percent. Such a situation is obviously unjust and, worse, unstable. Yet Earth, in the face of such injustice, has always been willing to treat this problem as soluble by degrees. It is still so willing. We should agree to reasonable quotas and reasonable restrictions. Yet the Outer Worlds have refused to discuss this matter. Over a space of five decades, they have rebuffed all efforts on the part of Earth to open negotiations.

Q. If such an attitude on the part of the Outer Worlds continues, do you *then* think there will be war?

A. I cannot believe that this attitude will continue. Our government will not cease hoping that the Outer Worlds will eventually reconsider their stand on the matter; that their sense of justice and right is not dead, but only sleeping.

Q. Mr Secretary, let us pass on to another subject. Do you think that the United Worlds Commission set up by the Outer Worlds recently to control trade with Earth represents a danger to peace?

A. In the sense that its actions indicate a desire on the part of the Outer Worlds to isolate Earth, and to weaken it economically, I can say that it does.

Q. To what actions do you refer, sir?

A. To its actions in restricting interstellar trade with Earth to the point where, in credit values, the total stands now at less than ten percent of what it did three months ago.

Q. But do such restrictions really represent an economic danger to Earth? For instance, is it not true that trade with the Outer Worlds represents an almost insignificant part of total Terrestrian trade? And is it not true that the importations from the Outer Worlds reach only a tiny minority of the population at best?

A. Your questions now are representative of a profound fallacy which is very common among our isolationists. In credit values, it is true that interstellar trade represents only five percent of our total trade, but ninety-five percent of our atomic engines are imported. Eighty percent of our thorium, sixty-five percent of our cesium, sixty percent of our molybdenum and tin are imported. The list can be extended almost indefinitely, and it is quite easy to see that the five percent is an extremely important, a vital, five percent. Furthermore, if a large manufacturer receives a shipment of atomic steel-shapers from Rhea, it does not follow that the benefit redounds only to him. Every man on Earth who uses steel implements or objects manufactured by steel implements benefits.

Q. But is it not true that the current restrictions on Earth's interstellar trade have cut our grain and cattle exports to almost nothing? And far from harming Earth, isn't this really a boon to our own hungry people?

A. This is another serious fallacy. That Earth's good food supply is tragically inadequate is true. The government would be the last to deny it. But our food exports do not represent any serious drain upon this supply. Less than one fifth of one percent of Earth's food is exported, and in return we obtain, for instance, fertilizers and farm machinery which more than make up for that small loss by increasing agricultural efficiency. Therefore, by buying less food from us, the Outer Worlds are engaged, in effect, in cutting our already inadequate food supply.

Q. Are you ready to admit, then, Secretary Moreno, that at least part of the blame for this situation should rest with Earth itself? In other words, we come to my next question: Was it not a diplomatic blunder of the first magnitude for the government to issue its inflammatory note denouncing the intentions of the Outer Worlds before those intentions had been made clear at the Interplanetary Conference?

A. I think those intentions were quite clear at the time.

Q. I beg pardon, sir, but I was at the conference. At the time the note was issued, there was almost a stalemate among the Outer World delegates. Those of Rhea and Tethys strongly opposed economic action against Earth, and there was considerable chance that Aurora and its block might have been defeated. Earth's note ended that possibility instantly.

A. Well, what is your question, Mr Keilin?

Q. In view of my statements, do you or do you not think Earth's note to have been a criminal error of diplomacy which can now be made up only by a policy of intelligent conciliation?

A. You use strong language. However, I cannot answer the question directly, since I do not agree with your major premise. I cannot believe that the delegates of the Outer Worlds could behave in the manner you describe. In the first place, it is well known that the Outer Worlds are proud of their boast that the percentage of insanity, psychoses, and even relatively minor maladjustments of personality are almost at the vanishing point in their society. It is one of their strongest arguments against Earth, that we have more psychiatrists than plumbers and yet are more pinched for want of the former. The delegates to the conference represented the best of this so-stable society. And now you would have me believe that these demigods would, in a moment of pique, have reversed their opinions and instituted a major change in the economic policy of fifty worlds. I cannot believe them capable of such childish and perverse activity, and must therefore insist that any action they took was based not upon any note from Earth, but upon motivations that go deeper.

Q. But I saw the effect upon them with my own eyes, sir. Remember, they were being scolded in what they considered to be insolent language from an inferior people. There can be no doubt, sir, that as a whole, the men of the Outer Worlds are a remarkably stable people, despite your sarcasm, but their attitude toward Earth represents a weak point in this stability.

A. Are you asking me questions, or are you defending the racist views and policies of the Outer Worlds?

Q. Well, accepting your viewpoint that Earth's note did no harm, what good could it have done? Why should it have been sent?

A. I think we were justified in presenting our side of the question before the bar of Galactic public opinion. I believe we have exhausted the subject. What is your next question, please? It is the last, isn't it?

Q. It is. It has recently been reported that the Terrestrian government will take stern measures against those dealing in smuggling operations. Is this consistent with the government's view that lowered trade relations are detrimental to Earth's welfare?

A. Our primary concern is peace, and not our own immediate welfare. The Outer Worlds have adopted certain trade restrictions.

We disapprove of them, and consider them a great injustice. Nevertheless, we shall adhere to them, so that no planet may say that we have given the slightest pretext for hostilities. For instance, I am privileged to announce here for the first time that in the past month, five ships, traveling under false Earth registry, were stopped while being engaged in the smuggling of Outer World materiel into Earth. Their goods were confiscated and their personnel imprisoned. This is an earnest of our good intentions.

Q. Outer World ships?

A. Yes. But traveling under false Earth registry, remember.

Q. And the men imprisoned are citizens of the Outer Worlds?

A. I believe so. However, they were breaking not only our laws, but those of the Outer Worlds as well, and therefore doubly forfeited their interplanetary rights. I think the interview had better close, now.

Q. But this—

It was at this point that the broadcast came to a sudden end. The conclusion of Keilin's last sentence was never heard by anyone but Moreno. It ended like this:

'—means war.'

But Luiz Moreno was no longer on the air. So as he drew on his gloves, he smiled and, with infinite meaning, shrugged his shoulders in a little gesture of indifference.

There were no witnesses to that shrug.

The Gathering at Aurora was still in session. Franklin Maynard had dropped out for the moment in utter weariness. He faced his son, whom he now saw for the first time in naval uniform.

'At least *you're* sure of what will happen, aren't you?'

In the young man's response, there was no weariness at all, no apprehension; nothing but utter satisfaction. 'This is it, dad!'

'Nothing bothers you, then? You don't think we've been maneuvered into this.'

'Who cares if we have? It's Earth's funeral.'

Maynard shook his head: 'But you realize that we've been put in the wrong. The Outer World citizens they hold are law-breakers. Earth is within its rights.'

His son frowned: 'I hope you're not going to make statements like that to the Gathering, dad. I don't see that Earth is justified at all. All right, what if smuggling was going on? It was just because some Outer Worlders are willing to pay black market prices for Terrestrial food. If Earth had any sense, she could look the other way, and everyone would benefit. She makes enough noise about how she needs our trade, so why doesn't she do something about it? Anyway, I don't see that we ought to leave any good Aurorans or other Outer Worlders in the hands of those apemen. Since they won't give them up, we'll make them. Otherwise, none of us will be safe next time.'

'I see that you've adopted the popular opinions, anyway.'

'The opinions are my own. If they're popular opinion also, it's because they make sense. Earth *wants* a war. Well, they'll get it.'

'But why do they want a war, eh? Why do they force our hands? Our entire economic policy of the past months was only intended to force a change in their attitude without war.'

He was talking to himself, but his son answered with the final argument: 'I don't care why they wanted war. They've *got* it now, and were going to smash them.'

Maynard returned to the Gathering, but even as the drone of debate re-filled the room, he thought, with a twinge, that there would be no Terrestrian alfalfa that year. He regretted the milk. In fact, even the beef seemed, somehow, to be just a little less savory— The vote came in the early hours of the morning. Aurora declared war. Most of the worlds of the Aurora bloc joined it by dawn.

In the history books, the war was later known as the Three Weeks' War. In the first week, Auroran forces occupied several of the transPlutonian asteroids, and at the beginning of the third week, the bulk of Earth's home fleet was all but completely destroyed in a battle within the orbit of Saturn by an Aurora fleet not one-quarter its size, numerically.

Declarations of war from the Outer Worlds yet neutral followed like the *pop-pop* of a string of firecrackers.

On the twenty-first day of the war, lacking two hours, Earth surrendered.

The negotiations of peace terms took place among the Outer Worlds. Earth's activities were concerned with signing only. The conditions of peace were unusual, perhaps unique, and under the force of an unprecedented humiliation, all the hordes of Earth seemed suddenly struck with a silence that came from a shamed anger too strong for words.

The terms mentioned were perhaps best commented upon by a voice on the Auroran video two days after they were made public. It can be quoted in part:

'... There is nothing in or on Earth that we of the Outer Worlds can need or want. All that was ever worthwhile on Earth left it centuries ago in the persons of our ancestors.

'They call us the children of Mother Earth, but that is not so, for we are the descendants of a Mother Earth that no longer exists, a Mother that we brought with us. The Earth of today bears us at best a cousinly relation. No more.

'Do we want their resources? Why, they have none for themselves. Can we use their industry or science? They are almost dead for lack of ours. Can we use their man power? Ten of them are not worth a single robot. Do we even want the dubious glory of ruling them? There is no such glory. As our helpless and incompetent inferiors, they would be only a drag upon us. They would divert from our own use food, labor, and administrative ability.

'So they have nothing to give us but the space they occupy in our thought. They have nothing to free us from but themselves. They cannot benefit us in any way other than in their absence.

'It is for that reason that the peace terms have been defined as they have been. We wish them no harm, so let them have their own solar system. Let them live there in peace. Let them mold their own destiny in their own way, and we will not disturb them there by even the least hint of our presence. But we in turn want peace. We in turn would guide our own future in our own way. So we do not want *their* presence. And with that end in view, an Outer World fleet will patrol the boundaries of their system, Outer World bases will be established on their outermost asteroids, so that we may make sure they do not intrude on our territory.

'There will be no trade, no diplomatic relationships, no travel, no communications. They are fenced off, locked out, hermetically sealed away. Out here we have a new universe, a second creation of Man, a higher Man—

'They ask us: What will become of Earth? We answer: That is Earth's problem. Population growth can be controlled. Resources can be efficiently exploited. Economic systems can be revised. We know, for we have done so. If they cannot, let them go the way of the dinosaur, and make room.

'Let them make room, instead of forever demanding room!'

And so an impenetrable curtain swung slowly shut about the Solar System. The stars in Earth's sky became only stars again, as in the long-dead days before the first ship had penetrated the barrier of light's speed.

The government that had made war and peace resigned, but there was no one, really, to take their place. The legislature elected Luiz Moreno – ex-Ambassador to Aurora, ex-Secretary without Portfolio – as President *pro tem*, and the Earth as a whole was too numbed to agree or disagree. There was only a widespread relief that someone existed who would be willing to take the job of trying to guide the destinies of a world in prison.

Very few realized how well-planned an ending this was, or with what calculation Moreno found himself in the president's chair.

Ernest Keilin said hopelessly from the video screen: 'We are only ourselves now. For us, there is no universe and no past – only Earth, and the future.'

That night he heard from Luiz Moreno once again, and before morning he left for the capital.

Moreno's presence seemed incongruent within the stiffly formal president's mansion. He was suffering from a cold again, and snuffled when he talked.

Keilin regarded him with a self-terrifying hostility; an almost singeing hatred in which he could feel his fingers begin to twitch in the first gestures of choking. Perhaps he shouldn't have come— Well, what was the difference; the orders had been plain. If he had not come, he would have been brought.

The new president looked at him sharply: 'You have to alter your attitude toward me, Keilin. I know you regard me as one of the Gravediggers of Earth – isn't that the phrase you used last night? – but you must listen to me quietly for a while. In your present state of suppressed rage, I doubt if you could hear me.'

'I will hear whatever you have to say, Mr President.'

'Well – the external amenities, at least. That's hopeful. Or do you think a video-tracer is attached to the room?'

Keilin merely lifted his eyebrows.

Moreno said: 'It isn't. We are quite alone. We *must* be alone; otherwise, how could I tell you safely that it is being arranged for you to be elected president under a constitution now being devised? Eh, what's the matter?'

Then he grinned at the look of bloodless amazement in Keilin's face. 'Oh, you don't believe it. Well, it's past your stopping. And before an hour is up, you'll understand.'

'I'm to be president?' Keilin struggled with a strange, hoarse voice. Then, more firmly: 'You are mad.'

'No. Not I. Those out there, rather. Out there in the Outer Worlds.' There was a sudden vicious intensity in Moreno's eyes, and face, and voice, so that you forgot he was a little monkey of a man with a perpetual cold. You didn't notice the wrinkled, sloping forehead. You forgot the baldish head and ill-fitting clothes. There was only the bright and luminous look in his eyes, and the hard incision in his voice. *That* you noticed.

Keilin reached blindly backward for a chair, as Moreno came closer and spoke with increasing intensity.

'Yes,' said Moreno. 'Those out among the Stars. The godlike ones. The stately supermen. The strong, handsome master-race. *They* are mad. But only we on Earth know it.

'Come, you have heard of the Pacific Project. I know you have. You denounced it to Cellioni once, and called it a fake. But it isn't a fake. And almost none of it is a secret. In fact, the only secret about it was that almost none of it was a secret.

'You're no fool, Keilin. You just never stopped to work it all out. And yet you were on the track. You had the feel of it. What was it you said that time you were interviewing me on the program? Something about the attitude of the Outer Worldling toward the Earthman being the only flaw in the former's stability. That was it, wasn't it? Or something like that? Very well, then; good! You had the first third of the Pacific Project in your mind at the time, and it was no secret after all, was it?

'Ask yourself, Keilin – what was the attitude of the typical Auroran to a typical Earthman? A feeling of superiority? That's the first thought, I suppose. But, tell me, Keilin, if he really felt superior, *really* superior, would it be so necessary for him to call such continuous attention to it? What kind of superiority is it that must be continuously bolstered by the constant repetition of phrases such as "apemen", "submen", "half-animals of Earth", and so on? That is not the calm internal assurance of superiority. Do you waste epithets on earthworms? No, there is something else there.

'Or let us approach it from another tack. Why do Outer World tourists stay in special hotels, travel in inclosed ground-cars, and have rigid, if unwritten, rules against social intermingling? Are they afraid of pollution? Strange, then, that they are not afraid to eat our food and drink our wine and smoke our tobacco.

'You see, Keilin, there are no psychiatrists on the Outer

Worlds. The supermen are, so they say, too well adjusted. But here on Earth, as the proverb goes, there are more psychiatrists than plumbers, and they get lots of practice. So it is we, and not they, who know the truth about this Outer World superiority-complex, who know it to be simply a wild reaction against an overwhelming feeling of *guilt*.

'Don't you think that can be so? You shake your head as though you disagree. You don't see that a handful of men who clutch a Galaxy while billions starve for lack of room *must* feel a subconscious guilt, no matter what? And, since they won't share the loot, don't you see that the only way they can justify themselves is to try to convince themselves that Earthmen, after all, are inferior, that they do not deserve the Galaxy, that a new race of men have been created out there and that we here are only the diseased remnants of an old race that should die out like the dinosaur, through the working of inexorable natural laws?

'Ah, if they could only convince themselves of that, they would no longer be guilty, but merely superior. Only, it doesn't work; it never does. It requires constant bolstering; constant repetition, constant reinforcement. And still it doesn't quite convince.

'Best of all, if only they could pretend that Earth and its population do not exist at all. When you visit Earth, therefore, avoid Earthmen; or they might make you uncomfortable by not looking inferior enough. Sometimes they might look miserable instead, and nothing more. Or worse still, they might even seem intelligent – as I did, for instance, on Aurora.

'Occasionally, an Outer Worlder like Moreanu did crop up, and was able to recognize guilt for what it was without being afraid to say so out loud. He spoke of the duty the Outer Worlds owed Earth – and so he was dangerous to us. For if the others listened to him and had offered token assistance to Earth, their guilt might have been assuaged in their own minds; and that without any lasting help to Earth. So Moreanu was removed through our web-weaving, and the way left clear to those who were unbending, who refused to admit guilt, and whose reaction could therefore be predicted and manipulated.

'Send them an arrogant note, for instance, and they automatically strike back with a useless embargo that merely gives us the ideal pretext for war. Then lose a war quickly, and you are sealed off by the annoyed supermen. No communication, no contact. You no longer exist to annoy them. Isn't that simple? Didn't it work out nicely?'

Keilin finally found his voice, because Moreno gave him time by stopping. He said: 'You mean that all this was planned? You *did* deliberately instigate the war for the purpose of sealing Earth off from the Galaxy? You sent out the men of the Home Fleet to sure death because you wanted defeat? Why, you're a monster, a . . . a—'

Moreno frowned: 'Please relax. It was not as simple as you think, and I am not a monster. Do you think the war could simply be – instigated? It had to be nurtured gently in just the right way and to just the right conclusion. If we had made the first move, if we had been the aggressor, if we had in any way put the fault on our side – why, they of the Outer Worlds would have occupied Earth and ground it under. They would no longer feel guilty, you see, if *we* committed a crime against *them*. Or, again, if we fought a protracted war, or one in which we inflicted damage, they could succeed in shifting the blame.

'But we didn't. We merely imprisoned Auroran smugglers, and were obviously within our rights. They had to go to war over it because only so could they protect their superiority, which in turn protected them against the horrors of guilt. And we lost quickly. Scarcely an Auroran died. The guilt grew deeper and resulted in exactly the peace treaty our psychiatrists had predicted.

'And as for sending men out to die, that is a commonplace in every war – and a necessity. It was necessary to fight a battle, and, naturally, there were casualties.'

'But why?' interrupted Keilin, wildly. 'Why? *Why?* Why does all this gibberish seem to make sense to you? What have we gained? What can we possibly gain out of the present situation?'

'Gained, man? You ask what we've gained? Why, we've gained

the universe. What has held us back so far? *You* know what Earth has needed these last centuries. You yourself once outlined it forcefully to Cellioni. We need a positronic robot society and an atomic power technology. We need chemical farming and we need population control. Well, what's prevented that, eh? Only the customs of centuries which said robots were evil since they deprived human beings of jobs, that population control was merely the murder of unborn children, and so on. And worse, there was always the safety valve of emigration either actual or hoped-for.

'But now we cannot emigrate. We're *stuck* here. Worse than that, we have been humiliatingly defeated by a handful of men out in the stars, and we've had a humiliating treaty of peace forced upon us. What Earthman wouldn't subconsciously burn for revenge? Self-preservation has frequently knuckled under to that tremendous yearning to "get even".

'And that is the second third of the Pacific Project, the recognition of the revenge motive. As simple as that.

'And how can we know that this is really so? Why, it has been demonstrated in history scores of times. Defeat a nation, but don't crush it entirely, and in a generation or two or three it will be stronger than it was before. Why? Because in the interval, sacrifices will have been made for revenge that would not have been made for mere conquest.

'Think! Rome beat Carthage rather easily the first time, but was almost defeated the second. Every time Napoleon defeated the European coalition, he laid the groundwork for another just a little bit harder to defeat, until he himself was crushed by the eighth. It took four years to defeat Wilhelm of medieval Germany, and six much more dangerous years to stop his successor, Hitler.

'There you are! Until now, Earth needed to change its way of life only for greater comfort and happiness. A minor item like that could always wait. But now it must change for revenge, and that will not wait. And I want that change for its own sake.

'Only— I am not the man to lead. I am tarred with the failure of yesteryear, and will remain so until, long after I am bone-dust, Earth learns the truth. But you . . . *you*, and others like you, have always fought for the road to modernization. *You* will be in charge. It may take a hundred years. Grandchildren of men unborn may be the first to see its completion. But at least you will see the start.

'Eh, what, do you say?'

Keilin was fumbling at the dream. He seemed to see it in a misty distance – a new and reborn Earth. But the change in attitude was too extreme. It could not be done just yet: He shook his head. He said: 'What makes you think the Outer Worlds would allow such a change, supposing what you say to be true? They will be watching, I am sure, and they will detect a growing danger and put a stop to it. Can you deny that?'

Moreno threw his head back and laughed noiselessly. He gasped out: 'But we have still a third left of the Pacific Project, a last, subtle and ironic third—

'The Outer Worlders call the men of Earth the subhuman dregs of a great race, but *we* are the men of *Earth*. Do you realize what that means? We live on a planet upon which, for a billion years, life – the life that has culminated in Mankind – has been adapting itself. There is not a microscopic part of Man, not a tiny working of his mind, that has not as its reason some tiny facet of the physical make-up of Earth, or of the biological make-up of Earth's other life-forms, or of the sociological make-up of the society about him.

'No other planet can substitute for Earth, *in Man's present shape*.

'The Outer Worlders exist as they do, only because pieces of Earth have been transplanted. Soil has been brought out there; plants; animals; men. They keep themselves surrounded by an artificial Earthborn geology which has within it, for instance, those traces of cobalt, zinc, and copper which human chemistry must have. They surround themselves by Earth-born bacteria and algae which have the ability to make those inorganic traces available in just the right way and in just the right quantity.

'And they maintain that situation by continued imports – luxury imports, they call it – from Earth.

'But on the Outer Worlds, even with Terrestrian soil laid down to bedrock, they cannot keep rain from falling and rivers from flowing, so that there is an inevitable, if slow, admixture with the native soil; an inevitable contamination of Terrestrian soil bacteria with the native bacteria, and an exposure, in any case, to a different atmosphere and to solar radiations of different types. Terrestrian bacteria disappear or change. And then plant life changes. And then animal life.

'No great change, mind you. Plant life would not become poisonous or nonnutritious in a day, or year, or decade. But already, the men of the Outer Worlds can detect the loss or change of the trace compounds that are responsible for that infinitely elusive thing we call "flavor". It has gone that far.

'And it will go further. Do you know, for instance, that on Aurora, nearly one half the native bacterial species known have protoplasm based on a fluorocarbon rather than hydrocarbon chemistry? Can you imagine the essential foreignness of such an environment?

'Well, for two decades now, the bacteriologists and physiologists of Earth have studied various forms of Outer World life – the only portion of the Pacific Project that has been truly secret – and the transplanted Terrestrian life is already beginning to show certain changes on the subcellular level. *Even among the humans.*

'And here is the irony. The Outer Worlders, by their rigid racism and unbending genetic policies are consistently eliminating from among themselves any children that show signs of adapting themselves to their respective planets in any way that departs from the norm. They are maintaining – they *must* maintain as a result of their own thought processes – an artificial criterion of "healthy" humanity, which is based on Terrestrian chemistiy and not their own.

'But now that Earth has been cut off from them; now that not even a trickle of Terrestrian soil and life will reach them, change will be piled on change. Sicknesses will come, mortality will increase, child abnormalities will become more frequent—'

'And then?' asked Keilin, suddenly caught up.

'And then? Well, they are physical scientists – leaving such inferior sciences as biology to us. And they cannot abandon their sensation of superiority and their arbitrary standard of human perfection. They will never detect the change till it is too late to fight it. Not all mutations are clearly visible, and there will be an increasing revolt against the mores of those stiff Outer World societies. There will be a century of increasing physical and social turmoil which will prevent any interference on their part with us.

'We will have a century of rebuilding and revitalization, and at the end of it, we shall face an outer Galaxy which will either be dying or changed. In the first case, we will build a second Terrestrian Empire, more wisely and with greater knowledge than we did the first; one based on a strong and modernized Earth.

'In the second case, we will face perhaps ten, twenty, or even all fifty Outer Worlds, each with a slightly different variety of Man. Fifty humanoid species, no longer united against us, each increasingly adapted to its own planet, each with a sufficient tendency toward atavism to love Earth, to regard it as the great and original Mother.

'And racism will be dead, for variety will then be the great fact of Humanity, and not uniformity. Each type of Man will have a world of its own, for which no other world could quite substitute, and on which no other type could live quite as well. And other worlds can be settled to breed still newer varieties, until out of the grand intellectual mixture, Mother Earth will finally have given birth not to merely a Terrestrian, but to a *Galactic* Empire.'

Kellin said, fascinated, 'You foresee all this so certainly.'

'Nothing is *truly* certain; but the best minds on Earth agree on this. There may be unforeseen stumbling blocks on the way, but to remove those will be the adventure of our great-grandchildren. Of *our* adventure, one phase has been successfully concluded; and another phase is beginning. Join us, Keilin.'

Slowly, Keilin began to think that perhaps Moreno was not a monster after all—

Darwinian Pool Room

'*Of course* the ordinary conception of Genesis 1 is all wrong,' I said. 'Take a pool room, for instance.'

The other three mentally took a pool room. We were sitting in broken down swivel chairs in Dr Trotter's laboratory, but it was no trick at all to convert the lab benches into pool tables, the tall ring stands into cues, the reagent bottles into billiard balls, and then set the whole thing neatly before us.

Thetier even raised one finger, closed his eyes, and muttered softly, 'Pool room!' Trotter, as usual, said nothing at all, but nursed his second cup of coffee. The coffee, also as usual, was horrible, but then, I was the newcomer to the group and had not callused my gastric lining sufficiently yet.

'Now consider the end of a game of pocket pool,' I said. 'You've got each ball, except the cue ball, of course, in a given pocket—'

'Wait awhile,' said Thetier, always the purist, 'it doesn't matter which pocket as long as you put them in in a certain order or—'

'Beside the point. When the game is all over, the balls are in various pockets. Right? Now suppose you walk into the pool room when the game is all over, and observe only that final position and try to reconstruct the course of previous events. Obviously, you have a number of alternatives.'

'Not if you know the rules of the game,' said Madend.

'Assume complete ignorance,' I said. 'You *can* decide that the balls were pocketed by being struck with the cue ball, which in turn was struck by the cue. This would be the truth, but not an explanation that is very likely to occur to you spontaneously. It is much more likely that you would decide that the balls were individually placed in their corresponding pockets by hand, or else that the balls always existed in the pockets as you found them.'

'All right,' said Thetier, 'if you're going to skip back to Genesis, you will claim that by analogy we can account for the universe as either having always existed, having been created arbitrarily, as it is now, or having developed through evolution. So what?'

'That's not the alternative I'm proposing at all,' I said. 'Let us accept the fact of a purposeful creation, and consider only the methods by which such a creation could have been accomplished. It's easy to suppose that God said, "Let there be light," and there was light, but it's not esthetic.'

'It's simple,' said Madend, 'and Occam's Razor demands that of alternate possibilities, the simpler be chosen.'

'Then why don't you end a pool game by putting the balls in the pockets by hand? That's simpler, too, but it isn't esthetic. On the other hand, if you started with the primordial atom—'

'What is that?' asked Trotter, softly.

'Well, call it all the mass energy of the universe compressed into a single sphere, in a state of minimum entropy. If you were to explode that in such a way that all the constituent particles of matter and quanta of energy were to act, react, and interact in a precalculated way so that just our present universe is created, wouldn't that be much more satisfactory than simply waving your hand and saying, "Let there be light!"'

'You mean,' said Madend, 'like stroking the cue ball against one of the billiard balls and sending all fifteen into their predestined pockets.'

'In a pretty pattern,' I said. 'Yes.'

'There's more poetry in the thought of a huge act of direct will,' said Madend.

'That depends on whether you look at the matter as a mathematician or a theologian,' I said. 'As a matter of fact, Genesis 1 could be made to fit the billiard-ball scheme. The Creator could have spent his time calculating all the necessary variables and relationships into six gigantic equations. Count one "day" for each equation. After having applied the initial explosive impetus, he would then "rest" on the seventh "day", said seventh "day" being the entire interval of time from that beginning to 4004 BC. That interval, in which the infinitely complex pattern of billiard balls is sorting itself out, is obviously of no interest to the writers of the Bible. All the billions of years of it could be considered merely the developing single act of creation.'

'You're postulating a teleological universe,' said Trotter, 'one in which purpose is implied.'

'Sure,' I said, 'why not? A conscious act of creation without a purpose is ridiculous. Besides which, if you try to consider the course of evolution as the blind outcome of nonpurposive forces, you end up with some very puzzling problems.'

'As for instance?' asked Madend.

'As for instance,' I said, 'the passing away of the dinosaurs.'

'What's so hard to understand about that?'

'There's no logical reason for it. Try to name some.'

'Law of diminishing returns,' said Madend. 'The brontosaurus got so massive, it took legs like tree trunks to support him, and at that he had to stand in water and let buoyancy do most of the work. And he had to eat all the time to keep himself supplied with calories. I mean, *all the time*. As for the carnivores, they afflicted such armor upon themselves in their race against one another, offensive and defensive, that they were just crawling tanks, puffing under half a ton of bone and scale. It just got to the point where it didn't pay off.'

'Okay,' I said, 'so the big babies die off. But most of the dinosaurs were little running creatures where neither mass nor armor had become excessive. What happened to them?'

'As far as the small ones are concerned,' put in Thetier, 'there's the question of competition. If some of the reptiles developed hair and warm blood, those could adapt themselves to variations in climate more efficiently. They wouldn't have to stay out of direct sunlight. They wouldn't get sluggish as soon as the temperature dropped below eighty Fahrenheit. They wouldn't have to hibernate in the winter. Therefore, they would get out front in the race for food.'

'That doesn't satisfy me,' I said. 'In the first place, I don't think the various saurians are quite such pushovers. They held out for some three hundred million years, you know, which is 298 million more than genus *Homo* has to its credit. Secondly, cold-blooded animals still survive, notably insects and amphibia—'

'Powers of reproduction,' said Thetier.

'*And* some reptiles. The snakes, lizards, and turtles are doing very well, thank you. For that matter, what about the ocean. The saurians adapted to that in the shape of ichthyosaurs and plesiosaurs. They vanished, too, and there were no newly developed forms of life based on radical evolutionary advances to compete with them. As near as I can make out, the highest form of ocean life are the fish, and they antedate the ichthyosaurs. How do you account for that? The fish are just as cold-blooded and even more primitive. And in the ocean there's no question of mass and diminishing returns, since the water does all the work of support. The sulfurbottom whale is larger than any dinosaur that ever lived. Another thing. What's the use of talking about the inefficiency of cold blood and saying that at temperatures below eighty, cold-blooded animals become sluggish. Fish are very happy at continuous temperatures of about thirty-five, and there is nothing sluggish about a shark.'

'Then why did the dinosaurs quietly steal off the Earth, leaving their bones behind?' asked Madend.

'They were part of the plan. Once they had served their purpose, they were unnecessary and therefore gotten rid of.'

'How? In a properly arranged Velikovskian catastrophe? A striking comet? The finger of God?'

'No, of course not. They died out naturally and of necessity according to the original precalculation.'

'Then we ought to be able to find out what that natural, necessary cause of extinction was.'

'Not necessarily. It might have been some obscure failure of the saurian biochemistry, some developing vitamin deficiency—'

'It's all too complicated,' said Thetier.

'It just seems complicated,' I maintained. 'Supposing it were necessary to pocket a given billiard ball by making a four-cushion shot. Would you quibble at the relatively complicated course of the cue ball? A direct hit would be less complicated, but would accomplish nothing. And despite the apparent complication, the stroke would be no more difficult to the master. It would still be a single motion of the cue, merely in a different direction. The ordinary properties of elastic materials and the laws of conservation of momentum would then take over.'

'I take it, then,' said Trotter, 'that you suggest that the course of evolution represents the simplest way in which one could have progressed from original chaos to man.'

'That's right. Not a sparrow falls without a purpose, and not a pterodactyl, either.'

'And where do we go from here?'

'Nowhere. Evolution is finished with the development of man. The old rules don't apply anymore.'

'Oh, don't they?' said Madend. 'You rule out the continuing occurrence of environmental variation and of mutations.'

'In a sense, I do,' I insisted. 'More and more, man is controlling his environment, and more and more he is understanding the mechanism of mutations. Before man appeared on the scene, creatures could neither foresee and guard themselves against shifts in climatic conditions. Nor could they understand the increasing danger from newly developing species before the danger had become overwhelming. But now ask yourself this question: What species of organism can possibly replace us and how is it going to accomplish the task?'

'We can start off,' said Madend, 'by considering the insects. I think they're doing the job already.'

'They haven't prevented us from increasing in population about ten-fold in the last two hundred and fifty years. If man were ever to concentrate on the struggle with the insects instead of spending most of his spare effort on other types of fighting, said insects would not last long. No way of proving it, but that's my opinion.'

'What about bacteria, or, better still, viruses,' said Madend.

'The influenza virus of 1918 did a respectable job of getting rid of a sizable percentage of us.'

'Sure,' I said, 'just about one percent of us. Even the Black Death of the fourteenth century only managed to kill one third of the population of Europe, and that at a time when medical science was nonexistent. It was allowed to run its course at will, under the most appalling conditions of medieval poverty, filth and squalor, and still two thirds of our very tough species managed to survive. Disease can't do it; I'm sure.'

'What about man himself developing into a sort of superman and displacing the old-timers,' suggested Thetier.

'Not bloody likely,' I said. 'The only part of the human being which is worth anything, as far as being boss of the world is concerned, is his nervous system; the cerebral hemispheres of the brain, in particular. They are the most specialized part of his organism and therefore a dead end. If there is anything the course of evolution demonstrates, it is that once a certain degree of specialization sets in, flexibility is lost and further development can proceed only in the direction of greater specialization.'

'Isn't that exactly what's wanted?' said Thetier.

'Maybe it is, but, as Madend pointed out, specializations have a way of reaching a point of diminishing returns. It's the size of the human head at birth that makes the process difficult and painful.

It's the complexity of the human mentality that makes mental and emotional maturity lag so far behind sexual maturity in man, with *its* consequent harvest of troubles. It's the delicacy of mental equipment that makes most of all of the race neurotic. How much further can we go without complete disaster?'

'The development,' said Madend, 'might be in the direction of greater stability or quicker maturity rather than in that of higher intensity of brain power.'

'Maybe, but there are no signs of it. The Cro-Magnon man existed ten thousand years ago and there are some interesting indications that modem man is his inferior, if anything, in brain power, and in physique, too, for that matter.'

'Ten thousand years,' said Trotter, 'isn't much, evolutionarily speaking. Besides, there is always the possibility of other species of animals developing intelligence, or something better, if there is anything better.'

'We'd never let them. That's the point. It would take hundreds of thousands of years for, let us say, bears or rats to become intelligent, and we'd wipe them out as soon as we saw what was happening – or else use them as slaves.'

'All right,' said Thetier. 'What about obscure biochemical deficiencies, such as you insisted on in the case of the dinosaurs. Take vitamin C, for instance. The only organisms that can't make their own are guinea pigs, and primates, including man. Suppose this trend continues and we become impossibly dependent on too many essential food factors. Or what if the apparent increase in the susceptibility of man to cancer continues. Then what?'

'That's no problem,' I said. 'It's the essence of the new situation, that we are producing all known food-factors artificially and may eventually have a completely synthetic diet. And there's no reason to think we won't learn how to prevent or cure cancer someday.'

Trotter got up. He had finished his coffee but was still nursing his cup. 'All right, then, you say we've hit a dead end. But what if all this has been taken into the original account. The Creator was prepared to spend three hundred million years letting the dinosaurs develop something or other that would hasten the development of man, or so you say; why can't he have figured out a way in which man could use his intelligence and his control of the environment to prepare the next stage of the game? That might be a very amusing part of the billiard-ball pattern.'

That stopped me. 'How do you mean?' I asked.

Trotter smiled at me. 'Oh, I was just thinking that it might not be entirely coincidence, and that a new race may be coming and an old one going entirely through the efforts of this cerebral mechanism.' He tapped his temple.

'In what way?'

'Stop me if I'm wrong, but aren't the sciences of nucleonics and cybernetics reaching simultaneous peaks? Aren't we inventing hydrogen bombs and thinking machines at the same time? Is that coincidence or part of the divine purpose?'

That was about all for that lunch hour. It had begun as logic chopping on my part, but since then – I've been wondering!

Shah Guido G.

Once every year Philo Plat returned to the scene of his crime. It was a form of penance. On each anniversary he climbed the barren crest and gazed along the miles of smashed metal, concrete, and bones.

The area was desolate. The metal crumplings were still stainless and unrusted, their jagged teeth raised in futile anger. Somewhere among it all were the skeletons of the thousands who had died, of all ages and both sexes. Their skully sightlessness, for all he knew, was turning empty, curse-torn eye holes at him.

The stench had long since gone from the desert, and the lizards held their lairs untroubled. No man approached the fenced-off burial ground where what remained of bodies lay in the gashed crater carved out in that final fall.

Only Plat came. He returned year after year and always, as though to ward off so many Evil Eyes, he took his gold medal with him. It hung suspended bravely from his neck as he stood on the crest. On it was inscribed simply, 'To the Liberator!'

This time, Fulton was with him. Fulton had been a Lower One once in the days before the crash; the days when there had been Higher Ones and Lower Ones.

Fulton said, 'I am amazed you insist on coming here, Philo.'

Plat said, 'I must. You know the sound of the crash was heard for hundreds of miles; seismographs registered it around the world. My ship was almost directly above it; the shock vibrations caught me and flung me miles: Yet all I can remember of sound is that one composite scream as Atlantis began its fall.'

'It had to be done.'

'Words,' sighed Plat. 'There were babies and guiltless ones.'

'No one is guiltless.'

'Nor am I. Ought I to have been the executioner?'

'Someone had to be.' Fulton was firm. 'Consider the world now, twenty-five years later. Democracy re-established, education once more universal, culture available for the masses, and science once more advancing. Two expeditions have already landed on Mars.'

'I know. I know. But that, too, was a culture. They called it Atlantis because it was an island that ruled the world. It was an island in the sky, not the sea. It was a city and a world all at once, Fulton. You never saw its crystal covering and its gorgeous buildings. It was a single jewel carved of stone and metal. It was a dream.'

'It was concentrated happiness distilled out of the little supply distributed to billions of ordinary folk who lived on the Surface.'

'Yes, you are right. Yes, it had to be. But it might have been so different, Fulton. You know,' he seated himself on the hard rock, crossed his arms upon his knees and cradled his chin in them, 'I think, sometimes, of how it must have been in the old days, when there were nations and wars upon the Earth. I think of how much a miracle it must have seemed to the peoples when the United Nations first became a real world government, and what Atlantis must have meant to them.

'It was a capital city that governed Earth but was not of it. It was a black disc in the air, capable of appearing anywhere on Earth at any height; belonging to no one nation, but to all the planet; the product of no one nation's ingenuity but the first great achievement of all the race – and then, what it became!'

Fulton said, 'Shall we go? We'll want to get back to the ship before dark.'

Plat went on, 'In a way, I suppose it was inevitable. The human race never did invent an institution that didn't end as a cancer. Probably in prehistoric times, the medicine man who began as the repository of tribal wisdom ended as the last bar to tribal advance. In ancient Rome, the citizen army—'

Fulton was letting him speak – patiently. It was a queer echo of the past. And there had been other eyes upon him in those days, patiently waiting, while he talked.

'—the citizen army that defended the Romans against all comers from Veil to Carthage, became the professional Praetorian Guard that sold the Imperium and levied tribute on all the Empire. The Turks developed the Janissaries as their invincible advance guard against Europe and the Sultan ended as a slave of his Janissary slaves. The barons of medieval Europe protected the serfs against the Northmen and the Magyars, then remained six hundred years longer as a parasite aristocracy that contributed nothing.'

Plat became aware of the patient eyes and said, 'Don't you understand me?'

One of the bolder technicians said, 'With your kind permission, Higher One, we must needs be at work.'

'Yes, I suppose you must.'

The technician felt sorry. This Higher One was queer, but he meant well. Though he spoke a deal of nonsense, he inquired after their families, told them they were fine fellows, and that their work made them better than the Higher Ones.

So he explained, 'You see, there is another shipment of granite and steel for the new theater and we will have to shift the energy distribution. It is becoming very hard to do that. The Higher Ones will not listen.'

'Now that's what I mean. You should *make* them listen.'

But they just stared at him, and at that moment an idea crawled gently into Plat's unconscious mind.

Leo Spinney waited for him on the crystal level. He was Plat's age but taller and much more handsome. Plat's face was thin, his eyes were china-blue, and he never smiled. Spinney was straightnosed with brown eyes that seemed to laugh continuously.

Spinney called, 'We'll miss the game.'

'I don't want to go, Leo. Please.'

Spinney said, 'With the technicians again? Why do you waste your time?'

Plat said, 'They work. I respect them. What right have we to idle?'

'Ought I to ask questions of the world as it is when it suits me so well?'

'If you do not, someone will ask questions for you someday.'

'That will be someday, not this day. And, frankly, you had better come. The Sekjen has noticed that you are never present at the games and he doesn't like it. Personally, I think people have been telling him of your talks to the technicians and your visits to the Surface. He might even think you consort with Lower Ones.'

Spinney laughed heartily, but Plat said nothing. It would not hurt them if they consorted with Lower Ones a bit more, learned something of their thinking. Atlantis had its guns and its battalions of Waves. It might learn someday that that was not enough. Not enough to save the Sekjen.

The Sekjen! Plat wanted to spit. The full title was 'Secretary General of the United Nations.' Two centuries before it had been an elective office; an honorable one. Now a man like Guido Garshthavastra could fill it because he could prove he was the son of his equally worthless father.

'Guido G.' was what the Lower Ones on the Surface called him. And usually, with bitterness, 'Shah Guido G.', because 'Shah' had been the title of a line of despotic oriental kings. The Lower Ones knew him for what he was. Plat wanted to tell Spinney that, but it wasn't time yet.

The real games were held in the upper stratosphere, a hundred miles above Atlantis, though the Sky-Island was itself twenty miles above sea-level. The huge amphitheater was filled and the radiant globe in its center held all eyes. Each tiny one-man cruiser high above was represented by its own particular glowing symbol in the color that belonged to the fleet of which it was part. The little sparks reproduced in exact miniature the motions of the ships.

The game was starting as Plat and Spinney took their seats. The little dots were already flashing toward one another, skimming and missing, veering.

A large scoreboard blazoned the progress of the battle in conventional symbology that Plat did not understand. There was confused cheering for either fleet and for particular ships.

High up under a canopy was the Sekjen, the Shah Guido G. of the Lower Ones. Plat could barely see him but he could make out clearly the smaller replica of the game globe that was there for his private use.

Plat was watching the game for the first time. He understood none of the finer points and wondered at the reason for the particular shouts. Yet he understood that the dots were ships and that the streaks of light that licked out from them on frequent occasions represented energy beams which, one hundred miles above, were as real as flaring atoms could make them. Each time a dot streaked, there was a clamor in the audience that died in a great moan as a target dot veered and escaped.

And then there was a general yell and the audience, men and women up to the Sekjen himself, clambered to its feet. One of the shining dots had been hit and was going down – spiraling, spiraling. A hundred miles above, a real ship was doing the same; plunging down into the thickening air that would heat and consume its specially designed magnesium alloy shell to harmless powdery ash before it could reach the surface of the Earth.

Plat turned away. 'I'm leaving, Spinney.'

Spinney was marking his scorecard and saying, 'That's five ships the Greens have lost this week. We've got to have more.' He was on his feet, calling wildly, 'Another one!'

The audience was taking up the shout, chanting it. Plat said, 'A man died in that ship.'

'You bet. One of the Greens' best too. Damn good thing.'

'Do you realize that a man *died*.'

'They're only Lower Ones. What's bothering you?'

Plat made his slow way out among the rows of people. A few looked at him and whispered. Most had eyes for nothing but the game globe. There was perfume all about him and in the distance, occasionally heard amid the shouts, there was a faint wash of gentle music. As he passed through a main exit, a yell trembled the air behind him.

Plat fought the nausea grimly.

He walked two miles, then stopped.

Steel girders were swinging at the end of diamagnetic beams and the coarse sound of orders yelled in Lower accents filled the air.

There was always building going on upon Atlantis. Two hundred years ago, when Atlantis had been the genuine seat of government, its lines had been straight, its spaces broad. But now it was much more than that. It was the Xanadu pleasure dome that Coleridge spoke of.

The crystal roof had been lifted upward and outward many times in the last two centuries. Each time it had been thickened so that Atlantis might more safely climb higher; more safely withstand the possible blows of meteoric pebbles not yet entirely burnt by the thin wisps of air.

And as Atlantis became more useless and more attractive, more and more of the Higher Ones left their estates and factories in the hands of managers and foremen and took up permanent residence on the Sky-Island. All built larger, higher, more elaborately.

And here was still another structure.

Waves were standing by in stolid, duty-ridden obedience. The name applied to the females – if, Plat thought sourly, they could be called that – was taken from the Early English of the days when Earth was divided into nations. There, too, conversion and degeneration had obtained. The old Waves had done paper work behind the lines. These creatures, still called Waves, were front-line soldiers.

It made sense, Plat knew. Properly trained, women were more single-minded, more fanatic, less given to doubts and remorse than ever men could be.

They always had Waves present at the scene of any building, because the building was done by Lower Ones, and Lower Ones on Atlantis had to be guarded. Just as those on the Surface had to be cowed. In the last fifty years alone, the long-range atomic artillery that studded the underside of Atlantis had been doubled and tripled.

He watched the girder come softly down, two men yelling directions to each other as it settled in place. Soon there would be no further room for new buildings on Atlantis.

The idea that had nudged his unconscious mind earlier in the day gently touched his conscious mind.

Plat's nostrils flared.

Plat's nose twitched at the smell of oil and machinery. More than most of the perfume-spoiled Higher Ones, he was used to odors of all sorts. He had been on the Surface and smelled the pungence of its growing fields and the fumes of its cities.

He said to the technician, 'I am seriously thinking of building a new house and would like your advice as to the best possible location.'

The technician was amazed and gratified. 'Thank you, Higher One. It has become so difficult to arrange the available power.'

'It is why I come to you.'

They talked at length. Plat asked a great many questions and when he returned to crystal level his mind was a maze of speculation. Two days passed in an agony of doubt. Then he remembered the shining dot, spiraling and spiraling, and the young, wondering eyes upon his own as Spinney said, 'They're only Lower Ones.'

He made up his mind and applied for audience with the Sekjen.

The Sekjen's drawling voice accentuated the boredom he did not care to hide. He said, 'The Plats are of good family, yet you amuse yourself with technicians. I am told you speak to them as equals. I *hope* that it will not become necessary to remind you that your estates on the Surface require your care.'

That would have meant exile from Atlantis, of course.

Plat said, 'It is necessary to watch the technicians, Sire. They are of Lower extraction.'

The Sekjen frowned. 'Our Wave Commander has her job. She takes care of such matters.'

'She does her best, I have no doubt, Sire, but I have made friends with the technicians. They are not safe. Would I have any other reason to soil my hands with them, but the safety of Atlantis.'

The Sekjen listened. First, doubtfully; then, with fear on his soft face. He said, 'I shall have them in custody—'

'Softly, Sire,' said Plat. 'We cannot do without them meanwhile, since none of us can man the guns and the antigravs. It would be better to give them no opportunity for rebellion. In two weeks the new theater will be dedicated with games and feasting.'

'And what do they intend then?'

'I am not yet certain, Sire. But I know enough to recommend that a division of Waves be brought to Atlantis. Secretly, of course, and at the last minute so that it will be too late for the rebels to change any plans they have made. They will have to drop them altogether, and the proper moment, once lost, may never be regained. Thereafter, I will learn more. If necessary, we will train new men. It would be a pity, Sire, to tell anyone of this in advance. If the technicians learn our countermeasures prematurely, matters may go badly.'

The Sekjen, with his jeweled hand to his chin, mused – and believed.

Shah Guido G., thought Philo Plat. In history, you'll go down as Shah Guido G.

Philo Plat watched the gaiety from a distance. Atlantis's central squares were crawling black with people. That was good. He himself had managed to get away only with difficulty. And none too soon, since the Wave Division had already cross-hatched the sky with their ships.

They were maneuvering edgily now, adjusting themselves into final position over Atlantis's huge, raised air field, which was well able to take their ships all at once.

The cruisers were descending now vertically, in parade formation. Plat looked quickly toward the city proper. The populace had grown quieter as they watched the unscheduled demonstration, and it seemed to him that he had never seen so many Higher Ones upon the Sky-Island at one time. For a moment, a last misgiving arose. There was still time for a warning.

And even as he thought that he knew that there wasn't. The cruisers were dropping speedily. He would have to hurry if he were himself to escape in his own little craft. He wondered sickly, even as he grasped the controls, whether his friends on the Surface had received his yesterday's warning, or would believe it if they had received it. If they could not act quickly the Higher Ones would yet recover from the first blow, devastating though it was.

He was in the air when the Waves landed, seven thousand five hundred tear-drop ships covering the airfield like a descending net. Plat drove his ship upward, watching—

And Atlantis went dark! It was like a candle over which a mighty hand was suddenly cupped. One moment it blazed the night into brilliance for fifty miles around; the next it was black against blackness.

To Plat the thousands of screams blended into one thin, lost shriek of fear. He fled, and the shock vibrations of Atlantis's crash to Earth caught his ship and hurled it far.

He never stopped hearing that scream.

Fulton was staring at Plat. He said, 'Have you ever told this to anyone?'

Plat shook his head.

Fulton's mind went back a quarter century, too. 'We got your message, of course. It was hard to believe, as you expected. Many feared a trap even after report of the Fall arrived. But – well, it's history. The Higher Ones that remained, those on the Surface, were demoralized and before they could recover, they were done.

'But tell me,' he turned to Plat with sudden, hard curiosity. 'What was it you did? We've always assumed you sabotaged the power stations.'

'I know. The truth is so much less romantic, Fulton. The world would prefer to believe its myth. Let it.'

'May *I* have the truth?'

'If you will. As I told you, the Higher Ones built and built to saturation. The antigrav energy beams had to support a weight in buildings, guns, and enclosing shell that doubled and tripled as the years went on. Any requests the technicians might have made for newer or bigger motors were turned down, since the Higher Ones would rather have the room and money for their mansions and there was always enough power for the moment.

'The technicians, as I said, had already reached the stage where they were disturbed at the construction of single buildings. I questioned them and found exactly how little margin of safety remained. They were waiting only for the completion of the new theater to make a new request. They did *not* realize, however, that, at my suggestion, Atlantis would be called upon to support the sudden additional burden of a division of Wave cavalry in their ships. Seven thousand five hundred ships, fully rigged!

'When the Waves landed, by then almost two thousand tons, the antigrav power supply was overloaded. The motors failed and

Atlantis was only a vast rock, ten miles above the ground. What could such a rock do but fall.'

Plat arose. Together they turned back toward their ship.

Fulton laughed harshly. 'You know, there is a fatality in names.'

'What do you mean?'

'Why, that once more in history Atlantis sank beneath the Waves.'

Button, Button

It was the tuxedo that fooled me and for two seconds I didn't recognize him. To me, he was just a possible client, the first that had whiffed my way in a week – and he looked beautiful.

Even wearing a tuxedo at 9:45 a.m. he looked beautiful. Six inches of bony wrist and ten inches of knobby hand continued on where his sleeve left off; the top of his socks and the bottom of his trousers did not quite join forces; still he looked beautiful.

Then I looked at his face and it wasn't a client at all. It was my uncle Otto. Beauty ended. As usual, my uncle Otto's face looked like that of a bloodhound that had just been kicked in the rump by his best friend.

I wasn't very original in my reaction. I said, 'Uncle Otto!'

You'd know him too, if you saw that face. When he was featured on the cover of *Time* about five years ago (it was either '57 or '58), 204 readers by count wrote in to say that they would never forget that face. Most added comments concerning nightmares. If you want my uncle Otto's full name, it's Otto Schlemmelmayer. But don't jump to conclusions. He's my mother's brother. My own name is Smith.

He said, 'Harry, my boy,' and groaned.

Interesting, but not enlightening. I said, 'Why the tuxedo?'

He said, 'It's rented.'

'All right. But why do you wear it in the morning?'

'Is it morning already?' He stared vaguely about him, then went to the window and looked out.

That's my uncle Otto Schlemmelmayer.

I assured him it was morning and with an effort he deduced that he must have been walking the city streets all night.

He took a handful of fingers away from his forehead to say, 'But I was so upset, Harry. At the banquet—'

The fingers waved about for a minute and then folded into a quart of fist that came down and pounded holes in my desk top. 'But it's the end. From now on I do things my own way.'

My uncle Otto had been saying that since the business of the 'Schlemmelmayer Effect' first started up. Maybe that surprises you.

Maybe you think it was the Schlemmelmayer Effect that made my uncle Otto famous. Well, it's all how you look at it.

He discovered the Effect back in 1952 and the chances are that you know as much about it as I do. In a nutshell, he devised a germanium relay of such a nature as to respond to thoughtwaves, or anyway to the electromagnetic fields of the brain cells. He worked for years to build such a delay into a flute, so that it would play music under the pressure of nothing but thought. It was his love, his life, it was to revolutionize music. Everyone would be able to play; no skill necessary – only thought.

Then, five years ago, this young fellow at Consolidated Arms, Stephen Wheland, modified the Schlemmelmayer Effect and reversed it. He devised a field of supersonic waves that could activate the brain via a germanium relay, fry it, and kill a rat at twenty feet. Also, they found out later, men.

After that, Wheland got a bonus of ten thousand dollars and a promotion, while the major stockholders of Consolidated Arms proceeded to make millions when the government bought the patents and placed its orders.

My uncle Otto? He made the cover of *Time*.

After that, everyone who was close to him, say within a few miles, knew he had a grievance. Some thought it was the fact that he had received no money; others, that his great discovery had been made an instrument of war and killing.

Nuts! It was his flute! That was the real tack on the chair of his life. Poor Uncle Otto. He loved his flute. He carried it with him always, ready to demonstrate. It reposed in its special case on the back of his chair when he ate, and at the head of his bed when he slept. Sunday mornings in the university physics laboratories were made hideous by the sounds of my uncle Otto's flute, under imperfect mental control, flatting its way through some tearful German folk song.

The trouble was that no manufacturer would touch it. As soon as its existence was unveiled, the musicians' union threatened to silence every demiquaver in the land; the various entertainment industries called their lobbyists to attention and marked them off in brigades for instant action; and even old Pietro Faranini stuck his baton behind his ear and made fervent statements to the newspapers about the impending death of art.

Uncle Otto never recovered.

He was saying, 'Yesterday were my final hopes. Consolidated informs me they will in my honor a banquet give. Who knows, I say to myself. Maybe they will my flute buy.' Under stress, my uncle Otto's word order tends to shift from English to Germanic.

The picture intrigued me.

'What an idea,' I said. 'A thousand giant flutes secreted in key spots in enemy territories blaring out singing commercials just flat enough to—'

'Quiet! Quiet!' My uncle Otto brought down the flat of his hand on my desk like a pistol shot, and the plastic calendar jumped in fright and fell down dead. 'From you also mockery? Where is your respect?'

'I'm sorry, Uncle Otto.'

'Then listen. I attended the banquet and they made speeches

about the Schlemmelmayer Effect and how it harnessed the power of mind. Then when I thought they would announce they would my flute buy, they give me this!'

He took out what looked like a two-thousand-dollar gold piece and threw it at me. I ducked.

Had it hit the window, it would have gone through and brained a pedestrian, but it hit the wall. I picked it up. You could tell by the weight that it was only gold-plated. On one side it said: 'The Elias Bancroft Sudford Award' in big letters, and 'to Dr Otto Schlemmelmayer for his contributions to science' in small letters. On the other side was a profile, obviously not of my uncle Otto. In fact, it didn't look like any breed of dog; more like a pig.

'That,' said my uncle Otto, 'is Elias Bancroft Sudford, chairman of Consolidated Arms!'

He went on, 'So when I saw that was all, I got up and very politely said: "Gentlemen, dead drop!" and walked out.'

'Then you walked the streets all night,' I filled in for him, 'and came here without even changing your clothes. You're still in your tuxedo.'

My uncle Otto stretched out an arm and looked at its covering. 'A tuxedo?' he said.

'A tuxedo!' I said.

His long, jowled cheeks turned blotchy red and he roared, 'I come here on something of first-rate importance and you insist on about nothing but tuxedos talking. My own nephew!'

I let the fire burn out. My uncle Otto is the brilliant one in the family, so except for trying to keep him from falling into sewers and walking out of windows, we morons try not to bother him.

I said, 'And what can I do for you, Uncle?'

I tried to make it sound businesslike; I tried to introduce the lawyer-client relationship.

He waited impressively and said, 'I need money.'

He had come to the wrong place. I said, 'Uncle, right now I don't have—'

'Not from you,' he said.

I felt better.

He said, 'There is a new Schlemmelmayer Effect; a better one. This one I do *not* in scientific journals publish. My big mouth shut I keep. It entirely my own is.' He was leading a phantom orchestra with his bony fist as he spoke.

'From this new Effect,' he went on, 'I will make money and my own flute factory open.'

'Good,' I said, thinking of the factory and lying.

'But I don't know how.'

'Bad,' I said, thinking of the factory and lying.

'The trouble is my mind is brilliant. I can conceive concepts beyond ordinary people. Only, Harry, I can't conceive ways of making money. It's a talent I do not have.'

'Bad,' I said, not lying at all.

'So I come to you as a lawyer.'

I sniggered a little deprecating snigger.

'I come to you,' he went on, 'to make you help me with your crooked, lying, sneaking, dishonest lawyer's brain.'

I filed the remark, mentally, under unexpected compliments and said, 'I love you, too, Uncle Otto.'

He must have sensed the sarcasm because he turned purple with rage and yelled, 'Don't be touchy. Be like me, patient, understanding, and easygoing, lumphead. Who says anything about you as a man? As a man, you are an honest dunderkopf, but as a lawyer, you have to be a crook. Everyone knows that.'

I sighed. The Bar Association warned me there would be days like this.

'What's your new Effect, Uncle Otto?' I asked.

He said, 'I can reach back into Time and bring things out of the past.'

I acted quickly. With my left hand I snatched my watch out of the lower left vest pocket and consulted it with all the anxiety I could work up. With my right hand I reached for the telephone.

'Well, Uncle,' I said heartily, 'I just remembered an extremely important appointment I'm already hours late for. Always glad to see you. And now, I'm afraid I must say good-bye. Yes, sir, seeing you has been a pleasure, a real pleasure. Well, good-bye. Yes, sir—'

I failed to lift the telephone out of its cradle. I was pulling up all right, but my uncle Otto's hand was on mine and pushing down. It was no contest. Have I said my uncle Otto was once on the Heidelberg wrestling team in '32?

He took hold of my elbow gently (for him) and I was standing. It was a great saving of muscular effort (for me).

'Let's,' he said, 'to my laboratory go.'

He to his laboratory went. And since I had neither the knife nor the inclination to cut my left arm off at the shoulder, I to his laboratory went also . . .

My uncle Otto's laboratory is down a corridor and around a corner in one of the university buildings. Ever since the Schlemmelmayer Effect had turned out to be a big thing, he had been relieved of all course work and left entirely to himself. His laboratory looked it.

I said, 'Don't you keep the door locked anymore?'

He looked at me slyly, his huge nose wrinkling into a sniff. 'It *is* locked. With a Schlemmelmayer relay, it's locked. I think a word and the door opens. Without it, nobody can get in. Not even the president of the university. Not even the *janitor*.'

I got a little excited, 'Great guns, Uncle Otto. A thought-lock could bring you—'

'Hah! I should sell the patent for someone else rich to get? After last night? Never. In a while, I will myself rich become.'

One thing about my uncle Otto. He's not one of these fellows you have to argue and argue with before you can get him to see the light. You know in advance he'll never see the light.

So I changed the subject. I said, 'And the time machine?'

My uncle Otto is a foot taller than I am, thirty pounds heavier, and strong as an ox. When he puts his hands around my throat and shakes, I have to confine my own part in the conflict to turning blue.

I turned blue accordingly. He said, *'Ssh!'*

I got the idea.

He let go and said, 'Nobody knows about Project X.' He repeated, heavily, 'Project X. You understand?'

I nodded. I couldn't speak anyway with a larynx that was only slowly healing.

He said, 'I do not ask you to take my word for it. I will for you a demonstration make.'

I tried to stay near the door.

He said, 'Do you have a piece of paper with your own handwriting on it?'

I fumbled in my inner jacket pocket. I had notes for a possible brief for a possible client on some possible future day.

Uncle Otto said, 'Don't show it to me. Just tear it up. In little pieces tear it up and in this beaker the fragments put.'

I tore it into one hundred and twenty-eight pieces.

He considered them thoughtfully and began adjusting knobs on a – well, on a machine. It had a thick opal-glass slab attached to it that looked like a dentist's tray.

There was a wait. He kept adjusting.

Then he said, *'Aha!'* and I made a sort of queer sound that doesn't translate into letters.

About two inches above the glass tray there was what seemed to be a fuzzy piece of paper. It came into focus while I watched and— oh, well, why make a big thing out of it? It was my notes. My handwriting. Perfectly legible. Perfectly legitimate.

'Is it all right to touch it?' I was a little hoarse, partly out of astonishment and partly because of my uncle Otto's gentle ways of enforcing secrecy.

'You can't,' he said, and passed his hand through it. The paper remained behind, untouched. He said, 'It's only an image at one focus of a four-dimensional paraboloid. The other focus is at a point in time before you tore it up.'

I put my hand through it, too. I didn't feel a thing.

'Now watch,' he said. He turned a knob on the machine and the image of the paper vanished. Then he took out a pinch of paper from the pile of scrap, dropped them in an ashtray, and set a match to it. He flushed the ash down the sink. He turned a knob again and the paper appeared, but with a difference. Ragged patches in it were missing.

'The burned pieces?' I asked.

'Exactly. The machine must trace in time along the hypervectors of the molecules on which it is focused. If certain molecules are in the air dispersed – *pff-f-ft!*'

I had an idea. 'Suppose you just had the ash of a document.'

'Only those molecules would be traced back.'

'But they'd be so well distributed,' I pointed out, 'that you could get a hazy picture of the entire document.'

'Hmm. Maybe.'

The idea became more exciting. 'Well, then, look, Uncle Otto. Do you know how much police departments would pay for a machine like this. It would be a boon to the legal—'

I stopped. I didn't like the way he was stiffening. I said, politely, 'You were saying, Uncle?'

He was remarkably calm about it. He spoke in scarcely more than a shout. 'Once and for all, nephew. All my inventions I will myself from now on develop. First I must some initial capital obtain. Capital from some source other than my ideas selling. After that, I will for my flutes a factory to manufacture open. That comes first. Afterward, afterward, with my profits I can time-vector machinery manufacture. But first my flutes. Before anything, my flutes. Last night, I so swore.

'Through selfishness of a few the world of great music is being deprived. Shall my name in history as a murderer go down? Shall the Schlemmelmayer Effect a way to fry men's brains be? Or shall it beautiful music to mind bring? Great, wonderful, enduring music?'

He had a hand raised oracularly and the other behind his back. The windows gave out a shrill hum as they vibrated to his words.

I said quickly, 'Uncle Otto, they'll hear you.'

'Then stop shouting,' he retorted.

'But look,' I protested, 'how do you plan to get your initial capital, if you won't exploit this machinery?'

'I haven't told you. I can make an image real. What if the image is valuable?'

That did sound good. 'You mean, like some lost document, manuscript, first edition – things like that?'

'Well, no. There's a catch. Two catches. Three catches.'

I waited for him to stop counting, but three seemed the limit. 'What are they?' I asked.

He said, 'First, I must have the object in the present to focus on or I can't locate it in the past.'

'You mean you can't get anything that doesn't exist right now where you can see it?'

'Yes.'

'In that case, catches two and three are purely academic. But what are they, anyway?'

'I can only remove about a gram of material from the past.'

A gram! A thirtieth of an ounce!

'What's the matter? Not enough power?'

My uncle Otto said impatiently, 'It's an inverse exponential relationship. All the power in the universe more than maybe two grams couldn't bring.'

This left things cloudy. I said, 'The third catch?'

'Well.' He hesitated. 'The further the two foci separated are, the more flexible the bond. It must a certain length be before into the present it can be drawn. In other words, I must at least one hundred fifty years into the past go.'

'I see,' I said (not that I really did). 'Let's summarize.'

I tried to sound like a lawyer. 'You want to bring something from the past out of which you can coin a little capital. It's got to be something that exists and which you can see, so it can't be a lost object of historical or archaeological value. It's got to weigh less than a thirtieth of an ounce, so it can't be the Kullinan diamond or anything like that. It's got to be at least one hundred and fifty years old, so it can't be a rare stamp.'

'Exactly,' said my uncle Otto. 'You've got it.'

'Got what?' I thought two seconds. 'Can't think of a thing,' I said. 'Well, good-bye, Uncle Otto.'

I didn't think it would work, but I tried to go.

It didn't work. My uncle Otto's hands came down on my shoulders and I was standing tiptoe on an inch of air.

'You'll wrinkle my jacket, Uncle Otto.'

'Harold,' he said. 'As a lawyer to a client, you owe me more than a quick good-bye.'

'I didn't take a retainer,' I managed to gargle. My shirt collar was beginning to fit very tightly about my neck. I tried to swallow and the top button pinged off.

He reasoned, 'Between relatives a retainer is a formality. As a client and as an uncle, you owe me absolute loyalty. And besides, if you do not help me out I will tie your legs behind your neck and dribble you like a basketball.'

Well, as a lawyer, I am always susceptible to logic. I said, 'I give up. I surrender. You win.'

He let me drop.

And then – this is the part that seems most unbelievable to me when I look back at it all – I got an idea.

It was a whale of an idea. A piperoo. The one in a lifetime that everyone gets once in a lifetime.

I didn't tell Uncle Otto the whole thing at the time. I wanted a few days to think about it. But I told him what to do. I told him he would have to go to Washington. It wasn't easy to argue him into it, but, on the other hand, if you know my uncle Otto, there are ways.

I found two ten-dollar bills lurking pitifully in my wallet and gave them to him.

I said, 'I'll make out a check for the train fare and you can keep the two tens if it turns out I'm being dishonest with you.'

He considered. 'A fool to risk twenty dollars for nothing you aren't,' he admitted.

He was right, too ...

He was back in two days and pronounced the object focused. After all, it was on public view. It's in a nitrogen-filled, air-tight case, but my uncle Otto said that didn't matter. And back in the laboratory, four hundred miles away, the focusing remained accurate. My uncle Otto assured me of that, too.

I said, 'Two things, Uncle Otto, before we do anything.'

'What? What? What?' He went on at greater length, 'What? What? What? What?'

I gathered he was growing anxious. I said, 'Are you sure that if we bring into the present a piece of something out of the past, that piece won't disappear out of the object as it now exists?'

My uncle Otto cracked his large knuckles and said, 'We are creating new matter, not stealing old. Why else should we enormous energy need?'

I passed on to the second point. 'What about my fee?'

You may not believe this, but I hadn't mentioned money till then. My uncle Otto hadn't either, but then, that follows.

His mouth stretched in a bad imitation of an affectionate smile. 'A fee?'

'Ten per cent of the take,' I explained, 'is what I'll need.'

His jowls drooped. 'But how much is the take?'

'Maybe a hundred thousand dollars. That would leave you ninety.'

'Ninety thousand— Himmel! Then why do we wait?'

He leaped at his machine and in half a minute the space above the dentist's tray was agleam with an image of parchment.

It was covered with neat script, closely spaced, looking like an entry for an old-fashioned penmanship prize. At the bottom of the sheet there were names: one large one and fifty-five small ones.

Funny thing! I choked up. I had seen many reproductions, but this was the real thing. The real Declaration of Independence!

I said, 'I'll be damned. You did it.'

'And the hundred thousand?' asked my uncle Otto, getting to the point.

Now was the time to explain. 'You see, Uncle, at the bottom of the document there are signatures. These are the names of great Americans, fathers of their country, whom we all reverence. Anything about them is of interest to all true Americans.'

'All right,' grumbled my uncle Otto, 'I will accompany you by playing the "Stars and Stripes Forever" on my flute.'

I laughed quickly to show that I took that remark as a joke. The alternative to a joke would not bear thinking of. Have you ever heard my uncle Otto playing the 'Stars and Stripes Forever' on his flute?

I said, 'But one of these signers, from the state of Georgia, died in 1777, the year after he signed the Declaration. He didn't leave much behind him and so authentic examples of his signature are about the most valuable in the world. His name was Button Gwinnett.'

'And how does this help us cash in?' asked my uncle Otto, his mind still fixed grimly on the eternal verities of the universe.

'Here,' I said, simply, 'is an authentic, real-life signature of Button Gwinnett, right on the Declaration of Independence.'

My uncle Otto was stunned into absolute silence, and to bring absolute silence out of my uncle Otto, he's really got to be stunned!

I said, 'Now you see him right here on the extreme left of the signature space along with the two other signers for Georgia, Lyman Hall and George Walton. You'll notice they crowded their names although there's plenty of room above and below. In fact, the capital G of Gwinnett runs down into practical contact with Hall's name. So we won't try to separate them. We'll get them all. Can you handle that?'

Have you ever seen a bloodhound that looked happy? Well, my uncle Otto managed it.

A spot of brighter light centered about the names of the three Georgian signers.

My uncle Otto said, a little breathlessly, 'I have this never tried before.'

'What!' I screamed. *Now* he told me.

'It would have too much energy required. I did not wish the university to inquire, what was in here going on. But don't worry! My mathematics cannot wrong be.'

I prayed silently that his mathematics not wrong were.

The light grew brighter and there was a humming that filled the laboratory with raucous noise. My uncle Otto turned a knob, then another, then a third.

Do you remember the time a few weeks back when all of upper Manhattan and the Bronx were without electricity for twelve hours because of the damndest overload cut-off in the main power house? I won't say we did that, because I am in no mood to be sued for damages. But I will say this: The electricity went off when my uncle Otto turned the third knob.

Inside the lab, all the lights went out and I found myself on the floor with a terrific ringing in my ears. My uncle Otto was sprawled across me.

We worked each other to our feet and my uncle Otto found a flashlight.

He howled his anguish. 'Fused. Fused. My machine in ruins is. It has to destruction devoted been.'

'But the signatures?' I yelled at him. 'Did you get them?' He stopped in mid-cry. 'I haven't looked.'

He looked, and I closed my eyes. The disappearance of a hundred thousand dollars is not an easy thing to watch.

He cried, 'Ah, ha!' and I opened my eyes quickly. He had a square of parchment in his hand some two inches on a side. It had three signatures on it and the top one was that of Button Gwinnett.

Now, mind you, the signature was absolutely genuine. It was no fake. There wasn't an atom of fraud about the whole transaction. I want that understood. Lying on my uncle Otto's broad hand was a signature indited with the Georgian hand of Button Gwinnett himself on the authentic parchment of the honest-to-God, real-life Declaration of Independence.

It was decided that my uncle Otto would travel down to Washington with the parchment scrap. I was unsatisfactory for the purpose. I was a lawyer. I would be expected to know too much. He was merely a scientific genius, and wasn't expected to know anything. Besides, who could suspect Dr Otto Schlemmelmayer of anything but the most transparent honesty.

We spent a week arranging our story. I bought a book for the occasion, an old history of colonial Georgia, in a secondhand shop. My uncle Otto was to take it with him and claim that he had found a document among its leaves; a letter to the Continental Congress in the name of the state of Georgia. He had shrugged his shoulders at it and held it out over a Bunsen flame. Why should a physicist be interested in letters? Then he became aware of the peculiar odor it gave off as it burned and the slowness with which it was consumed. He beat out the flames but saved only the piece with the signatures. He looked at it and the name Button Gwinnett had stirred a slight fiber of memory.

He had the story cold. I burnt the edges of the parchment so that the lowest name, that of George Walton, was slightly singed.

'It will make it more realistic,' I explained. 'Of course, a signature, without a letter above it, loses value, but here we have three signatures, all signers.'

My uncle Otto was thoughtful. 'And if they compare the signatures with those on the Declaration and notice it is all even microscopically the same, won't they fraud suspect?'

'Certainly. But what can they do? The parchment is authentic. The ink is authentic. The signatures are authentic. They'll have to concede that. No matter how they suspect something queer, they can't prove anything. Can they conceive of reaching through time for it? In fact, I hope they do try to make a fuss about it. The publicity will boost the price.'

The last phrase made my uncle Otto laugh.

The next day he took the train to Washington with visions of flutes in his head. Long flutes, short flutes, bass flutes, flute tremolos, massive flutes, micro flutes, flutes for the individual and flutes for the orchestra. A world of flutes for mind-drawn music.

'Remember,' his last words were, 'the machine I have no money to rebuild. This must work.'

And I said, 'Uncle Otto, it can't miss.' Ha!

He was back in a week. I had made long-distance calls each day and each day he told me they were investigating.

Investigating.

Well, wouldn't you investigate? But what good would it do them?

I was at the station waiting for him. He was expressionless. I didn't dare ask anything in public. I wanted to say, 'Well, yes or no?' but I thought, let *him* speak.

I took him to my office. I offered him a cigar and a drink. I hid my hands under the desk but that only made the desk shake too, so I put them in my pocket and shook all over.

He said, 'They investigated.'

'Sure! I told you they would. Ha, ha, ha! Ha, ha?'

My uncle Otto took a slow drag at the cigar. He said, 'The man at the Bureau of Documents came to me and said, "Professor Schlemmelmayer," he said, "you are the victim of a clever fraud." I said, "So? And how can it a fraud be? The signature a forgery is?" So he answered, "It certainly doesn't look like a forgery, but it must be!" "And why must it be?" I asked.'

My uncle Otto put down his cigar, put down his drink, and leaned across the desk toward me. He had me so in suspense, I leaned forward toward him, so in a way I deserved everything I got.

'Exactly,' I babbled, 'why must it be? They can't prove a thing wrong with it, because it's genuine. Why must it be a fraud, eh? *Why?*'

My uncle Otto's voice was terrifyingly saccharine. He said, 'We got the parchment from the past?'

'Yes. Yes. You know we did.'

'Well in the past.'

'Over a hundred fifty years in the past. You said—'

'And a hundred fifty years ago the parchment on which the Declaration of Independence was written pretty new was. No?'

I was beginning to get it, but not fast enough.

My uncle Otto's voice switched gears and became a dull, throbbing roar, 'And if Button Gwinnett in 1777 died, you Godforsaken dunderlump, how can an authentic signature of his on a new piece of parchment be found?'

After that it was just a case of the whole world rushing backward and forward about me.

I expect to be on my feet soon. I still ache, but the doctors tell me no bones were broken.

Still, my uncle Otto didn't have to make me swallow the damned parchment.

Everest

In 1952 they were about ready to give up trying to climb Mount Everest. It was the photographs that kept them going.

As photographs go, they weren't much; fuzzy, streaked, and with just dark blobs against the white to be interested in. But those dark blobs were living creatures. The men swore to it.

I said, 'What the hell, they've been talking about creatures skidding along the Everest glaciers for forty years. It's about time we did something about it.'

Jimmy Robbons (pardon me, James Abram Robbons) was the one who pushed me into that position. He was always nuts on mountain climbing, you see. He was the one who knew all about how the Tibetans wouldn't go near Everest because it was the mountain of the gods. He could quote me every mysterious manlike footprint ever reported in the ice twenty-five thousand feet up; he knew by heart every tall story about the spindly white creatures, speeding along the crags just over the last heart-breaking camp which the climbers had managed to establish.

It's good to have one enthusiastic creature of the sort at Planetary Survey headquarters.

The last photographs put bite into his words, though. After all, you *might* just barely think they were men.

Jimmy said, 'Look, boss, the point isn't that they're there, the point is that they move fast. Look at that figure. It's blurred.'

'The camera might have moved.'

'The crag here is sharp enough. And the men swear it was running. Imagine the metabolism it must have to run at that oxygen pressure. Look, boss, would you have believed in deep-sea fish if you'd never heard of them? You have fish which are looking for new niches in environment which they can exploit, so they go deeper and deeper into the abyss until one day they find they can't return. They've adapted so thoroughly they can live only under tons of pressure.'

'Well—'

'Damn it, can't you reverse the picture? Creatures can be forced up a mountain, can't they? They can learn to stick it out in thinner air and colder temperatures. They can live on moss or on occasional birds, just as the deep-sea fish in the last analysis live on the upper fauna that slowly go filtering down. Then, someday, they find they can't go down again. I don't even say they're men. They can be chamois or mountain goats or badgers or anything.'

I said stubbornly, 'The witnesses said they were vaguely manlike, and the reported footprints are certainly manlike.'

'Or bearlike,' said Jimmy. 'You can't tell.'

So that's when I said, 'It's about time we did something about it.'

Jimmy shrugged and said, 'They've been trying to climb Mount Everest for forty years.' And he shook his head.

'For gossake,' I said. 'All you mountain climbers are nuts. That's for sure. You're not interested in getting to the top. You're just interested in getting to the top in a certain way. It's about time we stopped fooling around with picks, ropes, camps, and all the paraphernalia of the Gentlemen's Club that sends suckers up the slopes every five years or so.'

'What are you getting at?'

'They invented the airplane in 1903, you know?'

'You mean fly over Mount Everest!' He said it the way an English lord would say, 'Shoot a fox!' or an angler would say, 'Use worms!'

'Yes,' I said, 'fly over Mount Everest and let someone down on the top. Why not?'

'He won't live long. The fellow you let down, I mean.'

'Why not?' I asked again. 'You drop supplies and oxygen tanks, and the fellow wears a spacesuit. Naturally.'

It took time to get the Air Force to listen and to agree to send a plane and by that time Jimmy Robbons had swiveled his mind to the point where he volunteered to be the one to land on Everest's peak. 'After all,' he said in a half whisper, 'I'd be the first man ever to stand there.'

That's the beginning of the story. The story itself can be told very simply, and in far fewer words.

The plane waited two weeks during the best part of the year (as far as Everest was concerned, that is) for a siege of only moderately nasty flying weather, then took off. They made it. The pilot reported by radio to a listening group exactly what the top of Mount Everest looked like when seen from above and then he described exactly how Jimmy Robbons looked as his parachute got smaller and smaller.

Then another blizzard broke and the plane barely made it back to base and it was another two weeks before the weather was bearable again.

And all that time Jimmy was on the roof of the world by himself and I hated myself for a murderer.

The plane went back up two weeks later to see if they could spot his body. I don't know what good it would have done if they had, but that's the human race for you. How many dead in the last war? Who can count that high? But money or anything else is no object to the saving of one life, or even the recovering of one body.

They didn't find his body, but they did find a smoke signal; curling up in the thin air and whipping away in the gusts. They let down a grapple and Jimmy came up, still in his spacesuit, looking like hell, but definitely alive.

The p.s. to the story involves my visit to the hospital last week to see him. He was recovering very slowly. The doctors said shock, they said exhaustion, but Jimmy's eyes said a lot more.

I said, 'How about it, Jimmy, you haven't talked to the reporters, you haven't talked to the government. All right. How about talking to me?'

'I've got nothing to say,' he whispered.

'Sure you have,' I said. 'You lived on top of Mount Everest during a two-week blizzard. You didn't do that by yourself, not with all the supplies we dumped along with you. Who helped you, Jimmy boy?'

I guess he knew there was no use trying to bluff. Or maybe he was anxious to get it off his mind.

He said, 'They're intelligent, boss. They compressed air for me. They set up a little power pack to keep me warm. They set up the smoke signal when they spotted the airplane coming back.'

'I see.' I didn't want to rush him. 'It's like we thought. They've adapted to Everest life. They can't come down the slopes.'

'No, they can't. And we can't go up the slopes. Even if the weather didn't stop us, they would!'

'They sound like kindly creatures, so why should they object? They helped *you*.'

'They have nothing against us. They spoke to me, you know. Telepathy.'

I frowned. 'Well, then.'

'But they don't intend to be interfered with. They're watching us, boss. They've got to. We've got atomic power. We're about to have rocket ships. They're worried about us. And Everest is the only place they can watch us from!'

I frowned deeper. He was sweating and his hands were shaking.

I said, 'Easy, boy. Take it easy. What on Earth are these creatures?'

And he said, 'What do you suppose would be so adapted to thin air and subzero cold that Everest would be the only livable place on Earth to them. That's the whole point. They're nothing at all on Earth. They're Martians.'

And that's it.

The Pause

The white powder was confined within a thin-walled, transparent capsule. The capsule in turn was heat-sealed into a double strip of parafilm. Along that strip of parafilm were other capsules at six-inch intervals.

The strip moved. Each capsule in the course of events rested for one minute on a metal jaw immediately beneath a mica window. On another portion of the face of the radiation counter a number clicked out upon an unrolling cylinder of paper. The capsule moved on; the next took its place.

The number printed at 1:45 P.M. was 308. A minute later 256 appeared. A minute later, 391. A minute later, 477. A minute later, 202. A minute later, 251. A minute later, 000. A minute later, 000. A minute later, 000. A minute later, 000.

Shortly after 2 P.M. Mr Alexander Johannison passed by the counter and the corner of one eye stubbed itself over the row of figures. Two steps past the counter he stopped and returned.

He ran the paper cylinder backward, then restored its position and said, 'Nuts!'

He said it with vehemence. He was tall and thin, with bigknuckled hands, sandy hair, and light eyebrows. He looked tired and, at the moment, perplexed.

Gene Damelli wandered his way with the same easy carelessness he brought to all his actions. He was dark, hairy, and on the short side. His nose had once been broken and it made him look curiously unlike the popular conception of the nuclear physicist.

Damelli said, 'My damned Geiger won't pick up a thing, and I'm not in the mood to go over the wiring. Got a cigarette?'

Johannison held out a pack. 'What about the others in the building?'

'I haven't tried them, but I guess they haven't all gone.'

'Why not? My counter isn't registering either.'

'No kidding. You see? All the money invested, too. It doesn't mean a thing. Let's step out for a Coke.'

Johannison said with greater vehemence than he intended, 'No! I'm going to see George Duke. I want to see his machine. If *it's* off—'

Damelli tagged along. 'It won't be off, Alex. Don't be an ass.'

George Duke listened to Johannison and watched him disapprovingly over rimless glasses. He was an old-young man with little hair and less patience.

He said, 'I'm busy.'

'Too busy to tell me if your rig is working, for heaven's sake?'

Duke stood up. 'Oh, hell, when does a man have time to work around here?' His slide rule fell with a thud over a scattering of ruled paper as he rounded his desk.

He stepped to a cluttered lab table and lifted the heavy gray leaden top from a heavier gray leaden container. He reached in with a two-foot-long pair of tongs and took out a small silvery cylinder.

Duke said grimly, 'Stay where you are.'

Johannison didn't need the advice. He kept his distance. He had not been exposed to any abnormal dosage of radioactivity over the past month but there was no sense getting any closer than necessary to 'hot' cobalt.

Still using the tongs, and with arms held well away from his body, Duke brought the shining bit of metal that contained the concentrated radioactivity up to the window of his counter. At two feet, the counter should have chattered its head off. It didn't.

Duke said, 'Guk!' and let the cobalt container drop. He scrabbled madly for it and lifted it against the window again. Closer.

There was no sound. The dots of light on the scaler did not show.

Numbers did not step up and up.

Johannison said, 'Not even background noise.'

Damelli said, 'Holy jumping Jupiter!'

Duke put the cobalt tube back into its leaden sheath, as gingerly as ever, and stood there, glaring.

Johannison burst into Bill Everard's office, with Damelli at his heels. He spoke for excited minutes, his bony hands knuckly white on Everard's shiny desk. Everard listened, his smooth, fresh-shaven cheeks turning pink and his plump neck bulging out a bit over his stiff, white collar.

Everard looked at Damelli and pointed a questioning thumb at Johannison. Damelli shrugged, bringing his hands forward, palms upward, and corrugating his forehead.

Everard said, 'I don't see how they can all go wrong.'

'They *have*, that's all,' insisted Johannison. 'They all went dead at about two o'clock. That's over an hour ago now and none of them is back in order. Even George Duke can't do anything about it. I'm telling you, it isn't the counters.'

'You're saying it is.'

'I'm saying they're not working. But that's not their fault. There's nothing for them to work on.'

'What do you mean?'

'I mean there isn't any radioactivity in this place. In this whole building. Nowhere.'

'I don't believe you.'

'Listen, if a hot cobalt cartridge won't start up a counter, maybe there's something wrong with every counter we try. But when that same cartridge won't discharge a gold-leaf electroscope and when it won't even fog a photographic film, then there's something wrong with the cartridge.'

'All right,' said Everard, 'so it's a dud. Somebody made a mistake and never filled it.'

'The same cartridge was working this morning, but never mind that. Maybe cartridges can get switched somehow. But I got that hunk of pitchblende from our display box on the fourth floor and that doesn't register either. You're not going to tell me that someone forgot to put the uranium in it.'

Everard rubbed his ear. 'What do you think, Damelli?'

Damelli shook his head. 'I don't know, boss. Wish I did.'

Johannison said, 'It's not the time for thinking. It's a time for doing. You've got to call Washington.'

'What about?' asked Everard.

'About the A-bomb supply.'

'What?'

'That might be the answer, boss. Look, someone has figured out a way to stop radioactivity, all of it. It might be blanketing the country, the whole USA. If that's being done, it can only be to put our A-bombs out of commission. They don't know where we keep them, so they have to blank out the nation. And if *that's* right, it means an attack is due. Any minute, maybe. Use the phone, boss!'

Everard's hand reached for the phone. His eyes and Johannison's met and locked.

'No.'

He said into the mouthpiece, 'An outside call, please.'

It was five minutes to four. Everard put down the phone. 'Was that the commissioner?' asked Johannison.

'Yes,' said Everard. He was frowning.

'All right. What did he say?'

'Son,' said Everard, 'he said to me, "What A-bombs?"'

Johannison looked bewildered. 'What the devil does he mean, "What A-bombs?" I know! They've already found out they've got duds on their hands, and they won't talk. Not even to us. Now what?'

'Now nothing,' said Everard. He sat back in his chair and glowered at the physicist. 'Alex, I know the kind of strain you're under; so I'm not going to blow up about this. What bothers me is, how did you get *me* started on this nonsense?'

Johannison paled. 'This isn't nonsense. Did the commissioner say it was?'

'He said I was a fool, and so I am. What the devil do you mean coming here with your stories about A-bombs? What *are* A-bombs? I never heard of them.'

'You never heard of atom bombs? What is this? A gag?'

'I never heard of them. It sounds like something from a comic strip.'

Johannison turned to Damelli, whose olive complexion had seemed to deepen with worry. 'Tell him, Gene.'

Damelli shook his head. 'Leave me out of this.'

'All right.' Johannison leaned forward, looking at the line of books in the shelves about Everard's head. 'I don't know what this is all about, but I can go along with it. Where's Glasstone?'

'Right there,' said Everard.

'No. Not the *Textbook of Physical Chemistry*. I want his *Sourcebook on Atomic Energy*.'

'Never heard of it.'

'What are you talking about? It's been here in your shelf since I've been here.'

'Never heard of it,' said Everard stubbornly.

'I suppose you haven't heard of Kamen's *Radioactive Tracers in Biology* either?'

Johannison shouted, 'All right. Let's use Glasstone's *Textbook* then. It will do.'

He brought down the thick book and flipped the pages. First once, then a second time. He frowned and looked at the copyright page. It said: Third Edition, 1956. He went through the first two chapters page by page. It was there, atomic structure, quantum numbers, electrons and their shells, transition series – but no radioactivity, nothing about that.

He turned to the table of elements on the inside front cover. It took him only a few seconds to see that there were only eighty-one listed, the eighty-one nonradioactive ones.

Johannison's throat felt bricky-dry. He said huskily to Everard, 'I suppose you never heard of uranium.'

'What's that?' asked Everard coldly. 'A trade name?'

Desperately, Johannison dropped Glasstone and reached for the *Handbook of Chemistry and Physics*. He used the index. He looked up radioactive series, uranium, plutonium, isotopes. He found only the last. With fumbling, jittery fingers he turned to the table of isotopes. Just a glance. Only the stable isotopes were listed.

He said pleadingly, 'All right. I give up. Enough's enough. You've set up a bunch of fake books just to get a rise out of me, haven't you?' He tried to smile.

Everard stiffened. 'Don't be a fool, Johannison. You'd better go home. See a doctor.'

'There's nothing wrong with me.'

'You may not think so, but there is. You need a vacation, so take one. Damelli, do me a favor. Get him into a cab and see that he gets home.'

Johannison stood irresolute. Suddenly he screamed, 'Then what are all the counters in this place for? What do they do?'

'I don't know what you mean by counters. If you mean computers, they're here to solve our problems for us.'

Johannison pointed to a plaque on the wall. 'All right, then. See those initials. A! E! C! Atomic! Energy! Commission!' He spaced the words, staccato.

Everard pointed in turn. 'Air! Experimental! Commission! Get him home, Damelli.'

Johannison turned to Damelli when they reached the sidewalk.

Urgently he whispered, 'Listen, Gene, don't be a setup for that guy. Everard's sold out. They got to him some way. Imagine them setting up the faked books and trying to make me think I'm crazy.'

Damelli said levelly, 'Cool down, Alex boy. You're just jumping a little. Everard's all right.'

'You heard him. He never heard of A-bombs. Uranium's a trade name. How can he be all right?'

'If it comes to that, I never heard of A-bombs *or* uranium.'

He lifted a finger. 'Taxi!' It whizzed by.

Johannison got rid of the gagging sensation. 'Gene! You were there when the counters quit. You were there when the pitchblende went dead. You came with me to Everard to get the thing straightened out.'

'If you want the straight truth, Alex, you said you had something to discuss with the boss and you asked me to come along, and that's all I know about it. Nothing went wrong as far as I know, and what the devil would we be doing with this pitchblende? We don't use any tar in the place— Taxi!'

A cab drew up to the curb.

Damelli opened the door, motioned Johannison in. Johannison entered, then, with red-eyed fury, turned, snatched the door out of Damelli's hand, slammed it closed, and shouted an address at the cab driver. He leaned out the window as the cab pulled away, leaving Damelli stranded and staring.

Johannison cried, 'Tell Everard it won't work. I'm wise to all of you.'

He fell back into the upholstery, exhausted. He was sure Damelli had heard the address he gave. Would they get to the FBI first with some story about a nervous breakdown? Would they take Everard's word against his? They couldn't deny the stopping of the radioactivity. They couldn't deny the faked books.

But what was the good of it? An enemy attack was on its way and men like Everard and Damelli— How rotten with treason was the country?

He stiffened suddenly. 'Driver!' he cried. Then louder, *'Driver!'*

The man at the wheel did not turn around. The traffic passed smoothly by them.

Johannison tried to struggle up from his seat, but his head was swimming.

'Driver!' he muttered. This wasn't the way to the FBI. He was being taken home. But how did the driver know where he lived?

A planted driver, of course. He could scarcely see and there was a roaring in his ears.

Lord, what organization! There was no use fighting! He blacked out!

He was moving up the walk toward the small, two-story, brickfronted house in which Mercedes and he lived. He didn't remember getting out of the cab.

He turned. There was no taxicab in sight. Automatically, he felt for his wallet and keys. They were there. Nothing had been touched.

Mercedes was at the door, waiting. She didn't seem surprised at his return. He looked at his watch quickly. It was nearly an hour before his usual homecoming.

He said, 'Mercy, we've got to get out of here and—'

She said huskily, 'I know all about it, Alex. Come in.'

She looked like heaven to him. Straight hair, a little on the blond side, parted in the middle and drawn into a horse tail; wide-set blue eyes with that slight Oriental tilt, full lips, and little ears set close to the head. Johannison's eyes devoured her.

But he could see she was doing her best to repress a certain tension.

He said, 'Did Everard call you? Or Damelli?'

She said, 'We have a visitor.' He thought, They've got to *her*.

He might snatch her out of the doorway. They would run, try to make it to safety. But how could they? The visitor would be standing in the shadows of the hallway. It would be a sinister man, he imagined, with a thick, brutal voice and foreign accent, standing there with a hand in his jacket pocket and a bulge there that was bigger than his hand. Numbly he stepped inside.

'In the living room,' said Mercedes. A smile flashed momentarily across her face. 'I think it's all right.'

The visitor was standing. He had an unreal look about him, the unreality of perfection. His face and body were flawless and carefully devoid of individuality. He might have stepped off a billboard.

His voice had the cultured and unimpassioned sound of the professional radio announcer. It was entirely free of accent.

He said, 'It was quite troublesome getting you home, Dr Johannison.'

Johannison said, 'Whatever it is, whatever you want, I'm not cooperating.'

Mercedes broke in. 'No, Alex, you don't understand. We've been talking. He says all radioactivity has been stopped.'

'Yes, it has, and how I wish this collar-ad could tell me how it was done! Look here, you, are you an American?'

'You still don't understand, Alex,' said his wife. 'It's stopped all over the world. This man isn't from anywhere on Earth. Don't look at me like that, Alex. It's true. I know it's true. Look at him.'

The visitor smiled. It was a perfect smile. He said, 'This body in which I appear is carefully built up according to specification, but it is only matter. It's under complete control.' He held out a hand and the skin vanished. The muscles, the straight tendons, and crooked veins were exposed. The walls of the veins disappeared and blood flowed smoothly without the necessity of containment. All dissolved to the appearance of smooth gray bone. That went also.

Then all reappeared.

Johannison muttered, 'Hypnotism!'

'Not at all,' said the visitor, calmly.

Johannison said, 'Where are you from?'

The visitor said, 'That's hard to explain. Does it matter?'

'I've got to understand what's going on,' cried Johannison. 'Can't you see that?'

'Yes. I can. It's why I'm here. At this moment I am speaking to a hundred and more of your people all over your planet. In different bodies, of course, since different segments of your people have different preferences and standards as far as bodily appearance is concerned!'

Fleetingly, Johannison wondered if he was mad after all. He said, 'Are you from – from Mars? Any place like that? Are you taking over? Is this war?'

'You see,' said the visitor, 'that sort of attitude is what we're trying to correct. Your people are sick, Dr Johannison, very sick. For tens of thousands of your years we have known that your particular species has great possibilities. It has been a great disappointment to us that your development has taken a pathological pathway. Definitely pathological.' He shook his head.

Mercedes interrupted, 'He told me before you came that he was trying to cure us.'

'Who asked him?' muttered Johannison.

The visitor only smiled. He said, 'I was assigned the job a long time ago, but such illnesses are always hard to treat. For one thing, there is the difficulty in communication.'

'We're communicating,' said Johannison stubbornly.

'Yes. In a manner of speaking, we are. I'm using your concepts, your code system. It's quite inadequate. I couldn't even explain to you the true nature of the disease of your species. By your concepts, the closest approach I can make is that it is a disease of the spirit.'

'Huh.'

'It's a kind of social ailment that is very ticklish to handle. That's why I've hesitated for so long to attempt a direct cure. It would be sad if, through accident, so gifted a potentiality as that of your race were lost to us. What I've tried to do for millennia has been to work indirectly through the few individuals in each generation who had natural immunity to the disease. Philosophers, moralists, warriors, and politicians. All those who had a glimpse of world brotherhood. All those who—'

'All right. You failed. Let it go at that. Now suppose you tell me about your people, not mine.'

'What can I tell you that you would understand?'

'Where are you from? Begin with that.'

'You have no proper concept. I'm not from anywhere in the yard.'

'What yard?'

'In the universe, I mean. I'm from outside the universe.'

Mercedes interrupted again, leaning forward. 'Alex, don't you see what he means? Suppose you landed on the New Guinea coast and talked to some natives through television somehow. I mean to natives who had never seen or heard of anyone outside their tribe. Could you explain how television worked or how it made it possible for you to speak to many men in many places at once? Could you explain that the image wasn't you yourself but merely an illusion that you could make disappear and reappear? You couldn't even explain where you came from if all the universe they knew was their own island.'

'Well, then, we're savages to him. Is that it?' demanded Johannison.

The visitor said, 'Your wife is being metaphorical. Let me finish. I can no longer try to encourage your society to cure itself. The disease has progressed too far. I am going to have to alter the temperamental makeup of the race.'

'How?'

'There are neither words nor concepts to explain that either. You must see that our control of physical matter is extensive. It was quite simple to stop all radioactivity. It was a little more difficult to see to it that all things, including books, now suited a world in which radioactivity did not exist. It was still more difficult, and took more time, to wipe out all thought of radioactivity from the minds of men. Right now, uranium does not exist on Earth. No one ever heard of it.'

'I have,' said Johannison. 'How about you, Mercy?'

'I remember, too,' said Mercedes.

'You two are omitted for a reason,' said the visitor, 'as are over a hundred others, men and women, all over the world.'

'No radioactivity,' muttered Johannison. 'Forever?'

'For five of your years,' said the visitor. 'It is a pause, nothing more. Merely a pause, or call it a period of anesthesia, so that I can operate on the species without the interim danger of atomic war. In five years the phenomenon of radioactivity will return, together with all the uranium and thorium that currently do not exist. The knowledge will not return, however. That is where you will come in. You and the others like you. You will re-educate the world gradually.'

'That's quite a job. It took fifty years to get us to this point. Even allowing for less the second time, why not simply restore knowledge? You can do that, can't you?'

'The operation,' said the visitor, 'will be a serious one. It will take anywhere up to a decade to make certain there are no complications. So we want re-education slowly, on purpose.'

Johannison said, 'How do we know when the time comes? I mean when the operation's over.'

The visitor smiled. 'When the time comes, you will know. Be assured of that.'

'Well, it's a hell of a thing, waiting five years for a gong to ring in your head. What if it never comes? What if your operation isn't successful?'

The visitor said seriously, 'Let us hope that it is.'

'But if it isn't? Can't you clear our minds temporarily, too? Can't you let us live normally till it's time?'

'No. I'm sorry. I need your minds untouched. If the operation *is* a failure, if the cure does not work out, I will need a small reservoir of normal, untouched minds out of which to bring about the growth of a new population on this planet on whom a new variety of cure may be attempted. At all costs, your species must be preserved. It is valuable to us. It is why I am spending so much time trying to explain the situation to you. If I had left you as you were an hour ago, five days, let alone five years, would have completely ruined you.'

And without another word he disappeared.

Mercedes went through the motions of preparing supper and they sat at the table almost as though it had been any other day.

Johannison said, 'Is it true? Is it all real?'

'I saw it, too,' said Mercedes. 'I heard it.'

'I went through my own books. They're all changed. When this pause is over, we'll be working strictly from memory, all of us who are left. We'll have to build instruments again. It will take a long time to get it across to those who won't remember.' Suddenly he was angry, 'And what for, I want to know. What for?'

'Alex,' Mercedes began timidly, 'he may have been on Earth before and spoken to people. He's lived for thousands and thousands of years. Do you suppose he's what we've been thinking of for so long as – as—'

Johannison looked at her. 'As God? Is that what you're trying to say? How should I know? All I know is that his people, whatever they are, are infinitely more advanced than we, and that he's curing us of a disease.'

Mercedes said, 'Then I think of him as a doctor or what's equivalent to it in his society.'

'A doctor? All he kept saying was that the difficulty of communication was the big problem. What kind of a doctor can't communicate with his patients? A vet! An animal doctor!'

He pushed his plate away.

His wife said, 'Even so. If he brings an end to war—'

'Why should he want to? What are we to him? We're animals. We *are* animals to him. Literally. He as much as said so. When I asked him where he was from, he said he didn't come from the "yard" at all. Get it? The *barnyard*. Then he changed it to the "universe". He didn't come from the "universe" at all. His difficulty in communication gave him away. He used the concept for what our universe was to him rather than what it was to us. So the universe is a barnyard and we're— horses, chickens, sheep. Take your choice.'

Mercedes said softly, '"The Lord is my Shepherd. I shall not want..."'

'Stop it, Mercy. That's a metaphor; this is reality. If he's a shepherd, then we're sheep with a queer, unnatural desire, and ability, to kill one another. Why stop us?'

'He said—'

'I know what he said. He said we have great potentialities. We're very valuable. Right?'

'Yes.'

'But what are the potentialities and values of sheep to a shepherd? The sheep wouldn't have any idea. They couldn't. Maybe if they knew why they were coddled so, they'd prefer to live their own lives. They'd take their own chances with wolves or with themselves.'

Mercedes looked at him helplessly.

Johannison cried, 'It's what I keep asking myself now. Where are we going? Where are we going? Do sheep know? Do we know? Can we know?'

They sat staring at their plates, not eating.

Outside, there was the noise of traffic and the calling of children at play. Night was falling and gradually it grew dark.

Let's Not

Professor Charles Kittredge ran in long, unsteady strides. He was in time to bat the glass from the lips of Associate Professor Heber Vandermeer. It was almost like an exercise in slow motion.

Vandermeer, whose absorption had apparently been such that he had not heard the thud of Kittredge's approach, looked at once startled and ashamed. His glance sank to the smashed glass and the puddling liquid that surrounded it.

'What was it?' asked Kittredge grimly.

'Potassium cyanide. I'd kept a bit, when we left. Just in case . . .'

'How would that have helped? And it's one glass gone, too. Now it's got to be cleaned up . . . No, I'll do it.'

Kittredge found a precious fragment of cardboard to scoop up the glass fragments and an even more precious scrap of cloth to soak up the poisonous fluid. He left to discard the glass and, regretfully, the cardboard and cloth into one of the chutes that would puff them to the surface, a half mile up.

He returned to find Vandermeer sitting on the cot, eyes fixed glassily on the wall. The physicist's hair had turned quite white and he had lost weight, of course. There were no fat men in the Refuge.

Kittredge, who had been long, thin, and gray to begin with, had, in contrast, scarcely changed.

Vandermeer said, 'Remember the old days, Kitt.'

'I try not to.'

'It's the only pleasure left,' said Vandermeer. 'Schools were schools. There were classes, equipment, students, air, light, and people. People.'

'A school's a school as long as there is one teacher and one student.'

'You're almost right,' mourned Vandermeer. 'There are two teachers. You, chemistry. I, physics. The two of us, everything else we can get out of the books. And one graduate student. He'll be the first man ever to get his Ph.D. down here. Quite a distinction. Poor Jones.'

Kittredge put his hands behind his back to keep them steady. 'There are twenty other youngsters who will live to be graduate students someday.'

Vandermeer looked up. His face was gray. 'What do we teach them meanwhile? History? How man discovered what makes hydrogen go boom and was happy as a lark while it went boom and boom and boom? Geography? We can describe how the winds blew the shining dust everywhere and the water currents carried the dissolved isotopes to all the deeps and shallows of the ocean.'

Kittredge found it very hard. He and Vandermeer were the only qualified scientists who got away in time. The responsibility of the existence of a hundred men, women, and children was theirs as they hid from the dangers and rigors of the surface and from the terror Man had created here in this bubble of life half a mile below the planet's crust.

Desperately, he tried to put nerve into Vandermeer. He said, as forcefully as he could, 'You know what we must teach them. We must keep science alive so that someday we can repopulate the Earth. Make a new start.'

Vandermeer did not answer that. He turned his face to the wall. Kittredge said, 'Why not? Even radioactivity doesn't last forever.

Let it take a thousand years, five thousand. Someday the radiation level on Earth's surface will drop to bearable amounts.'

'Someday.'

'Of course. Someday. Don't you see that what we have here is the most important school in the history of man? If we succeed, you and I, our descendants will have open sky and free-running water again. They'll even have,' and he smiled wryly, 'graduate schools such as those we remember.'

Vandermeer said, 'I don't believe any of it. At first, when it seemed better than dying, I would have believed anything. But now, it just doesn't make sense. So we'll teach them all we know, down here, and then we die . . . *down here.*'

'But before long Jones will be teaching with us, and then there'll be others. The youngsters who hardly remember the old ways will become teachers, and then the youngsters who were born here will teach. This will be the critical point. Once the native-born are in charge, there will be no memories to destroy morale. This will be their life and they will have a goal to strive for, something to fight for . . . a whole world to win once more. *If,* Van, *if* we keep alive the knowledge of physical science on the graduate level. You understand why, don't you?'

'Of course I understand,' said Vandermeer irritably, 'but that doesn't make it possible.'

'Giving up will make it impossible. That's for sure.'

'Well, I'll try,' said Vandermeer in a whisper.

So Kittredge moved to his own cot and closed his eyes and wished desperately that he might be standing in his protective suit on the planet's surface. Just for a little while. Just for a little while. He would stand beside the shell of the ship that had been dismantled and cannibalized to create the bubble of life here below. Then he could rouse his own courage just after sunset by looking up and seeing once more, just once more as it gleamed through the thin, cold atmosphere of Mars, the bright, dead evening star that was Earth.

Youth

There was a spatter of pebbles against the window and the youngster stirred in his sleep. Another, and he was awake.

He sat up stiffly in bed. Seconds passed while he interpreted his strange surroundings. He wasn't in his own home, of course. This was out in the country. It was colder than it should be and there was green at the window.

'Slim!'

The call was a hoarse, urgent whisper, and the youngster bounded to the open window.

Slim wasn't his real name, but the new friend he had met the day before had needed only one look at his slight figure to say, 'You're Slim.' He added, 'I'm Red.'

Red wasn't his real name, either, but its appropriateness was obvious. They were friends instantly with the quick, unquestioning friendship of young ones not yet quite in adolescence, before even the first stains of adulthood began to make their appearance.

Slim cried, 'Hi, Red!' and waved cheerfully, still blinking the sleep out of himself.

Red kept to his croaking whisper, 'Quiet! You want to wake

somebody?' Slim noticed all at once that the sun scarcely topped the low hills in the east, that the shadows were long and soft, and that the grass was wet. Slim said more softly, 'What's the matter?'

Red only waved for him to come out.

Slim dressed quickly, gladly confining his morning wash to the momentary sprinkle of a little lukewarm water. He let the air dry the exposed portions of his body as he ran out, while bare skin grew wet against the dewy grass.

Red said, 'You've got to be quiet. If Mom wakes up or Dad or your dad or even any of the hands, then it'll be "Come on in or you'll catch your death of cold tramping bare in the dew."'

He mimicked voice and tone faithfully, so that Slim laughed and thought that there had never been so funny a fellow as Red.

Slim said eagerly, 'Do you come out here every day like this, Red? Real early? It's like the whole world is just yours, isn't it, Red? No one else around, and all like that.' He felt proud at being allowed entrance into this private world.

Red stared at him sidelong. He said carelessly, 'I've been up for hours. Didn't you hear it last night?'

'Hear what?'

'Thunder.'

'Was there a thunderstorm?' Slim was startled. He never slept through a thunderstorm.

'I guess not. But there was thunder. I heard it, and then I went to the window and it wasn't raining. It was all stars and the sky was just getting sort of almost gray. You know what I mean?'

Slim had never seen it so, but he nodded. 'So I just thought I'd go out,' said Red.

They walked along the grassy side of the concrete road that split the panorama right down the middle all the way down to where it vanished among the hills. The road was so old that Red's father couldn't tell Red when it had been built. It didn't have a crack or a rough spot in it.

Red said, 'Can you keep a secret?'

'Sure, Red. What kind of a secret?'

'Just a secret. Maybe I'll tell you and maybe I won't. I don't know yet.' Red broke a long, supple stem from a fern they passed, methodically stripped it of its leaflets, and swung what was left whip-fashion. For a moment, he was on a wild charger, which reared and champed under his iron control. Then he got tired, tossed the whip aside, and stowed the charger away in a corner of his imagination for future use.

He said, 'There'll be a circus around.'

Slim said, 'That's no secret. I knew that. My dad told me even before we came here—'

'That's not the secret. Fine secret! Ever see a circus?'

'Oh, sure. You bet.'

'Like it?'

'Say, there isn't anything I like better.'

Red was watching out of the corner of his eyes again. 'Ever think you would like to be with a circus? I mean, for good?'

Slim considered. 'I guess not. I think I'll be an astronomer like my dad. I think he wants me to be.'

'Huh! Astronomer!' said Red.

Slim felt the doors of the new, private world closing on him and astronomy became a thing of dead stars.

He said placatingly, 'A circus *would* be more fun.'

'You're just saying that.'

'No, I'm not. I mean it.'

Red grew argumentative. 'Suppose you had a chance to join the circus right now. What would you do?'

'I–I—'

'See!' Red affected scornful laughter.

Slim was stung. 'I'd join up.'

'Go on.'

'Try me.'

Red whirled at him, strange and intense. 'You mean that? You want to go in with me?'

'What do you mean?' Slim stepped back a bit.

'I got something that can get us into the circus. Maybe someday we can even have a circus of our own. We could be the biggest circus fellows in the world. That's if you want to go in with me. Otherwise— Well, I guess I can do it on my own. I just thought, Let's give good old Slim a chance.'

The world was strange and glamorous, and Slim said, 'Sure thing, Red. I'm in! What is it, huh, Red? Tell me what it is.'

'Figure it out. What's the most important thing in circuses?'

Slim thought desperately. He wanted to give the right answer. Finally he said, 'Acrobats?'

'Holy smokes! I wouldn't go five steps to look at acrobats.'

'I don't know then.'

'Animals, that's what! What's the best side show? Where are the biggest crowds? Even in the main rings the best acts are animal acts.'

'Do you think so?'

'Everyone thinks so. You ask anyone. Anyway, I found animals this morning. Two of them.'

'And you've got them?'

'Sure. That's the secret. Are you telling?'

'Of course not.'

'Okay. I've got them in the barn. *Do* you want to see them?'

They were almost at the barn; its huge open door black. Too black: They had been heading there all the time. Slim stopped in his tracks.

He tried to make his words casual. 'Are they big?'

'Would I fool with them if they were big? They can't hurt you. They're only about so long. I've got them in a cage.'

They were in the barn now and Slim saw the large cage suspended from a hook in the roof. It was covered with stiff canvas.

Red said, 'We used to have some bird there or something. Anyway, they can't get away from there. Come on, let's go up to the loft.'

They clambered up the wooden stairs and Red hooked the cage toward them. Slim pointed and said, 'There's sort of a hole in the canvas.'

Red frowned. 'How'd that get there?' He lifted the canvas, looked in, and said with relief, 'They're still there.'

'The canvas looks burned,' worried Slim.

'You want to look or don't you?'

Slim nodded slowly. He wasn't sure he wanted to, after all. They might be—

But the canvas had been jerked off and there they were. Two of them, the way Red said. They were small and sort of disgusting-looking. The animals moved quickly as the canvas lifted and were on the side toward the youngsters. Red poked a cautious finger at them.

'Watch out,' said Slim in agony.

'They don't hurt you,' said Red. 'Ever see anything like them?'

'No.'

'Can't you see how a circus would jump at a chance to have these?'

'Maybe they're too small for a circus.'

Red looked annoyed. He let go the cage which swung back and forth pendulum-fashion. 'You're just backing out.'

'No, I'm not. It's just—'

'They're not too small, don't worry. Right now, I've only got one worry.'

'What's that?'

'Well, I've got to keep them till the circus comes, don't I? I've got to figure out what to feed them meanwhile.'

The cage swung and the little trapped creatures clung to its bars, gesturing at the youngsters with queer, quick motions – almost as though they were intelligent.

The Astronomer entered the dining room with decorum. He felt very much the guest.

He said, 'Where are the youngsters? My son isn't in his room.'

The Industrialist smiled. 'They've been out for hours. However, breakfast was forced into them by the women some time ago, so there is nothing to worry about. Youth, Doctor, youth!'

'Youth!' The word seemed to depress the Astronomer.

They ate breakfast in silence. The Industrialist said once, 'You really think they'll come. The day looks so – *normal.*'

The Astronomer said, 'They'll come.'

That was all.

Afterward the Industrialist said, 'You'll pardon me. I can't conceive your playing so elaborate a hoax. You really spoke to them?'

'As I speak to you. At least, in a sense. They can project thoughts.'

'I gathered that must be so from your letter. How, I wonder.'

'I could not say. I asked them and, of course, they were vague. Or perhaps it was just that I could not understand. It involves a projector for the focusing of thought and, even more than that, conscious attention on the part of both projector and receptor. It was quite a while before I realized they were trying to think at me. Such thought projectors may be part of the science they will give us.'

'Perhaps,' said the Industrialist. 'Yet think of the changes it would bring to society. A thought projector!'

'Why not? Change would be good for us.'

'I don't think so.'

'It is only in old age that change is unwelcome,' said the Astronomer, 'and races can be old as well as individuals.'

The Industrialist pointed out the window. 'You see that road. It was built Beforethewars. I don't know exactly when. It is as good now as the day it was built. We couldn't possibly duplicate it now. The race was young when that was built, eh?'

'Then? Yes! At least they weren't afraid of new things.'

'No. I wish they had been. Where is the society of Beforethewars? Destroyed, Doctor. What good were youth and new things? We are better off now. The world is peaceful and jogs along. The race goes nowhere but after all, there is nowhere to go. *They* proved that. The men who built the road. I will speak with your visitors as I agreed, if they come. But I think I will only ask them to go.'

'The race is not going nowhere,' said the Astronomer earnestly. 'It is going toward final destruction. My university has a smaller student body each year. Fewer books are written. Less work is done. An old man sleeps in the sun and his days are peaceful and unchanging, but each day finds him nearer death all the same.'

'Well, well,' said the Industrialist.

'No, don't dismiss it. Listen. Before I wrote you, I investigated your position in the planetary economy.'

'And you found me solvent?' interrupted the Industrialist, smiling.

'Why, yes. Oh, I see, you are joking. And yet – perhaps the joke is not far off. You are less solvent than your father and he was less solvent than his father. Perhaps your son will no longer be solvent. It becomes too troublesome for the planet to support even the industries that still exist, though they are toothpicks to the oak trees of Beforethewars. We will be back to village economy, and then to what? The caves?'

'And the infusion of fresh technological knowledge will be the changing of all that?'

'Not just the new knowledge. Rather the whole effect of change, of a broadening of horizons. Look, sir, I chose you to approach in this matter not only because you were rich and influential with government officials, but because you had an unusual reputation, for these days, of daring to break with tradition. Our people will resist change and you would know how to handle them, how to see to it that – that—'

'That the youth of the race is revived?'

'Yes.'

'With its atomic bombs?'

'The atomic bombs,' returned the Astronomer, 'need not be the end of civilization. These visitors of mine had their atomic bomb, or whatever their equivalent was on their own worlds, and survived it, because they didn't give up. Don't you see? It wasn't the bomb that defeated us, but our own shell shock. This may be the last chance to reverse the process.'

'Tell me,' said the Industrialist, 'what do these friends from space want in return?'

The Astronomer hesitated. He said, 'I will be truthful with you. They come from a denser planet. Ours is richer in the lighter atoms.'

'They want magnesium? Aluminum?'

'No, sir. Carbon and hydrogen. They want coal and oil.'

'Really?'

The Astronomer said quickly, 'You are going to ask why creatures who have mastered space travel, and therefore atomic power, would want coal and oil. I can't answer that.'

The Industrialist smiled. 'But I can. This is the best evidence yet of the truth of your story. Superficially, atomic power would seem to preclude the use of coal and oil. However, quite apart from the energy gained by their combustion, they remain, and always will remain, the basic raw material for all organic chemistry. Plastics, dyes, pharmaceuticals, solvents. Industry could not exist without them, even in an atomic age. Still, if coal and oil are the low price for which they would sell us the troubles and tortures of racial youth, my answer is that the commodity would be dear if offered gratis.'

The Astronomer sighed and said, 'There are the boys!'

They were visible through the open window, standing together in the grassy field and lost in animated conversation. The Industrialist's son pointed imperiously and the Astronomer's son nodded and made off at a run toward the house.

The Industrialist said, 'There is the youth you speak of. Our race has as much of it as it ever had.'

'Yes, but we age them quickly and pour them into the mold.' Slim scuttled into the room, the door banging behind him.

The Astronomer said in mild disapproval, 'What's this?'

Slim looked up in surprise and came to a halt. 'I beg your pardon. I didn't know anyone was here. I am sorry to have interrupted.' His enunciation was almost painfully precise.

The Industrialist said, 'It's all right, youngster.'

But the Astronomer said, 'Even if you had been entering an empty room, son, there would be no cause for slamming a door.'

'Nonsense,' insisted the Industrialist. 'The youngster has done no harm. You simply scold him for being young. You, with your views!'

He said to Slim, 'Come here, lad.' Slim advanced slowly.

'How do you like the country, eh?'

'Very much, sir, thank you.'

'My son has been showing you about the place, has he?'

'Yes, sir. Red— I mean—'

'No, no. Call him Red. I call him that myself. Now tell me, what are you two up to, eh?'

Slim looked away. 'Why – just exploring, sir.'

The Industrialist turned to the Astronomer. 'There you are, youthful curiosity and adventure lust. The race has not yet lost it.'

Slim said, 'Sir?'

'Yes, lad.'

The youngster took a long time in getting on with it. He said, 'Red sent me in for something good to eat, but I don't exactly know what he meant. I didn't like to say so.'

'Why, just ask Cook. She'll have something good for young'uns to eat.'

'Oh no, sir. I mean for animals.'

'For animals?'

'Yes, sir. What do animals eat?'

The Astronomer said, 'I am afraid my son is city-bred.'

'Well,' said the Industrialist, 'there's no harm in that. What kind of an animal, lad?'

'A small one, sir.'

'Then try grass or leaves, and if they don't want that, nuts or berries would probably do the trick.'

'Thank you, sir.' Slim ran out again, closing the door gently behind him.

The Astronomer said, 'Do you suppose they've trapped an animal alive?' He was obviously perturbed.

'That's common enough. There's no shooting on my estate and it's tame country, full of rodents and small creatures. Red is always coming home with pets of one sort or another. They rarely maintain his interest for long.'

He looked at the wall clock. 'Your friends should have been here by now, shouldn't they?'

*

The swaying had come to a halt and it was dark. The Explorer was not comfortable in the alien air. It felt as thick as soup and he had to breath shallowly. Even so—

He reached out in a sudden need for company. The Merchant was warm to the touch. His breathing was rough, he moved in an occasional spasm, and was obviously asleep. The Explorer hesitated and decided not to wake him. It would serve no real purpose.

There would be no rescue, of course. That was the penalty paid for the high profits which unrestrained competition could lead to. The Merchant who opened a new planet could have a ten-year monopoly of its trade, which he might hug to himself or, more likely, rent out to all comers at a stiff price. It followed that planets were searched for in secrecy and preferably away from the usual trade routes. In a case such as theirs then, there was little or no chance that another ship would come within range of their subetherics except for the most improbable of coincidences. Even if they were in their ship, that is, rather than in this – this – *cage*.

The Explorer grasped the thick bars. Even if they blasted those away, as they could, they would be stuck too high in open air for leaping.

It was too bad. They had landed twice before in the scout ship. They had established contact with the natives, who were grotesquely huge, but mild and unaggressive. It was obvious that they had once owned a flourishing technology, but hadn't faced up to the consequences of such a technology. It would have been a wonderful market.

And it was a tremendous world. The Merchant, especially, had been taken aback. He had known the figures that expressed the planet's diameter, but from a distance of two light-seconds, he had stood at the visiplate and muttered, 'Unbelievable!'

'Oh, there are larger worlds,' the Explorer said. It wouldn't do for an Explorer to be too easily impressed.

'Inhabited?'

'Well, no.'

'Why, you could drop your planet into that large ocean and drown it.'

The Explorer smiled. It was a gentle dig at his Arcturian homeland, which was smaller than most planets. He said, 'Not quite.'

The Merchant followed along the line of his thoughts. 'And the inhabitants are large in proportion to their world?' He sounded as though the news struck him less favorably now.

'Nearly ten times our height.'

'Are you sure they are friendly?'

'That is hard to say. Friendship between alien intelligences is an imponderable. They are not dangerous, I think. We've come across other groups that could not maintain equilibrium after the atomic war stage and you know the results. Introversion. Retreat. Gradual decadence and increasing gentleness.'

'Even if they are such monsters?'

'The principle remains.'

It was about then that the Explorer felt the heavy throbbing of the engines. He frowned and said, 'We are descending a bit too quickly.'

There had been some speculation on the dangers of landing several hours before. The planetary target was a huge one for an oxygen-water world. Though it lacked the size of the uninhabitable hydrogen-ammonia planets and its low density made its surface gravity fairly normal, its gravitational forces fell off, but slowly with distance. In short, its gravitational potential was high and the ship's calculator was a run-of-the-mill model not designed to plot landing trajectories at that potential range. That meant the Pilot would have to use manual controls. It would have been wiser to install a more high-powered model, but that would have meant a trip to some outpost of civilization; lost time; perhaps a lost secret.

The Merchant demanded an immediate landing.

The Merchant felt it necessary to defend his position now. He said angrily to the Explorer, 'Don't you think the Pilot knows his job? He landed you safely twice before.'

Yes, thought the Explorer, in a scout ship, not in this unmaneuverable freighter. Aloud, he said nothing.

He kept his eye on the visiplate. They were descending too quickly. There was no room for doubt. Much too quickly.

The Merchant said peevishly, 'Why do you keep silence?'

'Well then, if you wish me to speak, I would suggest that you strap on your floater and help me prepare the ejector.'

The Pilot fought a noble fight. He was no beginner. The atmosphere, abnormally high and thick in the gravitational potential of this world, whipped and burned about the ship, but to the very last, it looked as though he might bring it under control despite that.

He even maintained course, following the extrapolated line to the point on the northern continent toward which they were headed. Under other circumstances, with a shade more luck, the story eventually would have been told and retold as a heroic and masterly reversal of a lost situation. But within sight of victory, tired body and tired nerves clamped a control bar with a shade too much pressure. The ship, which had almost leveled off, dipped down again.

There was no room to retrieve the final error. There was only a mile left to fall. The Pilot remained at his post to the actual landing, his only thought that of breaking the force of the crash, of maintaining the spaceworthiness of the vessel. He did not survive. With the ship bucking madly in a soupy atmosphere, few ejectors could be mobilized and only one of them in time.

When afterward the Explorer lifted out of unconsciousness and rose to his feet, he had the definite feeling that but for himself and the Merchant, there were no survivors. And perhaps that was an overcalculation. His floater had burned out while still sufficiently distant from surface to have the fall stun him. The Merchant might have had less luck, even, than that.

He was surrounded by a world of thick, ropy stalks of grass, and in the distance were trees that reminded him vaguely of similar structures on his native Arcturian world except that their lowest branches were high above what he would consider normal treetops.

He called, his voice sounding basso in the thick air, and the

Merchant answered. The Explorer made his way toward him, thrusting violently at the coarse stalks that barred his path.

'Are you hurt?' he asked.

The Merchant grimaced, 'I've sprained something. It hurts to walk.'

The Explorer probed gently. 'I don't think anything is broken. You'll have to walk despite the pain.'

'Can't we rest first?'

'It's important to try to find the ship. If it is spaceworthy or if it can be repaired, we may live. Otherwise, we won't.'

'Just a few minutes. Let me catch my breath.'

The Explorer was glad enough for those few minutes. The Merchant's eyes were already closed. He allowed his to do the same.

He heard the trampling and his eyes snapped open. 'Never sleep on a strange planet,' he told himself futilely.

The Merchant was awake too and his steady screaming was a rumble of terror.

The Explorer called, 'It's only a native of this planet. It won't harm you.'

But even as he spoke, the giant had swooped down, and in a moment, they were in its grasp, being lifted closer to its monstrous ugliness.

The Merchant struggled violently and, of course, quite futilely. 'Can't you talk to it?' he yelled.

The Explorer could only shake his head. 'I can't reach it with the projector. It won't be listening.'

'Then blast it. Blast it down.'

'We can't do that.' The phrase 'you fool' had almost been added. The Explorer struggled to keep his self-control. They were swallowing space as the monster moved purposefully away.

'Why not?' cried the Merchant. 'You can reach your blaster. I see it in plain sight. Don't be afraid of falling.'

'It's simpler than that. If this monster is killed, you'll never trade with this planet. You'll never even leave it. You probably won't live the day out.'

'Why? Why?'

'Because this is one of the young of the species. You should know what happens when a trader kills a native young, even accidentally. What's more, if this is the target point, then we are on the estate of a powerful native. This might be one of his brood.'

That was how they entered their present prison. They had carefully burned away a portion of the thick, stiff covering and it was obvious that the height from which they were suspended was a killing one.

Now, once again, the prison cage shuddered and lifted in an upward arc. The Merchant rolled to the lower rim and startled awake. The cover lifted and light flooded in. As was the case the time before, there were two specimens of the young. They were not very different in appearance from adults of the species, reflected the Explorer, though, of course, they were considerably smaller.

A handful of reedy green stalks was stuffed between the bars. Its odor was not unpleasant but it carried clods of soil at its ends.

The Merchant drew away and said huskily, 'What are they doing?'

The Explorer said, 'Trying to feed us, I should judge. At least, this seems to be the native equivalent of grass.'

The cover was replaced and they were set swinging again, alone with their fodder.

Slim started at the sound of footsteps and brightened when it turned out to be only Red.

He said, 'No one's around. I had my eye peeled, you bet.'

Red said, 'Ssh. Look. You take this stuff and stick it in the cage. I've got to scoot back to the house.'

'What is it?' Slim reached reluctantly.

'Ground meat. Holy smokes, haven't you ever seen ground meat? That's what you should've got when I sent you to the house instead of coming back with that stupid grass.'

Slim was hurt. 'How'd I know they don't eat grass? Besides, ground meat doesn't come loose like that, it comes in cellophane and it isn't that color.'

'Sure – in the city. Out here we grind our own and it's always this color till it's cooked.'

'You mean it isn't cooked?' Slim drew away quickly.

Red looked disgusted. 'Do you think animals eat *cooked* food? Come on, take it. It won't hurt you. I tell you there isn't much time.'

'Why? What's doing back at the house?'

'I don't know. Dad and your father are walking around. I think maybe they're looking for me. Maybe the cook told them I took the meat. Anyway, we don't want them coming here after me.'

'Didn't you ask the cook before you took this stuff?'

'Who? That crab? Shouldn't wonder if she only let me have a drink of water because Dad makes her. Come on. Take it.'

Slim took the large glob of meat though his skin crawled at the touch. He turned toward the barn and Red sped away in the direction from which he had come.

Red slowed when he approached the two adults, took a few deep breaths to bring himself back to normal, and then carefully and nonchalantly sauntered past. (They were walking in the general direction of the barn, he noticed, but not dead on.)

He said, 'Hi, Dad. Hello, sir.'

The Industrialist said, 'Just a moment, Red. I have a question to ask you.'

Red turned a carefully blank face to his father. 'Yes, Dad?'

'Mother tells me you were out early this morning.'

'Not real early, Dad. Just a little before breakfast.'

'She said you told her it was because you had been awakened during the night.'

Red waited before answering. Should he have told Mom that? Then he said, 'Yes, sir.'

'What was it that awakened you?'

Red saw no harm in it. He said, 'I don't know, Dad. It sounded like thunder, sort of, and like a collision, sort of.'

'Could you tell where it came from?'

'It *sounded* like it was out by the hill.' That was truthful, and useful as well, since the direction was almost opposite that in which the barn lay.

The Industrialist looked at his guest. 'I suppose it would do no harm to walk toward the hill.'

The Astronomer said, 'I am ready.'

Red watched them walk away, and when he turned, he saw Slim peering cautiously out from among the briers of a hedge.

Red waved at him. 'Come on.'

Slim stepped out and approached. 'Did they say anything about the meat?'

'No. I guess they don't know about that. They went down to the hill.'

'What for?'

'Search me. They kept asking about the noise I heard. Listen, did the animals eat the meat?'

'Well,' said Slim cautiously, 'they were sort of *looking* at it and smelling it or something.'

'Okay,' Red said, 'I guess they'll eat it. Holy smokes, they've got to eat *something*. Let's walk along toward the hill and see what Dad and your father are going to do.'

'What about the animals?'

'They'll be all right. A fellow can't spend all his time on them. Did you give them water?'

'Sure. They drank that.'

'See. Come on. We'll look at them after lunch. I tell you what. We'll bring them fruit. Anything'll eat fruit.'

Together they trotted up the rise, Red, as usual, in the lead.

The Astronomer said, 'You think the noise was their ship landing?'

'Don't you think it could be?'

'If it were, they may all be dead.'

'Perhaps not.' The Industrialist frowned.

'If they have landed and are still alive, where are they?'

'Think about that for a while.' He was still frowning.

The Astronomer said, 'I don't understand you.'

'They may not be friendly.'

'Oh no. I've spoken with them. They've—'

'You've spoken with them. Call that reconnaissance. What would their next step be? Invasion?'

'But they only have one ship, sir.'

'You know that only because they say so. They might have a fleet.'

'I've told you about their size. They—'

'Their size would not matter if they have hand weapons that may well be superior to our artillery.'

'That is not what I meant.'

'I had this partly in mind from the first.' The Industrialist went on. 'It is for that reason I agreed to see them after I received your letter. Not to agree to an unsettling and impossible trade, but to judge their real purposes. I did not count on their evading the meeting.'

He sighed and added, 'I suppose it isn't our fault. You are right in one thing, at any rate. The world has been at peace too long. We are losing a healthy sense of suspicion.'

The Astronomer's mild voice rose to an unusual pitch and he said, 'I *will* speak. I tell you that there is no reason to suppose they can possibly be hostile. They are small, yes, but that is only important because it is a reflection of the fact that their native worlds are small. Our world has what is for them a normal gravity, but because of our much higher gravitational potential, our atmosphere is too dense to support them comfortably over sustained periods. For a similar reason, the use of the world as a base for interstellar travel, except for trade in certain items, is uneconomical. And there are important differences in chemistry of life due to the basic differences in soils. They couldn't eat our food or we theirs.'

'Surely all this can be overcome. They can bring their own food, build domed stations of lowered air pressure, devise specially designed ships.'

'They can. And how glibly you can describe feats that are easy to a race in its youth. It is simply that they don't have to do any of that.

There are millions of worlds suitable for them in the Galaxy. They don't need this one which isn't.'

'How do you know? All this is their information again.'

'This I was able to check independently. I am an astronomer, after all.'

'That is true. Let me hear what you have to say then while we walk.'

'Then, sir, consider that for a long time our astronomers have believed that two general classes of planetary bodies existed. First, the planets which formed at differences far enough from their stellar nuclei to become cool enough to capture hydrogen. These would be large planets rich in hydrogen, ammonia, and methane. We have examples of these in the giant outer planets. The second class would include those planets formed so near the stellar center that the high temperature would make it impossible to capture much hydrogen. These would be smaller planets, comparatively poorer in hydrogen and richer in oxygen. We know that type very well since we live on one. Ours is the only solar system we know in detail, however, and it has been reasonable for us to assume that these were the *only* two planetary classes.'

'I take it then that there is another.'

'Yes. There is a super-dense class, still smaller, poorer in hydrogen than the inner planets of the solar system. The ratio of occurrence of hydrogen-ammonia planets and these super-dense water-oxygen worlds of theirs over the entire Galaxy – and remember that they have actually conducted a survey of significant sample volumes of the Galaxy, which we, without interstellar travel, cannot do – is about three to one. This leaves them several million super-dense worlds for exploration and colonization.'

The Industrialist looked at the blue sky and the green-crowned trees among which they were making their way. He said, 'And worlds like ours?'

The Astronomer said softly, 'Ours is the first solar system they have found which contains them. Apparently the development of our solar system was unique and did not follow the ordinary rules.'

The Industrialist considered that. 'What it amounts to is that these creatures from space are asteroid dwellers.'

'No, no. The asteroids are something else again. They occur, I was told, in one out of eight stellar systems, but they're completely different from what we've been discussing.'

'And how does your being an astronomer change the fact that you are still only quoting their unsupported statements?'

'But they did not restrict themselves to bald items of information. They presented me with a theory of stellar evolution which I had to accept and which is more nearly valid than anything our own astronomy has ever been able to devise, if we except possible lost theories dating from Beforethewars. Mind you, their theory had a rigidly mathematical development and it predicted just such a galaxy as they describe. So you see, they have all the worlds they wish. They are not land-hungry. Certainly not for our land.'

'Reason would say so, if what you say is true. But creatures may be intelligent and not reasonable. Our forefathers were presumably intelligent, yet they were certainly not reasonable. Was it reasonable to destroy almost all their tremendous civilization in atomic warfare over causes our historians can no longer accurately determine?' The Industrialist brooded over it. 'From the dropping of the first atom bomb over the Eastern Islands of the Sun – I forget the ancient name – there was only one end in sight, and in plain sight. Yet events were allowed to proceed to that end.'

He looked up, said briskly, 'Well, where are we? I wonder if we are not on a fool's errand after all.'

But the Astronomer was a little in advance and his voice came thickly. 'No fool's errand, sir. Look there.'

Red and Slim had trailed their elders with the experience of youth, aided by the absorption and anxiety of their fathers. Their view of the final object of the search was somewhat obscured by the underbrush behind which they remained.

Red said, 'Holy smokes. Look at that. It's all shiny silver or something.'

But it was Slim who was really excited. He caught at the other. 'I know what this is. It's a spaceship. That must be why my father came here. He's one of the biggest astronomers in the world and your father would have to call him if a spaceship landed on his estate.'

'What are you talking about? Dad didn't even know that thing was there. He only came here because I told him I heard the thunder from here. Besides, there isn't any such thing as a spaceship.'

'Sure, there is. Look at it. See those round things. They're ports. And you can see the rocket tubes.'

'How do you know so much?'

Slim was flushed. He said, 'I read about them. My father has books about them. Old books. From Beforethewars.'

'Huh. Now I know you're making it up. Books from Beforethewars!'

'My father *has* to have them. He teaches at the University. It's his job.'

His voice had risen and Red had to pull at him. 'You want them to hear us?' he whispered indignantly.

'Well, it is, too, a spaceship.'

'Look here, Slim, you mean that's a ship from another world.'

'It's *got* to be. Look at my father going round and round it. He wouldn't be so interested if it was anything else.'

'Other worlds! Where are there other worlds?'

'Everywhere. How about the planets? They're worlds just like ours, some of them. And other stars probably have planets. There's probably zillions of planets.'

Red felt outweighed and outnumbered. He muttered, 'You're crazy!'

'All right, then. I'll show you.'

'Hey! Where are you going?'

'Down there. I'm going to ask my father. I suppose you'll believe it if *he* tells you. I suppose you'll believe a Professor of Astronomy knows what—'

He had scrambled upright.

Red said, 'Hey. You don't want them to see us. We're not supposed to be here. Do you want them to start asking questions and find out about our animals?'

'I don't care. You said I was crazy.'

'Snitcher! You promised you wouldn't tell.'

'I'm *not* going to tell. But if they find out themselves, it's your fault for starting an argument and saying I was crazy.'

'I take it back then,' grumbled Red.

'Well, all right. You better.'

In a way, Slim was disappointed. He wanted to see the spaceship at closer quarters. Still, he could not break his vow of secrecy even in spirit without at least the excuse of personal insult.

Red said, 'It's awfully small for a spaceship.'

'Sure, because it's probably a scout ship.'

'I'll bet Dad couldn't even get into the old thing.'

So much Slim realized to be true. It was a weak point in his argument and he made no answer.

Red rose to his feet; an elaborate attitude of boredom all about him. 'Well, I guess we better be going. There's business to do and I can't spend all day here looking at some old spaceship or whatever it is. We've got to take care of the animals if we're going to be circus folks. That's the first rule with circus folks. They've got to take care of the animals. And,' he finished virtuously, 'that's what I aim to do, anyway.'

Slim said, 'What for, Red? They've got plenty of meat. Let's watch.'

'There's no fun in watching. Besides Dad and your father are going away and I guess it's about lunch time.'

Red became argumentative. 'Look, Slim, we can't start acting suspicious or they're going to start investigating. Holy smokes, don't you ever read any detective stories? When you're trying to work a big deal without being caught, it's practically the main thing to keep on acting just like always. Then they don't suspect anything. That's the first law—'

'Oh, all right.'

Slim rose resentfully. At the moment, the circus appeared to him a rather tawdry and shoddy substitute for the glories of astronomy, and he wondered how he had come to fall in with Red's silly scheme.

Down the slope they went, Slim, as usual, in the rear.

The industrialist said, 'It's the workmanship that gets me. I never saw such construction.'

'What good is it now?' said the Astronomer bitterly. 'There's nothing left. There'll be no second landing. This ship detected life on our planet through accident. Other exploring parties would come no closer than necessary to establish the fact that no super-dense worlds existed in our solar system.'

'Well, there's no quarreling with a crash landing.'

'The ship hardly seems damaged. If only some had survived, the ship might have been repaired.'

'If they had survived, there would be no trade in any case. They're too different. Too disturbing. In any case – it's over.'

They entered the house and the Industrialist greeted his wife calmly. 'Lunch about ready, dear?'

'I'm afraid not. You see—' She looked hesitantly at the Astronomer.

'Is anything wrong?' asked the Industrialist. 'Why not tell me? I'm sure our guest won't mind a little family discussion.'

'Pray don't pay any attention whatever to me,' muttered the Astronomer. He moved miserably to the other end of the living room.

The woman said in low, hurried tones, 'Really, dear, Cook's that upset. I've been soothing her for hours and honestly I don't know why Red should have done it.'

'Done what?' The Industrialist was more amused than otherwise. It had taken the united efforts of himself and his son months to argue his wife into using the name 'Red' rather than the perfectly ridiculous (viewed youngster-fashion) name which was his real one.

She said, 'He's taken most of the chopped meat.'

'He's eaten it?'

'Well, I hope not. It was raw.'

'Then what would he want it for?'

'I haven't the slightest idea. I haven't seen him since breakfast. Meanwhile Cook's just furious. She caught him vanishing out the kitchen door and there was the bowl of chopped meat just about empty and she was going to use it for lunch. Well, you know Cook. She had to change the lunch menu and that means she won't be worth living with for a week. You'll just have to speak to Red, dear, and make him promise not to do things in the kitchen any more. And it wouldn't hurt to have him apologize to Cook.'

'Oh, come. She works for us. If we don't complain about a change in lunch menu, why should she?'

'Because she's the one who has double work made for her, and she's talking about quitting. Good cooks aren't easy to get. Do you remember the one before her?'

It was a strong argument.

The Industrialist looked about vaguely, He said, 'I suppose you're right. He isn't here, I suppose. When he comes in, I'll talk to him.'

'You'd better start. Here he comes.'

Red walked into the house and said cheerfully, 'Time for lunch, I guess.' He looked from one parent to the other in quick speculation at their fixed stares and said, 'Got to clean up first, though,' and made for the other door.

The Industrialist said, 'One moment, son.'

'Sir?'

'Where's your little friend?'

Red said carelessly, 'He's around somewhere. We were just sort of walking and I looked around and he wasn't there.' This was perfectly true, and Red felt on safe ground. 'I told him it was lunch time. I said, "I suppose it's about lunch time." I said, "We got to be getting back to the house." And he said, "Yes." And I just went on, and then when I was about at the creek, I looked around and—'

The Astronomer interrupted the voluble story, looking up from a magazine he had been sightlessly rummaging through. 'I wouldn't worry about my youngster. He is quite self-reliant. Don't wait lunch for him.'

'Lunch isn't ready in any case, Doctor.' The Industrialist turned once more to his son. 'And talking about that, son, the reason for it is that something happened to the ingredients. Do you have anything to say?'

'Sir?'

'I hate to feel that I have to explain myself more fully. Why did you take the chopped meat?'

'The chopped meat?'

'The chopped meat.' He waited patiently.

Red said, 'Well, I was sort of—'

'Hungry?' prompted his father. 'For raw meat?'

'No, sir. I just sort of needed it.'

'For what exactly?'

Red looked miserable and remained silent.

The Astronomer broke in again. 'If you don't mind my putting in a few words – you'll remember that just after breakfast, my son came in to ask what animals ate.'

'Oh, you're right. How stupid of me to forget. Look here, Red, did you take it for an animal pet you've got?'

Red recovered indignant breath. He said, 'You mean Slim came in here and said I had an animal? He came in here and said that? He said I had an animal?'

'No, he didn't. He simply asked what animals ate. That's all. Now if he promised he wouldn't tell on you, he didn't. It's your own foolishness in trying to take something without permission that gave you away. That happened to be stealing. Now have you an animal? I ask you a direct question.'

'Yes, sir.' It was a whisper so low as hardly to be heard. 'All right, you'll have to get rid of it. Do you understand?'

Red's mother intervened. 'Do you mean to say you're keeping a meat-eating animal, Red? It might bite you and give you blood poison.'

'They're only small ones,' quavered Red. 'They hardly budge if you touch them.'

'They? How many do you have?'

'Two.'

'Where are they?'

The Industrialist touched her arm. 'Don't chivvy the child any further,' he said in a low voice. 'If he says he'll get rid of them, he will, and that's punishment enough.'

He dismissed the matter from his mind.

Lunch was half over when Slim dashed into the dining room. For a moment, he stood abashed, and then he said in what was almost hysteria, 'I've got to speak to Red. I've got to say something.'

Red looked up in fright, but the Astronomer said, 'I don't think, son, you're being very polite. You've kept lunch waiting.'

'I'm sorry, Father.'

'Oh, don't rate the lad,' said the Industrialist's wife. 'He can speak to Red if he wants to, and there was no damage done to the lunch.'

'I've got to speak to Red alone,' Slim insisted.

'Now that's enough,' said the Astronomer with a kind of gentleness that was obviously manufactured for the benefit of strangers and which had beneath it an easily recognized edge. 'Take your seat.'

Slim did so, but he ate only when someone looked directly upon him. Even then he was not very successful.

Red caught his eyes. He made soundless words, 'Did the animals get loose?'

Slim shook his head slightly. He whispered, 'No, it's—' The Astronomer looked at him hard and Slim faltered to a stop.

With lunch over, Red slipped out of the room, with a microscopic motion at Slim to follow.

They walked in silence to the creek.

Then Red turned fiercely upon his companion. 'Look here, what's the idea of telling my dad we were feeding animals?'

Slim said, 'I didn't. I asked what you feed animals. That's not the same as saying we were doing it. Besides, it's something else, Red.'

But Red had not used up his grievances. 'And where did you go, anyway? I thought you were coming to the house. They acted like it was my fault you weren't there.'

'But I'm trying to tell you about that, if you'd only shut *up* a second and let me talk. You don't give a fellow a chance.'

'Well, go on and tell me if you've got so much to say.'

'I'm *trying* to. I went back to the spaceship. The folks weren't there any more and I wanted to see what it was like.'

'It isn't a spaceship,' said Red sullenly. He had nothing to lose.

'It is, too. I looked inside. You could look through the ports and I looked inside and they were *dead*.' He looked sick. 'They were dead.'

'*Who* were dead?'

Slim screeched, 'Animals! Like *our* animals! Only they *aren't* animals. They're people things from other planets.'

For a moment, Red might have been turned to stone. It didn't occur to him to disbelieve Slim at this point. Slim looked too genuinely the bearer of just such tidings. He said finally, 'Oh, my.'

'Well, what are we going to do? Golly, will we get a whopping if they find out!' He was shivering.

'We better turn them loose,' said Red. 'They'll tell on us.'

'They can't talk our language. Not if they're from another planet.'

'Yes, they can. Because I remember my father talking about some stuff like that to my mother when he didn't know I was in the room. He was talking about visitors who could talk with the mind. Telepathery or something. I thought he was making it up.'

'Well, holy smokes. I mean – holy smokes.' Red looked up. 'I tell you. My dad said to get rid of them. Let's sort of bury them somewhere or throw them in the creek.'

'He *told* you to do that?'

'He made me say I had animals and then he said, "Get rid of them." I got to do what he says. Holy smokes, he's my dad.'

Some of the panic left Slim's heart. It was a thoroughly legalistic way out. 'Well, let's do it right now then, before they find out. Oh, golly, if they find out, will we be in trouble!'

They broke into a run toward the barn, unspeakable visions in their minds.

It was different, looking at them as though they were 'people'. As animals, they had been interesting; as 'people', horrible. Their eyes, which were neutral little objects before, now seemed to watch them with active malevolence.

'They're making noises,' said Slim in a whisper.

'I guess they're talking or something,' said Red. Funny that those noises which they had heard before had not had significance earlier. He was making no move toward them. Neither was Slim.

The canvas was off but they were just watching. The ground meat, Slim noticed, hadn't been touched.

Slim said, 'Aren't you going to do something?'

'Aren't you?'

'You found them.'

'It's your turn now.'

'No, it isn't. You found them. It's your fault, the whole thing. I was just watching.'

'You joined in, Slim. You know you did.'

'I don't care. You found them and that's what I'll say when they come here looking for us.'

Red said, 'All right for you.' But the thought of the consequences inspired him anyway, and he reached for the cage door. Slim said, 'Wait!'

Red was glad to. He said, 'Now what's biting you?'

'One of them's got something on him that looks like it might be iron or something.'

'Where?'

'Right there. I saw it before but I thought it was just part of him. But if he's "people", maybe it's a disintegrator gun.'

'What's that?'

'I read about it in the books from Beforethewars. Mostly people with spaceships have disintegrator guns. They point them at you and you get disintegratored.'

'They didn't point it at us till now,' pointed out Red with his heart not quite in it.

'I don't care. I'm not hanging around here and getting disintegratored. I'm getting my father.'

'Cowardy-cat. Yellow cowardy-cat.'

'I don't care. You can call all the names you want, but if you bother them now, you'll get disintegratored. You wait and see, and it'll be all your fault.' He made for the narrow spiral stairs that led to the main floor of the barn, stopped at its head, then backed away.

Red's mother was moving up, panting a little with the exertion and smiling a tight smile for the benefit of Slim in his capacity as guest.

'Red! You, Red! Are you up there? Now don't try to hide. I know this is where you're keeping them. Cook saw where you ran with the meat.'

Red quavered, 'Hello, Ma!'

'Now show me those nasty animals. I'm going to see to it that you get rid of them right away.'

It was over! And despite the imminent corporal punishment, Red felt something like a load fall from him. At least the decision was out of his hands. 'Right there, Ma. I didn't do anything to them, Ma. I didn't know. They just looked like little animals and I thought you'd let me keep them, Ma. I wouldn't have taken the meat only they wouldn't eat grass or leaves and we couldn't find good nuts or berries and Cook never lets me have anything or I would have asked her and I didn't know it was for lunch and—'

He was speaking on the sheer momentum of terror and did not realize that his mother did not hear him but, with eyes frozen and popping at the cage, was screaming in thin, piercing tones.

The Astronomer was saying, 'A quiet burial is all we can do. There is no point in any publicity now,' when they heard the screams.

She had not entirely recovered by the time she reached them, running and running. It was minutes before her husband could extract sense from her.

She was saying finally, 'I tell you they're in the barn. I don't know what they are. No, no—'

She barred the Industrialist's quick movement in that direction. She said, 'Don't *you* go. Send one of the hands with a shotgun. I tell you I never saw anything like it. Little horrible beasts with – with— I can't describe it. To think that Red was touching them and trying to feed them. He was *holding* them, and feeding them meat.'

Red began, 'I only—'

And Slim said, 'It wasn't—'

The Industrialist said quickly, 'Now you boys have done enough harm today. March! Into the house! And not a word; not one word! I'm not interested in anything you have to say. After this is all over, I'll hear you out and as for you, Red, I'll see that you're properly punished.'

He turned to his wife, 'Now whatever the animals are, we'll have them killed.' He added quietly once the youngsters were out of hearing, 'Come, come. The children aren't hurt, and after all, they haven't done anything really terrible. They've just found a new pet.'

The Astronomer spoke with difficulty. 'Pardon me, ma'am, but can you describe these animals?'

She shook her head. She was quite beyond words. 'Can you just tell me if they—'

'I'm sorry,' said the Industrialist apologetically, 'but I think I had better take care of her. Will you excuse me?'

'A moment. Please. One moment. She said she had never seen such animals before. Surely it is not usual to find animals that are completely unique on an estate such as this.'

'I'm sorry. Let's not discuss that now.'

'Except that unique animals might have landed during the night.'

The Industrialist stepped away from his wife. 'What are you implying?'

'I think we had better go to the barn, sir!'

The Industrialist stared a moment, turned, and suddenly and quite uncharacteristically began running. The Astronomer followed and the woman's wail rose unheeded behind them.

The industrialist stared, looked at the Astronomer, turned to stare again.

'Those?'

'Those,' said the Astronomer. 'I have no doubt we appear as strange and repulsive to them.'

'What do they say?'

'Why, that they are uncomfortable and tired and even a little sick, but that they are not seriously damaged, and that the youngsters treated them well.'

'Treated them well! Scooping them up, keeping them in a cage, giving them grass and raw meat to eat? Tell me how to speak to them.'

'It may take a little time. Think *at* them. Try to listen. It will come to you, but perhaps not right away.'

The Industrialist tried. He grimaced with the effort of it, thinking over and over again, The youngsters were ignorant of your identity.

And the thought was suddenly in his mind, We were quite aware of it and because we knew they meant well by us according to their own view of the matter, we did not attempt to attack them.

Attack them? thought the Industrialist, and said it aloud in his concentration.

Why, yes, came the answering thought. We are armed.

One of the revolting little creatures in the cage lifted a metal object and there was a sudden hole in the top of the cage and another in the roof of the barn, each hole rimmed with charred wood.

We hope, the creatures thought, it will not be too difficult to make repairs.

The Industrialist found it impossible to organize himself to the point of directed thought. He turned to the Astronomer. 'And with that weapon in their possession, they let themselves be handled and caged? I don't understand it.'

But the calm thought came, We would not harm the young of an intelligent species.

It was twilight. The Industrialist had entirely missed the evening meal and remained unaware of the fact.

He said, 'Do you really think the ship will fly?'

'If they say so,' said the Astronomer, 'I'm sure it will. They'll be back, I hope, before too long.'

'And when they do,' said the Industrialist energetically, 'I will keep my part of the agreement. What is more I will move sky and earth to have the world accept them. I was entirely wrong, Doctor. Creatures that would refuse to harm children under such provocation as they received are admirable. But you know I almost hate to say this—'

'Say what?'

'The kids. Yours and mine. I'm almost proud of them. Imagine seizing these creatures, feeding them or trying to, and keeping them hidden. The amazing gall of it. Red told me it was his idea to get a job in a circus on the strength of them. Imagine!'

The Astronomer said, 'Youth!'

The Merchant said, 'Will we be taking off soon?'

'Half an hour,' said the Explorer.

It was going to be a lonely trip back. All the remaining seventeen of the crew were dead and their ashes were to be left on a strange planet. Back they would go with a limping ship and the burden of the controls entirely on himself.

The Merchant said, 'It was a good business stroke, not harming the young ones. We will get very good terms; *very* good terms.'

The Explorer thought, Business!

The Merchant said, 'They've lined up to see us off. All of them. You don't think they're too close, do you? It would be bad to burn any of them with the rocket blast at this stage of the game.'

'They're safe.'

'Horrible-looking things, aren't they?'

'Pleasant enough, inside. Their thoughts are perfectly friendly.'

'You wouldn't believe it of them. That immature one, the one that first picked us up'

'They call him Red.'

'That's a queer name for a monster. Makes me laugh. He actually feels *bad* that we're leaving. Only I can't make out exactly why. The nearest I can come to it is something about a lost opportunity with some organization or other that I can't quite interpret.'

'A circus,' said the Explorer briefly.

'What? Why, the impertinent monstrosity.'

'Why not? What would you have done if you had found *him* wandering on *your* native world; found him sleeping in a field on Earth, red tentacles, six legs, pseudopods and all?'

Red watched the ship leave. His red tentacles, which gave him his nickname, quivered their regret at lost opportunity to the very last, and the eyes at their tips filled with drifting yellowish crystals that were the equivalent of Earthly tears.

Sucker Bait

The ship *Triple G.* flashed silently out of the nothingness of hyperspace and into the allness of space-time. It emerged into the glitter of the great star cluster of Hercules.

It poised gingerly in space, surrounded by suns and suns and suns, each centering a gravitational field that wrenched at the little bubble of metal. But the ship's computers had done well and it had pin-pricked squarely into position. It was within a day's journey – ordinary space-drive journey – of the Lagrange System.

This face had varying significance to the different men aboard ship. To the crew, it was another day's work and another day's flight pay and then shore rest. The planet for which they were aiming was uninhabited, but shore rest could be a pleasant interlude even on an asteroid. They did not trouble themselves concerning a possible difference of opinion among the passengers.

The crew, in fact, were rather contemptuous of the passengers, and avoided them.

Eggheads!

And so they were, every one of them but one – Scientists, in politer terms – and a heterogeneous lot. Their nearest approach to a common emotion at that moment was a final anxiety for their instruments, a vague desire for a last check. And perhaps just a small increase of tension and anxiety. It *was* an uninhabited planet. Each had expressed himself as firmly of that belief a number of times.

Still, each man's thoughts are his own.

As for the one unusual man on board ship – not a crewman and not really a scientist – his strongest feeling was one of bone-weariness. He stirred to his feet weakly and fought off the last dregs of space-sickness. He was Mark Annuncio, and he had been in bed now for four days, feeding on almost nothing, while the ship wove in and out of the Universe, jumping its light-years of space.

But now he felt less certain of imminent death and he had to answer the summons of the Captain. In his inarticulate way, Mark resented that summons.

He was used to having his own way, seeing what he felt like seeing. Who was the Captain to—

The impulse kept returning to tell Dr Sheffield about this and let it rest there. But Mark was curious, so he knew he would have to go.

It was his one great vice. Curiosity!

It also happened to be his profession and his mission in life.

Captain Follenbee of the *Triple G.* was a hardheaded man. It was how he habitually thought of himself. He had made government-sponsored runs before. For one thing, they were profitable. The Confederacy didn't haggle. It meant a complete overhaul of his ship each time, replacement of defective parts, liberal terms for the crew. It was good business. Damned good business.

This run, of course, was a little different.

It wasn't so much the particular gang of passengers he had taken aboard. (He had expected temperament, tantrums, and unbearable foolishness but it turned out eggheads were much like normal people.) It wasn't that half his ship had been torn down and rebuilt into what the contract called a 'universal centralaccess laboratory.'

Actually, and he hated the thought, it was 'Junior' – the planet that lay ahead of them.

The crew didn't know, of course, but he, himself, hard head and all, was beginning to find the matter unpleasant.

But only beginning—

At the moment, he told himself, it was this Mark Annuncio, if that was the name, who was annoying him. He slapped the back of one hand against the palm of the other and thought angrily about it. His large, round face was ruddy with annoyance.

Insolence!

A boy of not more than twenty, with no position that he knew of among the passengers, to make a request like that.

What was behind it? *That* at least ought to be straightened out.

In his present mood, he would like to straighten it out by means of a jacket collar twisted in a fist and a rattle of teeth, but better not – better not—

After all, this was a curious kind of flight for the Confederacy of Worlds to sponsor, and a twenty-year-old, overcurious rubberneck might be an integral part of the strangeness. What was he on board *for?* There was this Dr Sheffield, for instance, who seemed to have no job but to play nursemaid for the boy. Now why was that? Who *was* this Annuncio?

He had been space-sick for the entire trip, or was that just a device to keep to his cabin—

There was a light buzzing as the door signal sounded. It would be the boy.

Easy now, thought the Captain. Easy now.

Mark Annuncio entered the Captain's cabin and licked his lips in a futile attempt to get rid of the bitter taste in his mouth. He felt lightheaded and heavyhearted.

At the moment, he would have given up his Service status to be back on Earth. He thought wishfully of his own famihar quarters; small but private; alone with his own kind. It was just a bed, desk, chair, and closet, but he had all of Central Library on free call. Here there was nothing. He had thought there would be a lot to learn on board ship. He had never been on board ship before. But he hadn't expected days and days of space-sickness.

He was so homesick he could cry, and he hated himself because he knew that his eyes were red and moist and that the Captain would see it. He hated himself because he wasn't large and wide; because he looked like a mouse.

In a word, that was it. He had mouse-brown hair with nothing but silken straightness to it; a narrow, receding chin, a small mouth, and a pointed nose. All he needed were five or six delicate vibrissae on each side of the nose to make the illusion complete. And he was below average in height.

And then he saw the star field in the Captain's observation port and the breath went out of him.

Stars!

Stars as he had never seen them.

Mark had never left the planet Earth before. (Dr Sheffield told him that was why he was space-sick. Mark didn't believe him. He had read in fifty different books that space-sickness was psychogenic. Even Dr Sheffield tried to fool him sometimes.)

He had never left Earth before, and he was used to Earth's sky. He was accustomed to viewing two thousand stars spread over half a celestial sphere, with only ten of the first magnitude.

But here they crowded madly. There were ten times the number in Earth's sky in that small square alone. And *bright!*

He fixed the star pattern greedily in his mind. It overwhelmed him. He knew the figures on the Hercules cluster, of course. It contained between one million and ten million stars (no exact census had been taken as yet), but figures are one thing and stars are another.

He wanted to count them. It was a sudden overwhelming desire. He was curious about the number. He wondered if they all had names; if there were astronomic data on all of them. Let's see . . .

He counted them in groups of hundreds. Two – three – he might have used the mental pattern alone, but he liked to watch the actual physical objects when they were so startlingly beautiful – six – seven—

The Captain's hearty voice splattered over him and brought him back to the ship's interior.

'Mr Annuncio. Glad to meet you.'

Mark looked up, startled, resentful. Why was his count being interrupted? He said irritably, 'The stars!' and pointed.

The Captain turned to stare. 'What about them? What's wrong?'

Mark looked at the Captain's wide back and his overdeveloped posterior. He looked at the gray stubble that covered the Captain's head, at the two large hands with thick fingers that clasped one another in the small of the Captain's back and flapped rhythmically against the shiny plastex of his jacket.

Mark thought, What does *he* care about the stars? Does *he* care about their size and brightness and spectral classes?

His lower lip trembled. The Captain was just one of the noncompos. Everyone on ship was a noncompos. That's what they called them back in the Service. Noncompos. All of them. Couldn't cube fifteen without a computer.

Mark felt very lonely.

He let it go (no use trying to explain) and said, 'The stars get so thick here. Like pea soup.'

'All appearance, Mr Annuncio.' (The Captain pronounced the *c* in Mark's name like an *s* rather than a *ch* and the sound grated Mark's ear.) 'Average distance between stars in the thickest cluster is over a light-year. Plenty of room, eh? Looks thick, though. Grant you that. If the light were out, they'd shine like a trillion Chisholm points in an oscillating force field.'

But he didn't offer to put the lights out and Mark wasn't going to ask him to. The Captain said, 'Sit down, Mr Annuncio. No use standing, eh? You smoke? Mind if I do? Sorry you couldn't be here this morning. Had an excellent view of Lagrange I and II at six space-hours. Red and green. Like traffic lights, eh? Missed you all trip. Space legs need strengthening, eh?'

He barked out his 'eh's' in a high-pitched voice that Mark found devilishly irritating.

Mark said in a low voice, 'I'm all right now.'

The Captain seemed to find that unsatisfactory. He puffed at his cigar and stared down at Mark with eyebrows hunched down over his eyes. He said slowly, 'Glad to see you now, anyway. Get acquainted a little. Shake hands. The *Triple G.*'s been on a good many government-chartered cruises. No trouble. Never had trouble. Wouldn't want trouble. You understand.'

Mark didn't. He was tired of trying to. His eyes drifted back hungrily to the stars. The pattern had changed a little.

The Captain caught his eyes for a moment. He was frowning and his shoulders seemed to tremble at the edge of a shrug. He walked to the control panel, and like a gigantic eyelid, metal slithered across the studded observation port.

Mark jumped up in a fury, shrieking, 'What's the idea? I'm counting them, you fool.'

'*Counting*—' The Captain flushed, but maintained a quality of politeness in his voice. He said, 'Sorry! Little matter of business we must discuss.'

He stressed the word 'business' lightly.

Mark knew what he meant. 'There's nothing to discuss. I want to see the ship's log. I called you hours ago to tell you that. You're delaying me.'

The Captain said, 'Suppose you tell me why you want to see it, eh? Never been asked before. Where's your authority?'

Mark felt astonished. 'I can look at anything I want to. I'm in Mnemonic Service.'

The Captain puffed strongly at his cigar. (It was a special grade manufactured for use in space and on enclosed space objects. It had an oxidant included so that atmospheric oxygen was not consumed.)

He said cautiously, 'That so? Never heard of it. What is it?'

Mark said indignantly, 'It's the Mnemonic Service, that's all. It's my job to look at anything I want to and to ask anything I want to. And I've got the right to do it.'

'Can't look at the log if I don't want you to.'

'You've got no say in it, you – you *noncompos*.'

The Captain's coolness evaporated. He threw his cigar down violently and stamped at it, then picked it up and poked it carefully into the ash vent. 'What the Galactic drift is this?' he demanded. 'Who are you, anyway? Security agent? What's up? Let's have it straight. Right now.'

'I've told you all I have to.'

'Nothing to hide,' said the Captain, 'but I've got rights.'

'Nothing to hide?' squeaked Mark. 'Then why is this ship called the *Triple G.*?'

'That's its name.'

'Go on. No such ship with an Earth registry. I knew that before I got on. I've been waiting to ask you.'

The Captain blinked. He said, 'Official name is *George G. Grundy. Triple G.* is what everyone calls it.'

Mark laughed. 'All right, then. And after I see the logbook, I want to talk to the crew. I have the right. You ask Dr Sheffield.'

'The crew, too, eh?' The Captain seethed. 'Let's talk to Dr Sheffield, and then let's keep you in quarters till we land. Sprout!' He snatched at the intercom box.

The scientific complement of the *Triple G.* were few in number for the job they had to do, and, as individuals, young. Not as young as Mark Annuncio, perhaps, who was in a class by himself, but even the oldest of them, Emmanuel George Cimon (astrophysicist), was not quite thirty-nine. And with his dark, unthinned hair and large, brilliant eyes, he looked still younger. To be sure, the optic brilliance was partly due to the wearing of contact lenses.

Cimon, who was perhaps overconscious of his relative age, and of the fact that he was the titular head of the expedition (a fact most of the others were inclined to ignore) usually affected an undramatic view of the mission. He ran the dotted tape through his fingers, then let it snake silently back into its spool.

'Run of the mill,' he sighed, seating himself in the softest chair in the small passengers' lounge. 'Nothing.'

He looked at the latest color photographs of the Lagrange binary and was impervious to their beauty. Lagrange I, smaller and hotter than Earth's own sun, was a brilliant green blue, with a pearly green-yellow corona surrounding it like the gold setting of an emerald. It appeared to be the size of a lentil or of a ball bearing out of a Lenser ratchet. A short distance away (as distances go on a photograph) was Lagrange II. It appeared twice the size of Lagrange I, due to its position in space. (Actually, it was only four fifths the diameter of Lagrange I, half its volume, and two thirds its mass.) Its orange red, toward which the film was less sensitive, comparatively, than was the human retina, seemed dimmer than ever against the glory of its sister sun.

Surrounding both, undrowned by the near-by suns, as the result of the differentially polarized lens specifically used for the purpose, was the unbelievable brilliance of the Hercules cluster. It was diamond dust, scattered thickly, yellow, white, blue, and red.

'Nothing,' said Cimon.

'Looks good to me,' said the other man in the lounge. He was Groot Knoevenaagel (physician; short, plump, and known to man by no name other than Novee).

He went on to ask, 'Where's Junior?' then bent over Cimon's shoulder, peering out of slightly myopic eyes.

Cimon looked up and shuddered. 'Its name is not Junior. You can't see the planet, Troas, if *that's* what you mean, in this damned wilderness of stars. This picture is *Scientific Earthman* material. It isn't particularly useful.'

'Oh, space and back!' Novee was disappointed.

'What difference is it to you, anyway?' demanded Cimon. 'Suppose I said one of those dots was Troas. Any one of them. You wouldn't know the difference and what good would it do you?'

'Now wait, Cimon. Don't be so damned superior. It's legitimate sentiment. We'll be living on Junior for a while. For all we know, we'll be dying on it.'

'There's no audience, Novee, no orchestra, no mikes, no trumpets, so why be dramatic? We won't be dying on it. If we do, it'll be our own fault, and probably as a result of overeating.' He said it with the peculiar emphasis men of small appetite use when speaking to men of hearty appetite, as though a poor digestion were something that came only of rigid virtue and superior intellect. 'A thousand people did die,' said Novee softly.

'Sure. About a billion men a day die all over the Galaxy.'

'Not this way.'

'Not what way?'

With an effort, Novee kept to his usual drawl. 'No discussions except at official meetings. That was the decision.'

'I'll have nothing to discuss,' said Cimon gloomily. 'They're just two ordinary stars. Damned if I know why I volunteered. I suppose it was just the chance of seeing an abnormally large Trojan system from close up. It was the thought of looking at a habitable planet with a double sun. I don't know why I should have thought there'd be anything amazing about it.'

'Because you thought of a thousand dead men and women,' said Novee, then went on hastily, 'Listen, tell me something, will you? What's a Trojan planet, anyway?'

The physician bore the other's look of contempt for a moment, then said, 'All right. All right. So I don't know. You don't know everything either. What do you know about ultrasonic incisions?'

Cimon said, 'Nothing, and I think that's fine. It's my opinion that information outside a professional man's specialty is useless and a waste of psycho-potential. Sheffield's point of view leaves me cold.'

'I still want to know. That is if you can explain it.'

'I can explain it. As a matter of fact, it was mentioned in the original briefing, if you were listening. Most multiple stars, and that means one third of all stars, have planets of a sort. The trouble is that the planets are never habitable. If they're far enough away from the center of gravity of the stellar system to have a fairly circular orbit, they're cold enough to have helium oceans. If they're close enough to get heat, their orbit is so erratic that at least once in each revolution, they get close enough to one or another of the stars to melt iron.

'Here in the Lagrange System, however, we have an unusual case. The two stars, Lagrange I and Lagrange II, and the planet, Troas (along with its satellite, Ilium), are at the corners of an imaginary equilateral triangle. Got that? Such an arrangement happens to be a stable one, and for the sake of anything you like, don't ask me to tell you why. Just take it as my professional opinion.'

Novee muttered under his breath, 'I wouldn't dream of doubting it.'

Cimon looked displeased and continued, 'The system revolves as a unit. Troas is always a hundred million miles from each sun, and the suns are always a hundred million miles from one another.'

Novee rubbed his ear and looked dissatisfied. 'I know all that. I *was* listening at the briefing. But why is it a *Trojan* planet? Why *Trojan*?'

Cimon's thin lips compressed for a moment as though holding back a nasty word by force. He said, 'We have an arrangement like that in the Solar System. The Sun, Jupiter, and a group of small asteroids form a stable equilateral triangle. It so happens that the asteroids had been given such names as Hector, Achilles, Ajax, and other heroes of the Trojan War, hence— Or do I have to finish?'

'Is that all?' said Novee.

'Yes. Are you through bothering me?'

'Oh, boil your head.'

Novee rose to leave the indignant astrophysicist but the door slid open a moment before his hand touched the activator and Boris Vemadsky (geochemist; dark eyebrows, wide mouth, broad face, and with an inveterate tendency to polka-dot shirts and magnetic clip-ons in red plastic) stepped in.

He was oblivious to Novee's flushed face and Cimon's frozen expression of distaste.

He said lightly, 'Fellow scientists, if you listen very carefully, you will probably hear an explosion to beat the Milky Way from up yonder in Captain's quarters.'

'What happened?' asked Novee.

'The Captain got hold of Annuncio, Sheffield's little pet wizard, and Sheffield went charging updeck, bleeding heavily at each eyeball.' Cimon, having listened so far, turned away, snorting.

Novee said, 'Sheffield! The man can't get angry. I've never even heard him raise his voice.'

'He did this time. When he found out the kid had left his cabin without telling him and that the Captain was bullyragging him— Wow! Did you know he was up and about, Novee?'

'No, but I'm not surprised. Space-sickness is one of those things. When you have it, you think you're dying. In fact, you can hardly wait. Then, in two minutes it's gone and you feel all right. Weak, but all right. I told Mark this morning we'd be landing next day and I suppose it pulled him through. The thought of a planetary surface in clear prospect does wonders for space-sickness. We *are* landing soon, aren't we, Cimon?'

The astrophysicist made a peculiar sound that could have been interpreted as a grunt of assent. At least, Novee so interpreted it.

'Anyway,' said Novee, 'what happened?'

Vernadsky said, 'Well, Sheffield's been bunking with me since the kid twirled on his toes and went over backward with space-sickness and he's sitting there at the desk with his damn charts and his fist computer chug-chugging away, when the room phone signals and it's the Captain. Well, it turns out he's got the boy with him and he wants to know what the blankety-blank and assorted dot and dash the government means by planting a spy on him. So Sheffield yells back at him that he'll stab him in the groin with a Collamore macro-leveling-tube if he's been fooling with the kid and off he goes, leaving the phone activated and the Captain frothing.'

'You're making this up,' said Novee. 'Sheffield wouldn't say anything like that.'

'Words to that effect.'

Novee turned to Cimon. 'You're heading our group. Why don't you do something about this?'

Cimon snarled, 'In cases like this, I'm heading the group. My responsiblities always come on suddenly. Let them fight it out. Sheffield talks an excellent fight and the Captain never takes his hands out of the small of his back. Vernadsky's jitterbugging description doesn't mean there'll be physical violence.'

'All right, but there's no point in having feuds of any kind in an expedition like ours.'

'You mean our mission!' Vernadsky raised both hands in mock awe and rolled his eyes upward. 'How I dread the time when we must find ourselves among the rags and bones of the first expedition.'

And as though the picture brought to mind by that was not one that bore levity well after all, there was suddenly nothing to say. Even the back of Cimon's head, which was all that showed over the back of the easy chair, seemed a bit the stiffer for the thought.

Oswald Mayer Sheffield (psychologist, thin as a string and as tall as a good length of it, and with a voice that could be used either for singing an operatic selection with surprising virtuosity or for making a point of argument, softly but with stinging accuracy) did not show the anger one would have expected from Vernadsky's account.

He was even smiling when he entered the Captain's cabin.

The Captain broke out mauvely as soon as he entered. 'Look here, Sheffield—'

'One minute, Captain Follenbee,' said Sheffield. 'How are you, Mark?'

Mark's eyes fell and his words were muffled. 'All right, Dr Sheffield.'

'I wasn't aware you'd gotten out of bed.'

There wasn't the shade of reproach in his voice, but Mark grew apologetic. 'I was feeling better, Dr Sheffield, and I feel bad about not working. I haven't done anything in all the time I've been on the ship.

So I put in a call to the Captain to ask to see the logbook and he had me come up here.'

'All right. I'm sure he won't mind if you go back to your room now.'

'Oh, won't I?' began the Captain.

Sheffield's mild eyes rose to meet the Captain. 'I'm responsible for him, sir.'

And somehow the Captain could think of nothing further to say.

Mark turned obediently and Sheffield watched him leave and waited till the door was well closed behind him.

Then he turned again to the Captain. 'What's the bloody idea, Captain?'

The Captain's knees bent a little, then straightened and bent again with a sort of threatening rhythm. The invisible slap of his hands, clasped behind his back, could be heard distinctly. 'That's my question. I'm Captain here, Sheffield.'

'I know that.'

'Know what it means, eh? This ship, in space, is a legally recognized planet. I'm absolute ruler. In space, what I say goes. Central Committee of the Confederacy can't say otherwise. I've got to maintain discipline, and no spy—'

'All right, and now let me tell *you* something, Captain. You're chartered by the Bureau of Outer Provinces to carry a government-sponsored research expedition to the Lagrange System, to maintain it there as long as research necessity requires and the safety of the crew and vessel permits, and then to bring us home. You've signed that contract and you've assumed certain obligations, Captain or not. For instance, you can't tamper with our instruments and destroy their research usefulness.'

'Who in space is doing that?' The Captain's voice was a blast of indignation.

Sheffield replied calmly, 'You are. Hands off Mark Annuncio, Captain. Just as you've got to keep your hands off Cimon's monochrome and Vailleux's micropics, you've got to keep your hands off my Annuncio. And that means each one of your ten, four-striped fingers. Got it?'

The Captain's uniformed chest expanded. 'I take no order on board my own ship. Your language is a breach of discipline, *Mister* Sheffield. Any more like that and it's cabin arrest. You *and* your Annuncio. Don't like it, then speak to Board of Review back on Earth. Till then, it's tongue behind teeth.'

'Look, Captain, let me explain something. Mark is in the Mnemonic Service—'

'Sure, he said so. Nummonic Service. Nummonic Service. It's plain secret police as far as I'm concerned. Well, not on board *my* ship, eh?'

'Mnemonic Service,' said Sheffield patiently. '*Em-en-ee-em-oh-en-eye-see* Service. You don't pronounce the first *em*. It's from a Greek word meaning memory.'

The Captain's eyes narrowed. 'He remembers things?'

'Correct, Captain. Look, in a way this is my fault. I should have briefed you on this. I would have, too, if the boy hadn't gotten so sick right after the take-off. It drove most other matters out of my mind. Besides, it didn't occur to me that he might be interested in the workings of the ship itself. Space knows why not. He should be interested in everything.'

'He should, eh?' The Captain looked at the timepiece on the wall. 'Brief me now, eh? But no fancy words. Not many of any other kind, either. Time limited.'

'It won't take long, I assure you. Now you're a space-going man, Captain. How many inhabited worlds would you say there were in the Confederation?'

'Eighty thousand,' said the Captain promptly.

'Eighty-three thousand two hundred,' said Sheffield. 'What do you suppose it takes to run a political organization that size?'

Again the Captain did not hesitate. 'Computers,' he said.

'All right. There's Earth, where half the population works for the government and does nothing but compute and there are computing subcenters on every other world. And even so data gets lost. Every world knows something no other world knows. Almost every man. Look at our little group. Vemadsky doesn't know any biology and

I don't know enough chemistry to stay alive. There's not one of us can pilot the simplest space cruiser, except for Fawkes. So we work together, each one supplying the knowledge the others lack.

'Only there's a catch. Not one of us knows exactly which of our own data is meaningful to the other under a given set of circumstances. We can't sit and spout everything we know. So we guess, and sometimes we don't guess right. Two facts, A and B, can go together beautifully sometimes. So Person A, who knows Fact A, says to Person B, who knows Fact B, "Why didn't you tell me this ten years ago?" and Person B answers, "I didn't think it was important," or, "I thought everyone knew that."'

The Captain said, 'That's what computers are for.'

Sheffield said, 'Computers are limited, Captain. They have to be asked questions. What's more, the questions have to be the kind that can be put into a limited number of symbols. What's more, computers are very literal-minded. They answer exactly what you ask and not what you have in mind. Sometimes it never occurs to anyone to ask just the right question or feed the computer just the right symbols, and when that happens, the computer doesn't volunteer information.

'What we need, what all mankind needs, is a computer that is nonmechanical; a computer with imagination. There's one like that, Captain.' The psychologist tapped his temple. 'In everyone, Captain.'

'Maybe,' grunted the Captain, 'but I'll stick to the usual, eh? Kind you punch a button.'

'Are you sure? Machines don't have hunches. Did *you* ever have a hunch?'

'Is this on the point?' The Captain looked at the timepiece again.

Sheffield said, 'Somewhere inside the human brain is a record of every datum that has impinged upon it. Very little of it is consciously remembered, but all of it's there, and a small association can bring an individual datum back without a person's knowing where it comes from. So you get a "hunch" or a "feeling". Some people are better at it than others. And some can be trained. Some are almost perfect, like Mark Annuncio and a hundred like him.

Someday, I hope, there'll be a billion like him, and we'll *really* have a Mnemonic Service.

'All their lives,' Sheffield went on, 'they do nothing but read, look, and listen. And train to do that better and more efficiently. It doesn't matter what data they collect. It doesn't have to have obvious sense or obvious significance. It doesn't matter if any man in the Service wants to spend a week going over the records of the space-polo teams of the Canopus Sector for the last century. *Any* datum may be useful someday. That's the fundamental axiom.

'Every once in a while one of the Service may correlate across a gap no machine could possibly manage. The machine would fail because no one machine is likely to possess those two pieces of thoroughly unconnected information, or else, if the machine does have them, no man would be insane enough to ask the right question. One good correlation out of the Service can pay for all the money appropriated for it in ten years or more.'

The Captain raised his broad hand. He looked troubled. He said, 'Wait a minute. Annuncio said no ship named *Triple G.* was under Earth registry. You mean he knows all registered ships by heart?'

'Probably,' said Sheffield. 'He may have read through the Merchant-Ship Register. If he did, he knows all the names, tonnages, years of construction, ports of call, numbers of crews, and anything else the register would contain.'

'And he was counting stars.'

'Why not? It's a datum.'

'I'm damned.'

'Perhaps, Captain. But the point is that a man like Mark is different from other men. He's got a queer, distorted upbringing and a queer, distorted view of life. This is the first time he's been away from Service grounds since he entered them at the age of five. He's easily upset – and he can be ruined. That mustn't happen, and I'm in charge to see it doesn't. He's my instrument; a more valuable instrument than everything else on this entire ship baled into a neat little ball of plutonium wire. There are only a hundred like him in all the Milky Way.'

Captain Follenbee assumed an air of wounded dignity. 'All right, then. Logbook. Strictly confidential, eh?'

'Strictly. He talks only to me, and I talk to no one unless a correlation has been made.'

The Captain did not look as though that fell under his classification of the word 'strictly' but he said, 'But no crew.' He paused significantly. 'You know what I mean.'

Sheffield stepped to the door. 'Mark knows about that. The crew won't hear about it from him, believe me.'

And as he was about to leave, the Captain called out, 'Sheffield!'

'Yes?'

'What in space is a noncompos?'

Sheffield suppressed a smile. 'Did he call you that?'

'What is it?'

'Just short for *non compos mentis*. Everyone in the Service uses it for everyone not in the Service. You're one. I'm one. It's Latin for 'not of sound mind'. And you know, Captain – I think they're quite right.' He stepped out the door quickly.

Mark Annuncio went through ship's log in some fifteen seconds. He found it incomprehensible, but then most of the material he put into his mind was that. That was no trouble. Nor was the fact that it was dull. The disappointment was that it did not satisfy his curiosity, so he left it with a mixture of relief and displeasure.

He had then gone into the ship's library and worked his way through three dozen books as quickly as he could work the scanner. He had spent three years of his early teens learning how to read by total gestalt and he still recalled proudly that he had set a school record at the final examinations.

Finally he wandered into the laboratory sections of the ship and watched a bit here and a bit there. He asked no questions and he moved on when any of the men cast more than a casual glance at him.

He hated the insufferable way they looked at him, as though he were some sort of queer animal. He hated their air of knowledge, as though there were something of value in spending an entire brain on one tiny subject and remembering only a little of that.

Eventually, of course, he would *have* to ask them questions. It was his job, and even if it weren't, curiosity would drive him. He hoped, though, he could hold off till they had made planetary surface.

He found it pleasant that they were inside a stellar system. Soon he would see a new world with new suns – two of them – and a new moon. Four objects with brand-new information in each; immense storehouses of facts to be collected lovingly and sorted out.

It thrilled him just to think of the amorphous mountain of data waiting for him. He thought of his mind as a tremendous filing system with index, cross index, cross cross index. He thought of it as stretching indefinitely in all directions. Neat. Smooth. Well oiled. Perfect precision.

He thought of the dusty attic that the noncompos called minds and almost laughed. He could see it even talking to Dr Sheffield, who was a nice fellow for a noncompos. He tried hard and sometimes he almost *understood*. The others, the men on board ship, their minds were lumberyards. Dusty lumberyards with splintery slats of wood tumbled every which way; and only whatever happened to be on top could be reached.

The poor fools! He could be sorry for them if they weren't so sloppy-nasty. If only they *knew* what they were like. If only they *realized*.

Whenever he could, Mark haunted the observation posts and watched the new worlds come closer.

They passed quite close to the satellite Ilium. (Cimon, the astrophysicist, was very meticulous about calling their planetary destination 'Troas' and the satellite 'Ilium', but everyone else aboard ship called them 'Junior' and 'Sister' respectively.) On the other side of the two suns, in the opposite Trojan position, were a group of asteroids. Cimon called them 'Lagrange Epsilon' but everyone else called them 'The Puppies'.

Mark thought of all this with vague simultaneity at the moment the thought 'Ilium' occurred to him. He was scarcely conscious of it, and let it pass as material of no immediate interest. Still more vague, and still further below his skin of mental consciousness were the dim stirrings of five hundred such homely misnomers of astronomical dignities of nomenclature. He had read about some, picked up others on subetheric programs, heard about still others in ordinary conversation, come across a few in news reports. The material might have been told him directly, or it might have been a carelessly overheard word. Even the substitution of *Triple G.* for *George G. Grundy* had its place in the shadowy file.

Sheffield had often questioned him about what went on in his mind – very gently, very cautiously.

'We want many more like you, Mark, for the Mnemonic Service. We need millions. Billions, eventually, if the race fills up the entire Galaxy, as it will someday. But where do we get them? Relying on inborn talent won't do. We all have that more or less. It's the training that counts, and unless we find out a little about what goes on, we won't know how to train.'

And urged by Sheffield, Mark had watched himself, listened to himself, turned his eyes inward and tried to become *aware*. He learned of the filing cases in his head. He watched them marshal past. He observed individual items pop up on call, always tremblingly ready. It was hard to explain, but he did his best. His own confidence grew with it. The anxieties of his childhood, those first years in Service, grew less. He stopped waking in the middle of the night, perspiration dripping, screaming with fear that he would forget. And his headaches stopped.

He watched Ilium as it appeared in the viewport at closest approach. It was brighter than he could imagine a moon to be. (Figures for albedos of three hundred inhabited planets marched through his mind, neatly arrayed in decreasing order. It scarcely stirred the skin of his mind. He ignored them.)

The brightness he blinked at was concentrated in the vast,

irregular patches that Cimon said (he overheard him, in weary response to another's question) had once been sea bottom. A fact popped into Mark's mind. The original report of Hidosheki Makoyama had given the composition of those bright salts as 78.6 per cent sodium chloride, 19.2 per cent magnesium carbonate, 1.4 per cerit potassium sulf . . . The thought faded out. It wasn't necessary.

Ilium had an atmosphere. A total of about 100 mm. of mercury. (A little over an eighth of Earth's, ten times Mars', 0.254 that of Coralemon, 0.1376 that of Aurora.) Idly he let the decimals grow to more places. It was a form of exercise, but he grew bored. Instant arithmetic was fifth-grade stuff. Actually, he still had trouble with integrals and wondered if that was because he didn't know what an integral was. A half dozen definitions flashed by, but he had never had enough mathematics to understand the definitions, though he could quote them well enough.

At school, they had always said, 'Don't ever get too interested in any one thing or group of things. As soon as you do that, you begin selecting your facts and you must never do that. *Everything, anything* is important. As long as you have the facts on file, it doesn't matter whether you understand them or not.'

But the noncompos didn't think so. Arrogant minds with holes in them!

They were approaching Junior itself now. It was bright, too, but in a different way. It had icecaps north and south. (Textbooks of Earth's paleo-climatology drifted past and Mark made no move to stop them.) The icecaps were retreating. In a million years, Junior would have Earth's present climate. It was just about Earth's size and mass and it rotated in a period of thirty-six hours.

It might have been Earth's twin. What differences there were, according to Makoyama's reports, were to Junior's advantage. There was nothing on Junior to threaten mankind as far as was known. Nor would anyone imagine there possibly might be were it not for the fact that humanity's first colony on the planet had been wiped out to the last soul.

What was worse, the destruction had occurred in such a way that a study of all surviving information gave no reasonable clue whatever as to what had happened.

Sheffield entered Mark's cabin and joined the boy two hours before landing. He and Mark had orginally been assigned a room together. That had been an experiment. Mnemonics didn't like the company of noncompos. Even the best of them. In any case, the experiment had failed. Almost immediately after take-off, Mark's sweating face and pleading eyes made privacy absolutely essential for him.

Sheffield felt responsible. He felt responsible for everything about Mark whether it was actually his fault or not. He and men like himself had taken Mark and children like him and trained them into personal ruin. They had been force-grown. They had been bent and molded. They had been allowed no normal contact with normal children lest they develop normal mental habits. No Mnemonic had contracted a normal marriage, even within the group.

It made for a terrible guilt feeling on Sheffield's part.

Twenty years ago there had been a dozen lads trained at one school under the leadership of U Karaganda, as mad an Asiatic as had ever roused the snickers of a group of interviewing newsmen. Karaganda had committed suicide eventually, under some vague motivation, but other psychologists, Sheffield for one, of greater respectability and undoubtedly of lesser brilliance, had had time to join him and learn of him.

The school continued and others were established. One was even founded on Mars. It had an enrollment of five at the moment. At latest count, there were one hundred three living graduates with full honors (naturally, only a minority of those enrolled actually absorbed the entire course). Five years ago, the Terrestrial-planetary government (not to be confused with the Central Galactic Committee, based on Earth, and ruling the Galactic Confederation) allowed the establishment of the Mnemonic Service as a branch of the Department of the Interior.

It had already paid for itself many times over, but few people knew that. Nor did the Terrestrial government advertise the fact, or any other fact about the Mnemonics. It was a tender subject with them. It was an 'experiment.' They feared that failure might be politically expensive. The opposition (with difficulty prevented from making a campaign issue out of it as it was) spoke at the planetary conferences of 'crackpotism' and 'waste of the taxpayers' money.' And the latter despite the existence of documentary proof of the precise opposite. In the machine-centered civilization that filled the Galaxy, it was difficult to learn to appreciate the achievements of naked mind without a long apprenticeship.

Sheffield wondered how long.

But there was no use being depressed in Mark's company. Too much danger of contagion. He said instead, 'You're looking fine, sport.'

Mark seemed glad to see him. He said thoughtfully, 'When we get back to Earth, Dr Sheffield—'

He stopped, flushed slightly, and said, 'I mean supposing we get back, I intend to get as many books and films as I can on folkways. I've hardly read anything on that subject. I was down in the ship's library and they had nothing.'

'Why the interest?'

'It's the Captain. Didn't you say he told you that the crew were not to know we were visiting a world on which the first expedition had died?'

'Yes, of course. Well?'

'Because spacemen consider it bad luck to touch on a world like that, especially one that looks harmless? "Sucker bait," they call it.'

'That's right.'

'So the Captain *says*. It's just that I don't see how that can be true. I can think of seventeen habitable planets from which the first expeditions never returned and never established residence. And each one was later colonized and now is a member of the Confederation. Sarinatia is one of them, and it's a pretty big world now.'

'There are planets of continuous disaster, too.' Sheffield deliberately put that as a declarative statement.

(Never ask informational questions. That was one of the Rules of Karaganda. Mnemonic correlations weren't a matter of the conscious intelligence; they weren't volitional. As soon as a direct question was asked, the resultant correlations were plentiful but only such as any reasonably informed man might make. It was the unconscious mind that bridged the wide, unlikely gaps.)

Mark, as any Mnemonic would, fell into the trap. He said energetically, 'No, I've never heard of one. Not where the planet was at all habitable. If the planet is solid ice, or complete desert, that's different. Junior isn't like that.'

'No, it isn't,' agreed Sheffield.

'Then why should the crew be afraid of it? I kept thinking about that all the time I was in bed. That's when I thought of looking at the log. I'd never actually seen one, so it would be a valuable thing to do in any case. And certainly, I thought, I would find the truth there.'

'Uh-huh,' said Sheffield.

'And, well – I may have been wrong. In the whole log, the purpose of the expedition was never mentioned. Now that wouldn't be so unless the purpose were secret. It was as if he were even keeping it *from* the other ship's officers. And the name of the ship *is* given as the *George G. Grundy*.'

'It would be, of course,' said Sheffield.

'I don't know. I suspected that business about *Triple G.*,' said Mark darkly.

Sheffield said, 'You seem disappointed that the Captain wasn't lying.'

'Not disappointed. Relieved, I think. I thought – I thought—' He stopped, and looked acutely embarrassed, but Sheffield made no effort to rescue him. He was forced to continue. 'I thought everyone might be lying to me, not just the Captain. Even *you* might, Dr Sheffield. I thought you just didn't want me to talk to the crew for some reason.'

Sheffield tried to smile and managed to succeed. The occupational disease of the Mnemonic Service was suspicion. They were isolated, these Mnemonics, and they were different. Cause and effect were obvious.

Sheffield said lightly, 'I think you'll find in your reading on folkways that these superstitions are not necessarily based on logical analysis. A planet which has become notorious has evil expected of it. The good which happens is disregarded; the bad is cried up, advertised, and exaggerated. The thing snowballs.'

He moved away from Mark. He busied himself with an inspection of the hydraulic chairs. They would be landing soon. He felt unnecessarily along the length of the broad webbing of the straps, keeping his back to the youngster. So protected, he said, almost in a whisper, 'And, of course, what makes it worse is that Junior is so different.'

(Easy now, easy. Don't push. He had tried that trick before this and—)

Mark was saying, 'No, it isn't. Not a bit. The other expeditions that failed were different. That's true.'

Sheffield kept his back turned. He waited.

Mark said, 'The seventeen other expeditions that failed on planets that are now inhabited were all small exploring expeditions. In sixteen of the cases, the cause of death was shipwreck of one sort or another, and in the remaining case, Coma Minor that one was, the failure resulted from a surprise attack by indigenous life forms, not intelligent, of course. I have the details on all of them—'

(Sheffield couldn't forbear holding his breath. Mark *could* give the details on all of them. All the details. It was as easy for him to quote all the records on each expedition, word for word, as it was to say yes or no. And he might well choose to. A Mnemonic had no selectivity. It was one of the things that made ordinary companionship between Mnemonics and ordinary people impossible. Mnemonics were dreadful bores by the nature of things. Even Sheffield, who was trained and inured to listen to it all, and who had no intention of stopping Mark if he were really off on a talk jag, sighed softly.)

'—but what's the use,' Mark continued, and Sheffield felt rescued from a horror. 'They're just not in the same class with the Junior expedition. That consisted of an actual settlement of 789 men, 207 women, and fifteen children under the age of thirteen. In the course of the next year, 315 women, nine men, and two children were added by immigration. The settlement survived almost two years and the cause of death isn't known, except that from their report, it might be disease.

'Now *that* part is different. But Junior itself has nothing unusual about it, except – of course—'

Mark paused as though the information were too unimportant to bother with and Sheffield almost yelled. He forced himself to say calmly, '*That* difference, of course.'

Mark said, 'We all know about that. It has two suns and the others only have one.'

The psychologist could have cried his disappointment. Nothing!

But what was the use? Better luck next time. If you don't have patience with a Mnemonic, you might as well not have a Mnemonic.

He sat down in the hydraulic chair and buckled himself in tightly. Mark did likewise. (Sheffield would have liked to help, but that would have been injudicious.) He looked at his watch. They must be spiraling down even now. Under his disappointment, Sheffield felt a stronger disturbance. Mark Annuncio had acted wrongly in following up his own hunch that the Captain and everybody else had been lying. Mnemonics had a tendency to believe that because their store of facts was great, it was complete. This, obviously, is a prime error. It is therefore necessary (thus spake Karaganda) for them to present their correlations to properly constituted authority and never to act upon it themselves.

Well, how significant was this error of Mark's? He was the first Mnemonic to be taken away from Service headquarters; the first to be separated from all of his kind; the first to be isolated among noncompos. What did that do to him? What would it continue to do to him? Would it be bad? If so, how to stop it?

To all of which questions, Dr Oswald Mayer Sheffield knew no answer.

The men at the controls were the lucky ones. They and, of course, Cimon, who, as astrophysicist and director of the expedition, joined them by special dispensation. The others of the crew had their separate duties, while the remaining scientific personnel preferred the relative comfort of their hydraulic seats during the spiral around and down to Junior.

It was while Junior was still far enough away to be seen as a whole that the scene was at its grandest.

North and south, a third of the way to the equator, lay the icecaps, still at the start of their millennial retreat. Since the *Triple G.* was spiraling on a north-south great circle (deliberately chosen for the sake of viewing the polar regions, as Cimon, at the cost of less than maximum safety, insisted), each cap in turn was laid out below them.

Each burned equally with sunlight, the consequence of Junior's untilted axis. And each cap was in sectors, cut like a pie with a rainbowed knife.

The sunward third of each was illuminated by both suns simultaneously into a brilliant white that slowly yellowed westward, and as slowly greened eastward. To the east of the white sector lay another, half as wide, which was reached by the light of Lagrange I only, and the snow there blazed a response of sapphire beauty. To the west, another half sector, exposed to Lagrange II alone, shone in the warm orange red of an Earthly sunset. The three colors graded into one another bandwise, and the similarity to a rainbow was increased thereby.

The final third was dark in contrast, but if one looked carefully enough, it, too, was in parts – unequal parts. The smaller portion was black indeed, but the larger portion had a faint milkiness about it.

Cimon muttered to himself, 'Moonlight. Of course,' then looked about hastily to see if he had been overheard. He did not like people to observe the actual process by which conclusions were brought to fruition in his mind. Rather they were to be presented to his students and listeners, to all about him in short, in a polished perfection that showed neither birth nor growth.

But there were only spacemen about and they did not hear him. Despite all their space-hardening, they were fixing whatever concentration they could spare from their duties and instruments upon the wonder before them.

The spiral curved, veered away from north-south to northeast-southwest, finally to the east-west, in which a safe landing was most feasible. The dull thunder of atmosphere carried into the pilot room, thin and shrill at first, but gathering body and volume as the minutes passed.

Until now, in the interests of scientific observation (and to the considerable uneasiness of the Captain) the spiral had been tight, deceleration slight, and the planetary circumnavigations numerous. As they bit into Junior's air covering, however, deceleration pitched high and the surface rose to meet them.

The icecaps vanished on either side and there began an equal alternation of land and water. A continent, mountainous on either seacoast and flat in between, like a soup plate with two ice-topped rims, flashed below at lengthening intervals. It spread halfway around Junior and the rest was water.

Most of the ocean at the moment was in the dark sector, and what was not lay in the red-orange light of Lagrange II. In the light of that sun, the waters were a dusky purple with a sprinkling of ruddy specks that thickened north and south. Icebergs!

The land was distributed at the moment between the red-orange half sector and the full white light. Only the eastern seacoast was in the blue green. The eastern mountain range was a startling sight, with its western slopes red and its eastern slopes green.

The ship was slowing rapidly now; the final trip over ocean was done. Next – landing!

The first steps were cautious enough. Slow enough, too. Cimon inspected his photochromes of Junior as taken from space with minute care. Under protest, he passed them among the others of the expedition, and more than a few groaned inwardly at the thought of having placed comfort before a chance to see the original of *that*.

Boris Vernadsky bent over his gas analyzer interminably, a symphony in loud clothes and soft grunts.

'We're about at sea level, I should judge,' he said, 'going by the value of g.'

Then, because he was explaining himself to the rest of the group, he added negligently, 'The gravitational constant, that is,' which didn't help most of them.

He said, 'The atmospheric pressure is just about eight hundred millimeters of mercury, which is about 5 per cent higher than on earth. And two hundred forty millimeters of that is oxygen as compared to only one hundred fifty on Earth. Not bad.'

He seemed to be waiting for approval, but scientists found it best to comment as little as possible on data in another man's specialty.

He went on, 'Nitrogen, of course. Dull, isn't it, the way nature repeats itself like a three-year-old who knows three lessons, period. Takes the fun away when it turns out that a water world always has an oxygen-nitrogen atmosphere. Makes the whole thing yawn-worthy.'

'What else in the atmosphere?' asked Cimon irritably. 'So far all we have is oxygen, nitrogen, and homely philosophy from kindly Uncle Boris.'

Vernadsky hooked his arm over his seat and said, amiably enough, 'What are you? Director or something?'

Cimon, to whom the directorship meant little more than the annoyance of preparing composite reports for the Bureau, flushed and said grimly, 'What else in the atmosphere, Dr Vernadsky?'

Vernadsky said, without looking at his notes, 'Under 1 per cent and over a hundredth of 1 per cent: hydrogen, helium, and carbon dioxide in that order. Under a hundredth of 1 per cent and over a ten thousandth of 1 per cent: methane, argon, and neon in that order. Under a ten thousandth of 1 per cent and over a millionth of a per cent: radon, krypton, and xenon in that order.

'The figures aren't very informative. About all I can get out of them is that Junior is going to be a happy hunting ground for uranium, that it's low in potassium, and that it's no wonder it's such a lovely little double icecap of a world.'

He did that deliberately, so that someone could ask him how he knew, and someone, with gratifying wonder, inevitably did.

Vernadsky smiled blandly and said, 'Atmospheric radon is ten to a hundred times as high here as on Earth. So is helium. Both radon and helium are produced as by-products of the radioactive breakdown of uranium and thorium. Conclusion: Uranium and thorium minerals are ten to a hundred times as copious in Junior's crust as in Earth's.

'Argon, on the other hand, is over a hundred times as low as on Earth. Chances are Junior has none of the argon it originally started with. A planet of this type has only the argon which forms from the breakdown of K^{40}, one of the potassium isotopes. Low argon; low potassium. Simple, kids.'

One of the assembled groups asked, 'What about the icecaps?'

Cimon, who knew the answer to that, asked, before Vernadsky could answer the other, 'What's the carbon dioxide content exactly?'

'Zero point zero one six em em,' said Vernadsky.

Cimon nodded, and vouchsafed nothing more.

'Well?' asked the inquirer impatiently.

'Carbon dioxide is only about half what it is on Earth, and it's the carbon dioxide that gives the hothouse effect. It lets the short waves of sunlight pass through to the planet's surface, but doesn't allow the long waves of planetary heat to radiate off. When carbon dioxide concentration goes up as a result of volcanic action, the planet heats up a bit and you have a carboniferous age, with oceans high and land surface at a minimum. When carbon dioxide goes down as a result of the vegetation refusing to let a good thing alone, fattening up on the good old CO_2 and losing its head about it, temperature drops, ice forms, a vicious cycle of glaciation starts, and *voila*—'

'Anything else in the atmosphere?' asked Cimon.

'Water vapor and dust. I suppose there are a few million air-borne spores of various virulent diseases per cubic centimeter in addition to that.' He said it lightly enough, but there was a stir in the room. More than one of the bystanders looked as though he were holding his breath.

Vemadsky shrugged and said, 'Don't worry about it for now. My analyzer washes out dust and spores quite thoroughly. But then, that's not my angle. I suggest Rodriguez grow his damn cultures under glass right away. Good thick glass.'

Mark Annuncio wandered everywhere. His eyes shone as he listened, and he pressed himself forward to hear better. The group suffered him to do so with various degrees of reluctance, in accordance with individual personalities and temperaments. None spoke to him.

Sheffield stayed close to Mark. He scarcely spoke either. He bent all his effort on remaining in the background of Mark's consciousness. He wanted to refrain from giving Mark the feeling of being haunted by himself; give the boy the illusion of freedom instead. He wanted to seem to be there each time by accident only.

It was a most unsuccessful pretense, he felt, but what could he do? He *had* to keep the kid from getting into trouble.

Miguel Antonio Rodriguez y Lopez (microbiologist; small, tawny, with intensely black hair, which he wore rather long, and with a reputation, which he did nothing to discourage, of being a Latin in the grand style as far as the ladies were concerned) cultured the dust from Vernadsky's gas-analyzer trap with a combination of precision and respectful delicacy.

'Nothing,' he said eventually. 'What foolish growths I get look harmless.' It was suggested that Junior's bacteria need not necessarily look harmful; that toxins and metabolic processes could not be analyzed by eye, even by microscopic eye.

This was met with hot contempt, as almost an invasion of professional function. He said, with an eyebrow lifted, 'One gets a feeling for these things. When one has seen as much of the microcosm as I have, one can sense danger or lack of danger.'

This was an outright lie, and Rodriguez proved it by carefully transferring samples of the various germ colonies into buffered, isotonic media and injecting hamsters with the concentrated result. They did not seem to mind.

Raw atmosphere was trapped in large jars and several specimens of minor animal life from Earth and other planets were allowed to disport themselves within. None of them seemed to mind either.

Nevile Fawkes (botanist; a man who appreciated his own handsomeness by modeling his hair style after that shown on the traditional busts of Alexander the Great, but from whose appearance the presence of a nose far more aquiline than Alexander ever possessed noticeably detracted) was gone for two days, by Junior chronology, in one of the *Triple G.*'s atmospheric coasters. He could navigate one like a dream and was, in fact, the only man outside the crew who could navigate one at all, so he was the natural choice for the task. Fawkes did not seem noticeably overjoyed about that.

He returned, completely unharmed and unable to hide a grin of relief. He submitted to irradiation for the sake of sterilizing the exterior of his flexible air suit (designed to protect men from the deleterious effect of the outer environment, where no pressure differential existed; the strength and jointedness of a true space suit being obviously unnecessary within an atmosphere as thick as Junior's). The coaster was subjected to a more extended irradiation and pinned down under a plastic coverall.

Fawkes flaunted color photographs in great number. The central valley of the continent was fertile almost beyond Earthly dreams. The rivers were mighty, the mountains rugged and snow-covered (with the usual pyrotechnic solar effects). Under Lagrange II alone, the vegetation looked vaguely repellent, seeming rather dark, like dried blood. Under Lagrange I, however, or under the suns together, the brilliant, flourishing green and the glisten of the numerous lakes (particularly north and south along the dead rims of the departing glaciers) brought an ache of homesickness to the hearts of many.

Fawkes said, 'Look at these.'

He had skimmed low to take a photochrome of a field of huge

flowers dripping with scarlet. In the high ultra-violet radiation of Lagrange I, exposure times were of necessity extremely short, and despite the motion of the coaster, each blossom stood out as a sharp blotch of strident color.

'I swear,' said Fawkes, 'each one of those was six feet across.'

They admired the flowers unrestrainedly.

Fawkes then said, 'No intelligent life whatever, of course.'

Sheffield looked up from the photographs with instant sharpness. Life and intelligence, after all, were by way of being his province. 'How do you know?'

'Look for yourself,' said the botanist. 'There are the photos. No highways, no cities, no artificial waterways, no signs of anything man-made.'

'No machine civilization,' said Sheffield. 'That's all.'

'Even ape men would build shelters and use fire,' said Fawkes, offended.

'The continent is ten times as large as Africa and you've been over it for two days. There's a lot you could miss.'

'Not as much as you'd think,' was the warm response. 'I followed every sizable river up and down and looked over both seacoasts. Any settlements are bound to be there.'

'In allowing seventy-two hours for two eight thousand-mile seacosts ten thousand miles apart, plus how many thousand miles of river, that had to be a pretty quick lookover.'

Cimon interrupted, 'What's this all about? *Homo sapiens* is the only intelligence ever discovered in the Galaxy through a hundred thousand and more explored planets. The chances of Troas possessing intelligence is virtually nil.'

'Yes?' said Sheffield. 'You could use the same argument to prove there's no intelligence on Earth.'

'Makoyama,' said Cimon, 'in his report mentioned no intelligent life.'

'And how much time did he have? It was a case of another quick feel through the haystack with one finger and a report of no needle.'

'What the eternal Universe,' said Rodriguez waspishly. 'We argue like madmen. Call the hypothesis of indigenous intelligence unproven and let it go. We are not through investigating yet, I hope.'

Copies of those first pictures of Junior's surface were added to what might be termed the open files. After a second trip, Fawkes returned in more somber mood and the meeting was correspondingly more subdued.

New photographs went from hand to hand and were then placed by Cimion himself in the special safe that nothing could open short of Cimon's own hands or an all-destroying nuclear blast.

Fawkes said, 'The two largest rivers have a generally north-south course along the eastern edges of the western mountain range. The larger river comes down from the northern icecap, the smaller up from the southern one. Tributaries come in westward from the eastern range, interlacing the entire central plain. Apparently the central plain is tipped, the eastern edge being higher. It's what ought to be expected maybe. The eastern mountain range is the taller, broader, and more continuous of the two. I wasn't able to make actual measurements, but I wouldn't be surprised if they beat the Himalayas. In fact, they're a lot like the Wu Ch'ao range on Hesperus. You have to hit the stratosphere to get over them, and rugged— Wow!

'Anyway' – he brought himself back to the immediate subject at hand with an effort – 'the two main rivers join about a hundred miles south of the equator and pour through a gap in the western range. They make it to the ocean after that in just short of eighty miles.

'Where it hits the ocean is a natural spot for the planetary metropolis. The trade routes into the interior of the continent have to converge there so it would be the inevitable emporium for space trade. Even as far as surface trade is concerned, the continental east coast has to move goods across the ocean. Jumping the eastern range isn't worth the effort. Then, too, there are the islands we saw when we were landing.

'So right there is where I would have looked for the settlement even if we didn't have a record of the latitude and longitude. And those settlers had an eye for the future. It's where they set up shop.'

Novee said in a low voice, 'They thought they had an eye for the future, anyway. There isn't much left of them, is there?'

Fawkes tried to be philosophic about it. 'It's been over a century. What do you expect? There's a lot more left of them than I honestly thought there would be. Their buildings were mostly prefab. They've tumbled, and vegetation has forced its way over and through them. The fact that the climate of Junior is glacial is what's preserved it. The trees – or the objects that rather look like trees – are small and obviously very slow-growing.

'Even so, the clearing is gone. From the air, the only way you could tell there had once been a settlement in that spot was that the new growth had a slightly different color and – and, well, *texture* than the surrounding forests.'

He pointed at a particular photograph. 'This is just a slag heap. Maybe it was machinery once. I think those are burial mounds.'

Novee said, 'Any actual remains? Bones?' Fawks shook his head.

Novee said, 'The last survivors didn't bury themselves, did they?'

Fawkes said, 'Animals, I suppose.' He walked away, his back to the group. 'It was raining when I poked my way through. It went splat, splat on the flat leaves above me and the ground was soggy and spongy underneath. It was dark, gloomy. There was a cold wind. The pictures I took don't get it across. I felt as though there were a thousand ghosts, waiting—'

The mood was contagious.

Cimon said savagely, 'Stop that!'

In the background, Mark Annuncio's pointed nose fairly quivered with the intensity of his curiosity. He turned to Sheffield, who was at his side, and whispered, 'Ghosts? No authentic case of seeing—'

Sheffield touched Mark's thin shoulder lightly. 'Only a way of speaking, Mark. But don't feel badly that he doesn't mean it literally. You're watching the birth of a superstition, and that's something, isn't it?'

A semi-sullen Captain Follenbee sought out Cimon the evening after Fawkes' second return and said in his harumphy way, 'Never do, Dr Cimon. My men are unsettled. Very unsettled.'

The port shields were open. Lagrange I was six hours gone, and Lagrange II's ruddy light, deepened to crimson in setting, flushed the Captain's face and tinged his short gray hair with red.

Cimon, whose attitude toward the crew in general and the Captain in particular was one of controlled impatience, said, 'What is the trouble, Captain?'

'Been here two weeks, Earth time. Still no one leaves without suits. Always irradiate before you come back. Anything wrong with the air?'

'Not as far as we know.'

'Why not breathe it then?'

'Captain, that's for me to decide.'

The flush on the Captain's face became a real one. He said, 'My papers say I don't have to stay if ship's safety is endangered. A frightened and mutinous crew is something I don't want.'

'Can't you handle your own men?'

'Within reason.'

'Well, what really bothers them? This is a new planet and we're being cautious. Can't they understand that?'

'Two weeks and still cautious. They think we're hiding something. And we are. You know that. Besides, surface leave is necessary. Crew's got to have it. Even if it's just on a bare rock a mile across. Gets them out of the ship. Away from the routine. Can't deny them that.'

'Give me till tomorrow,' said Cimon contemptuously.

The scientists gathered in the observatory the next day.

Cimon said, 'Vernadsky tells me the data on air is still negative, and Rodriguez has discovered no air-borne pathogenic organism of any type.'

There was a general air of dubiety over the last statement. Novee said, 'The settlement died of disease. I'll swear to that.'

'Maybe so,' said Rodriguez at once, 'but can you explain how? It's impossible. I tell you that and I tell you. See here. Almost all Earth-type planets give birth to life and that life is always protein in nature and always either cellular or virus in organization. But that's all. There the resemblance ends.

'You laymen think it's all the same; Earth or any planet. Germs are germs and viruses are viruses. I tell you you don't understand the infinite possibilities for variation in the protein molecule. Even on Earth, every species has its own diseases. Some may spread over several species but there isn't one single pathogenic life form of any type on Earth that can attack all other species.

'You think that a virus or a bacterium developing independently for a billion years on another planet with different amino acids, different enzyme systems, a different scheme of metabolism altogether is just going to happen to find *Homo sapiens* succulent like a lollipop. I tell you it is childishness.'

Novee, his physician's soul badly pierced at having been lumped under the phrase, 'You laymen,' was not disposed to let it go that easily. '*Homo sapiens* brings its own germs with it wherever it goes, Rod. Who's to say the virus of the common cold didn't mutate under some planetary influence into something that was suddenly deadly? Or influenza. Things like that have happened even on Earth. The 2755 para-meas—'

'I know all about the 2755 para-measles epidemic,' said Rodriguez, 'and the 1918 influenza epidemic, and the Black Death, too. But when has it happened lately? Granted the settlement was a matter of a century and more ago – still that wasn't exactly pre-atomic times, either. They included doctors. They had supplies of antibiotics and for space's sake, they knew the techniques of antibody induction. They're simple enough. And there was the medical relief expedition, too.'

Novee patted his round abdomen and said stubbornly, 'The symptoms were those of a respiratory infection; dyspnea—'

'I know the list, but I tell you it wasn't a germ disease that got them. It couldn't be.'

'What was it, then?'

'That's outside my professional competence. Talking from inside, I tell you it wasn't infection. Even mutant infection. It couldn't be. It *mathematically* couldn't be.' He leaned heavily on the adverb.

There was a stir among his listeners as Mark Annuncio shoved his thin body forward into the space immediately before Rodriguez.

For the first time, he spoke at one of these gatherings. 'Mathematically?' he asked eagerly.

Sheffield followed after, his long body all elbows and knees as he made a path. He murmured 'Sorry' half a dozen times.

Rodriguez, in an advanced stage of exasperation, thrust out his lower lip and said, 'What do *you* want?'

Mark flinched. Less eagerly, he said, 'You said you knew it wasn't infection mathematically. I was wondering how-mathematics . . .' He ran down.

Rodriguez said, 'I have stated my professional opinion.'

He said it formally, stiltedly, then turned away. No man questioned another's professional opinion unless he was of the same specialty. Otherwise the implication, clearly enough, was that the specialist's experience and knowledge was sufficiently dubious to be brought into question by an outsider.

Mark knew this, but then he was of the Mnemonic Service. He tapped Rodriguez's shoulder, while the others standing about listened in stunned fascination, and said, 'I know it's your professional opinion, but still I'd like to have it explained.'

He didn't mean to sound peremptory. He was just stating a fact.

Rodriguez whirled. 'You'd like to have it explained? Who the eternal Universe are *you* to ask me questions?'

Mark was startled at the other's vehemence, but Sheffield had reached him now, and he gained courage. With it, anger. He disregarded Sheffield's quick whisper and said shrilly, 'I'm Mark Annuncio of Mnemonic Service and I've asked you a question. I want your statement explained.'

'It won't be explained. Sheffield, take this young nut out of here and tuck him into bed, will you? And keep him away from me after this. Damn young jackass.' The last was a clearly heard aside.

Sheffield took Mark's wrist but it was wrenched out of his grasp. The young Mnemonic screamed, 'You stupid noncompos. You– you moron. You forgettery on two feet. Sievemind. Let me *go*, Dr Sheffield – You're no expert. You don't remember anything you've learned, and you haven't learned much in the first place. You're not a specialist; none of you—'

'For space's sake,' cried Cimon, 'take the young idiot out of here, Sheffield.'

Sheffield, his long cheeks burning, stooped and lifted Mark bodily into the air. Holding him close, he made his way out of the room.

Tears squeezed out of Mark's eyes, and just outside the door, he managed to speak with difficulty. 'Let me down. I want to hear – I want to hear what they say.'

Sheffield said, 'Don't go back in. Please, Mark.'

'I won't. Don't worry. But—' He didn't finish the but.

Inside the observatory room, Cimon, looking haggard, said, ' All right. All right. Let's get back to the point. Come on, now. Quiet! I'm accepting Rodriguez's viewpoint. It's good enough for me and I don't suppose there's anyone else here who questions Rodriguez's professional opinion.'

('Better not,' muttered Rodriguez, his dark eyes hot with sustained fury.) Cimon went on. 'And since there's nothing to fear as far as infection is concerned, I'm telling Captain Follenbee that the crew may take surface leave without special protection against the atmosphere. Apparently the lack of surface leave is bad for morale. Are there any objections?' There weren't any.

Cimon said, 'I see no reason also why we can't pass on to the next stage of the investigation. I propose that we set up camp at the site of the original settlement. I appoint a committee of five to trek out there. Fawkes, since he can handle the coaster; Novee and Rodriguez to handle the biological data; Vernadsky and myself to take care of the chemistry and physics.

'The rest of you will, naturally, be apprised of all pertinent data in your own specialties, and will be expected to help in suggesting lines of attack, et cetera. Eventually, we may all be out there, but for the while only this small group. And until further notice, communication between ourselves and the main group on ship will be by radio only, since if the trouble, whatever it is, turns out to be localized at settlement site, five men are enough to lose.'

Novee said, 'The settlement lived on Junior several years before dying out. Over a year, anyway. It could be a long time before we are certain we're safe.'

'We,' said Cimon, 'are not a settlement. We are a group of specialists who are looking for trouble. We'll find it if it's there to find, and when we do find it, we'll beat it. And it won't take us a couple of years, either. Now, are there any objections?'

There were none, and the meeting broke up.

Mark Annuncio sat on his bunk, hands clasped about his knees, chin sunken and touching his chest. He was dry-eyed now, but his voice was heady with frustration.

'They're not taking me,' he said. 'They won't let me go with them.' Sheffield was in the chair opposite the boy, bathed in an agony of perplexity.

He said, 'They may take you later on.'

'No,' said Mark fiercely, 'they won't. They hate me. Besides, I want to go now. I've never been on another planet before. There's so much to see and find out. They've got no right to hold me back if I want to go.'

Sheffield shook his head. Mnemonics were so firmly trained into this belief that they *must* collect facts and that no one or nothing could or ought to stop them. Perhaps when they returned, he might recommend a certain degree of counterindoctrination. After all, Mnemonics had to live in the real world occasionally. More and more with each generation, perhaps, as they grew to play an increasing role in the Galaxy.

He tried an experiment. He said, 'It may be dangerous, you know.'

'I don't care. I've got to know. I've *got* to find out about this planet. Dr Sheffield, you go to Dr Cimon and tell him I'm going along.'

'Now, Mark.'

'If you don't, I will.' He raised his small body from the bed in earnest of leaving that moment.

'Look, you're excited.'

Mark's fists clenched. 'It's not fair, Dr Sheffield. I found this planet. It's *my* planet.'

Sheffield's conscience hit him badly. What Mark said was true in a way. No one, except Mark, knew that better than Sheffield. And no one, again except Mark, knew the history of Junior better than Sheffield.

It was only in the last twenty years that, faced ith the rising tide of population pressure in the older planets and the recession of the Galactic frontier from those same older planets, the Confederation of Worlds began exploring the Galaxy systematically. Before that, human expansion went on hit or miss. Men and women in search of new land and a better life followed rumor as to the existence of habitable planets or sent out amateur groups to find something promising. A hundred ten years before, one such group found Junior. They didn't report their find officially because they didn't want a crowd of land speculators, promotion men, exploiters and general riffraff following. In the next months, some of the unattached men arranged to have women brought in, so the settlement must have flourished for a while.

It was a year later, when some had died and most or all the rest were sick and dying, that they beamed a cry of help to Pretoria, the nearest inhabited planet. The Pretorian government was in some sort of crisis at the time and relayed the message to the Sector government at Altmark. Pretoria then felt justified in forgetting the matter.

The Altmark government, acting in reflex fashion, sent out a medical ship to Junior. It dropped anti-sera and various other supplies. The ship did not land because the medical officer diagnosed the matter from a distance as influenza and minimized the danger. The medical supplies, his report said, would handle the matter perfectly. It was quite possible that the crew of the ship, fearing contagion, had prevented a landing, but nothing in the official report indicated that.

There was a final report from Junior three months later to the effect that only ten people were left alive and that they were dying. They begged for help. This report was forwarded to Earth itself along with the previous medical report. The Central government, however, was a maze in which reports regularly were forgotten unless someone had sufficient personal interest, and influence, to keep them alive. No one had much interest in a far-off, unknown planet with ten dying men and women on it.

Filed and forgotten – and for a century, no human foot was felt on Junior.

Then, with the new furor over Galactic exploration, hundreds of ships began darting through the empty vastness, probing here and there. Reports trickled in, then flooded in. Some came from Hidosheki Mikoyama, who passed through the Hercules cluster twice (dying in a crash landing the second time, with his tight and despairing voice coming over the subether in a final message: 'Surface coming up fast now; ship walls frictioning into red he—' and no more.)

Last year the accumulation of reports, grown past any reasonable human handling, was fed into the overworked Washington computer on a priority so high that there was only a five-month wait. The operators checked out the data for planetary habitability and lo, Abou· ben Junior led all the rest.

Sheffield remembered the wild hoorah over it. The stellar system was enthusiastically proclaimed to the Galaxy and the name Junior was thought up by a bright young man in the Bureau of Outer Provinces who felt the need for personal friendliness between man and world. Junior's virtues were magnified. Its fertility, its climate ('a New England perpetual spring'), and most of all, its vast future, were put across without any feeling of need for discretion. 'For the next million years,' propagandists declared, 'Junior will grow richer. While other planets age, Junior will grow younger as the ice recedes and fresh soil is exposed. Always a new frontier; always untapped resources.'

For a million years!

It was the Bureau's masterpiece. It was to be the tremendously successful start of a program of government-sponsored colonization. It was to be the beginning, at long last, of the scientific exploitation of the Galaxy for the good of humanity.

And then came Mark Annuncio, who heard much of all this and was as thrilled at the prospect as any Joe Earthman, but who one day thought of something he had seen while sniffing idly through the 'dead matter' files of the Bureau of Outer Provinces. He had seen a medical report about a colony on a planet of a system whose description and position in space tallied with that of the Lagrange group.

Sheffield remembered the day Mark came to him with that news.

He also remembered the face of the Secretary for the Outer Provinces when the news was passed on to *him*. He saw the Secretary's square jaw slowly go slack and a look of infinite trouble come into his eyes.

The government was committed! It was going to ship millions of people to Junior. It was going to grant farmland and subsidize the first seed supplies, farm machinery, factories. Junior was going to be a paradise for numerous voters and a promise of more paradise for a myriad others.

If Junior turned out to be a killer planet for some reason or other, it would mean political suicide for all government figures concerned in the project. That meant some pretty big men, not least the Secretary for the Outer provinces.

After days of checking and indecision, the Secretary had said to Sheffield, 'It looks as though we've got to find out what happened and weave it into the propaganda somehow. Don't you think we could neutralize it that way?'

'If what happened isn't too horrible to neutralize.'

'But it can't be, can it? I mean what can it be?' The man was miserably unhappy.

Sheffield shrugged.

The Secretary said, 'See here. We can send a ship of specialists to the planet. Volunteers only and good reliable men, of course. We can give it the highest priority rating we can move, and Project Junior carries considerable weight, you know. We'll slow things up here, and hold on till they get back. That might work, don't you think?'

Sheffield wasn't sure, but he got the sudden dream of going on that expedition, of taking Mark with him. He could study a Mnemonic in an off-trail environment, and if Mark *should* be the means of working out the mystery—

From the beginning, a mystery was assumed. After all, people don't die of influenza. And the medical ship hadn't landed; they hadn't *really* observed what was going on. It was fortunate, indeed, that that medical man was now dead thirty-seven years, or he would be slated for court-martial now.

If Mark *should* help solve the matter, the Mnemonic Service would be enormously strengthened. The government had to be grateful.

But now—

Sheffield wondered if Cimon knew the story of how the matter of the first settlement had been brought to light. He was fairly certain that the rest of the crew did not. It was not something the Bureau would willingly speak about. Nor would it be politic to use the story as a lever to pry concessions out of Cimon. If Mark's correction of Bureau 'stupidity' (that would undoubtedly be the opposition's phrasing) were overpublicized, the Bureau would look bad. If they could be grateful, they could be vengeful, too. Retaliation against the Mnemonic Service would not be too petty a thing to expect.

Still—

Sheffield stood up with quick decision. 'All right, Mark. I'll get you out to the settlement site. I'll get us both out there. Now you sit down and wait for me. Promise you'll try nothing on your own.'

'All right,' said Mark. He sat down on his bunk again.

'Well now, Dr Sheffield, what is it?' said Cimon. The astrophysicist sat at his desk, on which papers and film formed rigidly arranged heaps about a small Macfreed integrator, and watched Sheffield step over the threshold.

Sheffield sat carelessly down upon the tautly yanked top sheet of Cimon's bunk. He was aware of Cimon's annoyed glance in that direction and it did not worry him. In fact, he rather enjoyed it.

He said, 'I have a quarrel with your choice of men to go to the expedition site. It looks as though you've picked two men for the physical sciences and three for the biological sciences. Right?'

'Yes.'

'I suppose you think you've covered the ground like a Danielski ovospore at perihelion.'

'Oh, space! Have you anything to suggest?'

'I would like to come along myself.'

'Why?'

'You have no one to take care of the mental sciences.'

'The *mental* sciences! Good Galaxy! Dr Sheffield, five men are quite enough to risk. As a matter of fact, Doctor, you and your – uh – ward were assigned to the scientific personnel of this ship by order of the Bureau of Outer Provinces without any prior consultation of myself. I'll be frank. If I had been consulted, I would have advised against you. I don't see the function of mental science in an investigation such as this, which, after all, is purely physical. It is too bad that the Bureau wishes to experiment with Mnemonics on an occasion such as this. We can't afford scenes like that one with Rodriguez.'

Sheffield decided that Cimon did not know of Mark's connection with the original decision to send out the expedition.

He sat upright, hands on knees, elbows cocked outward, and let a freezing formality settle over him. 'So you wonder about the function of mental science in an investigation such as this, Dr Cimon. Suppose I told you that the end of the first settlement might possibly be explained on a simple, psychological basis.'

'It wouldn't impress me. A psychologist is a man who can explain anything and prove nothing.' Cimon smirked like a man who had made an epigram and was proud of it.

Sheffield ignored it. He said, 'Let me go into a little detail. In what way is Junior different from every one of the eighty-three thousand inhabited worlds?'

'Our information is as yet incomplete, I cannot say.'

'Oh, cobber-vitals. You had the necessary information before you ever came here. Junior has two suns.'

'Well, of course.' But the astrophysicist allowed a trace of discomfiture to enter his expression.

'Colored suns, mind you. Colored suns. Do you know what that means? It means that a human being, yourself or myself, standing in the full glare of the two suns, would cast two shadows. One blue green, one red orange. The length of each would naturally vary with the time of day. Have you taken the trouble to verify the color distribution in those shadows? The what-do-you-call-'em-reflection spectrum?'

'I presume,' said Cimon loftily, 'they'd be about the same as the radiation spectra of the suns. What are you getting at?'

'You should check. Wouldn't the air absorb some wave lengths? And the vegetation? What's left? And take Junior's moon, Sister. I've been watching it in the last few nights. It's in colors, too, and the colors change position.'

'Well, of course, damn it. It runs through its phases independently with each sun.'

'You haven't checked its reflection spectrum, either, have you?'

'We have that somewhere. There are no points of interest about it. Of what interest is it to you, anyway?'

'My dear Dr Cimon, it is a well established psychological fact that combinations of red and green colors exert a deleterious effect on mental stability. We have a case here where the red-green chromopsychic picture (to use a technical term) is inescapable and is presented under circumstances which seem most unnatural to the human mind. It is quite possible that chromopsychosis could reach the fatal level by inducing hypertrophy of the trinitarian follicles, with consequent cerebric catatonia.'

Cimon looked floored. He said, 'I never heard of such a thing.'

'Naturally not,' said Sheffield (it was his turn to be lofty). 'You are not a psychologist. Surely you are not questioning my professional opinion.'

'No, of course not. But it's quite plain from the last reports of the expedition that they were dying of something that sounded like a respiratory disease.'

'Correct, but Rodriguez denies that and you accepted his professional opinion.'

'I didn't say it was a respiratory disease. I said it sounded like one. Where does your red-green chromothingumbob come in?'

Sheffield shook his head. 'You laymen have your misconceptions. Granted that there is a physical effect, it still does not imply that there may not be a mental cause. The most convincing point about my theory is that red-green chromopsychosis has been recorded to exhibit itself first as a psychogenic respiratory infection. I take it you are not acquainted with psychogenics.'

'No. It's out of my field.'

'Well, yes. I should say so. Now my own calculations show me that under the heightened oxygen tension of this world, the psychogenic respiratory infection is both inevitable and particularly severe. For instance, you've observed the moon – Sister, I mean – in the last few nights.'

'Yes, I have observed Ilium.' Cimon did not forget Sister's official name even now.

'You watched it closely and over lengthy periods? Under magnification?'

'Yes.' Cimon was growing uneasy.

'Ah,' said Sheffield. 'Now the moon colors in the last few nights have been particularly virulent. Surely you must be noticing just a small inflammation of the mucus membrane of the nose, a slight itching in the throat. Nothing painful yet, I imagine. Have you been coughing or sneezing? Is it a little hard to swallow?'

'I believe I—' Cimon swallowed, then drew in his breath sharply. He was testing.

Then he sprang to his feet, fists clenched and mouth working. 'Great galaxy, Sheffield, you had no right to keep quiet about this. I can feel it now. What do I do, Sheffield? It's not incurable, is it? Damn it, Sheffield' – his voice went shrill – 'why didn't you tell us this before?'

'Because,' said Sheffield calmly, 'there's not a word of truth in anything I've said. Not one word. There's no harm in colors. Sit down, Dr Cimon. You're beginning to look foolish.'

'You said,' said Cimon, thoroughly confused, and in a voice that was beginning to strangle, 'that it was your professional opinion that—'

'My professional opinion! Space and little comets, Cimon, what's so magic about a professional opinion? A man can be lying or he can just plain be ignorant, even about the final details of his own specialty. A professional can be wrong because he's ignorant of a neighboring specialty. He may be certain he's right and still be wrong.

'Look at you. You know all about what makes the Universe tick and I'm lost completely except that I know that a star is something that twinkles and a light-year is something that's long. And yet you'll swallow gibberish psychology that a freshman student of mentics would laugh his head off at. Don't you think, Cimon, it's time we worried less about professional opinion and more about over-all co-ordination?'

The color washed slowly out of Cimon's face. It turned waxy-pale. His lips trembled. He whispered, 'You used professional status as a cloak to make a fool of me.'

'That's about it,' said Sheffield.

'I have never, *never*—' Cimon gasped and tried a new start. 'I have never witnessed anything as cowardly and unethical.'

'I was trying to make a point.'

'Oh, you made it. You made it.' Cimon was slowly recovering, his voice approaching normality. 'You want me to take that boy of yours with us.'

'That's right.'

'No. No. Definitely no. It was no before you came in here and it's no a million times over now.'

'What's your reason? I mean before I came in.'

'He's psychotic. He can't be trusted with normal people.'

Sheffield said grimly, 'I'll thank you not to use the word, 'psychotic.' You are not competent to use it. If you're so precise in your feeling for professional ethics, remember to stay out of my specialty in my presence. Mark Annuncio is perfectly normal.'

'After that scene with Rodriguez? Yes. Oh, yes.'

'Mark had the right to ask his question. It was his job to do so and his duty. Rodriguez had no right to be boorish about it.'

'I'll have to consider Rodriguez first, if you don't mind.'

'Why? Mark Annuncio knows more than Rodriguez. For that matter, he knows more than you or I. Are you trying to bring back an intelligent report or to satisfy a petty vanity?'

'Your statements about what your boy knows do not impress me. I am quite aware he is an efficient parrot. He understands nothing, however. His my duty to see to it that data is made available to him because the Bureau has ordered that. They did not consult me, but very well. I will co-operate that far. He will receive his data here in the ship.'

Sheffield said, 'Not adequate, Cimon. He should be on the spot. He may see things our precious specialists will not.'

Cimon said freezingly, 'Very likely. The answer, Sheffield, is no. There is no argument that can possibly persuade me.' The astrophysicist's nose was pinched and white.

'Because I made a fool of you?'

'Because you violated the most fundamental obligation of a professional man. No respectable professional would ever use his specialty to prey on the innocence of a non-associate professional.'

'So I made a fool of you.'

Cimon turned away. 'Please leave. There will be no further communication between us, outside the most necessary business, for the duration of the trip.'

'If I go,' said Sheffield, 'the rest of the boys may get to hear about this.'

Cimon started. 'You're going to repeat our little affair?' A cold smile rested on his lips, then went its transient and contemptuous way. 'You'll broadcast the dastard you were.'

'Oh, I doubt they'll take it seriously. Everyone knows psychologists will have their little jokes. Besides, they'll be so busy laughing at you. You know – the very impressive Dr Cimon scared into a sore throat and howling for mercy after a few mystic words of gibberish.'

'Who'd believe you?' cried Cimon.

Sheffield lifted his right hand. Between thumb and forefinger was a small rectangular object, studded with a line of control toggles.

'Pocket recorder,' he said. He touched one of the toggles and Cimon's voice was suddenly saying, 'Well, now, Dr Sheffield, what is it?'

It sounded pompous, peremptory, and even a little smug.

'Give me that!' Cimon hurled himself at the lanky psychologist.

Sheffield held him off. 'Don't try force, Cimon. I was in amateur wrestling not too long ago. Look, I'll make a deal with you.'

Cimon was still writhing toward him, dignity forgotten, panting his fury. Sheffield kept him at arm's length, backing slowly.

Sheffield said, 'Let Mark and myself come along and no one will ever see or hear this.'

Slowly Cimon simmered down. He gasped, 'Will you let me have it, then?'

'After Mark and I are out at the settlement site.'

'I'm to trust *you*.' He seemed to take pains to make that as offensive as possible.

'Why not? You can certainly trust me to broadcast this if you *don't* agree. I'll play it off for Vernadsky first. He'll love it. You know his corny sense of humor.'

Cimon said in a voice so low it could hardly be heard, 'You and the boy can come along.' Then vigorously, 'But remember this, Sheffield. When we get back to Earth, I'll have you before the Central Committee of the G.A.A.S. That's a promise. You'll be de-professionalized.'

Sheffield said, 'I'm not afraid of the Galactic Association for the Advancement of Science.' He let the syllables resound. 'After all, what will you accuse me of? Are you going to play this recording before the Central Committee as evidence? Come, come, let's be friendly about this. You don't want to broadcast your own – uh – mistake before the primest stuffed shirts in eighty-three thousand worlds.'

Smiling gently, he backed out the door.

But when he closed the door between himself and Cimon, his smile vanished. He hadn't liked to do this. Now that he had done it, he wondered if it were worth the enemy he had made.

Seven tents had sprung up near the site of the original settlement on Junior. Nevile Fawkes could see them all from the low ridge on which he stood. They had been there seven days now.

He looked up at the sky. The clouds were thick overhead and pregnant with rain. That pleased him. With both suns behind those clouds, the diffused light was gray white. It made things seem almost normal.

The wind was damp and a little raw, as though it were April in

Vermont. Fawkes was a New Englander and he appreciated the resemblance. In four or five hours, Lagrange I would set and the clouds would turn ruddy while the landscape would become angrily dim. But Fawkes intended to be back in the tents by then. So near the equator, yet so cool! Well, that would change with the millennia. As the glaciers retreated, the air would warm up and the soil would dry out. Jungles and deserts would make their appearance. The water level in the oceans would slowly creep higher, wiping out numberless islands. The two large rivers would become an inland sea, changing the configuration of Junior's one large continent; perhaps making several smaller ones out of it.

He wondered if the settlement site would be drowned. Probably, he decided. Maybe that would take the curse off it.

He could understand why the Confederation were so damned anxious to solve the mystery of that first settlement. Even if it were a simple matter of disease, there would have to be proof. Otherwise, who would settle the world? The 'sucker bait' superstition held for more than merely spacemen.

He, himself— Well, his first visit to the settlement site hadn't been so bad, though he had been glad to leave the rain and the gloom. Returning was worse. It was difficult to sleep with the thought that a thousand mysterious deaths lay all about, separated from him only by that insubstantial thing time.

With medical coolness, Novee had dug up the moldering graves of a dozen of the ancient settlers. (Fawkes could not and did not look at the remains.) There had been only crumbling bones, Novee had said, out of which nothing could be made.

'There seem to be abnormalities of bone deposition,' he said.

Then on questioning, he admitted that the effects might be entirely owing to a hundred years' exposure to damp soil.

Fawkes had constructed a fantasy that followed him even into his waking hours. It concerned an elusive race of intelligent beings dwelling underground, never being seen but haunting that first settlement a century back with a deadly perserverance.

He pictured a silent bacteriological warfare. He could see them in laboratories beneath the tree roots, culturing their molds and spores, waiting for one that could live on human beings. Perhaps they captured children to experiment upon.

And when they found what they were looking for, spores drifted silently out over the settlement in venomous clouds—

Fawkes knew all this to be fantasy. He had made it up in the wakeful nights out of no evidence but that of his quivering stomach. Yet alone in the forest, he whirled more than once in a sudden horror-filled conviction that bright eyes were staring out of the duskiness of a tree's Lagrange I shadow.

Fawkes' botanist's eye did not miss the vegetation he passed, absorbed as he was. He had deliberately struck out from camp in a new direction, but what he saw was what he had already seen. Junior's forests were neither thick nor tangled. They were scarcely a barrier to travel. The small trees (few were higher than ten feet, although their trunks were nearly as thick as the average Terrestrial tree) grew with considerable room between them.

Fawkes had constructed a rough scheme for arranging the plant life of Junior into some sort of taxonomic order. He was not unaware of the fact that he might be arranging for his own immortality.

There was the scarlet 'bayonet tree,' for instance. Its huge scarlet flowers attracted insect-like creatures that built small nests within it. Then (at what signal or what impulse Fawkes had not divined) all the flowers on some one given tree would grow a glistening white pistil over night. Each pistil stood two feet high, as though every bloom had been suddenly equipped with a bayonet.

By the next day, the flower had been fertilized and the petals closed shut – about pistil, insects, and all. The explorer, Makoyama, had named it the 'bayonet tree,' but Fawkes had made so bold as to rename it *Migrania Fawkesii*.

One thing the trees had in common. Their wood was incredibly tough. It would be the task of the biochemist to determine the physical state of the cellulose molecule and that of the biophysicist to determine how water could be transported through the wood's impervious texture. What Fawkes knew from experience was that the blossoms would break if pulled, that the stems would bend only with difficulty and break not at all. His pocketknife was blunted without so much as making a scratch.

The original settlers, in order to clear land, had obviously had to dig out the trees, roots and all.

Compared to Earth, the woods were almost free of animal life. That might be due to the glacial slaughter. Fawkes didn't know.

The insect-like creatures were all two winged. And those wings were feathery little fronds that beat noiselessly. None, apparently, were bloodsuckers.

The only major experience with animals that they had had was the sudden appearance of a large flying creature over the camp. It took high-speed photography to reveal the actual shape of the beast, for the specimen they observed, apparently overcome with curiosity, swooped low over the tents again and again at speeds too great for comfortable, naked-eye observation. It was four-winged, the forward wings terminating in powerful claws, being membranous and nearly naked, serving the office of gliding planes. The hind pair, covered with a hairlike fuzz, beat rapidly.

Rodriguez suggested the name *Tetrapterus*.

Fawkes paused in his reminiscence to look at a variety of grass he had not seen before. It grew in a dense patch and each stem forked in three toward the top. He brought out his magnifying glass and felt one of the stems gingerly with his finger. Like other grasses on Junior, it—

It was here that he heard the rustle behind him – unmistakable. He listened for a moment, his own heartbeat drowning the sound, then whirled. A small manlike object dodged behind a tree.

Fawkes' breathing nearly stopped: He fumbled for the blaster he wore and his hand seemed to be moving through molasses.

Was his fantasy no fantasy at all? Was Junior inhabited after all?

Numbly Fawkes found himself behind another tree. He couldn't leave it at this. He knew that. He could not report to the rest: 'I saw something alive. It might have been the answer to everything. But I was afraid and let it get away.'

He would have to make some attempt.

There was a 'chalice tree' just behind the tree that hid the creature. It was in bloom, the white and cream flowers lifted turgidly upward, waiting to catch the rain that would soon fall. There was the sharp tinkle of a breaking flower and cream slivers twisted and turned downward.

It wasn't imagination. Something *was* behind the tree.

Fawkes took a deep breath and dashed out, holding his blaster before him, nerving himself to shoot at the slightest sign of danger.

But a voice called out, 'Don't. It's only I.' A frightened but definitely human face looked out from behind the tree. It was Mark Annuncio.

Fawkes stopped in mid-stride and stared. Finally, he managed to croak, 'What are you doing here?'

Mark said, staring at the blaster in the other's hand, 'I was following you.'

'Why?'

'To see what you would do. I was interested in what you might find. I thought if you saw me, you would send me away.'

Fawkes became conscious of the weapon he was still holding and put it away.

It took three tries to get it into the holster.

The first fat drops of rain began to fall. Fawkes said harshly, 'Don't say anything about this to the others.'

He glared hostilely at the youngster and they walked back to camp separately and in silence.

A central hall of prefab had been added to the seven tents now, and the group was together within it, sitting about the long table.

It was a great moment, but a rather subdued one. Vernadsky, who had cooked for himself in his college days, was in charge. He lifted the steaming stew off the short-wave heater and said, 'Calories, anyone?'

He ladled the stuff lavishly.

'It smells very good,' said Novee doubtfully.

He lifted a piece of meat with his fork. It was purplish and still felt tough despite internal heating. The shredded herbs that surrounded it seemed softer, but looked less edible.

'Well,' said Vernadsky, 'eat it. Put it in your mouth. I've tasted it and it's—' He crammed his mouth and chewed. He kept on chewing. 'Tough, but good.'

Fawkes said gloomily, 'It'll probably kill us.'

'Nuts,' said Vernadsky. 'The rats have been living on it for two weeks.'

'Two weeks isn't much,' said Novee.

Rodriguez said, 'Well, one bite won't kill. Say, it *is* good.'

And it was. They all agreed eventually. So far, it seemed that whenever Junior's life could be eaten at all, it was good. The grains were almost impossible to grind into flour, but that done, a protein-high bread could be baked. There was some on the table now, dark and heavy. It wasn't bad, either.

Fawkes had studied the herb life on Junior and come to the conclusion that an acre of Junior's surface, properly seeded and watered, could support ten times the number of grazing animals that an acre of Earthly alfalfa could.

Sheffield had been impressed; had spoken of Junior as the granary of a hundred worlds, but Fawkes dismissed his own statements with a shrug.

He said, 'Sucker bait.'

About a week earlier, the party had been agitated by the sudden refusal of the hamsters and white rats to touch certain new herbs Fawkes had brought in. Mixing small quantities with regular rations had resulted in the death of those that fed on it.

Solution?

Not quite. Vernadsky came in a few hours later and said calmly, 'Copper, lead, and mercury.'

'What?' said Cimon.

'Those plants. They're high in heavy metals. Probably an evolutionary development to keep from being eaten.'

'The first settlers—' began Cimon.

'No. That's impossible. Most of the plants are perfectly all right. Just these, and no person would eat them.'

'How do you know?'

'The rats didn't.'

'They're just rats.'

It was what Vernadsky was waiting for. He said dramatically, 'You may hail a modest martyr to science. I tasted the stuff.'

'What?' yelled Novee.

'Just a lick. Don't worry. I'm the careful-type martyr. Anyway, the stuff is as bitter as strychnine. What do you expect? If a plant is going to fill itself with lead just to keep the animals off, what good does it do the plant to have the animal find out by dying after he's eaten it? A little bitter stuff in addition acts as a warning. The combination warning and punishment does the trick.'

'Besides,' said Novee, 'it wasn't heavy metal poisoning that killed the settlers. The symptoms aren't right for it.'

The rest knew the symptoms well enough. Some in lay terms and some in more technical language. Difficult and painful breathing that grew steadily worse. That's what it amounted to.

Fawkes put down his fork. 'Look here, suppose this stuff contains some alkaloid that paralyzes the nerves that control the lung muscles.'

'Rats have lung muscles,' said Vernadsky. 'It doesn't kill them.'

'Maybe it's a cumulative thing.'

'All right. All right. Any time your breathing gets painful, go back to ship rations and see if you improve. But no fair counting psychosomatics.'

Sheffield grunted, 'That's my job. Don't worry about it.'

Fawkes drew a deep breath, then another. Glumly he put another piece of meat into his mouth.

At one corner of the table, Mark Annuncio, eating more slowly than the rest, thought of Norris Vinograd's monograph on 'Taste and Smell.' Vinograd had made a taste-smell classification based on enzyme inhibition patterns within the taste buds. Annuncio did not know what that meant exactly but he remembered the symbols, their values, and the descriptive definitions.

While he placed the taste of the stew to three subclassifications, he finished his helping. His jaws ached faintly because of the difficult chewing.

Evening was approaching and Lagrange I was low in the sky. It had been a bright day, reasonably warm, and Boris Vernadsky felt pleased. He had made interesting measurements and his brilliantly colored sweater had showed fascinating changes from hour to hour as the suns' positions shifted.

Right now his shadow was a long red thing, with the lowest third of it gray, where the Lagrange II shadow coincided. He held out one arm and it cast two shadows. There was a smeared orange one some fifteen feet away and a denser blue one in the same direction but only five feet away. If he had time, he could work out a beautiful set of shadowgrams.

He was so pleased with the thought that he felt no resentment at seeing Mark Annuncio skirting his trail in the distance.

He put down his nucleometer and waved his hand. 'Come here!'

The youngster approached diffidently. 'Hello.'

'Want something?'

'Just – just watching.'

'Oh? Well, go ahead and watch. Do you know what I'm doing?' Mark shook his head.

'This is a nucleometer,' said Vernadsky. 'You jab it into the ground like this. It's got a force-field generator at the top so it will penetrate any rock.' He leaned on the nucleometer as he spoke, and it went two feet into the stony outcropping. 'See?'

Mark's eyes shone, and Vernadsky felt pleased. The chemist said, 'Along the sides of the uniped are microscopic atomic furnaces, each of which vaporizes about a million molecules or so in the surrounding rock and decomposes them into atoms. The atoms are then differentiated in terms of nuclear mass and charge and the results may be read off directly on the dials above. Do you follow all that?'

'I'm not sure. But it's a good thing to know?'

Vernadsky smiled and said, 'We end up with figures on the different elements in the crust. It's pretty much the same on all oxygen water planets.'

Mark said seriously, 'The planet with the most silicon I know of is Lepta, with 32.765 per cent. Earth is only 24.862. That's by weight.'

Vernadsky's smile faded. He said dryly, 'You have the figures on all the planets, pal?'

'Oh no. I couldn't. I don't think they've all been surveyed. Bischon and Spenglow's *Handbook of Planetary Crusts* only lists figures for 21,854 planets. I know all those, of course.'

Vernadsky, with a definite feeling of deflation, said, 'Now Junior has a more even distribution of elements than is usually met up with. Oxygen is low. So far my average is a lousy 42.113. So is silicon, with 22.722. The heavy metals are ten to a hundred times as concentrated as on Earth. That's not just a local phenomenon, either, since Junior's over-all density is 5 per cent higher than Earth's.'

Vernadsky wasn't sure why he was telling the kid all this. Partly, he felt, because it was good to find someone who would listen. A man gets lonely and frustrated when there is no one of his own field to talk to.

He went on, beginning to relish the lecture. 'On the other hand, the lighter elements are also better distributed. The ocean solids aren't predominantly sodium chloride, as on Earth. Junior's oceans contain a respectable helping of magnesium salts. And take what they call the 'rare lights'. Those are the elements lithium, beryllium, and boron. They're lighter than carbon, all of them, but they are of very rare occurrence on Earth, and in fact, on all planets. Junior, on the other hand, is quite rich in them. The three of them total almost four tenths of a per cent of the crust as compared to about four thousandths on Earth.'

Mark plucked at the other's sleeve. 'Do you have a list of figures on all the elements? May I see?'

'I suppose so.' He took a folded piece of paper out of his hip pocket.

He grinned as Mark took the sheet and said, 'Don't publish those figures before I do.'

Mark glanced at them once and returned the paper. 'Are you through?' asked Vernadsky in surprise.

'Oh yes,' said Mark thoughtfully, 'I have it all.' He turned on his heel and walked away with no word of parting.

The last glimmer of Lagrange I faded below the horizon.

Vernadsky gazed after Mark and shrugged. He plucked his nucleometer out of the ground, and followed after, walking back toward the tents.

Sheffield was moderately pleased. Mark had been doing better than expected. To be sure, he scarcely talked but that was not very serious. At least, he showed interest and didn't sulk. And he threw no tantrums.

Vernadsky was even telling Sheffield that last evening Mark had spoken to him quite normally, without raised voices on either side, about planetary crust analyses. Vernadsky had laughed a bit about it, saying that Mark knew the crust analyses of twenty thousand planets and someday he'd have the boy repeat them all just to see how long it would take.

Mark, himself, had made no mention of the matter. In fact, he had spent the morning sitting in his tent. Sheffield had looked in, seen him on his cot, staring at his feet, and had left him to himself.

What he really needed at the moment, Sheffield felt, was a bright idea for himself. A really bright one.

So far, everything had come to nothing. A whole month of nothing. Rodriguez held fast against any infection. Vernadsky absolutely barred food poisoning. Novee shook his head with vehement negativeness at suggestions of disturbed metabolism. 'Where's the evidence?' he kept saying.

What it amounted to was that every physical cause of death was eliminated on the strength of expert opinion. But men, women, and children had died. There must be a reason. Could it be psychological?

He had satirized the matter to Cimon for a purpose before they had come out here, but it was now time and more than time to be serious about it. Could the settlers have been driven to suicide? Why? Humanity had colonized tens of thousands of planets without its having seriously affected mental stability. In fact, the suicide rate, as well as the incidence of psychoses, was higher on Earth than anywhere else in the Galaxy.

Besides, the settlement had called frantically for medical help. They didn't want to die.

Personality disorders? Something peculiar to that one group? Enough to affect over a thousand people to the death? Unlikely. Besides, how could any evidence be uncovered? The settlement site had been ransacked for any films or records, even the most frivolous. Nothing. A century of dampness left nothing so fragile as purposeful records.

So he was working in a vacuum. He felt helpless. The others, at least, had data; something to chew on. He had nothing.

He found himself at Mark's tent again and looked inside automatically. It was empty. He looked about and spied Mark walking out of the camp and into the woods.

Sheffield cried out after him, 'Mark! Wait for me!'

Mark stopped, made as though to go on, thought better of it, and let Sheffield's long legs consume the distance between them.

Sheffield said, 'Where are you off to?' (Even after running, it was unnecessary to pant in Junior's rich atmosphere.)

Mark's eyes were sullen. 'To the air-coaster.'

'Oh?'

'I haven't had a chance to look at it.'

'Why, of course you've had a chance,' said Sheffield. 'You were watching Fawkes like a hawk on the trip over.'

Mark scowled. 'Everyone was around. I want to see it for myself.'

Sheffield felt disturbed. The kid was angry. He'd better tag along and try to find out what was wrong. He said, 'Come to think of it, I'd like to see the coaster myself. You don't mind having me along, do you?'

Mark hesitated. Then he said, 'We-ell. If you want to.' It wasn't exactly a gracious invitation.

Sheffield said, 'What are you carrying, Mark?'

'Tree branch. I cut it off with the buzz-field gun. I'm taking it with me just in case anyone wants to stop me.' He swung it so that it whistled through the thick air.

'Why should anyone want to stop you, Mark? I'd throw it away. It's hard and heavy. You could hurt someone.'

Mark was striding on. 'I'm not throwing it away.'

Sheffield pondered briefly, then decided against a quarrel at the moment. It would be better to get to the basic reason for this hostility first. 'All right,' he said.

The air-coaster lay in a clearing, its clear metal surface throwing back green highlights. (Lagrange II had not yet risen.)

Mark looked carefully about.

'There's no one in sight, Mark,' said Sheffield.

They climbed aboard. It was a large coaster. It had carried seven men and the necessary supplies in only three trips.

Sheffield looked at its control panel with something quite close to awe. He said, 'Imagine a botanist like Fawkes learning to run one of these things. It's so far outside his specialty.'

'I can run one,' said Mark suddenly.

Sheffield stared at him in surprise. 'You can?'

'I watched Dr Fawkes when we came: I know everything he did. And he has a repair manual for the coaster. I sneaked that out once and read it.'

Sheffield said lightly, 'Well, that's very nice. We have a spare navigator for an emergency, then.'

He turned away from Mark then, so he never saw the tree limb as it came down on his head. He didn't hear Mark's troubled voice saying, 'I'm sorry, Dr Sheffield.' He didn't even, properly speaking, feel the concussion that knocked him out.

It was the jar of the coaster's landing, Sheffield later thought, that first brought consciousness back. It was a dim, aching sort of thing that had no understanding in it at first.

The sound of Mark's voice was floating up to him. That was his first sensation. Then as he tried to roll over and get a knee beneath him, he could feel his head throbbing.

For a while, Mark's voice was only a collection of sounds that meant nothing to him. Then they began to coalesce into words. Finally, when his eyes fluttered open and light entered stabbingly so that he had to close them again, he could make out sentences. He remained where he was, head hanging, one quivering knee holding him up.

Mark was saying in a breathless, high-pitched voice, '. . . a thousand people all dead. Just graves. And nobody knows why.'

There was a rumble Sheffield couldn't make out. A hoarse, deep voice.

Then Mark again, 'It's true. Why do you suppose all the scientists are aboard?'

Sheffield lifted achingly to his feet and rested against one wall. He put his hand to his head and it came away bloody. His hair was caked and matted with it. Groaning, he staggered toward the coaster's cabin door. He fumbled for the hook and yanked it inward.

The landing ramp had been lowered. For a moment, he stood there, swaying, afraid to trust his legs.

He had to take in everything by installments. Both suns were high in the sky and a thousand feet away the giant steel cylinder of the *Triple G.* reared its nose high above the runty trees that ringed it.

Mark was at the foot of the ramp, semi-circled by members of the crew. The crewmen were stripped to the waist and browned nearly black in the ultraviolet of Lagrange I. (Thanks only to the thick atmosphere and the heavy ozone coating in the upper reaches for keeping UV down to a livable range.)

The crewman directly before Mark was leaning on a baseball bat. Another tossed a ball in the air and caught it. Many of the rest were wearing gloves.

Funny, thought Sheffield erratically, Mark landed right in the middle of a ball park.

Mark looked up and saw him. He screamed excitedly, 'All right, ask him. Go ahead, ask him. Dr Sheffield, wasn't there an expedition to this planet once and they all died mysteriously?'

Sheffield tried to say, 'Mark, what are you doing?' He couldn't. When he opened his mouth, only a moan came out.

The crewman with the bat said, 'Is this little gumboil telling the truth, mister?'

Sheffield held on to the railing with two perspiring hands. The crewman's face seemed to waver. The face had thick lips on it and small eyes buried under bristly eyebrows. It wavered very badly.

Then the ramp came up and whirled about his head. There was ground gripped in his hands suddenly and a cold ache on his cheekbone. He gave up the fight and let go of consciousness again.

He came awake less painfully the second time. He was in bed now and two misty faces leaned over him. A long, thin object passed across his line of vision and a voice, just heard above the humming in his ears, said, 'He'll come to now, Cimon.'

Sheffield closed his eyes. Somehow he seemed to be aware of the fact that his skull was thoroughly bandaged.

He lay quietly for a minute, breathing deeply. When he opened his eyes again, the faces above him were clear. There was Novee's round face, a small, professionally serious line between his eyes that cleared away when Sheffield said, 'Hello, Novee.'

The other man was Cimon, jaws set and angry, yet with a look of something like satisfaction in his eyes.

Sheffield said, 'Where are we?'

Cimon said coldly, 'In space, Dr Sheffield. Two days out in space.'

'Two days out—' Sheffield's eyes widened.

Novee interposed. 'You've had a bad concussion, nearly a fracture, Sheffield. Take it easy.'

'Well, what hap— Where's Mark? *Where's Mark?*'

'Easy. Easy now.' Novee put a hand on each of Sheffield's shoulders and pressed him down.

Cimon said, 'Your boy is in the brig. In case you want to know why, he deliberately caused mutiny on board ship, thus endangering the safety of five men. We were almost marooned at our temporary camp because the crew wanted to leave immediately. He persuaded them, the Captain did, to pick us up.'

Sheffield remembered now, very vaguely. There was just that fuzzy memory of Mark and a man with a bat. Mark saying '. . . a thousand people all dead.'

The psychologist hitched himself up on one elbow with a tremendous effort.

'Listen, Cimon, I don't know why Mark did it, but let me talk to him. I'll find out.'

Cimon said, 'No need of that. It will all come out at the trial.'

Sheffield tried to brush Novee's restraining arm to one side. 'But why make it formal? Why involve the Bureau? We can settle this among ourselves.'

'That's exactly what we intend to do. The Captain is empowered by the laws of space to preside over trials involving crimes and misdemeanors in deep space.'

'The Captain. A trial here? On board ship? Cimon, don't let him do it. It will be murder.'

'Not at all. It will be a fair and proper trial. I'm in full agreement with the Captain. Discipline demands a trial.'

Novee said uneasily, 'Look, Cimon, I wish you wouldn't. He's in no shape to take this.'

'Too bad,' said Cimon.

Sheffield said, 'But you don't understand. I'm responsible for the boy.'

'On the contrary, I do understand,' said Cimon. 'It's why we've been waiting for you to regain consciousness. You're standing trial with him.'

'What!'

'You are generally responsible for his actions. Specifically, you were with him when he stole the air-coaster. The crew saw you at the coaster's cabin door while Mark was inciting mutiny.'

'But he cracked my skull in order to take the coaster. Can't you see that's the act of a seriously disturbed mind? He can't be held responsible.'

'We'll let the Captain decide, Sheffield. You stay with him, Novee.' He turned to go.

Sheffield called on what strength he could muster. 'Cimon,' he shouted, 'you're doing this to get back at me for the lesson in psychology I taught you. You're a narrow – petty—'

He fell back on his pillow, breathless.

Cimon, from the door, said, 'And by the way, Sheffield, the penalty for inciting mutiny on board ship is death!'

Well, it was a *kind* of trial, Sheffield thought grimly. Nobody was following accurate legal procedure, but then, the psychologist felt certain, no one knew the accurate legal procedure, least of all the Captain.

They were using the large assembly room where, on ordinary cruises, the crew got together to watch subetheric broadcasts. At this time, the crew were rigidly excluded, though all the scientific personnel were present.

Captain Follenbee sat behind a desk just underneath the subetheric reception cube. Sheffield and Mark Annuncio sat by themselves at his left, faces toward him.

The Captain was not at ease. He alternated between informal exchanges with the various 'witnesses' and sudden super-judicial blasts against whispering among the spectators.

Sheffield and Mark, having met one another in the 'courtroom' for the first time since the flight of the air-coaster, shook hands solemnly on the former's initiative. Mark had hung back at first, looking up briefly at the crisscross of tape still present on the shaven patch on Sheffield's skull. 'I'm sorry, Dr Sheffield: I'm very sorry.'

'It's all right, Mark. How have they been treating you?'

'All right, I guess.'

The Captain's voice boomed out, 'No talking among the accused.'

Sheffield retorted in a conversational tone, 'Listen, Captain, we haven't had lawyers. We haven't had time to prepare a case.'

'No lawyers necessary,' said the Captain. 'This isn't a court trial on Earth. Captain's investigation. Different thing. Just interested in facts, not legal fireworks. Proceedings can be reviewed back on Earth.'

'And we can be dead by then,' said Sheffield hotly.

'Let's get on with it,' said the Captain, banging his desk with an aluminum T-wedge.

Cimon sat in the front row of the audience, smiling thinly. It was he whom Sheffield watched most uneasily.

The smile never varied as witnesses were called upon to state that they had been informed that the crew were on no account to be told of the true nature of the trip; that Sheffield and Mark had been present when told. A mycologist testified to a conversation he had with Sheffield which indicated the latter to be well aware of the prohibition.

It was brought out that Mark had been sick for most of the trip out to Junior, that he had behaved erratically after they had landed on Junior. 'How do you explain all that?' asked the Captain.

From the audience, Cimon's calm voice suddenly sounded. 'He was frightened. He was willing to do anything that would get him off the planet.'

Sheffield sprang to his feet. 'His remarks are out of order. He's not a witness.'

The Captain banged his T-wedge and said, 'Sit down!'

The trial went on. A crew member was called in to testify that Mark had informed them of the first expedition and that Sheffield had stood by while that was done.

Sheffield cried, 'I want to cross-examine!'

The Captain said, 'You'll get your chance later.' The crewman was shooed out.

Sheffield studied the audience. It seemed obvious that their sympathy was not entirely with the Captain. He was pyschologist enough to be able to wonder, even at this point, how many of them were secretly relieved at having left Junior and actually grateful to Mark for having precipitated the matter as he did. Then, too, the obvious kangaroo nature of the court didn't sit well with them.

Vernadsky was frowning darkly while Novee stared at Cimon with obvious distaste.

It was Cimon who worried Sheffield. He, the psychologist felt, must have argued the Captain into this and it was he who might insist on the extreme penalty. Sheffield was bitterly regretful of having punctured the man's pathological vanity.

But what really puzzled Sheffield above all was Mark's attitude. He was showing no signs of space-sickness or of unease of any kind. He listened to everything closely but seemed moved by nothing. He acted as though nothing mundane concerned him at the moment; as though certain information he himself held made everything else of no account.

The Captain banged his T-wedge and said, 'I guess we have it all. Facts all clear. No argument. We can finish this.'

Sheffield jumped up again. 'Hold on. Aren't we getting our turn?'

'Quiet,' ordered the Captain.

'*You* keep quiet.' Sheffield turned to the audience. 'Listen, we haven't had a chance to defend ourselves. We haven't even had the right to cross-examine. Is that just?'

There was a murmur that buzzed up above the sound of the T-wedge. Cimon said coldly, 'What's there to defend?'

'Maybe nothing,' shouted back Sheffield, 'in which case what have you to lose by hearing us? Or are you afraid we have considerable to defend?'

Individual calls from the audience were sounding now. 'Let him talk!'

Cimon shrugged. 'Go ahead.'

The Captain said sullenly, 'What do you want to do?'

Sheffield said, 'Act as my own lawyer and call Mark Annuncio as witness.'

Mark stood up calmly enough. Sheffield turned his chair to face the audience and motioned him down again.

Sheffield decided there was no use in trying to imitate the courtroom dramas he had watched on the subether. Pompous questions on name and condition of past life would get nowhere. Better to be direct.

So he said, 'Mark, did you know what would happen when you told the crew about the first expedition?'

'Yes, Dr Sheffield.'

'Why did you do it then?'

'Because it was important that we all get away from Junior without losing a minute. Telling the crew the truth was the fastest way of getting us off the planet.'

Sheffield could feel the bad impression that answer made on the audience, but he could only follow his instinct. That, and his psychologist's decision that only special knowledge could make Mark or any Mnemonic so calm in the face of adversity. After all, special knowledge was their business.

He said, 'Why was it important to leave Junior, Mark?'

Mark didn't flinch. He looked straight at the watching scientists. 'Because I know what killed the first expedition, and it was only a question of time before it killed us. In fact, it may be too late already. We may be dying now. We may, every one of us, be dead men.'

Sheffield let the murmur from the audience swell up and subside. Even the Captain seemed shocked into T-wedge immobility while Cimon's smile grew quite faint.

For the moment, Sheffield was less concerned with Mark's 'knowledge,' whatever it was, than that he had acted independently on the basis of it. It had happened before. Mark had searched the ship's log on the basis of a theory of his own. Sheffield felt pure chagrin at not having probed that tendency to the uttermost then and there.

So his next question, asked in a grim enough voice, was, 'Why didn't you consult me about this, Mark?'

Mark faltered a trifle. 'You wouldn't have believed me. It's why I had to hit you to keep you from stopping me. None of them would have believed me. They all hated me.'

'What makes you think they hated you?'

'Well, you remember about Dr Rodriguez.'

'That was quite a while ago. The others had no arguments with you.'

'I could tell the way Dr Cimon looked at me. And Dr Fawkes wanted to shoot me with a blaster.'

'What?' Sheffield whirled, forgetting in his own turn any formality due the trial. 'Say, Fawkes, did you try to shoot him?'

Fawkes stood up, face crimson, as all turned to look at him. He said, 'I was out in the woods and he came sneaking up on me. I thought it was an animal and took precautions. When I saw it was he, I put the blaster away.'

Sheffield turned back to Mark. 'Is that right?'

Mark turned sullen again. 'Well – I asked Dr Vernadsky to see some data he had collected and he told me not to publish it before he did. He tried to make out that I was dishonest.'

'For the love of Earth, I was only joking,' came a yell from the audience.

Sheffield said hurriedly, 'Very well, Mark, you didn't trust us and you felt you had to take action on your own. Now, Mark, let's get to the point. What did you think killed the first settlers?'

Mark said, 'It might have killed the explorer, Makoyama, too, for all I know except that he died in a crash two months and three days after reporting on Junior, so we'll never know.'

'All right, but what is it you're talking about?' A hush fell over everyone.

Mark looked about and said, 'The dust.'

There was general laughter, and Mark's cheeks flamed. Sheffield said, 'What do you mean?'

'The dust! The dust in the air. It has beryllium in it. Ask Dr Vernadsky.'

Vernadsky stood up and pushed his way forward. 'What's this?'

'Sure,' said Mark. 'It was in the data you showed me. Beryllium was very high in the crust, so it must be in the dust in the air as well.'

Sheffield said, 'What if beryllium is there? Let me ask the questions, Vernadsky. Please.'

'Beryllium poisoning, that's what. If you breathe beryllium dust, non-healing granulomata, whatever they are, form in the lungs. Anyway, it gets hard to breathe and eventually you die.'

A new voice, quite agitated, joined the melee. 'What are you talking about? You're no physician.' It was Novee.

'I know that,' said Mark earnestly, 'but I once read a very old book about poisons. It was so old it was printed on actual sheets of paper. The library had some and I went through them because it was such a novelty, you know.'

'All right,' said Novee. 'What did you read? Can you tell me?'

Mark's chin lifted. 'I can quote it. Word for word. 'A surprising variety of enzymatic reactions in the body are activated by any of a number of divalent metallic ions of similar ionic radius. Among these are magnesium, manganous, zinc, ferrous, cobaltous, and nickelous ions, as well as others. Against all of these, the beryllium ion, which has a similar charge and size, acts as an inhibitor. Beryllium therefore serves to derange a number of enzyme-catalyzed reactions: Since the lungs have, apparently, no way of excreting beryllium, diverse metabolic derangements causing serious illness and death can result from inhaling dust containing certain beryllium salts. Cases exist in which one known exposure has resulted in death. The onset of symptoms is insidious, being delayed sometimes for as long as three years after exposure. Prognosis is not good.'

The Captain leaned forward in agitation. 'What's all this, Novee? Is what he's saying making sense?'

Novee said, 'I don't know if he's right or not; but there's nothing absurd in what he's saying.'

Sheffield said sharply, 'You mean you don't know if beryllium is poisonous or not.'

'No, I don't,' said Novee. 'I've never read anything about it. No case has ever come up.'

'Isn't beryllium used for anything?' Sheffield turned to Vernadsky. 'Is it?'

Vernadsky said in vast surprise, 'No, it isn't. Damn it, I can't think of a single use. I tell you what, though. In the early days of atomic power, it was used in the primitive uranium piles as a neutron decelerator, along with other things like paraffin and graphite. I'm almost sure of that.'

'It isn't used now, though?' asked Sheffield.

'No.'

An electronics man said quite suddenly, 'I think beryllium-zinc coatings were used in the first fluorescent lights. I seem to recall a mention of that.'

'No more, though?' asked Sheffield.

'No.'

Sheffield said, 'Well then, listen, all of you. In the first place, anything Mark quotes is accurate. That's what the book said. It's my opinion that beryllium is poisonous. In ordinary life, it doesn't matter because the beryllium content of the soil is so low. When man concentrates beryllium to use in nuclear piles or in fluorescent lights or even in alloys, he comes across the toxicity and looks for substitutes.

'He finds substitutes, forgets about beryllium, and eventually forgets about its toxicity. And then we come across an unusual beryllium-rich planet like Junior and we can't figure out what hits us.'

Cimon didn't seem to be listening. He said in a low voice, 'What does that mean, "Prognosis is not good."'

Novee said abstractedly, 'It means that if you've got beryllium poisoning, you won't recover.'

Cimon fell back in his chair, chewing his lip.

Novee said to Mark, 'I suppose the symptoms of beryllium poisoning—'

Mark said at once, 'I can give you the full list. I don't understand the words but—'

'Was one of them "dyspnea"?'

'Yes.'

Novee sighed and said, 'I say that we get back to Earth as quickly as possible and get under medical investigation.'

Cimon said weakly, 'But if we won't recover, what use is it?'

Novee said, 'Medical science has advanced since the days of books printed on paper. Besides, we may not have received the toxic dose. The first settlers survived for over a year of continuous exposure. We've had only a month, thanks to Mark Annuncio's quick and drastic action.'

Fawkes, miserably unhappy, yelled, 'For space's sake, Captain, get out of here and get this ship back to Earth.'

It amounted to the end of the trial. Sheffield and Mark walked out among the first.

Cimon was the last to stir out of his chair, and when he did, it was with the listless gait of a man already dead in all but fact.

The Lagrange System was only a star lost in the receding cluster. Sheffield looked at that large patch of light and said, 'So beautiful a planet.'

He sighed. 'Well, let's hope we live. In any case, the government will watch out for beryllium-high planets in the future. There'll be no catching mankind with that particular variety of sucker bait any more.'

Mark did not respond to that idealism. The trial was over; the excitement was gone. There were tears in his eyes. He could only think that he might die; and that if he did, there were so many things, so many, many things in the Universe that he would never learn.

What's in a Name?

If you think it's hard to get hold of potassium cyanide, think again. I stood there with a pound bottle in my hand. Brown glass, a nice clear label saying 'Potassium Cyanide CP' (the initials, I was told, meaning 'chemically pure') with a small skull and crossbones underneath.

The fellow who owned the bottle polished his glasses and blinked at me. He was Associate Professor Helmuth Rodney of Carmody University. He was of middle height, stocky, with a soft chin, plump lips, a budding paunch, a shock of brown hair, and a look of complete indifference to the fact that I was holding in my hand enough poison to kill a regiment.

I said, 'Do you mean to say this just stands on your shelf, Professor?'

He said in the kind of deliberate tone he probably used in lecturing his students, 'Yes, it always has, Inspector. Along with the rest of the chemicals in alphabetic order.'

I glanced about the cluttered room. Shelves lined the upper reaches of all the walls, and bottles, large and small, filled them all.

'This one,' I pointed out, 'is poison.'

'A great many of them are,' he said with composure.

'Do you keep track of what you've got?'

'In a general way.' He rubbed his chin. 'I know I have that bottle.'

'But suppose someone came in here and helped himself to a spoonful of this stuff. Would you be able to tell?'

Professor Rodney shook his head. 'I couldn't possibly.'

'Well, then, who could get into this laboratory? Is it kept locked?'

He said, 'It's locked when I leave in the evening, unless I forget. During the day, it isn't locked, and I'm in and out.'

'In other words, Professor, anyone could come in here, even someone from the street, walk off with some of the cyanide, and no one would ever know.'

'I'm afraid so.'

'Tell me, Professor, why do you keep this much cyanide in the place anyway? To kill rats?'

'Good heavens, no.' He seemed faintly repelled at the thought. 'Cyanide is sometimes used in organic reactions to form necessary intermediates, to provide a proper basic medium, to catalyze—'

'I see. I see. Now in what other labs is cyanide available in this way?'

'In most of them,' he answered at once. 'Even in the student labs. After all, it's a common chemical, routinely used in syntheses.'

'I wouldn't call its use today routine,' I said.

He sighed and said, 'No, I suppose not.' He added thoughtfully, 'They used to call them the "Library Twins".'

I nodded. I could see the reason for the nickname. The two girl librarians were very alike.

Not close up, of course. One had a small pointed chin on a round face, and the other had a square jaw and a long nose. Still, bend them over a desk and both had honey-blond hair parted in the middle, with a similar wave. Look them quickly in the face and you would probably notice first wide-set eyes of about the same shade of blue. See them standing together at a moderate distance and you could see they were both of a height and both, probably, with the same brand and size uplift brassiere. Both had trim waists and neat legs. Today they had even dressed similarly. Both wore blue.

There was no confusing the two now, though. The one with the small chin and round face was full of cyanide, and quite dead.

The similarity was the first thing that struck me when I arrived with my partner, Ed Hathaway. There was one girl slumped in her chair and dead, her eyes open, one arm dangling straight down, with a broken teacup on the floor beneath like a period under an exclamation point. Her name, it turned out, was Louella-Marie Busch. There was a second girl, like the first one brought back to life, white and shaken, staring straight ahead and letting the police and their work flow about her without seeming to notice. Her name was Susan Morey.

The first question I asked was, 'Relatives?' They weren't. Not even second cousins.

I looked about the library. There were whole shelves of books in similar bindings, then other shelves with books in another set of bindings. They were volumes of different research journals. In another room were stacks of what I found later to be textbooks, monographs, and older books. In the back was a special alcove containing recent numbers of unbound research periodicals in dull and closely printed paper covers. From wall to wall were long tables that might have seated a hundred people if all were fully occupied. Fortunately that wasn't the case.

We got the story out of Susan Morey in flat, toneless pieces. Mrs Nettler, the old Senior Librarian had taken off for the afternoon and had left the two girls in charge. That, apparently, was not unusual.

At two o'clock, give or take five minutes, Louella-Marie took herself into the back room behind the library desk. There, in addition to new books that awaited cataloguing, stacks of periodicals that awaited binding, reserved books that awaited their reservers, there was also a small hot-plate, a small kettle, and the fixings for weak tea.

Two o'clock tea was apparently usual, too.

I said, 'Did Louella-Marie prepare the tea every day?'

Susan looked at me out of her blank blue eyes. 'Sometimes Mrs Nettler does, but usually Lou-Louella-Marie did.'

When the tea was ready, Louella-Marie emerged to say so and after a few moments the two retired.

'Both of you?' I asked sharply. 'Who took care of the library?' Susan shrugged as though this were a minor 'point to worry about, and said, 'We can see out the door. If anyone came to the desk, one of us could have gone out.'

'Did anyone come to the desk?'

'No one. It's intersession. Hardly anyone's around.'

By intersession she meant that the spring semester was over and the summer sessions had not yet started. I learned quite a bit about college life that day.

What was left of the story was little enough. The tea bags were already out of the gently steaming cups and the sugar had been added.

I interrupted. 'You both take sugar?'

Susan said slowly, 'Yes. But mine didn't have any.'

'No?'

'She never forgot before. She knows I take it. I just took a sip or two and I was going to reach for the sugar and tell her, you know, when—'

When Louella-Marie gave a queer strangled cry, dropped the cup, and was dead in a minute.

After that Susan screamed and eventually we came.

The routine passed smoothly enough. Photographs and fingerprints had been taken. The names and addresses of the men and women in the building were taken and they were sent home. Cause of death was obviously cyanide and the sugar bowl was the obvious villain. Samples were taken for official testing.

There had been six men in the library at the time of the murder.

Five were students, who looked frightened, confused, or sick, depending, I suppose, on their personalities. The sixth was a middleaged man, an outsider, who talked with a German accent and had no connection with the college at all. He looked frightened, confused, and sick, all three.

My sidekick, Hathaway, was leading them out of the library. The idea was to get them to the Co-educational Lounge and have them stay put till we could get to them in detail.

One of the students broke away and strode past me without a glance. Susan flew to meet him, clutching each sleeve above the elbow. 'Pete. Pete.'

Pete was built like a football player except that his profile looked as though he had never been within half a mile of the playing field. He was too good-looking for my taste, but then I get jealous easily.

Pete was looking past the girl, his face coming apart at the seams till its prettiness was drowned in uneasy horror. He said in a hoarse, choking way, 'How did Lolly come to . . .'

Susan gasped, 'I don't know. I don't know.' She kept trying to meet his eye.

Pete pulled away. He never looked at Susan once, kept staring over her shoulder. Then he responded to Hathaway's grip on his elbow and let himself be led away.

I said, 'Boy friend?'

Susan tore her eyes from the departing student. 'What?'

'Is he your boy friend?'

She looked down at her twisting hands. 'We've been out on dates.'

'How serious?'

She whispered, 'Pretty serious.'

'Does he know the other girl, too? He called her Lolly?'

Susan shrugged. 'Well . . .'

'Let's put it this way. Did he go out with her?'

'Sometimes.'

'Seriously.'

She snapped, 'How should I know?'

'Come on, now. Was she jealous of you?'

'What's all this about?'

'Someone put the cyanide in the sugar and put the mixture in only one cup. Suppose Louella-Marie was jealous enough of you to try to poison you and leave herself a clear field with our friend Pete. And suppose she took the wrong teacup herself by mistake.'

Susan said, 'That's crazy. Louella-Marie wouldn't do such a thing.'

But her lips were thin, her eyes sparkled, and I can tell hate in a voice when I hear it.

Professor Rodney came into the library. He was the first man I had met on entering the building and my feelings toward him had grown no warmer.

He had begun by informing me that as senior faculty member present, he was in charge.

I said, 'I'm in charge now, Professor.'

He said, 'Of the investigation perhaps, Inspector, but it is I who am responsible to the Dean and I propose to fulfill my responsibilities.'

And although he hadn't the figure of an aristocrat, more like a shopkeeper, if you follow me, he managed to look at me as though there were a microscope between us with himself on the large side. Now he said, 'Mrs Nettler is in my office. She heard the news bulletin, apparently, and came at once. She is quite agitated. You will see her?' He made it sound like an order.

'Bring her in, Professor.' I made it sound like permission.

Mrs Nettler was in the usual quandary of the average old lady. She didn't know whether to be horrified or fascinated at the closeness with which death had struck. Horror won out after she looked into the inner office and noticed what was left of the tea things. The body was gone by then, of course.

She flopped into a chair and began crying. 'I had tea here myself,' she moaned. 'It might have been . . .'

I said as quietly and soothingly as I could manage, 'When did you drink tea here, Mrs Nettler?'

She turned in her seat, looked up. 'Why – why, just after one, I think. I offered Professor Rodney a cup, I remember. It was just after one, Professor Rodney, wasn't it?'

A trace of annoyance crossed Rodney's plump face. He said to me, 'I was here a moment just after lunch to consult a reference. Mrs Nettler did offer a cup. I was too busy, I'm afraid, to accept or to note the time exactly.'

I grunted and turned back to the old lady. 'Do you take sugar, Mrs Nettler?'

'Yes, sir.'

'*Did* you take sugar?'

She nodded and started crying again.

I waited a bit. Then, 'Did you notice the condition of the sugar bowl?'

'It was— it was—' A sudden surprise at the question seemed to put her on her feet. 'It was empty and I filled it myself. I used the two-pound box of granulated sugar and I remember saying to myself that whenever I wanted tea the sugar was gone and I wished the girls would—'

Maybe it was the mention of the girls in the plural. She broke out again.

I nodded to Hathaway to lead her away.

Between 1 and 2 p.m., obviously, someone had emptied the sugar bowl and then added just a bit of laced sugar – very neatly laced sugar.

Maybe it was Mrs Nettler's appearance that pumped librarianship back into Susan, because when Hathaway came back and reached for one of his cigars – he already had the match lit – the girl said, 'No smoking in the library, sir.'

Hathaway was so surprised he blew the match out and replaced the cigar in his pocket.

Then the girl stepped briskly to one of the long tables and reached for a large volume that lay open on it.

Hathaway was ahead of her. 'What are you going to do, Miss?'

Susan looked completely astonished. 'I'm just going to put it back on the shelves.'

'Why? What is it?' He looked down at the open page. I was there too, by then. I looked over his shoulder.

It was German. I can't read the language, but I can recognize it when I see it. The printing was small, and there were geometrical figures on the page with lines of letters attached at various places. I knew enough, too, to know those were chemical formulas.

I put my finger in the place, closed the book and looked at the backstrap. It said, 'Beilstein – Organische Chemie – Band VI – System Nummer 499–608.' I opened to the page again. It was 233 and the first words, just to give you an idea, were 4'-chlor-4-brom-2-nitrodiphenylather-$C_{12}H_7O_3NClBr$.

Hathaway was busy copying things down.

Professor Rodney was at the table too, which made four of us all gathered round the book.

The professor said in a cool voice, as though he were on a platform with a pointer in one hand and a piece of chalk in the other, 'This is a volume of Beilstein.' (He pronounced it Bile-shtine.) 'It's a kind of encyclopedia of organic compounds. It lists hundreds of thousands of them.'

'In this book?' demanded Hathaway.

'This book is only one of more than sixty volumes and supplementary volumes. It is a tremendous German work which is years out of date because, first, organic chemistry is progressing at an ever-increasing pace and, second, because of the interference of politics and war. Even so, there is nothing even faintly approaching its usefulness in English. For all research men in organic chemistry, these volumes are an absolute necessity.'

The professor actually patted the book as he spoke, a fond pat. 'Before dealing with any unfamiliar compound,' he said, 'it is good practice to look it up in Beilstein. It will give you methods of preparation, properties, references, and so on. It acts as a starting point. The various compounds are listed according to a logical system which is clear but not obvious. I myself give several lectures in my course on organic syntheses which deal entirely with methods for finding a particular compound somewhere in the sixty volumes.'

I don't know how long he might have continued, but I wasn't there to learn organic syntheses and it was time to get down to cases. I said abruptly, 'Professor, I want to speak to you in your laboratory.'

I suppose I had some notion that cyanide was kept in a safe, that every bit of it was accounted for, that people had to sign out for it when they wanted some. I thought the question of opportunity to get some illicitly might supply what proof we needed.

And there I stood with a pound of it in my hand and the knowledge that anyone could have any amount for the asking, or without asking.

And he said thoughtfully, 'They used to call them the "Library Twins".'

I nodded. 'So?'

'Only that it proves how superficial the judgment of most people is. There was nothing alike about them except the accident of hair and eyes. What happened in the library, Inspector?'

I told him Susan's story briefly and watched him.

He shook his head. 'I suppose you think the dead girl planned murder.'

My thoughts weren't for sale at the moment. I said, 'Don't you?'

'No. She was incapable of it. Her attitude toward her duties was a pleasant and helpful one. Besides, why would she?'

'There's a student,' I said. 'Peter is his first name.'

'Peter van Norden,' he said at once. 'A reasonably bright student, but, somehow, worthless.'

'Girls look at these things differently, Professor. Both librarians were apparently interested. Susan may have been the more successful and Louella-Marie may have decided on direct measures.'

'And then proceeded to take the wrong cup?'

I said, 'People do queer things under tension.'

'Not this queer,' he said. 'One cup was left unsugared, so the murderess wasn't taking chances. Presumably even if she had not carefully memorized which cup was which, she could count on the sweetness to give it away. She could easily have avoided a fatal dose.'

I said dryly, 'Both girls usually took sugar. The dead girl was used to sweet tea. In the excitement the accustomed sweetness didn't ring a bell.'

'I don't believe it.'

'What's the alternative, Professor? The sugar was hocused after Mrs Nettler's tea at one o'clock. Did Mrs Nettler do it?'

He looked up sharply. 'What possible motive?'

I shrugged. 'She might have been afraid the girls were going to be taking her job away.'

'That's nonsense. She's retiring before the fall session begins.'

'You were there, Professor,' I said softly.

He took it in stride, to my surprise. 'Motive?' he said.

I said, 'You're not too old to have been interested in Louella-Marie, Professor. Suppose she had threatened to report some word or act of yours to the Dean.'

The professor smiled bitterly. 'How did I manage to make sure the right girl got the cyanide? Why should one cup remain unsugared? I may have hocused the sugar but I didn't prepare the tea.' I began to change my mind about Professor Rodney. He hadn't bothered to work up indignation or register shock. He simply pointed out the logical weakness and let it go at that. I liked that.

I said, 'What do you think happened?'

He said, 'The mirror-image. The reverse. I think the survivor told the truth inside out. Suppose it was Louella-Marie who was getting the boy and Susan who didn't like it, rather than the reverse. Suppose it was Susan who for once was preparing the tea and Louella-Marie who was at the front desk rather than the reverse. In that case, the girl who prepared the tea would have taken the right cup and remained safe. Everything would be logical instead of ridiculously improbable.'

That did it. The man had come to the same conclusion I had and so I had to like him after all. I have a habit of feeling soft toward guys who agree with me. It comes of being Homo sapiens, I think. I said, 'We've got to prove that beyond reasonable doubt. How? I'd come up here, hoping to prove someone had had access to potassium cyanide and others had not. That's out. Everyone had access. Now what?'

The professor said, 'Check on which girl was really at the desk at two o'clock when the tea was being prepared.'

It was obvious to me that the professor read detective stories and had faith in witnesses. I didn't, but I got up anyway.

'All right, Professor. I'll do that.'

The professor rose also. He said urgently, 'May I be present?'

I considered. 'Why? Your responsibilities to the Dean?'

'In a way. I would like to see a quick, clean end to this.'

I said, 'Come along, if you think that will help.'

Ed Hathaway was waiting for me when I came down. He was sitting in an empty library. He said, 'I got it.'

'Got what?' I wanted to know.

'How it happened. I figured it out by deduction.'

'Oh?'

He was paying no attention to Professor Rodney. 'The cyanide had to be smuggled in. By whom? By the joker in the deck, the outsider, the guy with the accent – whatzisname.'

He started scrabbling through a series of cards on which he had filed information on the various presumably innocent bystanders.

I knew who he meant so I said, 'All right, never mind the name. What's in a name? Go on' – which shows that I can be as unbright as anyone.

'All right. The foreigner comes in with the cyanide in a little envelope. He tapes the envelope to a page in the German book, that organish whatzisname with all the volumes...'

The professor and I both nodded.

Hathaway went on. 'He was German, so was the book. He was probably familiar with it. He put the envelope on a prearranged page according to a particular formula that had been picked out. The professor said there was a way to find any formula if you only knew how. Isn't that right, Professor?'

'That is right,' said Rodney coldly.

'All right. The librarian knew the formula so she could find the page too. She picks up the cyanide and uses it for the tea. In the excitement, she forgets to close the book—'

I said, 'Look, Hathaway. Why should that little guy be doing this?

'What's his excuse for being here?'

'He says he's a furrier reading up on moth repellents and insecticides. Now isn't that phony right off? Ever hear anything so phony?'

'Sure,' I said, 'your theory. Look, no one is going to hide an envelope with cyanide in a book. You don't have to find a particular formula or page with an envelope bulging a volume out of shape. Anyone who took the volume off the shelf would find that the book would fall open to the right page automatically. A hell of a hiding place.'

Hathaway began to look foolish.

I drove on pitilessly, 'Besides, cyanide doesn't have to be smuggled in from the outside. They've got tons of it here. They can use it to make snow-slides. Anyone who wants a pound or two can help himself.'

'What?'

'Ask the professor.'

Hathaway's eyes widened and then he fumbled in his jacket pocket and drew out an envelope. 'Then what do I do with this?'

'What is it?'

He took out a printed page with German on it and said, 'It's the page out of that German volume that—'

Professor Rodney grew suddenly scarlet. 'You tore a page out of Beilstein?'

He shrieked it and surprised the hell out of me. I wouldn't have thought him capable of shrieking.

Hathaway said, 'I thought we could test it for stickum from the scotch tape, or maybe for a little cyanide that leaked out.'

'Give it to me!' yelled the professor. 'You ignorant fool.'

He smoothed out the sheet and looked at both sides as though to make sure that none of the print had been rubbed off.

'Vandal!' he said, and I'm sure that at the moment he could have killed Hathaway and laughed during the entire process.

Professor Rodney might be morally certain of Susan's guilt and so, for that matter, might I. Nevertheless, moral certainty cannot be taken before a jury. Evidence was needed.

So, lacking faith in witnesses, I attacked through the one weakness of any possibly guilty person – the possibly guilty person.

I brought her in to witness the new line of questioning, and if the questioning didn't pin her to her guilt, her own nerves might. From her appearance I couldn't tell how good that 'might' would be. Susan Morey sat at her desk, hands clasped before her, eyes cold, and the skin around her nostrils tight-looking.

The little German furrier was in first, looking sick with worry. 'I did nothing,' he babbled. 'Please. I have business. How long must I stay?'

Hathaway had his name and vital statistics, so I skipped all that and got to the point.

'You came here a little before two o'clock. Right?'

'Yes. I wanted to know about moth repellents—'

'All right. When you came in you went to the desk. Right?'

'Yes. I told her my name, who I was, what I wanted—'

'Told whom?' That was the key question.

The little fellow stared at me. He had curly hair and a mouth that fell in as though he were toothless, but that was just appearance, for when he talked, small yellow teeth were plainly visible. He said, 'Her. I told her. The girl sitting there.'

'That's right,' said Susan tonelessly. 'He spoke to me.'

Professor Rodney was gazing at her with a look of concentrated detestation. It occurred to me that his reason for wishing to see justice done quickly might be more personal than idealistic at that. However, that was none of my business.

I said to the furrier, 'Are you *sure* this is the girl?'

He said, 'Yes. I told her my name and my business, and she smiled. She told me where to find books on insecticides. Then, as I was stepping away, another girl came out from inside there.'

'Good!' I said at once. 'Now here's a photograph of another girl. 'Tell me, was it the girl at the desk you spoke to and the girl in the photograph who came out of the back room? Or was it the girl in the photograph you spoke to and the girl at the desk who came out of the back room?'

For a long minute, the furrier stared at the girl, then at the photograph, then at me. 'They are alike.'

I swore to myself. The faintest smile had passed over Susan's lips, hovering there a moment before vanishing. She must have counted on this. It was intersession. Hardly anyone would be in the library. None of them would pay much attention to the librarians who are fixtures like the bookshelves, and if any did, he could never swear which of the Library Twins he had seen.

I *knew* she was guilty now, but knowing meant nothing.

I said, 'Well, which was it?'

He said, like one anxious to put an end to questioning, 'I spoke to her, the girl right there at the desk.'

'That's right,' said Susan, perfectly calm.

My hope in her nerves hit bottom.

I said to the furrier, 'Would you swear?'

He said at once, 'No.'

'All right. Hathaway, take him away. Send him home.'

Professor Rodney leaned over to touch my elbow. He whispered, 'Why did she smile at the fellow when he stated his business.'

I whispered back, 'Why not?' but put the question to her anyway.

Her eyebrows went up a fraction of an inch. 'I was just being pleasant. Is there anything wrong with that?'

She was almost enjoying herself. I could swear to that.

The professor shook his head slightly. He whispered to me again, 'She's not the type to smile at a troublesome stranger. It had to be Louella-Marie at the desk.'

I shrugged. I could see myself bringing that kind of evidence to the Commissioner.

Four of the students were a blank and took up little time. They were engaged in research, they knew what books they wanted, what shelves the books would be on. They went straight there without stopping at the desk. None could say whether Susan or Louella-Marie had been at the desk at any particular time. None had even looked up from their books, to hear them tell it, before the scream roused everything.

The fifth was Peter van Norden. He kept his eyes fixed firmly on his right thumb, which had a badly bitten nail. He did not look up at Susan as he was brought in.

I let him sit awhile and soften up.

Finally I said, 'What are you doing here this time of year? I understand it's between sessions.'

He muttered, 'My Qualifyings are coming up next month. I'm studying. Qualifying examinations. If I pass, I can go on for my Ph.D., see?'

I said, 'I suppose you stopped at the desk when you came in here'

He mumbled.

I said, 'What?'

He said in a low voice that was hardly an improvement, 'I didn't. I don't think I stopped at the desk.'

'You don't *think*?'

'I didn't.'

I said, 'Isn't that strange? I understand you're good friends of both Susan and Louella-Marie. Don't you say hello?'

'I was worried. I had this test in my mind. I had to study. I—'

'So you couldn't even take time out for a hello.' I looked at Susan to see how this was going over. She seemed paler, but that might have been my imagination.

I said, 'Isn't it true that you were practically engaged to one of them?'

He looked up with uneasy indignation. 'No! I can't get engaged before I get my degree. Who told you I was engaged?'

'I said practically engaged.'

'*No!* I had a few dates, maybe. So what! What's a date or two?'

I said smoothly, 'Come on, Pete, which one was your girl?'

'I tell you it wasn't like that.'

He was washing his hands of the whole matter so hard, he seemed buried and smothered in an invisible lather.

'How about it?' I asked suddenly, addressing Susan. 'Did he stop at your desk?'

'He waved as he passed,' she said. 'Did you, Pete?'

'I don't remember,' he said sullenly. 'Maybe I did. So what?'

'Nothing,' I said. Inside me, I wished Susan joy of her bargain. If she had killed for the sake of this specimen, she had done it for nothing. To me it seemed a certainty that henceforward he would ignore her even if she fell off a two-story building and hit him on the head.

Susan must have realized that too. From the look she was giving Peter van Norden, I marked him down as a second candidate for cyanide – assuming she went free – and it certainly seemed as though she would.

I nodded to Hathaway to take him away. Hathaway rose to do that and said, 'Say, you ever use those books?' and he pointed to the shelves where the sixty-odd volumes of the organic chemistry encyclopedia stretched from floor to ceiling.

The boy looked over his shoulder and said in honest astonishment. 'Sure. I've got to. Lord, is something wrong with looking up compounds in Beilst—'

'It's all right,' I assured him. 'Come on, Ed.'

Ed Hathaway scowled at me and led the boy out. He hates letting go of an exploded theory.

It was about six and I didn't see that anything more could be done. As it stood, it was Susan's word against no word. If she had been a hood with a record, we could have sweated out the truth in any of several effective, if tedious, ways. In this case, such a procedure was inadvisable.

I turned to the professor to say so, but he was staring at Hathaway's cards. At one of them, anyway, which he was holding in his hand. You know, people always talk about other people's hands shaking with excitement, but it's something you don't often see. Rodney's hand was shaking, though, shaking like the clapper of an old-fashioned alarm clock.

He cleared his throat. 'Let me ask her something. Let me . . .'

I stared at him, then pushed my chair back. 'Go ahead,' I said. At this point, there was nothing to lose.

He looked at the girl, putting the card clown on the desk, blank side up.

He said shakily, 'Miss Morey?' He seemed to be deliberately avoiding the familiarity of her first name.

She stared at him. For a moment she had seemed nervous, but that passed and she was calm again. 'Yes, Professor?'

The professor said, 'Miss Morey, you smiled when the furrier told you his business here. Why was that?'

'I told you, Professor Rodney,' she said, 'I was being pleasant.'

'Perhaps there was something peculiar about what he said? Something amusing?'

'I was just trying to be pleasant,' she insisted.

'Perhaps you found his name amusing, Miss Morey?'

'Not particularly,' she said indifferently.

'Well, no one has mentioned his name here. I didn't know it till I happened to look at this card.' Then suddenly, tensely, he cried, 'What *was* his name, Miss Morey?'

She paused before answering, 'I don't remember.'

'You *don't*? He gave it to you, didn't he?'

There was an edge to her voice now. 'What if he did? It's just a name. After all that's happened, you can't expect me to remember some peculiar foreign name I happened to hear one time.'

'It was *foreign*, then?'

She pulled up short, avoiding the trap. 'I don't remember,' she said. 'I think it was a typically German name, but I don't remember. For all I know it was John Smith.'

I had to admit I didn't see the professor's point. I said, 'What are you trying to prove, Professor Rodney?'

'I'm trying to prove,' he said tightly, 'in fact I *am* proving, that it was Louella-Marie, the dead girl, who was at the desk when the furrier came in. He announced his name to Louella-Marie and she smiled in consequence. It was Miss Morey who was coming out of the inner office as he turned away. It was Miss Morey, *this* girl, who had just finished preparing and poisoning the tea.'

'You're basing that on the fact I can't remember a man's name!' shrilled Susan Morey. 'That's ridiculous.'

'No, it isn't,' said the professor. 'If you had been the girl at the desk, you would remember his name. It would be *impossible* for you to forget it. *If* you were the girl at the desk.' He was holding Hathaway's card up now. He said, 'That furrier's first name is Ernest, but his last name is Beilstein. *His name is Beilstein!*'

The air went out of Susan as though she had been kicked in the stomach. She turned white as talcum powder.

The professor went on intensely, 'No chemical librarian could possibly forget the name of anyone who came in and announced himself to be Beilstein. The sixty-volume encyclopedia we've mentioned half a dozen times today is referred to invariably by the name of its editor, Beilstein. The name is like Mother Goose to a chemical librarian, like George Washington, like Christopher Columbus. It is more second nature to her than any of them.

'If this girl claims to have forgotten the name, it is only because she never heard it. And she never heard it because she wasn't at the desk.'

I rose and said grimly, 'Well, Miss Morey' – I abandoned the first name too – 'what about it?'

She was screaming in earsplitting hysteria. Half an hour later, we had her confession.

The Dust of Death

Like all men who worked under the great Llewes, Edmund Farley reached the point where he thought with longing of the pleasure it would give him to kill that same great Llewes.

No man who did not work for Llewes would quite understand the feeling. LIewes (men forgot his first name or grew, almost unconsciously, to think it was Great, with a capital G) was Everyman's idea of the great prober into the unknown: both relentless and brilliant, neither giving up in the face of failure nor ever at a loss for a new and more ingenious attack.

Llewes was an organic chemist who had brought the Solar System to the service of his science. It was he who first used the Moon for large-scale reactions to be run in vacuum, at the temperature of boiling water or liquid air, depending on the time of month. Photochemistry became something new and wonderful when carefully designed apparatus was set floating freely in orbits about space stations.

But, truth to tell, Llewes was a credit stealer, a sin almost impossible to forgive. Some nameless student had first thought of setting up apparatus on the Lunar surface; a forgotten technician had designed the first self-contained space reactor. Somehow both achievements became associated with the name of Llewes.

And nothing could be done. An employee who resigned in anger would lose his recommendation and find it difficult to obtain another job. His unsupported word against that of Llewes would be worth nothing. On the other hand, those who remained with him, endured, and finally left with good grace and a recommendation were sure of future success.

But while they stayed, they at least enjoyed the dubious pleasure of voicing their hatred among themselves.

And Edmund Farley had full reason to join them. He had come from Titan, Saturn's largest satellite, where he had singlehanded – aided by robots only – set up equipment to make full use of Titan's reducing atmosphere. The major planets had atmospheres composed largely of hydrogen and methane, but Jupiter and Saturn were too large to deal with, and Uranus and Neptune were still too expensively far. Titan, however, was Mars-size, small enough to operate upon and large enough and cold enough to retain a medium-thin hydrogen-methane atmosphere.

Large-scale reactions could proceed there easily in the hydrogen atmosphere, where on Earth those same reactions were kinetically troublesome. Farley had designed and redesigned and endured Titan for half a year and had come back with amazing data. Yet somehow, almost at once, Farley could see it fragment and begin to come together as a Llewes achievement.

The others sympathized, shrugged their shoulders, and bade him welcome to the fraternity. Farley tensed his acne-scarred face, brought his thin lips together, and listened to the others as they plotted violence.

Jim Gorham was the most outspoken. Farley rather despised him, for he was a 'vacuum man' who had never left Earth. Gorham said, 'Llewes is an easy man to kill because of his regular habits, you see. You can rely on him. For instance, look at the way he insists on eating by himself. He closes his office at twelve sharp and opens it at one sharp. Right? No one goes into his office in that interval, so poison has plenty of time to work.'

Belinsky said dubiously, 'Poison?'

'Easy. Plenty of poison all over the place. You name it, we got it. Okay, then. Llewes eats one Swiss cheese on rye with a special kind of relish knee-deep in onions. We all know that, right? After all, we can smell him all afternoon and we all remember the miserable howl he raised when the lunchroom ran out of the relish once last spring. No one else in the place will ever touch the relish, so poison in it will hit only Llewes and no one else . . .'

It was all a kind of lunchtime make-believe, but not for Farley. Grimly, and in earnest, he decided to murder Llewes.

It became an obsession with him. His blood tingled at the thought of Llewes dead, of himself able to take the credit that was rightfully his for those months of living in a small bubble of oxygen and tramping across frozen ammonia to remove products and set up new reactions in the thin, chill winds of hydrogen and methane.

But it would have to be something which couldn't possibly harm anyone but Llewes. That sharpened the matter and focused things on Llewes' atmosphere room. It was a long, low room, isolated from the rest of the laboratories by cement blocks and fireproof doors. No one but Llewes ever entered, except in Llewes' presence and with his permission. Not that the room was ever actually locked. The effective tyranny Llewes had established made the faded slip of paper on the laboratory door, reading 'Do Not Enter' and signed with his initials, more of a barrier than any lock . . . except where the desire for murder superseded all else. Then what about the atmosphere room? Llewes' routine of testing, his almost infinite caution, left nothing to chance. Any tampering with the equipment itself, unless it were unusually subtle, would certainly be detected.

Fire then? The atmosphere room contained inflammable materials and to spare, but Llewes didn't smoke and was perfectly aware of the danger of fires. No one took greater precautions against one.

Farley thought impatiently of the man on whom it seemed so difficult to wreak a just vengeance; the thief playing with his little tanks of methane and hydrogen where Farley had used it by the cubic mile. Llewes for the little tanks and fame; Farley for the cubic miles and oblivion.

All those little tanks of gas; each its own color; each a synthetic atmosphere. Hydrogen gas in red cylinders and methane in striped red and white, a mixture of the two representing the atmosphere of the outer planets. Nitrogen in brown cylinders and carbon dioxide in silver for the atmosphere of Venus. The yellow cylinders of compressed air and the green cylinders of oxygen, where Earthly chemistry was good enough. A parade of the rainbow, each color dating back through centuries of convention.

Then he had the thought. It was not born painfully, but came all at once. In one moment it had all crystallized in Farley's mind and he knew what he had to do.

Farley waited a painful month for the eighteenth of September, which was Space Day. It was the anniversary of man's first successful space flight and no one would be working that night. Space Day was, of all holidays, the one most meaningful to the scientist in particular and even the dedicated Llewes would be making merry then.

Farley entered Central Organic Laboratories – to use its official title – that night, certain he was unobserved. The labs weren't banks or museums. They were not subject to thievery and such nightwatchmen as there were had a generally easy-going attitude toward their jobs.

Farley closed the main door carefully behind him and moved slowly down the darkened corridors toward the atmosphere room. His equipment consisted of a flashlight, a small vial of black powder, and a thin brush he had bought in an art-supply store at the other end of town three weeks before. He wore gloves.

His greatest difficulty came in actually entering the atmosphere room. Its 'forbiddenness' hampered him more than the general forbiddenness of murder. Once in, however, once past the mental hazard, the rest was easy.

He cupped the flashlight and found the cylinder without hesitation. His heart was beating so as almost to deafen him, while his breath came quickly and his hand trembled.

He tucked the flash under his arm, then dipped the tip of the artist's brush into the black dust. Grains of it adhered to the brush and Farley pointed it into the noztle of the gauge attached to the cylinder. It took eons-long seconds for that trembling tip to enter the nozzle.

Farley moved it about delicately, dipped it into the black dust again, and inserted it once more in the nozzle. He repeated it over and over, almost hypnotized by the intensity of his own concentration. Finally, using a bit of facial tissue dampened with saliva, he began to wipe off the outer rim of the nozzle, enormously relieved that the job was done and he'd soon be out. It was then his hand froze, and the sick uncertainty of fear surged through him. The flashlight dropped clattering to the floor. Fool! Incredible and miserable fool! He hadn't been *thinking*!

Under the stress of his emotion and anxiety, he had ended at the wrong cylinder!

He snatched up the flash, put it out, and, his heart thumping alarmingly, listened for any noise.

In the continuing dead silence, he regained a portion of his selfcontrol, and screwed himself to the realization that what could be done once could be done again. If the wrong cylinder had been tampered with, then the right one would take two minutes more. Once again, the brush and the black dust came into play. At least, he had not dropped the vial of dust; the deadly, burning dust. This time, the cylinder was the right one.

He finished, wiping the nozzle again, with a badly trembling hand. His flash then played about quickly and rested upon a reagent bottle of toluene. That would do. He unscrewed the plastic cap, splashed some of the toluene on the floor, and left the bottle open.

He then stumbled out of the building as in a dream, made his way to his rooming house and the safety of his own room. As nearly as he could tell, he was unobserved throughout.

He disposed of the facial tissue he had used to wipe the nozzles of the gas cylinders by cramming it into the flash-disposal unit. It vanished into molecular dispersion. So did the artist's brush that followed.

The vial of dust could not be so gotten rid of without adjustments to the disposal unit he did not think it safe to make. He would walk to work, as he often did, and toss it off the Grand Street bridge . . .

Farley blinked at himself in the mirror the next morning and wondered if he dared go to work. It was an idle thought; he didn't dare *not* go to work. He must do nothing that would attract attention to him on this day of all days.

With grayish desperation, he worked to reproduce normal acts of nothingness that made up so much of the day. It was a fine, warm morning and he walked to work. It was only a flicking motion of the wrist that was necessary to get rid of the vial. It made a tiny splash in the river, filled with water, and sank.

He sat at his desk, later that morning, staring at his hand computer. Now that it had all been done, would it work? Llewes might ignore the smell of toluene. Why not? The odor was unpleasant, but not disgusting. Organic chemists were used to it. Then, if Llewes were still hot on the trail of the hydrogenation procedures Farley had brought back from Titan, the gas cylinder would be put into use at once. It would have to be. With a day of holiday behind him, Llewes would be more than usually anxious to get back to work.

Then, as soon as the gauge cock was turned, a bit of gas would spurt out and turn into a sheet of flame. If there were the proper quantity of toluene in the air, it would turn as quickly into an explosion—

So intent was Farley in his reverie that he accepted the dull boom in the distance as the creation of his own mind, a counterpoint to his own thoughts, until footsteps thudded by.

Farley looked up, and out of a dry throat, cried, 'What – what—'

'Dunno,' yelled back the other. 'Something wrong in the atmosphere room. Explosion. Hell of a mess.'

The extinguishers were on and men beat out the flames and snatched the burned and battered Llewes out of the wreckage. He had the barest flicker of life left in him and died before a doctor had time to predict that he would.

On the outskirts of the group that hovered about the scene in grim and grisly curiosity stood Edmund Farley. His pallor and the glisten of perspiration on his face did not, at that moment, mark him as different from the rest. He tottered back to his desk. He could be sick now. No one would remark on it.

But somehow he wasn't. He finished out the day and in the evening the load began to lighten. Accident was accident, wasn't it? There were occupational risks all chemists ran, especially those working with inflammable compounds. No one would question the matter.

And if anyone did, how could they possibly trace anything back to Edmund Farley? He had only to go about his life as though nothing had happened.

Nothing? Good Lord, the credit for Titan would now be his.

He would be a great man.

The load lightened indeed and that night he slept.

Jim Gorham had faded a bit in twenty-four hours. His yellow hair was stringy and only the light color of his stubble masked the fact that he needed a shave badly.

'We all talked murder,' he said.

H. Seton Davenport of the Terrestrial Bureau of Investigation tapped one finger against the desktop methodically, and so lightly that it could not be heard. He was a stocky man with a firm face and black hair, a thin, prominent nose made for utility rather than beauty, and a star-shaped scar on one cheek.

'Seriously?' he asked.

'No,' said Gorham, shaking his head violently. 'At least, I didn't think it was serious. The schemes were wild: poisoned sandwich spreads and acid on the helicopter, you know. Still, someone must have taken the matter seriously after all ... The madman! For what reason?'

Davenport said, 'From what you've said, I judge because the dead man appropriated other people's work.'

'So what,' cried Gorham. 'It was the price he charged for what he did. He held the entire team together. He was its muscles and guts. Llewes was the one who dealt with Congress and got the grants. He was the one who got permission to set up projects in space and send men to the Moon or wherever. He talked spaceship lines and industrialists into doing millions of dollars of work for us. He *organized* Central Organic.'

'Have you realized all this overnight?'

'Not really. I've always known this, but what could I do? I've chickened out of space travel, found excuses to avoid it. I was a vacuum man, who never even visited the Moon. The truth was, I was afraid, and even more afraid to have the others think I was afraid.' He virtually spat self-contempt.

'And now you want to find someone to punish?' said Davenport. 'You want to make up to the dead Llewes your crime against the live one?'

'No! Leave psychiatry out of this. I tell you it *is* murder. It's *got* to be. You didn't know Llewes. The man was a monomaniac on safety. No explosion could possibly have happened anywhere near him unless it were carefully arranged.'

Davenport shrugged. 'What exploded, Dr Gorham?'

'It could have been almost anything. He handled organic compounds of all sorts – benzene, ether, pyridine – all of them inflammable.'

'I studied chemistry once, Dr Gorham, and none of those liquids is explosive at room temperature as I remember. There has to be some sort of heat, a spark, a flame.'

'There was fire all right.'

'How did that happen?'

'I can't imagine. There were no burners in the place and no matches. Electrical equipment of all sorts was heavily shielded. Even little ordinary things like clamps were specially manufactured out of beryllium copper or other non-sparking alloys. Llewes didn't smoke and would have fired on the spot anyone who approached within a hundred feet of the room with a lighted cigarette.'

'What was the last thing he handled, then?'

'Hard to tell. The place was a shambles.'

'I suppose it has been straightened out by now, though.'

The chemist said with instant eagerness, 'No, it hasn't. I took care of that. I said we had to investigate the cause of the accident to prove it wasn't neglect. You know, to avoid bad publicity. So the room hasn't been touched.'

Davenport nodded. 'All right. Let's take a look at it.'

In the blackened, disheveled room, Davenport said, 'What's the most dangerous piece of equipment in the place?'

Gorham looked about. 'The compressed oxygen tanks,' he said, pointing.

Davenport looked at the variously colored cylinders standing against the wall cradled in a binding chain. Some leaned heavily against the chain, tipped by the force of the explosion.

Davenport said, 'How about this one?' He toed a red cylinder which lay flat on the ground in the middle of the room. It was heavy and didn't budge.

'That one's hydrogen,' said Gorham.

'Hydrogen is explosive, isn't it?'

'That's right – when heated.'

Davenport said, 'Then why do you say the compressed oxygen is the most dangerous. Oxygen doesn't explode, does it?'

'No. It doesn't even burn, but it supports combustion, see. Things burn in it.'

'So?'

'Well, look here.' A certain vivacity entered Gorham's voice; he was the scientist explaining something simple to the intelligent layman. 'Sometimes a person might accidentally put some lubricant on the valve before tightening it onto the cylinder, to make a tighter seal, you know. Or he might get something inflammable smeared on it by mistake. When he opens the valve then, the oxygen rushes out, and whatever goo is on the valve explodes, wrenching off the valve. Then the rest of the oxygen blows out of the cylinder, which would then take off like a miniature jet and go through a wall; the heat of the explosion would fire other inflammable liquids nearby.'

'Are the oxygen tanks in this place intact?'

'Yes, they are.'

Davenport kicked the hydrogen cylinder at his feet. 'The gauge on this cylinder reads zero. I suppose that means it was in use at the time of explosion and has emptied itself since then.'

Gorham nodded. 'I suppose so.'

'Could you explode hydrogen by smearing oil on the gauge?'

'Definitely not.'

Davenport rubbed his chin. 'Is there anything that would make hydrogen burst into flame outside of a spark of some sort?'

Gorham muttered, 'A catalyst, I suppose. Platinum black is the best. That's powdered platinum.'

Davenport looked astonished. 'Do you have such a thing?'

'Of course. It's expensive, but there's nothing better for catalyzing hydrogenations.' He fell silent and stared down at the hydrogen cylinder for a long moment. 'Platinum black,' he finally whispered. 'I wonder—'

Davenport said, 'Platinum black would make hydrogen burn, then?'

'Oh, yes. It brings about the combination of hydrogen and oxygen at room temperature. No heat necessary. The explosion would be just as though it were caused by heat, just the same.' Excitement was building up in Gorham's voice and he fell to his knees beside the hydrogen cylinder. He passed his finger over the blackened tip. It might be just soot and it might be—

He got to his feet, 'Sir, that must be the way it was done. I'm going to get every speck of foreign material off that nozzle and run a spectrographic analysis.'

'How long will it take?'

'Give me fifteen minutes.'

Gorham came back in twenty. Davenport had made a meticulous round of the burned-out laboratory. He looked up. 'Well?'

Gorham said triumphantly, 'It's there. Not much, but there.' He held up a strip of photographic negative against which there were short white parallel lines, irregularly spaced and of different degrees of brightness. 'Mostly extraneous material, but you see those lines . . .'

Davenport peered closely. '*Very* faint. Would you swear in court that platinum was present?'

'Yes,' said Gorham at once.

'Would any other chemist? If this photo were shown a chemist hired by the defense, could he claim the lines were too faint to be certain evidence?'

Gorham was silent.

Davenport shrugged.

The chemist cried, 'But it *is* there. The stream of gas and the explosion would have blown most of it out. You wouldn't expect much to be left. You see that, don't you?'

Davenport looked about thoughtfully. 'I do. I admit there's a reasonable chance this is murder. So now we look for more and better evidence. Do you suppose this is the only cylinder that might have been tampered with?'

'I don't know.'

'Then the first thing we do is check every other cylinder in the place. Everything else, too. If there is a murderer, he might conceivably have set other booby traps in the place. It's got to be checked.'

'I'll get started—' began Gorham eagerly.

'Uh – not you,' said Davenport. 'I'll have a man from our labs do it.'

The next morning, Gorham was in Davenport's office again.

This time he had been summoned.

Davenport said, 'It's murder, all right. A second cylinder had been tampered with.'

'*You see!*'

'An oxygen cylinder. There was platinum black inside the tip of the nozzle. Quite a bit of it.'

'Platinum black? On the *oxygen* cylinder?'

Davenport nodded. 'Right. Now why do you suppose that would be?'

Gorham shook his head. 'Oxygen won't burn and nothing will make it burn. Not even platinum black.'

'So the murderer must have put it on the oxygen cylinder by mistake in the tension of the moment. Presumably he corrected himself and tampered with the right cylinder, but meanwhile he left final evidence that this is murder and not accident.'

'Yes. Now it's only a matter of finding the person.'

The scar on Davenport's cheek crinkled alarmingly as he smiled. '*Only*, Dr Gorham? How do we do that? Our quarry left no calling card. There are a number of people in the laboratories with motive; a greater number with the chemical knowledge required to commit the crime and with the opportunity to do so. Is there any way we can trace the platinum black?'

'No,' said Gorham hesitantly. 'Any of twenty people could have gotten into the special supply room without trouble. What about alibis?'

'For what time?'

'For the night before.'

Davenport leaned across his desk. 'When was the last time, previous to the fatal moment, that Dr Llewes used that hydrogen cylinder?'

'I – I don't know. He worked alone. Very secretly. It was part of his way of making sure he had sole credit.'

'Yes, I know. We've been making our own inquiries. So the platinum black might have been put on the cylinder a week before for all we know.'

Gorham whispered disconsolately, 'Then what do we do?'

Davenport said, 'The only point of attack, it seems to me, is the platinum black on the oxygen cylinder. It's an irrational point and the explanation may hold the solution. But I'm no chemist and you are, so if the answer is anywhere it's inside you. Could it have been a mistake – could the murderer have confused the oxygen with the hydrogen?'

Gorham shook his head at once. 'No. You know about the colors. A green tank is oxygen; a red tank is hydrogen.'

'What if he were color blind?' asked Davenport.

This time Gorham took more time. Finally he said, 'No. Colorblind people don't generally go in for chemistry. Detection of color in chemical reactions is too important. And if anybody in this organization were color blind, he'd have enough trouble with one thing or another so that the rest of us would know about it.'

Davenport nodded. He fingered the scar on his cheek absently. 'All right. If the oxygen cylinder wasn't smeared by ignorance or accident, could it have been done on purpose? Deliberately?'

'I don't understand you.'

'Perhaps the murderer had a logical plan in mind when he smeared the oxygen cylinder, then changed his mind. Are there any conditions where platinum black would be dangerous in the presence of oxygen? Any conditions at all? You're the chemist, Dr Gorham.'

There was a puzzled frown on the chemist's face. He shook his head. 'No, none. There can't be. Unless—'

'Unless?'

'Well, this is ridiculous, but if you stuck the oxygen jet into a container of hydrogen gas, platinum black on the gas cylinder could be dangerous. Naturally you'd need a big container to make a satisfactory explosion.'

'Suppose,' said Davenport, 'our murderer had counted on filling the room with hydrogen and then having the oxygen tank turned on.'

Gorham said, with a half-smile, 'But why bother with the hydrogen atmosphere when—' The half-smile vanished completely while a complete pallor took its place. He cried, 'Farley! Edmund Farley!'

'What's that?'

'Farley just returned from six months on Titan,' said Gorham in gathering excitement. 'Titan has a hydrogen-methane atmosphere. He is the only man here to have had experience in such an atmosphere, and it all makes sense now. On Titan a jet of oxygen will combine with the surrounding hydrogen if heated, or treated with platinum black. A jet of hydrogen won't. The situation is exactly the reverse of what it is here on Earth. It *must* have been Farley. When he entered Llewes' lab to arrange an explosion, he put the platinum black on the oxygen, out of recent habit. By the time he recalled that the situation was the other way round on Earth, the damage was done.'

Davenport nodded in grim satisfaction. 'That does it, I think.' His hand reached out to an intercom and he said to the unseen recipient at the other end, 'Send out a man to pick up Dr Edmund Farley at Central Organic.'

Blank!

'Presumably,' said August Pointdexter, 'there is such a thing as overweening pride. The Greeks called it *hubris*, and considered it to be defiance of the gods, to be followed always by *ate*, or retribution.' He rubbed his pale blue eyes uneasily.

'Very pretty,' said Dr Edward Barron impatiently. 'Has that any connection with what I said?' His forehead was high and had horizontal creases in it that cut in sharply when he raised his eyebrows in contempt.

'Every connection,' said Pointdexter. 'To construct a time machine is itself a challenge to fate. You make it worse by your flat confidence. How can you be *sure* that your time-travel machine will operate through all of time without the possibility of paradox?'

Barron said, 'I didn't know you were superstitious. The simple fact is that a time machine is a machine like any other machine, no more and no less sacrilegious. Mathematically, it is analogous to an elevator moving up and down its shaft. What danger of retribution lies in that?'

Pointdexter said energetically, 'An elevator doesn't involve paradoxes. You can't move from the fifth floor to the fourth and kill your grandfather as a child.'

Dr Barron shook his head in agonized impatience. 'I was waiting for that. For *exactly* that. Why couldn't you suggest that I would meet myself or that I would change history by telling McClellan that Stonewall Jackson was going to make a flank march on Washington, or anything else? Now I'm asking you point blank. Will you come into the machine with me?'

Pointdexter hesitated. 'I . . . I don't think so.'

'Why do you make things difficult? I've explained already that time is invariant. If I go into the past it will be because I've already been there. Anything I decided to do and proceed to do, I will have already done in the past all along, so I'll be changing nothing and no paradoxes will result. If I decided to kill my grandfather as a baby, and *did* it, I would not be here. But I *am* here. Therefore I did not kill my grandfather. No matter how I try to kill him and plan to kill him, the fact is I didn't kill him and so I won't kill him. Nothing would change that. Do you understand what I'm explaining?'

'I understand what you say, but are you right?'

'Of course I'm right. For God's sake, why couldn't you have been a mathematician instead of a machinist with a college education?' In his impatience, Barron could scarcely hide his contempt. 'Look, this machine is only possible because certain mathematical relationships between space and time hold true. You understand that, don't you, even if you don't follow the details of the mathematics? The machine exists, so the mathematical relations I worked out have some correspondence in reality. Right? You've seen me send rabbits a week into the future. You've seen them appear out of nothing. You've watched me send a rabbit a week into the past one week after it appeared. And they were unharmed.'

'All right. I admit all that.'

'Then will you believe me if I tell you that the equations upon which this machine is based assume that time is composed of particles that exist in an unchanging order; that time is invariant. If the order of the particles could be changed in any way – any way at all – the equations would be invalid and this machine wouldn't work; this particular method of time travel would be impossible.'

Pointdexter rubbed his eyes again and looked thoughtful. 'I wish I knew mathematics.'

Barron said, 'Just consider the facts. You tried to send the rabbit *two* weeks into the past when it had arrived only one week in the past. That would have created a paradox, wouldn't it? But what happened? The indicator stuck at one week and wouldn't budge. You *couldn't* create a paradox. Will you come?'

Pointdexter shuddered at the edge of the abyss of agreement and drew back. He said, 'No.'

Barron said, 'I wouldn't ask you to help if I could do this alone, but you know it takes two men to operate the machine for intervals of more than a month. I need someone to control the Standards so that we can return with precision. And you're the one I want to use. We share the – the glory of this thing now. Do you want to thin it out, cut in a third person? Time enough for that after we've established ourselves as the first time travelers in history. Good Lord, man, don't you want to see where we'll be a hundred years from now, or a thousand; don't you want to see Napoleon, or Jesus, for that matter? We'll be like – like' – Barron seemed carried away – 'like gods.'

'Exactly,' mumbled Pointdexter. '*Hubris*. Time travel isn't godlike enough to risk being stranded out of my own time.'

'*Hubris*. Stranded. You keep making up fears. We're just moving along the particles of time like an elevator along the floors of a building. Time travel is actually safer because an elevator cable can break, whereas in the time machine there'll be no gravity to pull us down destructively. Nothing wrong can possibly happen. I guarantee it,' said Barron, tapping his chest with the middle finger of his right hand. 'I guarantee it.'

'*Hubris*,' muttered Pointdexter, but fell into the abyss of agreement nevertheless, overborne at last.

Together they entered the machine.

Pointdexter did not understand the controls in the sense Barron did, for he was no mathematician, but he knew how they were supposed to be handled.

Barron was at one set, the Propulsions. They supplied the drive that forced the machine along the time axis. Pointdexter was at the Standards that kept the point of origin fixed so that the machine could move back to the original starting point at any time.

Pointdexter's teeth chattered as the first motion made itself felt in his stomach. Like an elevator's motion it was, but not quite. It was something more subtle, yet very real. He said, 'What if—'

Barron snapped out, 'Nothing can go wrong. Please!'

And at once there was a jar and Pointdexter fell heavily against the wall.

Barron said, 'What the devil!'

'What happened?' demanded Pointdexter breathlessly.

'I don't know, but it doesn't matter. We're only twenty-two hours into the future. Let's step out and check.'

The door of the machine slid into its recessed panel and the breath went out of Pointdexter's body in a panting whoosh. He said, 'There's nothing there.'

Nothing. No matter. No light. Blank!

Pointdexter screamed. 'The Earth moved. We forgot that. In twenty-two hours, it moved thousands of miles through space, traveling around the sun.'

'No,' said Barron faintly, 'I didn't forget that. The machine is designed to follow the time path of Earth wherever that leads. Besides, even if Earth moved, where is the sun? Where are the stars?'

Barron went back to the controls. Nothing budged. Nothing worked. The door would no longer slide shut. Blank!

Pointdexter found it getting difficult to breathe, difficult to move. With effort he said, 'What's wrong, then?'

Barron moved slowly toward the center of the machine. He said painfully, 'The particles of time. I think we happened to stall . . . between two . . . particles.'

Pointdexter tried to clench a fist but couldn't. 'Don't understand.'

'Like an elevator. Like an elevator.' He could no longer sound the words, but only move his lips to shape them. 'Like an elevator, after all . . . stuck between the floors.'

Pointdexter could not even move his lips. He thought: Nothing can proceed in nontime. All motion is suspended, all consciousness, all everything. There was an inertia about themselves that had carried them along in time for a minute or so, like a body leaning forward when an automobile comes to a sudden halt – but it was dying fast.

The light within the machine dimmed and went out. Sensation and awareness chilled into nothing.

One last thought, one final, feeble, mental sigh: *Hubris, ate!*

Then thought stopped, too.

Stasis! Nothing! For all eternity, where even eternity was meaningless, there would only be – blank!

Silly Asses

Naron of the long-lived Rigellian race was the fourth of his line to keep the galactic records.

He had the large book which contained the list of the numerous races throughout the galaxies that had developed intelligence, and the much smaller book that listed those races that had reached maturity and had qualified for the Galactic Federation. In the first book, a number of those listed were crossed out; those that, for one reason or another, had failed. Misfortune, biochemical or biophysical shortcomings, social maladjustment took their toll. In the smaller book, however, no member listed had yet blanked out.

And now Naron, large and incredibly ancient, looked up as a messenger approached.

'Naron,' said the messenger. 'Great One!'

'Well, well, what is it? Less ceremony.'

'Another group of organisms has attained maturity.'

'Excellent. Excellent. They are coming up quickly now. Scarcely a year passes without a new one. And who are these?'

The messenger gave the code number of the galaxy and the coordinates of the world within it.

'Ah, yes,' said Naron. 'I know the world.' And in flowing script he noted it in the first book and transferred its name into the second, using, as was customary, the name by which the planet was known to the largest fraction of its populace. He wrote: Earth.

He said, 'These new creatures have set a record. No other group has passed from intelligence to maturity so quickly. No mistake, I hope.'

'None, sir,' said the messenger.

'They have attained to thermonuclear power, have they?'

'Yes, sir.'

'Well, that's the criterion.' Naron chuckled. 'And soon their ships will probe out and contact the Federation.'

'Actually, Great One,' said the messenger, reluctantly, 'the Observers tell us they have not yet penetrated space.'

Naron was astonished. 'Not at all? Not even a space station?'

'But if they have thermonuclear power, where then do they conduct their tests and detonations?'

'On their own planet, sir.'

Naron rose to his full twenty feet of height and thundered, 'On their own planet?'

'Yes, sir.'

Slowly Naron drew out his stylus and passed a line though the latest addition in the smaller book. It was an unprecedented act, but, then, Naron was very wise and could see the inevitable as well as anyone in the galaxy.

'Silly asses,' he muttered.

Buy Jupiter

He was a simulacron, of course, but so cleverly contrived that the human beings dealing with him had long since given up thinking of the real energy-entities, waiting in white-hot blaze in their field-enclosure 'ship' miles from Earth.

The simulacron, with a majestic golden beard and deep brown, wide-set eyes, said gently, 'We understand your hesitations and suspicions, and we can only continue to assure you we mean you no harm. We have, I think, presented you with proof that we inhabit the coronal haloes of 0-spectra stars; that your own sun is too weak for us; while your planets are of solid matter and therefore completely and eternally alien to us.'

The Terrestrial Negotiator (who was Secretary of Science and, by common consent, had been placed in charge of negotiations with the aliens) said, 'But you have admitted we are now on one of your chief trade routes.'

'Now that our new world of Kimmonoshek has developed new fields of protonic fluid, yes.'

The Secretary said, 'Well, here on Earth, positions on trade routes can gain military importance out of proportion to their intrinsic value. I can only repeat, then, that to gain our confidence you must tell us exactly why you need Jupiter.'

And as always, when that question or a form of it was asked, the simulacron looked pained. 'Secrecy is important. If the Lamberj people—'

'Exactly,' said the Secretary. 'To us it sounds like war. You and what you call the Lamberj people—'

The simulacron said hurriedly, 'But we are offering you a most generous return. You have only colonized the inner planets of your system and we are not interested in those. We ask for the world you call Jupiter, which, I understand, your people can never expect to live on, or even land on. Its size' (he laughed indulgently) 'is too much for you.'

The Secretary, who disliked the air of condescension, said stiffly, 'The Jovian satellites are practical sites for colonization, however, and we intend to colonize them shortly.'

'But the satellites will not be disturbed in any way. They are yours in every sense of the word. We ask only Jupiter itself, a completely useless world to you, and for that the return we offer is generous. Surely you realize that we could take your Jupiter, if we wished, without your permission. It is only that we prefer payment and a legal treaty. It will prevent disputes in the future. As you see, I'm being completely frank.'

The Secretary said stubbornly, 'Why do you need Jupiter?'

'The Lamberj—'

'Are you at war with the Lamberj?'

'It's not quite—'

'Because you see that if it is war and you establish some sort of fortified base on Jupiter, the Lamberj may, quite properly, resent that, and retaliate against us for granting you permission. We cannot allow ourselves to be involved in such a situation.'

'Nor would I ask you to be involved. My word that no harm would come to you. Surely' (he kept coming back to it) 'the return is generous. Enough power boxes each year to supply your world with a full year of power requirement.'

The Secretary said, 'On the understanding that future increases in power consumption will be met.'

'Up to a figure five times the present total. Yes.'

'Well, then, as I have said, I am a high official of the government and have been given considerable powers to deal with you – but not infinite power. I, myself, am inclined to trust you, but I could not accept your terms without understanding exactly why you want Jupiter. If the explanation is plausible and convincing, I could perhaps persuade our government and, through them, our people, to make the agreement. If I tried to make an agreement without such an explanation, I would simply be forced out of office and Earth would refuse to honor the agreement. You could then, as you say, take Jupiter by force, but you would be in illegal possession and you have said you don't wish that.'

The simulacron clicked its tongue impatiently. 'I cannot continue forever in this petty bickering. The Lamberj—' Again he stopped, then said, 'Have I your word of honor that this is all not a device inspired by the Lamberj people to delay us until—'

'My word of honor,' said the Secretary.

The Secretary of Science emerged, mopping his forehead and looking ten years younger. He said softly, 'I told him his people could have it as soon as I obtained the President's formal approval. I don't think he'll object, or Congress, either. Good Lord, gentlemen, think of it; free power at our fingertips in return for a planet we could never use in any case.'

The Secretary of Defense, growing purplish with objection, said, 'But we had agreed that only a Mizzarett-Lamberj war could explain their need for Jupiter. Under those circumstances, and comparing their military potential with ours, a strict neutrality is essential.'

'But there is no war, sir,' said the Secretary of Science. 'The simulacron presented an alternate explanation of their need for Jupiter so rational and plausible that I accepted at once. I think the President will agree with me, and you gentlemen, too, when you understand. In fact, I have here their plans for the new Jupiter, as it will soon appear.'

The others rose from their seats, clamoring. 'A new Jupiter?' gasped the Secretary of Defense.

'Not so different from the old, gentlemen,' said the Secretary of Science. 'Here are the sketches provided in form suitable for observation by matter beings such as ourselves.'

He laid them down. The familiar banded planet was there before them on one of the sketches: yellow, pale green, and light brown with curled white streaks here and there and all against the speckled velvet background of space. But across the bands were streaks of blackness as velvet as the background, arranged in a curious pattern.

'That,' said the Secretary of Science, 'is the day side of the planet. The night side is shown in this sketch.' (There, Jupiter was a thin crescent enclosing darkness, and within that darkness were the same thin streaks arranged in similar pattern, but in a phosphorescent glowing orange this time.)

'The marks,' said the Secretary of Science, 'are a purely optical phenomenon, I am told, which will not rotate with the planet, but will remain static in its atmospheric fringe.'

'But what is it?' asked the Secretary of Commerce.

'You see,' said the Secretary of Science, 'our solar system is now on one of their major trade routes. As many as seven of their ships pass within a few hundred million miles of the system in a single day, and each ship has the major planets under telescopic observation as they pass. Tourist curiosity, you know. Solid planets of any size are a marvel to them.'

'What has that to do with these marks?'

'That is one form of their writing. Translated, those marks read: "Use Mizzarett Ergone Vertices For Health and Glowing Heat."'

'You mean Jupiter is to be an advertising billboard?' exploded the Secretary of Defense.

'Right. The Lamberj people, it seems, produce a competing ergone tablet, which accounts for the Mizzarett anxiety to establish full legal ownership of Jupiter – in case of Lamberj lawsuits. Fortunately, the Mizzaretts are novices at the advertising game, it appears.'

'Why do you say that?' asked the Secretary of the Interior.

'Why, they neglected to set up a series of options on the other planets. The Jupiter billboard will be advertising our system, as well as their own product. And when the competing Lamberj people come storming in to check on the Mizzarett title to Jupiter, we will have Saturn to sell to *them*. *With* its rings. As we will be easily able to explain to them, the rings will make Saturn much the better spectacle.'

'And therefore,' said the Secretary of the Treasury, suddenly beaming, 'worth a *much* better price.'

And they all suddenly looked very cheerful.

Author! Author!

It occurred to Graham Dorn, and not for the first time, either, that there was one serious disadvantage in swearing you'll go through fire and water for a girl, however beloved. Sometimes she takes you at your miserable word.

This is one way of saying that he had been waylaid, shanghaied and dragooned by his fiancee into speaking at her maiden aunt's Literary Society. Don't laugh! It's not funny from the speaker's rostrum. Some of the faces you have to look at!

To race through the details, Graham Dorn had been jerked onto a platform and forced upright. He had read a speech on 'The Place of the Mystery Novel in American Literature' in full appalled tone. Not even the fact that his own eternally precious June had written it (part of the bribe to get him to speak in the first place) could mask the fact that it was essentially tripe.

And then when he was weltering, figuratively speaking, in his own mental gore, the harpies closed in, for lo, it was time for the informal discussion and assorted feminine gush.

—Oh, Mr Dorn, do you work from inspiration? I mean, do you just sit down and then an idea strikes you – all at once? And you must sit up all night and drink black coffee to keep you awake till you get it down?

—Oh, yes. Certainly. (His working hours were two to four in the afternoon every other day, and he drank milk.)

—Oh, Mr Dorn, you must do the most awful research to get all those bizarre murders. About how much must you do before you can write a story?

—About six months, usually. (The only reference books he ever used were a six-volume encyclopedia and year-before-last's World Almanac.)

—Oh, Mr Dorn, did you make up your Reginald de Meister from a real character? You must have. He's oh, so convincing in his every detail.

—He's modeled after a very dear boyhood chum of mine. (Dorn had never known *anyone* like de Meister. He lived in continual fear of meeting someone like him. He had even a cunningly fashioned ring containing a subtle Oriental poison for use just in case he did. So much for de Meister.)

Somewhere past the knot of women, June Billings sat in her seat and smiled with sickening and proprietary pride.

Graham passed a finger over his throat and went through the pantomime of choking to death as unobtrusively as possible. June smiled, nodded, threw him a delicate kiss, and did nothing.

Graham decided to pass a stern, lonely, woman-less life and to have nothing but villainesses in his stories forever after.

He was answering in monosyllables, alternating yesses and noes. Yes, he did take cocaine on occasion. He found it helped the creative urge. No, he didn't think he could allow Hollywood to take over de Meister. He thought movies weren't true expressions of real Art. Besides, they were just a passing fad. Yes, he would read Miss Crum's manuscripts if she brought them. Only too glad to. Reading amateur manuscripts was such fun, and editors are really such brutes. And then refreshments were announced, and there was a sudden vacuum. It took a split-second for Graham's head to clear. The mass of femininity had coalesced into a single specimen. She was four feet ten and about eighty-five pounds in weight. Graham was six-two and two hundred ten worth of brawn. He could probably have handled her without difficulty, especially since both her arms were occupied with a pachyderm of a purse. Still, he felt a little delicate, to say nothing of queasy, about knocking her down. It didn't seem quite the thing to do.

She was advancing, with admiration and fervor disgustingly clear in her eyes, and Graham felt the wall behind him. There was no doorway within armreach on either side.

'Oh, Mr de Meister – do, do please let me call you Mr de Meister. Your creation is so real to me, that I can't think of you as simply Graham Dorn. You don't mind, do you?'

'No, no, of course not,' gargled Graham, as well as he could through thirty-two teeth simultaneously set on edge. 'I often think of myself as Reginald in my more frivolous moments.'

'Thank you. You can have no idea, *dear* Mr de Meister, how I have looked *forward* to meeting you. I have read *all* your works, and I think they are wonderful.'

'I'm glad you think so.' He went automatically into the modesty routine. 'Really nothing, you know. Ha, ha, ha! Like to please the readers, but lots of room for improvement. Ha, ha, ha!'

'But you really are, you know.' This was said with intense earnestness. 'I mean good, *really* good. I think it is wonderful to be an author like you. It must be almost like being God.'

Graham stared blankly. 'Not to editors, sister.'

Sister didn't get the whisper. She continued, 'To be able to create living characters out of nothing; to unfold souls to all the world; to put thoughts into words; to build pictures and create worlds. I have often thought that an author was the most gloriously gifted person in creation. Better an inspired author starving in a garret than a king upon his throne. Don't you think so?'

'Definitely,' lied Graham.

'What are the crass material goods of the world to the wonders of weaving emotions and deeds into a little world of its own?'

'What, indeed?'

'And posterity, think of posterity!'

'Yes, yes. I often do.'

She seized his hand. 'There's only one little request. You might,' she blushed faintly, 'you might give poor Reginald – if you will allow me to call him that just once – a chance to marry Letitia Reynolds. You make her just a little too cruel to him. I'm sure I weep over it for hours together sometimes. But then he is too, too real to me.' And from somewhere, a lacy frill of handkerchief made its appearance, and went to her eyes. She removed it, smiled bravely, and scurried away. Graham Dorn inhaled, closed his eyes, and gently collapsed into June's arms.

His eyes opened with a jerk. 'You may consider,' he said severely, 'our engagement frazzled to the breaking point. Only my consideration for your poor, aged parents prevents your being known henceforward as the ex-fiancee of Graham Dorn.'

'Darling, you are so noble.' She massaged his sleeve with her cheek. 'Come, I'll take you home and bathe your poor wounds.'

'All right, but you'll have to carry me. Has your precious, loveable aunt got an axe?'

'But why?'

'For one thing, she had the gall to introduce me as the brain-father, God help me, of the famous Reginald de Meister.'

'And aren't you?'

'Let's get out of this creep-joint. And get this. I'm no relative by brain or otherwise, of that character. I disown him. I cast him into the darkness. I spit upon him. I declare him an illegitimate son, a foul degenerate, and the offspring of a hound, and I'll be damned if he ever pokes his lousy patrician nose into my typewriter again.'

They were in the taxi, and June straightened his tie. 'All right, Sonny, let's see the letter.'

'What letter?'

She held out her hand. 'The one from the publishers.'

Graham snarled and flipped it out of his jacket pocket. 'I've thought of inviting myself to his house for tea, the damned faintheart. He's got a rendezvous with a pinch of strychnine.'

'You may rave later. What does he say? Hmm – uh-huh – doesn't quite come up to what is expected— feel that de Meister isn't in his usual form— a little revision perhaps towards— feel sure the novel can be adjusted— are returning under separate cover—'

She tossed it aside. 'I told you you shouldn't have killed off Sancha Rodriguez. She was what you needed. You're getting skimpy on the love interest.'

'*You* write it! I'm through with de Meister. It's getting so clubwomen call me Mr de Meister, and my picture is printed in newspapers with the caption Mr de Meister. I have no individuality. No one ever heard of Graham Dorn. I'm always: Dorn, Dorn, you know, the guy who writes the de Meister stuff, *you* know.'

June squealed, 'Silly! You're jealous of your own detective.'

'I am not jealous of my own character. Listen! I hate detective stories. I never read them after I got into the two-syllable words. I wrote the first as a clever, trenchant, biting satire. It was to blast the entire false school of mystery writers. That's why I invented this de Meister. He was the detective to end all detectives. The Compleat Ass, by Graham Dorn.

'So the public, along with snakes, vipers, and ungrateful children takes this filth to its bosom. I wrote mystery after mystery trying to convert the public—'

Graham Dorn drooped a little at the futility of it all.

'Oh, well.' He smiled wanly, and the great soul rose above adversity. 'Don't you see? I've got to write other things. I can't waste my life. But who's going to read a serious novel by Graham Dorn, now that I'm so thoroughly identified with de Meister?'

'You can use a pseudonym.'

'I will not use a pseudonym. I'm proud of my name.'

'But you can't drop de Meister. Be sensible, dear.'

'A normal fiancee,' Graham said bitterly, 'would want her future husband to write something really worthwhile and become a great name in literature.'

'Well, I do want you to, Graham. But just a little de Meister once in a while to pay the bills that accumulate.'

'Ha!' Graham knocked his hat over his eyes to hide the sufferings of a strong spirit in agony. 'Now you say that I can't reach prominence unless I prostitute my art to that unmentionable. Here's your place. Get out. I'm going home and write a good scorching letter on asbestos to our senile Mr MacDunlap.'

'Do exactly as you want to, cookie,' soothed June. 'And tomorrow when you feel better, you'll come and cry on my shoulder, and we'll plan a revision of *Death on the Third Deck* together, shall we?'

'The engagement,' said Graham, loftily, 'is broken.'

'Yes, dear. I'll be home tomorrow at eight.'

'That is of no possible interest to me. Good-bye!'

Publishers and editors are untouchables, of course. Theirs is a heritage of the outstretched hand and the well-toothed smile; the nod of the head and the slap of the back.

But perhaps somewhere, in the privacy of the holes to which authors scurry when the night falls, a private revenge is taken. There, phrases may be uttered where no one can overhear, and letters may be written that need not be mailed, and perhaps a picture of an editor, smiling pensively, is enshrined above the typewriter to act the part of bulls-eye in an occasional game of darts.

Such a picture of MacDunlap, so used, enlightened Graham Dorn's room. And Graham Dorn himself, in his usual writing costume (streetclothes and typewriter), scowled at the fifth sheet of paper in his typewriter. The other four were draped over the edge of the wastebasket, condemned for their milk-and-watery mildness.

He began:

'Dear Sir—' and added slowly and viciously, 'or Madam, as the case may be.'

He typed furiously as the inspiration caught him, disregarding the faint wisp of smoke curling upward from the overheated keys:

'You say you don't think much of de Meister in this story. Well, I don't think much of de Meister, period. You can handcuff your slimy carcass to his and jump off the Brooklyn Bridge. And I hope they drain the East River just before you jump.

'From now on, my works will be aimed higher than your scurvy press. And the day will come when I can look back on this period of my career with the loathing that is its just—'

Someone had been tapping Graham on the shoulder during the last paragraph. Graham twitched it angrily and ineffectively at intervals.

Now he stopped, turned around, and addressed the stranger in his room courteously: 'Who the devilish damnation are you? And you can leave without bothering to answer. I won't think you rude.' The newcomer smiled graciously. His nod wafted the delicate aroma of some unobtrusive hair-oil toward Graham. His lean, hardbitten jaw stood out keenly, and he said in a well-modulated voice:

'De Meister is the name. Reginald de Meister.'

Graham rocked to his mental foundations and heard them creak. 'Glub,' he said.

'Pardon?'

Graham recovered. 'I said, "glub", a little code word meaning *which* de Meister.'

'*The* de Meister,' explained de Meister, kindly. 'My character? My detective?'

De Meister helped himself to a seat, and his finely-chiseled features assumed that air of well-bred boredom so admired in the best circles. He lit a Turkish cigarette, which Graham at once recognized as his detective's favorite brand, tapping it slowly and carefully against the back of his hand first, a mannerism equally characteristic. 'Really, old man,' said de Meister. 'This is really excruciatin'ly funny. I suppose I am your character, y'know, but let's not work on that basis. It would be so devastatin'ly awkward.'

'Glub,' said Graham again, by way of rejoinder.

His mind was feverishly setting up alternatives. He didn't drink, more, at the moment, was the pity, so he wasn't drunk. He had a chrome-steel digestion and he wasn't overheated, so it wasn't a hallucination. He never dreamed, and his imagination – as befitted a paying commodity – was under strict control. And since, like all authors, he was widely considered more than half a screwball, insanity was out of the question.

Which left de Meister simply an impossibility, and Graham felt relieved. It's a very poor author indeed who hasn't learned the fine art of ignoring impossibilities in writing a book.

He said smoothly, 'I have here a volume of my latest work. Do you mind naming your page and crawling back into it. I'm a busy man and God knows I have enough of you in the tripe I write.'

'But I'm here on business, old chap. I've got to come to a friendly arrangement with you first. Things are deucedly uncomfortable as they are.'

'Look, do you know you're bothering me? I'm not in the habit of talking to mythical characters. As a general thing, I don't pal around with them. Besides which, it's time your mother told you that you really don't exist.'

'My dear fellow, I always existed. Existence is such a subjective thing. What a mind thinks exists, *does* exist. I existed in your mind, for instance, ever since you first thought of me.'

Graham shuddered. 'But the question is, what are you doing *out* of my mind? Getting a little narrow for you? Want elbow room?'

'Not at all. Rather satisfact'ry mind in its way, but I achieved a more concrete existence only this afternoon, and so I seize the opportunity to engage you face to face in the aforementioned business conversation. You see, that thin, sentimental lady of your society—'

'What society?' questioned Graham hollowly. It was all awfully clear to him now.

'The one at which you made a speech' – de Meister shuddered in his turn – 'on the detective novel. She believed in my existence, so naturally, I exist.'

He finished his cigarette and flicked it out with a negligent twist of the wrist.

'The logic,' declared Graham, 'is inescapable. Now, what do you want and the answer is no.'

'Do you realize, old man, that if you stop writing de Meister stories, my existence will become that dull, wraithlike one of all superannuated fictional detectives. I'd have to gibber through the gray mists of Limbo with Holmes, Lecocq, and Dupin.'

'A very fascinating thought, I think. A very fitting fate.' Reginald de Meister's eyes turned icy, and Graham suddenly remembered the passage on page 123 of *The Case of the Broken Ashtray*:

His eyes, hitherto lazy and unattentive, hardened into twin pools of blue ice and transfixed the butler, who staggered back, a stifled cry on his lips.

Evidently, de Meister lost none of his characteristics out of the novels he adorned.

Graham staggered back, a stifled cry on his lip.

De Meister said menacingly, 'It would be better for you if the de Meister mysteries continue. Do you understand?'

Graham recovered and summoned a feeble indignation. 'Now, wait a while. You're getting out of hand. Remember: in a way, I'm your father. That's right. Your mental father. You can't hand me ultimatums or make threats. It isn't filial. It's lacking in the proper respect and love.'

'And another thing,' said de Meister, unmoved. 'We've got to straighten out this business of Letitia Reynolds. It's gettin' deucedly borin', y'know.'

'Now you're getting silly. My love scenes have been widely heralded as miracles of tenderness and sentiment not found in one murder mystery out of a thousand. – Wait, I'll get you a few reviews. I don't mind your attempts to dictate my actions so much, but I'm damned if you'll criticize my writing.'

'Forget the reviews. Tenderness and all that rot is what I don't want. I've been driftin' after the fair lady for five volumes now, and behavin' the most insufferable ass. This has got to stop.'

'In what way?'

'I've got to marry her in your present story. Either that, or make her a good, respectable mistress. And you'll have to stop making me so damned Victorian and gentlemanly towards ladies. I'm only human, old man.'

'Impossible!' said Graham, 'and that includes your last remark.'

De Meister grew severe. 'Really, old chap, for an author, you display the most appallin' lack of concern for the well-bein' of a character who has supported you for a good many years.'

Graham choked eloquently. 'Supported me? In other words, you think I couldn't sell real novels, hey? Well, I'll show you. I wouldn't write another de Meister story for a million dollars. Not even for a fifty percent royalty and all television rights. How's that?'

De Meister frowned and uttered those words that had been the sound of doom to so many criminals: 'We shall see, but you are not yet done with me.'

With firmly jutting jaw, he vanished.

Graham's twisted face straightened out, and slowly – very slowly – he brought his hands up to his cranium and felt carefully.

For the first time in a long and reasonably ribald mental life, he felt that his enemies were right and that a good dry cleaning would not hurt his mind at all.

The *things* that existed in it!

Graham Dorn shoved the doorbell with his elbow a second time. He distinctly remembered her saying she would be home at eight.

The peep-hole shoved open. 'Hello!'

'Hello!'

Silence!

Graham said plaintively, 'It's raining outside. Can't I come in to dry?'

'I don't know. Are we engaged, Mr Dorn?'

'If I'm not,' was the stiff reply, 'then I've been turning down the frenzied advances of a hundred passion-stricken girls – beautiful ones, all of them – for no apparent reason.'

'Yesterday, you said—'

'Ah, but who listens to what I say? I'm just quaint that way. Look, I brought you posies.' He flourished roses before the peep-hole.

June opened the door. 'Roses! How plebeian. Come in, cookie, and sully the sofa. Whoa, whoa, before you move a step, what have you got under the other arm? Not the manuscript of *Death on the Third Deck*?'

'Correct. Not that excrescence of a manuscript. This is something different.'

June's tone chilled. 'That isn't your precious novel, is it?'

Graham flung his head up, 'How did you know about it?'

'You slobbered the plot all over me at MacDunlap's silver anniversary party.'

'I did not. I couldn't unless I were drunk.'

'Oh; but you were. Stinking is the term. And on two cocktails too.'

'Well, if I was drunk, I couldn't have told you the right plot.'

'Is the setting a coal-mine district?'

'—Uh – yes.'

'And are the people concerned real, earthy, unartificial, downto-earth characters, speaking and thinking just like you and me? Is it a story of basic economic forces? Are the human characters lifted up and thrown down and whirled around, all at the mercy of the coal mine and mechanized industry of today?'

'—Uh – yes.'

She nodded her head retrospectively. 'I remember distinctly. First, you got drunk and were sick. Then you got better, and told me the first few chapters. Then I got sick.'

She approached the glowering author. 'Graham.' She leant her golden head upon his shoulder and cooed softly. 'Why don't you continue with the de Meister stories? You get such pretty checks out of them.'

Graham writhed out of her grasp. 'You are a mercenary wretch, incapable of understanding an author's soul. You may consider our engagement broken.'

He sat down hard on the sofa, and folded his arms. 'Unless you will consent to read the script of my novel and give me the usual story analysis.'

'May I give you my analysis of *Death on the Third Deck* first?'

'No.'

'Good! In the first place, your love interest is becoming sickening.'

'It is not.' Graham pointed his finger indignantly. 'It breathes a sweet and sentimental fragrance, as of an older day. I've got the review here that says it.' He fumbled in his wallet.

'Oh, bullfeathers. Are you going to start quoting that guy in the Pillsboro (Okla.) Clarion? He's probably your second cousin. You know that your last two novels were completely below par in royalties. And *Third Deck* isn't even being sold.'

'So much the better— Ow!' He rubbed his head violently. 'What did you do that for?'

'Because the only place I could hit as hard as I wanted to, without disabling you, was your head. Listen! The public is tired of your corny Letitia Reynolds. Why don't you let her soak her "gleaming golden crown of hair" in kerosene and get familiar with a match?'

'But June, that character is drawn from life. From you!'

'Graham Dorn! I am not here to listen to insults. The mystery market today is swinging towards action and hot, honest love and you're still in the sweet, sentimental stickiness of five years ago.'

'But that's Reginald de Meister's character.'

'Well, change his character. Listen! You introduce Sancha Rodriguez. That's fine. I approve of her. She's Mexican, flaming, passionate, sultry, and in love with him. So what do you do? First he behaves the impeccable gentleman, and then you kill her off in the middle of the story.'

'Hmm, I see— You really think it would improve things to have de Meister forget himself. A kiss or so—'

June clenched her lovely teeth and her lovely fists. 'Oh, darling, how glad I am love is blind! If it ever peeked one tiny little bit, I couldn't stand it. Look, you squirrels blue plate special, you're going to have de Meister and Rodriquez fall in love. They're going to have an affair through the entire book and you can put your horrible Letitia into a nunnery. She'd probably be happier there from the way you make her sound.'

'That's all *you* know about it, my sweet. It so happens that Reginald de Meister is in love with Letitia Reynolds and wants *her*, not this Roderiguez person.'

'And what makes you think that?'

'He told me so.'

'Who told you so?'

'Reginald de Meister.'

'What Reginald de Meister?'

'*My* Reginald de Meister.'

'What do you mean, your Reginald de Meister?'

'My *character*, Reginald de Meister.'

June got up, indulged in some deep-breathing and then said in a very calm voice, 'Let's start all over.'

She disappeared for a moment and returned with an aspirin. 'Your Reginald de Meister, from your books, told you, in person, he was in love with Letitia Reynolds?'

'That's right.'

June swallowed the aspirin.

'Well, I'll explain, June, the way he explained it to me. All characters really exist – at least, in the minds of the authors. But when people really begin to believe in them, they begin to exist in reality, because what people believe in, is, so far as they're concerned, and what is existence anyway?'

June's lips trembled. 'Oh, Gramie, please don't. Mother will never let me marry you if they put you in an asylum.'

'Don't call me Gramie, June, for God's sake. I tell you he was there, trying to tell me what to write and how to write it. He was almost as bad as you. Aw, come on, Baby, don't cry.'

'I can't help it. I always thought you were crazy, but I never thought you were *crazy*!'

'All right, what's the difference? Let's not talk about it, any more.

I'm never going to write another mystery novel. After all' – (he indulged in a bit of indignation) – 'when it gets so that my own character – my *own* character – tries to tell me what to do, it's going too far.'

June looked over her handkerchief. 'How do you know it was really de Meister?'

'Oh, golly. As soon as he tapped his Turkish cigarette on the back of his hand and started dropping g's like snowflakes in a blizzard, I knew the worst had come.'

The telephone rang. June leaped up. 'Don't answer, Graham. It's probably from the asylum. I'll tell them you're not here. Hello. Hello. Oh, Mr MacDunlap.' She heaved a sigh of relief, then covered the mouthpiece and whispered horasely, 'It might be a trap.'

'Hello, Mr MacDunlap! . . . No, he's not here . . . Yes, I think I can get in touch with him . . . At Martin's tomorrow, noon . . . I'll tell him . . . With who? . . . With who???' She hung up suddenly.

'Graham, you're to lunch with MacDunlap tomorrow.'

'At his expense! Only at his expense!'

Her great blue eyes got greater and bluer, 'And Reginald de Meister is to dine with you.'

'What Reginald de Meister?'

'Your Reginald de Meister.'

'*My* Reg—'

'Oh, Gramie, *don't*.' Her eyes misted, 'Don't you see, Gramie, now they'll put us both in an insane asylum – and Mr MacDunlap, too. And they'll probably put us all in the same padded cell. Oh, Gramie, three is such a dreadful crowd.'

And her face crumpled into tears.

Grew S. MacDunlap (that the S. stands for 'Some' is a vile untruth spread by his enemies) was alone at the table when Graham Dorn entered. Out of this fact, Graham extracted a few fleeting drops of pleasure.

It was not so much, you understand, the presence of MacDunlap that did it, as the absence of de Meister.

MacDunlap looked at him over his spectacles and swallowed a liver pill, his favorite sweetmeat.

'Aha. You're here. What is this corny joke you're putting over on me? You had no right to mix me up with a person like de Meister without warning me he was real. I might have taken precautions. I could have hired a bodyguard. I could have bought a revolver.'

'He's *not* real. God damn it! Half of him was *your* idea.

'That,' returned MacDunlap with heat, 'is libel. And what do you mean, he's not real? When he introduced himself, I took three liver pills at once and he didn't disappear. Do you know what three pills aie? Three pills, the kind I've got (the doctor should only drop dead), could make an elephant disappear – if he weren't real. I *know*.'

Graham said wearily, 'Just the same, he exists only in my mind.'

'In your mind, I know he exists. Your mind should be investigated by the Pure Food and Drugs Act.'

The several polite rejoinders that occurred simultaneously to Graham were dismissed almost immediately as containing too great a proportion of pithy Anglo-Saxon expletives. After all – ha, ha – a publisher is a publisher however Anglo-Saxony he may be.

Graham said, 'The question arises, then, how we're to get rid of de Meister.'

'Get rid of de Meister?' MacDunlap jerked the glasses off his nose in his sudden start, and caught them in one hand. His voice thickened with emotion. 'Who wants to get rid of him?'

'Do you want him around?'

'God forbid,' MacDunlap said between shudders. 'Next to him, my brother-in-law is an angel.'

'He has no business outside my books.'

'For my part, he has no business inside them. Since I started reading your manuscripts, my doctor added kidney pills and cough syrups to my medicines.' He looked at his watch, and took a kidney pill. 'My worst enemy should be a book publisher only a year.'

'Then why,' asked Graham patiently, 'don't you want to get rid of de Meister?'

'Because he is publicity.' Graham stared blankly.

'Look! What other writer has a real detective? All the others are fictional. Everyone knows that. But *yours* – *yours* is real. We can let him solve cases and have big newspaper writeups. He'll make the Police Department look silly. He'll make—'

'That,' interrupted Graham, categorically, 'is by all odds the most obscene proposal I have ever had my ears manured with.'

'It will make money.'

'Money isn't everything.'

'Name one thing it isn't . . . Shh!' He kicked a near-fracture into Graham's left ankle and rose to his feet with a convulsive smile, 'Mr de Meister!'

'Sorry, old dear,' came a lethargic voice. 'Couldn't quite make it, you know. Loads of engagements. Must have been most borin' for you.'

Graham Dorn's ears quivered spasmodically. He looked over his shoulder and reeled backward as far as a person could reel while in a sitting position. Reginald de Meister had sprouted a monocle since his last visitation, and his monocular glance was calculated to freeze blood.

De Meister's greeting was casual. 'My dear Watson! So glad to meet you. Overjoyed deucedly.'

'Why don't you go to hell?' Graham asked curiously.

'My dear fellow. Oh, my dear fellow.'

MacDunlap cackled, 'That's what I like. Jokes! Fun! Makes everything pleasant to start with. Now shall we get down to business?'

'Certainly. The dinner is on the way, I trust? Then I'll just order a bottle of wine. The usual, Henry.' The waiter ceased hovering, flew away, and skimmed back with a bottle that opened and gurgled into a glass.

De Meister sipped delicately, 'So nice of you, old chap, to make me a habitue of this place in your stories. It holds true even now, and it is most convenient. The waiters all know me. Mr MacDunlap, I take it you have convinced Mr Dorn of the necessity of continuing the de Meister stories.'

'Yes,' said MacDunlap.

'No,' said Graham.

'Don't mind him,' said MacDunlap. 'He's temperamental. You know these authors.'

'Don't mind him,' said Graham. 'He's microcephalic. You know these publishers.'

'Look, old chappie. I take it MacDunlap hasn't pointed out to you the unpleasanter side of acting stubborn.'

'For instance what, old stinkie?' asked Graham, courteously.

'Well, have you ever been haunted?'

'Like coming behind me and saying, Boo!'

'My dear fellow, I say. I'm much more subtle than that. I can really haunt one in modern, up-to-date methods. For instance, have you ever had your individuality submerged?'

He snickered.

There was something familiar about that snicker. Graham suddenly remembered. It was on page 103 of *Murder Rides the Range*:

His lazy eyelids flicked down and up. He laughed lightly and melodiously, and though he said not a word, Hank Marslowe cowered. There was hidden menace and hidden power in that light laugh, and somehow the burly rancher did not dare reach for his guns.

To Graham it still sounded like a nasty snicker, but he cowered, and did not dare reach for his guns.

MacDunlap plunged through the hole the momentary silence had created.

'You see, Graham. Why play around with ghosts? Ghosts aren't reasonable things. They're not *human*! If it's more royalties, you want—'

Graham fired up. 'Will you refrain from speaking of money? From now on, I write only great novels of tearing human emotions.'

MacDunlap's flushed face changed suddenly. 'No,' he said.

'In fact, to change the subject just a moment' – and Graham's tone became surpassingly sweet, as the words got all sticky with maple syrup – 'I have a manuscript here for you to look at.'

He grasped the perspiring MacDunlap by the lapel firmly. 'It is a novel that is the work of five years. A novel that will grip you with its intensity. A novel that will shake you to the core of your being. A novel that will open a new world. A novel that will—'

'No,' said MacDunlap.

'A novel that will blast the falseness of this world. A novel that pierces to the truth. A novel—'

MacDunlap, being able to stretch his hand no higher, took the manuscript. 'No,' he said.

'Why the bloody hell don't you read it?' inquired Graham.

'Now?'

'Well, start it.'

'Look, supposing I read it tomorrow, or even the next day. I have to take my cough syrup now.'

'You haven't coughed once since I got here.'

'I'll let you know immediately—'

'This,' said Graham, 'is the first page. Why don't you begin it? It will grip you instantly.'

MacDunlap read two paragraphs and said, 'Is this laid in a coal-mining town?'

'Yes.'

'Then I can't read it. I'm allergic to coal dust.'

'But it's not real coal dust, MacIdiot.'

'That,' pointed out MacDunlap, 'is what you said about de Meister.' Reginald de Meister tapped a cigarette carefully on the back of his hand in a subtle manner which Graham immediately recognized as betokening a sudden decision.

'That is all devastatin'ly borin', you know. Not quite gettin' to the point, you might say. Go ahead, MacDunlap, this is no time for half measures.'

MacDunlap girded his spiritual loins and said, 'All right Mister Dorn, with you it's no use being nice. Instead of de Meister, I'm getting coal dust. Instead of the best publicity in fifty years, I'm getting social significance. All right, Mister Smartaleck Dorn, if in one week you don't come to terms with me, *good* terms, you will be blacklisted in every reputable publishing firm in the United States and foreign parts.' He shook his finger and added in a shout, 'Including Scandinavian.'

Graham Dorn laughed lightly, 'Pish,' he said, 'tush. I happen to be an officer of the Author's Union, and if you try to push me around I'll have *you* blacklisted. How do you like that?'

'I like it fine. Because supposing I can prove you're a plagiarist.'

'Me,' gasped Graham, recovering narrowly from merry suffocation. 'Me, the most original writer of the decade.'

'Is that so? And maybe you don't remember that in each case you write up, you casually mention de Meister's notebooks on previous cases.'

'So what?'

'So he has them. Reginald, my boy, show Mister Dorn your notebook of your last case. – You see that. That's *Mystery of the Milestones* and it has, in detail, every incident in your book – and dated the year before the book was published. Very authentic.'

'Again so what?'

'Have you maybe got the right to copy his notebook and call it an original murder mystery?'

'Why, you case of mental poliomyelitis, that notebook is my invention.'

'Who says so? It's in de Meister's handwriting, as any expert can prove. And maybe you have a piece of paper, some little contract or agreement, you know, that gives you the right to use his notebooks?'

'How can I have an agreement with a mythical personage?'

'What mythical personage?'

'You and I know de Meister doesn't exist.'

'Ah, but does the jury know? When I testify that I took three strong liver pills and he didn't disappear, what twelve men will say he doesn't exist?'

'This is blackmail.'

'Certainly. I'll give you a week. Or in other words, seven days.'

Graham Dorn turned desperately to de Meister. 'You're in on this, too. In my books I give you the keenest sense of honor. Is this honorable?'

Meister shrugged. 'My dear fellow. All this – and haunting, too.'

Graham rose.

'Where are you going?'

'Home to write you a letter.' Graham's brows beetled defiantly. 'And this time I'll mail it. I'm not giving in. I'll fight to the last ditch. And, de Meister, you let loose with one single little haunt and I'll rip your head out of its socket and spurt the blood all over MacDunlap's new suit.'

He stalked out, and as he disappeared through the door, de Meister disappeared through nothing at all.

MacDunlap let out a soft yelp and then took a liver pill, a kidney pill, and a tablespoon of cough syrup in rapid succession.

Graham Dorn sat in June's front parlor, and having long since consumed his fingernails, was starting on the first knucldes.

June, at the moment, was not present, and this, Graham felt, was just as well. A dear girl; in fact, a dear, sweet girl. But his mind was not on her.

It was concerned instead with a miasmic series of flashbacks over the preceding six days:

—Say, Graham, I met your side-kick at the club yesterday. You know, de Meister. Got an awful shock. I always had the idea he was a sort of Sherlock Holmes that didn't exist. That's one on me, boy. Didn't know – Hey, where are you going?

—Hey, Dorn, I hear your boss de Meister is back in town. Ought to have material for more stories soon. You're lucky you've got someone to grind out your plots ready-made— Huh? Well, goodbye.'

—Why, Graham, darling, wherever were you last night? Ann's affair didn't get *anywhere* without you; or at least, it wouldn't have, if it hadn't been for Reggie de Meister. He asked after you; but then, I guess he felt lost without his Watson. It must feel wonderful to Watson for such— *Mister* Dorn! And the same to you, sir!

—You put one over on me. I thought you made up those wild things. Well, truth is stranger than fiction, ha, ha!

—Police officials deny that the famous amateur criminologist Reginald de Meister has interested himself in this case. Mr de Meister himself could not be reached by our reporters for comment. Mr de Meister is best known to the public for his brilliant solutions to over a dozen crimes, as chronicled in fiction form by his so-called 'Watson', Mr Grayle Doone.

Graham quivered and his arms trembled in an awful desire for blood. De Meister was haunting him – but good. He was losing his individuality, exactly as had been threatened.

It gradually dawned upon Graham that the monotonous ringing noise he heard was not in his head, but, on the contrary, from the front door.

Such seemed likewise the opinion of Miss June Billings, whose piercing call shot down the stairs and biffed Graham a sharp uppercut to the ear-drums.

'Hey, dope, see who's at the front door, before the vibration tears the house down. I'll be down in half an hour.'

'Yes, dear!'

Graham shuffled his way to the front door and opened it. 'Ah, there. Greetin's,' said de Meister, and brushed past.

Graham's dull eyes stared, and then fired high, as an animal snarl burst from his lips. He took up that gorilla posture, so comforting to red-blooded American males at moments like this, and circled the slightly-confused detective.

'My dear fellow, are you ill?'

'I,' explained Graham, 'am not ill, but you will soon be past all interest in that, for I am going to bathe my hands in your heart's reddest blood.'

'But I say, you'll only have to wash them afterwards. It would be such an obvious clue, wouldn't it?'

'Enough of this gay banter. Have you any last words?'

'Not particularly.'

'It's just as well. I'm not interested in your last words.'

He thundered into action, bearing down upon the unfortunate de Meister like a bull elephant. De Meister faded to the left, shot out an arm and a foot, and Graham described a parabolic arc that ended in the total destruction of an end table, a vase of flowers, a fish-bowl, and a five-foot section of wall.

Graham blinked, and brushed away a curious goldfish from his left eyebrow.

'My dear fellow,' murmured de Meister, 'oh, my dear fellow.' Too late, Graham remembered that passage in *Pistol Parade*:

De Meister's arms were whipcord lightning, as with sure, rapid thrusts, he rendered the two thugs helpless. Not by brute force, but by his expert knowledge of judo, he defeated them easily without hastening his breath. The thugs groaned in pain.

Graham groaned in pain.

He lifted his right thigh an inch or so to let his femur slip back into place.

'Hadn't you better get up, old chap?'

'I will stay here,' said Graham with dignity, 'and contemplate the floor in profile view, until such time as it suits me or until such time as I find myself capable of moving a muscle. I don't care which. And now, before I proceed to take further measures with you, what the hell do you want?'

Reginald de Meister adjusted his monocle to a nicety. 'You know, I suppose, that MacDunlap's ultimatum expires tomorrow?'

'And you and he with it, I trust.'

'You will not reconsider.'

'Ha!'

'Really,' de Meister sighed, 'this is borin' no end. You have made things comfortable for me in this world. After all, in your books you've made me well-known in all the clubs and better restaurants, the bosom friend, y'know, of the mayor and commissioner of police, the owner of a Park Avenue penthouse and a magnificent art collection. And it all lingers over, old chap. Really quite affectin'.'

'It is remarkable,' mused Graham, 'the intensity with which I am not listening and the distinctness with which I do not hear a word you say.'

'Still,' said de Meister, 'there is no denyin' my book world suits me better. It is somehow more fascinatin', freer from dull logic, more apart from the necessities of the world. In short, I must go back, and to active participation. You have till tomorrow!'

Graham hummed a gay little tune with flat little notes. 'Is this a new threat, de Meister?'

'It is the old threat intensified. I'm going to rob you of every vestige of your personality. And eventually public opinion will force you to write as, to paraphrase you, de Meister's Compleat Stooge. Did you see the name the newspaper chappies pinned on you today, old man?'

'Yes, Mr Filthy de Meister, and did you read a half-column item on page ten in the same paper. I'll read it *for* you: "Noted Criminologist in 1-A. Will be inducted shortly draft board says."'

For a moment, de Meister said and did nothing. And then one, after another, he did the following things: removed his monocle slowly, sat down heavily, rubbed his chin abstractedly, and lit a cigarette after long and careful tamping. Each of these, Graham Dorn's trained authorial eye recognized as singly representing perturbation and distress on the part of his character.

And never, in any of his books, did Graham remember a time when de Meister had gone through all four consecutively.

Finally, de Meister spoke. 'Why you had to bring up draft registrations in your last book, I really don't know. This urge to be topical; this fiendish desire to be up to the minute with the news is the curse of the mystery novel. A true mystery is timeless; should have no relation to current events; should—'

'There is one way,' said Graham, 'to escape induction—'

'You might at least have mentioned a deferred classification on some vital ground.'

'There is one way,' said Graham, 'to escape induction—'

'Criminal negligence,' said de Meister.

'Look! Go back to the books and you'll never be filled with lead.'

'Write them and I'll do it.'

'Think of the war.'

'Think of your ego.'

Two strong men stood face to face (or would have, if Graham weren't still horizontal) and neither flinched.

Impasse!

And the sweet, feminine voice of June Billings interrupted and snapped the tension:

'May I ask, Graham Dorn, what you are doing on the floor. It's been swept today and you're not complimenting me by attempting to improve the job.'

'I am not sweeping the floor. If you looked carefully,' replied Graham gently, 'you would see that your own adored fiance is lying here a mass of bruises and a hotbed of pains and aches.'

'You've ruined my end table!'

'I've broken my leg.'

'And my best lamp.'

'And two ribs.'

'And my fishbowl.'

'And my Adam's apple.'

'And you haven't introduced your friend.'

'And my cervical verte— What friend?'

'This friend.'

'Friend! Ha!' And a mist came over his eyes. She was so young, so fragile to come into contact with hard, brutal facts of life. 'This,' he muttered brokenly, 'is Reginald de Meister.'

De Meister at this point broke a cigarette sharply in two, a gesture pregnant with the deepest emotion.

June said slowly, 'Why – why, you're different from what I had thought.'

'How had you expected me to look?' asked de Meister, in soft, thrilling tones.

'I don't know. Differently than you do – from the stories I heard.'

'You remind me, somehow, Miss Billings, of Letitia Reynolds.'

'I think so. Graham said he drew her from me.'

'A very poor imitation, Miss Billings. Devastatin'ly poor.'

They were six inches apart now, eyes fixed with a mutual glue, and Graham yelled sharply. He sprang upright as memory smote him a nasty smite on the forehead.

A passage from *Case of the Muddy Overshoe* occurred to him. Likewise one from *The Primrose Murders*. Also one from *The Tragedy of Hartley Manor, Death of a Hunter, White Scorpion* and, to put it in a small nutshell, from every one of the others.

The passage read:

There was a certain fascination about de Meister that appealed irresistibly to women.

And June Billings was – as it had often, in Graham's idler moments, occurred to him – a woman.

And fascination simply gooed out of her ears and coated the floor six inches deep.

'Get out of this room, June,' he ordered.

'I will not.'

'There is something I must discuss with Mr de Meister, man to man. I demand that you leave this room.'

'Please go, Miss Billings,' said de Meister.

June hesitated, and in a very small voice said, 'Very well.'

'Hold on,' shouted Graham. 'Don't let him order you about. I demand that you stay.'

She closed the door very gently behind her.

The two men faced each other. There was that in either pair of eyes that indicated a strong man brought to bay. There was stubborn, undying antagonism; no quarter; no compromise. It was exactly the sort of situation Graham Dorn always presented his readers with, when two strong men fought for one hand, one heart, one girl.

The two said simultaneously, 'Let's make a deal!'

Graham said, 'You have convinced me, Reggie. Our public needs us. Tomorrow I shall begin another de Meister story. Let us shake hands and forget the past.'

De Meister struggled with his emotion. He laid his hand on Graham's lapel, 'My dear fellow, it is I who have been convinced by your logic. I can't allow you to sacrifice yourself for me. There are great things in you that must be brought out. Write your coal-mining novels. They count, not I.'

'I couldn't, old chap. Not after all you've done for me, and all you've meant to me. Tomorrow we start anew.'

'Graham, my – my spiritual father, I couldn't allow it. Do you think I have no feelings, *filial* feelings – in a spiritual sort of way.'

'But the war, think of the war. Mangled limbs. Blood. All that.'

'I must stay. My country needs me.'

'But if I stop writing, eventually you will stop existing. I can't allow that.'

'Oh, that!' De Meister laughed with a careless elegance. 'Things have changed since. So many people believe in my existence now that my grip upon actual existence has become too firm to be broken. I don't have to worry about Limbo any more.'

'Oh.' Graham clenched his teeth and spoke in searing sibilants: 'So that's your scheme, you snake. Do you suppose I don't see you're stuck on June?'

'Look here, old chap,' said de Meister haughtily. 'I can't permit you to speak slightingly of a true and honest love. I love June and she loves me – I know it. And if you're going to be stuffy and Victorian about it, you can swallow some nitro-glycerine and tap yourself with a hammer.'

'I'll nitro-glycerine you! Because I'm going home tonight and beginning another de Meister story. You'll be part of it and you'll get back into it, and what do you think of that?'

'Nothing, because you can't write another de Meister story. I'm too real now, and you can't control me just like *that*. And what do you think of that?'

It took Graham Dorn a week to make up his mind what to think of that, and then his thoughts were completely and startlingly unprintable.

In fact, it was impossible to write.

That is, startling ideas occurred to him for great novels, emotional dramas, epic poems, brilliant essays-but he couldn't write anything about Reginald de Meister.

The typewriter was simply fresh out of Capital R's.

Graham wept, cursed, tore his hair, and anointed his finger tips with liniment. He tried typewriter, pen, pencil, crayon, charcoal, and blood.

He could not write.

The doorbell rang, and Graham threw it open.

MacDunlap stumbled in, falling over the first drifts of torn paper directly into Graham's arms.

Graham let him drop. 'Hah!' he said, with frozen dignity.

'My heart!' said MacDunlap, and fumbled for his liver pills.

'Don't die there,' suggested Graham, courteously. 'The management won't permit me to drop human flesh into the incinerator.'

'Graham, my boy,' MacDunlap said, emotionally, 'no more ultimatums! No more threats! I come now to appeal to your finer feelings, Graham' – he went through a slight choking interlude – 'I love you like a son. This skunk de Meister must disappear. You must write more de Meister stories for my sake. Graham – I will tell you something in private. My wife is in love with this detective. She tells me I am not romantic. I! Not romantic! Can you understand it?'

'I can,' was the tragic response. 'He fascinates all women.'

'With that face? With that monocle?'

'It says so in all my books.'

MacDunlap stiffened. 'Ah ha. You again. Dope! If only you ever stopped long enough to let your mind know what your typewriter was saying.'

'You insisted. Feminine trade.' Graham didn't care any more. Women! He snickered bitterly. Nothing wrong with any of them that a block-buster wouldn't fix.

MacDunlap hemmed. 'Well, feminine trade. Very necessary. —But Graham, what shall I do? It's not only my wife. She owns fifty shares in MacDunlap, Inc. in her own name. If she leaves me, I lose control. Think of it, Graham. The catastrophe to the publishing world.'

'Grew, old chap,' Graham sighed a sigh so deep, his toenails quivered sympathetically. 'I might as well tell you. June, my fiancee, you know, loves this worm. And he loves her because she is the prototype of Letitia Reynolds.'

'The what of Letitia?' asked MacDunlap, vaguely suspecting an insult.

'Never mind. My life is ruined.' He smiled bravely and choked back the unmanly tears, after the first two had dripped off the end of his nose.

'My poor boy!' The two gripped hands convulsively.

'Caught in a vise by this foul monster,' said Graham.

'Trapped like a German in Russia,' said MacDunlap.

'Victim of an inhuman fiend,' said Graham.

'Exactly,' said MacDunlap. He wrung Graham's hand as if he were milking a cow. 'You've got to write de Meister stories and get him back where, next to Hell, he most belongs. Right?'

'Right! But there's one little catch.'

'What?'

'I can't write. He's *so* real now, I *can't* put him into a book.'

MacDunlap caught the significance of the massed drifts of used paper on the floor. He held his head and groaned, 'My corporation! My wife!'

'There's always the Army,' said Graham.

MacDunlap looked up. 'What about *Death on the Third Deck*, the novel I rejected three weeks ago?'

'That doesn't count. It's past history. It's already affected him.'

'Without being published?'

'Sure. That's the story I mentioned his draft board in. The one that put him in 1-A.'

'I could think of better places to put him.'

'MacDunlap!' Graham Dorn jumped up, and grappled MacDunlap's lapel. 'Maybe it can be revised.'

MacDunlap coughed hackingly, and stifled out a dim grunt.

'We can put anything we want into it.'

MacDunlap choked a bit.

'We can fix things up.'

MacDunlap turned blue in the face.

Graham shook the lapel and everything thereto attached, 'Say something, won't you?'

MacDunlap wrenched away and took a tablespoon of cough syrup. He held his hand over his heart and patted it a bit. He shook his head and gestured with his eyebrows.

Graham shrugged. 'Well, if you just want to be sullen, go ahead. I'll revise it without you.'

He located the manuscript and tried his fingers gingerly on the typewriter. They went smoothly, with practically no creaking at the joints. He put on speed, more speed, and then went into his usual race, with the portable jouncing along merrily under the accustomed head of steam.

'It's working,' he shouted. 'I can't write new stories, but I can revise old, unpublished ones.'

MacDunlap watched over his shoulder. He breathed only at odd moments.

'Faster,' said MacDunlap, 'faster!'

'Faster than thixty-five?' said Graham, sternly. 'OPA forbid! Five more minutes.'

'Will he be there?'

'He's always there. He's been at her house every evening this week.' He spat out the fine ivory dust into which he had ground the last inch of his incisors. 'But God help you if your secretary falls down on the job.'

'My boy, on my secretary you can depend.'

'She's got to read that revision by nine.'

'If she doesn't drop dead.'

'With my luck, she will. Will she believe it?'

'Every word. She's seen de Meister. She *knows* he exists.'

Brakes screeched, and Graham's soul cringed in sympathy with every molecule of rubber frictioned off the tires.

He bounded up the stairs, MacDunlap hobbling after.

He rang the bell and burst in at the door. Reginald de Meister standing directly inside received the full impact of a pointing finger, and only a rapid backward movement of the head kept him from becoming a one-eyed mythical character.

June Billings stood aside, silent and uncomfortable.

'Reginald de Meister,' growled Graham, in sinister tones, 'prepare to meet your doom.'

'Oh, boy,' said MacDunlap, 'are you going to get it.'

'And to what,' asked de Meister, 'am I indebted for your dramatic but unilluminatin' statement? Confusin', don't you know.' He lit a cigarette with a fine gesture and smiled.

'Hello, Gramie,' said June, tearfully.

'Scram, vile woman.'

June sniffed. She felt like a heroine out of a book, torn by her own emotions. Naturally, she was having the time of her life. So she let the tears dribble and looked forlorn.

'To return to the subject, what is this all about?' asked de Meister, wearily.

'I have rewritten *Death on the Third Deck*.'

'Well?'

'The revision,' continued Graham, 'is at present in the hands of MacDunlap's secretary, a girl on the style of Miss Billings, my fiancee. The Office of Price Administration was in charge of gasoline rationing at this period. Remember "A" stickers? D.R.B. that was. That is, she is a girl who aspires to the status of a moron, but has not yet quite attained it. She'll believe every word.'

'Well?'

Graham's voice grew ominous, 'You remember, perhaps, Sancha Rodriguez?'

For the first time, Reginald de Meister shuddered. He caught his cigarette as it dropped. 'She was killed by Sam Blake in the sixth chapter. She was in love with me. Really, old fellow, what messes you get me into.'

'Not half the mess you're in now, old chap. Sancha Rodriguez did *not* die in the revision.'

'Die!' came a sharp, but clear female voice, 'I'll show him if I died. And where have *you* been this last month, you two-crosser?' De Meister did not catch his cigarette this time. He didn't even try. He recognized the apparition. To an unprejudiced observer, it might have been merely a svelte Latin girl equipped with dark, flashing eyes, and long, glittering fingernails, but to de Meister, it was Sancha Rodriguez – *undead!*

MacDunlap's secretary had read and believed.

'Miss Rodriguez,' throbbed de Meister, charmingly, 'how fascinatin' to see you.'

'Mrs de Meister to you, you double-timer, you two-crosser, you scum of the ground, you scorpion of the grass. And who is this woman?'

June retreated with dignity behind the nearest chair.

'*Mrs* de Meister,' said Reginald pleadingly, and turned helplessly to Graham Dorn.

'Oh, you have forgotten, have you, you smooth talker, you low dog. I'll show you what it means to deceive a weak woman. I'll make you mince-meat with my fingernails.'

De Meister back-pedaled furiously. 'But darling—'

'Don't you make sweet talk. What are you doing with this woman?'

'But, darling—'

'Don't give me any explanation. What are you doing with this woman?'

'But darling—'

'Shut up! What are you doing with this woman?'

Reginald de Meister was up in a corner, and Mrs de Meister shook her fists at him. 'Answer me!'

De Meister disappeared.

Mrs de Meister disappeared right after him. June Billings collapsed into real tears.

Graham Dorn folded his arms and looked sternly at her. MacDunlap rubbed his hands and took a kidney pill.

'It wasn't my fault, Gramie,' said June. 'You said in your books he fascinated all women, so I couldn't help it. Deep inside, I hated him all along. You believe me, don't you?'

'A likely story!' said Graham, sitting down next to her on the sofa. 'A likely story. But I forgive you, maybe.'

MacDunlap said tremulously, 'My boy, you have saved my stocks. Also, my wife, of course. And remember – you promised me one de Meister story each year.'

Graham gritted, 'Just one, and I'll henpeck him to death, and keep one unpublished story forever on hand, just in case. And you're publishing my novel, aren't you, Grew, old boy?'

'Glug,' said MacDunlap.

'Aren't you?'

'Yes, Graham. Of course, Graham. Definitely, Graham. Positively, Graham.'

'Then leave us now. There are matters of importance I must discuss with my fiancee.'

MacDunlap smiled and tiptoed out the door.

Ah, love, love, he mused, as he took a liver pill and followed it up by a cough-syrup chaser.

The Proper Study

'The demonstration is ready,' said Oscar Harding softly, half to himself, when the phone rang to say that the general was on his way upstairs.

Ben Fife, Harding's young associate, pushed his fists deep into the pockets of his laboratory jacket. 'We won't get anywhere,' he said. 'The general doesn't change his mind.' He looked sideways at the older man's sharp profile, his pinched cheeks, his thinning gray hair. Harding might be a wizard with electronic equipment, but he couldn't seem to grasp the kind of man the general was.

And Harding said mildly, 'Oh, you can never tell.'

The general knocked once on the door, but it was for show only. He walked in quickly, without waiting for a response. Two soldiers took up their position in the corridor, one on each side of the door. They faced outward, rifles ready.

General Gruenwald said crisply, 'Professor Harding!' He nodded briefly in Fife's direction and then, for a moment, studied the remaining individual in the room. That was a blank-faced man who sat apart in a straight-backed chair, half-obscured by surrounding equipment.

Everything about the general was crisp; his walk, the way he held his spine, the way he spoke. He was all straight lines and angles, adhering rigidly at all points to the etiquette of the born soldier.

'Won't you sit down, General,' murmured Harding. 'Thank you. It's good of you to come; I've been trying to see you for some time. I appreciate the fact you're a busy man.'

'Since I am busy,' said the general, 'let us get to the point.'

'As near the point as I can, sir. I assume you know about our project here. You know about the Neurophotoscope.'

'Your top-secret project? Of course. My scientific aides keep me abreast of it as best they can. I won't object to some further clarification. What is it you want?'

The suddenness of the question made Harding blink. Then he said, 'To be brief – declassification. I want the world to know that—'

'Why do you want them to know anything?'

'Neurophotoscopy is an important problem, sir, and enormously complex. I would like all scientists of all nationalities working on it.'

'No, no. That's been gone over many times. The discovery is ours and we keep it.'

'It will remain a very small discovery if it remains ours. Let me explain once more.'

The general looked at his watch. 'It will be quite useless.'

'I have a new subject. A new demonstration. As long as you've come here at all, General, won't you listen for just a little while? I'll omit scientific detail as much as possible and say only that the varying electric potentials of brain cells can be recorded as tiny, irregular waves.'

'Electroencephalograms. Yes, I know. We've had them for a century. And I know what you do with it.'

'Uh – yes.' Harding grew more earnest. 'The brain waves by themselves carry their information too compactly. They give us the whole complex of changes from a hundred billion brain cells at once. My discovery was of a practical method for converting them to colored patterns.'

'With your Neurophotoscope,' said the general, pointing. 'You see, I recognize the machine.' Every campaign ribbon and medal on his chest lay in its proper place to within the millimeter.

'Yes. The 'scope produces color effects, real images that seem to fill the air and change very rapidly. They can be photographed and they're beautiful.'

'I have seen photographs,' the general said coldly.

'Have you seen the real thing, in action?'

'Once or twice. You were there at the time.'

'Oh, yes.' The professor was disconcerted. He said, 'But you haven't seen this man; our new subject.' He pointed briefly to the man in the chair, a man with a sharp chin, a long nose, no sign of hair on his skull, and still that vacant look in his eye.

'Who is he?' asked the general.

'The only name we use for him is Steve. He is mentally retarded but produces the most intense patterns we have yet found. Why this should be we don't know. Whether it has something to do with his mental—'

'Do you intend to show me what he does?' broke in the general.

'If you will watch, General.' Harding nodded at Fife, who went into action at once.

The subject, as always, watched Fife with mild interest, doing as he was told and making no resistance. The light plastic helmet fitted snugly over his shaved cranium and each of the complicated electrodes was adjusted properly. Fife tried to work smoothly under the unusual tension of the occasion. He was in agony lest the general look at his watch again, and leave.

He stepped away, panting. 'Shall I activate it now, Professor Harding?'

'Yes. Now.'

Fife closed a contact gently and at once the air above Steve's head seemed filled with brightening color. Circles appeared and circles within circles, turning, whirling, and splitting apart.

Fife felt a clear sensation of uneasiness but pushed it away impatiently. That was the subject's emotion – Steve's – not his own. The general must have felt it too, for he shifted in his chair and cleared his throat loudly.

Harding said casually, 'The patterns contain no more information than the brain waves, really, but are much more easily studied and analyzed. It is like putting germs under a strong microscope. Nothing new is added, but what is there can be seen more easily.'

Steve was growing steadily more uneasy. Fife could sense it was the harsh and unsympathetic presence of the general that was the cause. Although Steve did not change his position or give any outward sign of fear, the colors in the patterns his mind created grew harsher, and within the outer circles there were clashing interlocks.

The general raised his hand as though to push the flickering lights away. He said, 'What about all this, Professor?'

'With Steve, we can jump ahead even faster than we have been. Already we have learned more in the two years since I devised the first 'scope than in the fifty years before that. With Steve, and with others like him, perhaps, and with the help of the scientists of the world—'

'I have been told you can use this to reach minds,' said the general sharply.

'Reach minds?' Harding thought a moment. 'You mean telepathy? That's quite exaggerated. Minds are too different for that. The fine details of your way of thinking are not like mine or like anyone else's, and raw brain patterns won't match. We have to translate thoughts into words, a much cruder form of communication, and even then it is hard enough for human beings to make contact.'

'I don't mean telepathy! I mean emotion! If the subject feels anger, the receiver can be made to experience anger. Right?'

'In a manner of speaking.'

The general was clearly agitated. 'Those things – right there—'

His finger jabbed toward the patterns, which were whirling most unpleasantly now. 'They can be used for emotion control. With these, broadcast on television, whole populations can be emotionally manipulated. Can we allow such power to fall into the wrong hands?'

'If it were such power,' said Harding mildly, 'there would be no right hands.'

Fife frowned. That was a dangerous remark. Every once in a while Harding seemed to forget that the old days of democracy were gone.

But the general let it go. He said, 'I didn't know you had this thing so far advanced. I didn't know you had this – Steve. You get others like that. Meanwhile, the army is taking this over. *Completely!*'

'Wait, General, just ten seconds.' Harding turned to Fife. 'Give Steve his book, will you, Ben?'

Fife did so with alacrity. The book was one of the new Kaleido-volumes that told their stories by means of colored photographs that slowly twisted and changed once the book was opened. It was a kind of animated cartoon in hard-covers and Steve smiled as he reached out eagerly for it.

Almost at once the colored patterns that clustered above his plastic helmet changed in nature. They slowed their turning and the colors softened. The patterns within the circle grew less discordant.

Fife sighed his relief and let warmth and relaxation sweep over him.

Harding said, 'General, don't let the possibility of emotion control alarm you. The 'scope offers less possibility for that than you think. Surely there are men whose emotions can be manipulated, but the 'scope isn't necessary for them. They react mindlessly to catch words, music, uniforms, almost anything. Hitler once controlled Germany without even television, and Napoleon controlled France without even radio or mass-circulation newspapers. The 'scope offers nothing new.'

'I don't believe that,' muttered the general, but he had grown thoughtful again.

Steve stared earnestly at the Kaleido-volume, and the patterns over his head had almost stilled into warmly colored and intricately detailed circles that pulsed their pleasure.

Harding's voice was almost coaxing. 'There are always the people who resist conformity; who don't go along; and they are the important ones of society. They won't go along with colored patterns any more than with any other form of persuasion. So why worry about the useless bogey of emotion control? Let us instead see the Neurophotoscope as the first instrument through which mental function can be truly analyzed. That's what should concern us above all. The proper study of mankind is man, as Alexander Pope once said, and what is man but his brain?'

The general remained silent.

'If we can solve the manner of the brain's workings,' went on Harding, 'and learn at last what makes a man a man, we are on our way to understanding ourselves, and nothing more difficult – or more worthwhile – faces us. And how can this be done by just one man, by one laboratory? How can it be done in secrecy and fear? The whole world of science must cooperate. – General, declassify the project! Throw it open to all men!'

Slowly the general nodded. 'I think you're right after all.'

'I have the proper document. If you'll sign it and key it with your fingerprint; if you use your two guards outside as witnesses; if you alert the Executive Board by closed video; if you—'

It was all done. Before Fife's astonished eyes it was all done.

When the general was gone, the Neurophotoscope dismantled, and Steve taken back to his quarters, Fife finally overcame his amazement long enough to speak.

'How could he have been persuaded so easily, Professor Harding? You've explained your point of view at length in a dozen reports and it never helped a bit.'

'I've never presented it in this room, with the Neurophotoscope working,' said Harding. 'I've never had anyone as intensely projective as Steve before. Many people can withstand emotion control, as I said, but some people cannot withstand it. Those who have a tendency to conform are easily led to agree with others. I took the gamble that any man who feels comfortable in uniform and who lives by the military book is liable to be swayed, no matter how powerful he imagines himself to be.'

'You mean – Steve—'

'Of course, I let the general feel the uneasiness first, then you handed Steve the Kaleido-volume and the air filled with happiness. You felt it, didn't you?'

'Yes. Certainly.'

'It was my guess the general couldn't resist that happiness so suddenly following the unease, and he didn't. Anything would have sounded good at that moment.'

'But he'll get over it, won't he?'

'Eventually, I suppose, but so what? The key progress reports concerning Neurophotoscopy are being sent out right now to news media all over the world. The general might suppress it here in this country, but surely not elsewhere. – No, he will have to make the best of it. Mankind can begin its proper study in earnest, at last.'

Waterclap

Stephen Demerest looked at the textured sky. He kept looking at it and found the blue opaque and revolting.

Unwarily, he had looked at the Sun, for there was nothing to blank it out automatically, and then he had snatched his eyes away in panic. He wasn't blinded; just a few afterimages. Even the Sun was washed out.

Involuntarily, he thought of Ajax's prayer in Homer's *Iliad*. They were fighting over the body of Patroclus in the mist and Ajax said, 'O Father Zeus, save the Achaeans out of this mist! Make the sky clear, grant us to see with our eyes! Kill us in the light, since it is thy pleasure to kill us!'

Demerest thought: Kill us in the light –

Kill us in the clear light on the Moon, where the sky is black and soft, where the stars shine brightly, where the cleanliness and purity of vacuum make all things sharp.

– Not in this low-clinging, fuzzy blue.

He shuddered. It was an actual physical shudder that shook his lanky body, and he was annoyed. He was going to die. He was sure of it. And it wouldn't be under the blue, either, come to think of it, but under the black – but a different black.

It was as though in answer to that thought that the ferry pilot, short, swarthy, crisp-haired, came up to him and said, 'Ready for the black, Mr Demerest?'

Demerest nodded. He towered over the other as he did over most of the men of Earth. They were thick, all of them, and took their short, low steps with ease. He himself had to feel his footsteps, guide them through the air; even the impalpable bond that held him to the ground was textured.

'I'm ready,' he said. He took a deep breath and deliberately repeated his earlier glance at the Sun. It was low in the morning sky, washed out by dusty air, and he knew it wouldn't blind him. He didn't think he would ever see it again.

He had never seen a bathyscaphe before. Despite everything, he tended to think of it in terms of prototypes, an oblong balloon with a spherical gondola beneath. It was as though he persisted in thinking of space flight in terms of tons of fuel spewed backward in fire, and an irregular module feeling its way, spiderlike, toward the Lunar surface.

The bathyscaphe was not like the image in his thoughts at all. Under its skin, it might still be buoyant bag and gondola, but it was all engineered sleekness now.

'My name is Javan,' said the ferry pilot. 'Omar Javan.'

'Javan?'

'Queer name to you? I'm Iranian by descent; Earthman by persuasion. Once you get down there, there are no nationalities.' He grinned and his complexion grew darker against the even whiteness of his teeth. 'If you don't mind, we'll be starting in a minute. You'll be my only passenger, so I guess you carry weight.'

'Yes,' said Demerest dryly. 'At least a hundred pounds more than I'm used to.'

'You're from the Moon? I thought you had a queer walk on you. I hope it's not uncomfortable.'

'It's not exactly comfortable, but I manage. We exercise for this.'

'Well, come on board.' He stood aside and let Demerest walk down the gangplank. 'I wouldn't go to the Moon myself.'

'You go to Ocean-Deep.'

'About fifty times so far. That's different.'

Demerest got on board. It was cramped, but he didn't mind that. It might be a space module except that it was more – well, textured. There was that word again. There was the clear feeling everywhere that mass didn't matter. Mass was held up; it didn't have to be hurled up.

They were still on the surface. The blue sky could be seen greenishly through the clear thick glass. Javan said, 'You don't have to be strapped in. There's no acceleration. Smooth as oil, the whole thing. It won't take long; just about an hour. You can't smoke.'

'I don't smoke,' said Demerest.

'I hope you don't have claustrophobia.'

'Moon-men don't have claustrophobia.'

'All that open—'

'Not in our cavern. We live in a' – he groped for the phrase – 'a Lunar-Deep, a hundred feet deep.'

'A hundred feet!' The pilot seemed amused, but he didn't smile. 'We're slipping down now.'

The interior of the gondola was fitted into angles but here and there a section of wall beyond the instruments showed its basic sphericity. To Javan, the instruments seemed to be an extension of his arms; his eyes and hands moved over them lightly, almost lovingly.

'We're all checked out,' he said, 'but I like a last-minute lookover; we'll be facing a thousand atmospheres down there.' His finger touched a contact, and the round door closed massively inward and pressed against the beveled rim it met.

'The higher the pressure, the tighter that will hold,' said Javan. 'Take your last look at sunlight, Mr Demerest.'

The light still shone through the thick glass of the window. It was wavering now; there was water between the Sun and them now.

'The last look?' said Demerest.

Javan snickered. 'Not the *last* look. I mean for the trip. I suppose you've never been on a bathyscaphe before.'

'No, I haven't. Have many?'

'Very few,' admitted Javan. 'But don't worry. It's just an underwater balloon. We've introduced a million improvements since the first bathyscaphe. It's nuclear-powered now and we can move freely by water jet up to certain limits, but cut it down to basics and it's still a spherical gondola under buoyancy tanks. And it's still towed out to sea by a mother ship because it needs what power it carries too badly to waste it on surface travel. Ready?'

'Ready.'

The supporting cable of the mother ship flicked away and the bathyscaphe settled lower; then lower still, as sea water fed into the buoyancy tanks. For a few moments, caught in surface currents, it swayed, and then there was nothing. The bathyscaphe sank slowly through a deepening green.

Javan relaxed. He said, 'John Bergen is head of Ocean-Deep. You're going to see him?'

'That's right.'

'He's a nice guy. His wife's with him.'

'She is?'

'Oh, sure. They have women down there. There's a bunch down there, fifty people. Some stay for months.'

Demerest put his finger on the narrow, nearly invisible seam where door met wall. He took it away and looked at it. He said, 'It's oily.'

'Silicone, really. The pressure squeezes some out. It's supposed to . . . Don't worry. Everything's automatic. Everything's fail-safe. The first sign of malfunction, any malfunction at all, our ballast is released and up we go.'

'You mean nothing's ever happened to these bathyscaphes?'

'What can happen?' The pilot looked sideways at his passenger. 'Once you get too deep for sperm whales, nothing can go wrong.'

'Sperm whales?' Demerest's thin face creased in a frown.

'Sure, they dive as deep as half a mile. If they hit a bathyscaphe – well, the walls of the buoyancy chambers aren't particularly strong. They don't have to be, you know. They're open to the sea and when the gasoline, which supplies the buoyancy, compresses, sea water enters.'

It was dark now. Demerest found his gaze fastened to the viewport. It was light inside the gondola, but it was dark in that window. And it was not the darkness of space; it was a thick darkness.

Demerest said sharply, 'Let's get this straight, Mr Javan. You are not equipped to withstand the attack of a sperm whale. Presumably you are not equipped to withstand the attack of a giant squid. Have there been any actual incidents of that sort?'

'Well, it's like this—'

'No games, please, and don't try ragging the greenhorn. I am asking out of professional curiosity. I am head safety engineer at Luna City and I am asking what precautions this bathyscaphe can take against possible collision with large creatures.'

Javan looked embarrassed. He muttered, 'Actually, there have been no incidents.'

'Are any expected? Even as a remote possibility?'

'Anything is remotely possible. But actually sperm whales are too intelligent to monkey with us and giant squid are too shy.'

'Can they see us?'

'Yes, of course. We're lit up.'

'Do you have floodlights?'

'We're already past the large-animal range, but we have them, and I'll turn them on for you.'

Through the black of the window there suddenly appeared a snowstorm, an inverted upward-falling snowstorm. The blackness had come alive with stars in three-dimensional array and all moving upward.

Demerest said, 'What's that?'

'Just crud. Organic matter. Small creatures. They float, don't move much, and they catch the light. We're going down past them. They seem to be going up in consequence.'

Demerest's sense of perspective adjusted itself and he said, 'Aren't we dropping too quickly?'

'No, we're not. If we were, I could use the nuclear engines, if I wanted to waste power; or I could drop some ballast. I'll be doing that later, but for now everything is fine. Relax, Mr Demerest. The snow thins as we dive and we're not likely to see much in the way of spectacular life forms. There are small angler fish and such but they avoid us.'

Demerest said, 'How many do you take down at a time?'

'I've had as many as four passengers in this gondola, but that's crowded. We can put two bathyscaphes in tandem and carry ten, but that's clumsy. What we really need are trains of gondolas, heavier on the nukes – the nuclear engines – and lighter on the buoyancy. Stuff like that is on the drawing board, they tell me. Of course, they've been telling me that for years.'

'There are plans for large-scale expansion of Ocean-Deep, then?'

'Sure, why not? We've got cities on the continental shelves, why not on the deep-sea bottom? They way I look at it, Mr Demerest, where man can go, he will go and he should go. The Earth is ours to populate and we will populate it. All we need to make the deep sea habitable are completely maneuverable 'scaphes. The buoyancy chambers slow us, weaken us, and complicate the engineering.'

'But they also save you, don't they? If everything goes wrong at once, the gasoline you carry will still float you to the surface. What would do that for you if your nuclear engines go wrong and you had no buoyancy?'

'If it comes to that, you can't expect to eliminate the chances of accident altogether, not even fatal ones.'

'I know that very well,' said Demerest feelingly.

Javan stiffened. The tone of his voice changed. 'Sorry. Didn't mean anything by that. Tough about that accident.'

'Yes,' said Demerest. Fifteen men and five women had died. One of the individuals listed among the 'men' had been fourteen years old. It had been pinned down to human failure. What could a head safety engineer say after that?

'Yes,' he said.

A pall dropped between the two men, a pall as thick and as turgid as the pressurized sea water outside. How could one allow for panic and for distraction and for depression all at once? There were the Moon-Blues – stupid name – but they struck men at inconvenient times. It wasn't always noticeable when the Moon-Blues came but it made men torpid and slow to react.

How many times had a meteorite come along and been averted or smothered or successfully absorbed? How many times had a Moonquake done damage and been held in check? How many times had human failure been backed up and compensated for? How many times had accidents *not* happened?

But you don't pay off on accidents not happening. There were twenty dead—

Javan said (how many long minutes later?), 'There are the lights of Ocean-Deep!'

Demerest could not make them out at first. He didn't know where to look. Twice before, luminescent creatures had flicked past the windows at a distance and with the floodlights off again, Demerest had thought them the first sign of Ocean-Deep. Now he saw nothing.

'Down there,' said Javan, without pointing. He was busy now slowing the drop and edging the 'scaphe sideways.

Demerest could hear the distant sighing of the water jets, steamdriven, with the steam formed by the heat of momentary bursts of fusion power.

Demerest thought dimly: Deuterium is their fuel and it's all around them. Water is their exhaust and it's all around them.

Javan was dropping some of his ballast, too, and began a kind of distant chatter. 'The ballast used to be steel pellets and they were dropped by electromagnetic controls. Anywhere up to fifty tons of it were used in each trip. Conservationists worried about spreading rusting steel over the ocean floor, so we switched to metal nodules that are dredged up from the continental shelf. We put a thin layer of iron over them so they can still be electromagnetically handled and the ocean bottom gets nothing that wasn't sub-ocean to begin with. Cheaper, too . . . But when we get our real nuclear 'scaphes, we won't need ballast at all.'

Dernerest scarcely heard him. Ocean-Deep could be seen now. Javan had turned on his floodlights and far below was the muddy floor of the Puerto Rican Trench. Resting on that floor like a cluster of equally muddy pearls was the spherical conglomerate of Ocean-Deep.

Each unit was a sphere such as the one in which Dernerest was now sinking toward contact, but much larger, and as Ocean-Deep expanded-expanded-expanded, new spheres were added.

Dernerest thought: They're only five and a half miles from home, not a quarter of a million.

'How are we going to get through?' asked Demerest.

The 'scaphe had made contact. Demerest heard the dull sound of metal against metal but then for minutes there had been nothing more than a kind of occasional scrape as Javan bent over his instruments in rapt concentration.

'Don't worry about that,' Javan said at last, in belated answer. 'There's no problem. The delay now is only because I have to make sure we fit tightly. There's an electromagnetic joint that holds at every point of a perfect circle. When the instruments read correctly, that means we fit over the entrance door.'

'Which then opens?'

'It would if there were air on the other side, but there isn't. There's sea water, and that has to be driven out. *Then* we enter.'

Demerest did not miss this point. He had come here on this, the last day of his life, to give that same life meaning and he intended to miss nothing.

He said, 'Why the added step? Why not keep the air lock, if that's what it is, a real air lock, and have air in it at all times.'

'They tell me it's a matter of safety,' said Javan. '*Your* specialty. The interface has equal pressure on both sides at all times, *except* when men are moving across. This door is the weakest point of the whole system, because it opens and closes; it has joints; it has seams. You know what I mean?'

'I do,' murmured Demerest. There was a logical flaw here and that meant there was a possible chink through which – but later.

He said, 'Why are we waiting now?'

'The lock is being emptied. The water is being forced out.'

'By air.'

'Hell, no. They can't afford to waste air like that. It would take a thousand atmospheres to empty the chamber of its water, and filling the chamber with air at that density, even temporarily, is more air than they can afford to expend. Steam is what does it.'

'Of course. Yes.'

Javan said cheerfully, 'You heat the water. No pressure in the world can stop water from turning to steam at a temperature of more than 374° C. And the steam forces the sea water out through a one-way valve.'

'Another weak point,' said Demerest.

'I suppose so. It's never failed yet. The water in the lock is being pushed out now. When hot steam starts bubbling out the valve, the process automatically stops and the lock is full of overheated steam.'

'And then?'

'And then we have a whole ocean to cool it with. The temperature drops and the steam condenses. Once that happens, ordinary air can be let in at a pressure of one atmosphere and *then* the door opens.'

'How long must we wait?'

'Not long. If there were anything wrong, there'd be sirens sounding. At least, so they say. I never heard one in action.'

There was silence for a few minutes, and then there was a sudden sharp clap and a simultaneous jerk.

Javan said, 'Sorry, I should have warned you. I'm so used to it I forgot. When the door opens, a thousand atmospheres of pressure on the other side forces us hard against the metal of Ocean-Deep. No electromagnetic force can hold us hard enough to prevent that last hundredth-of-an-inch slam.'

Demerest unclenched his fist and released his breath. He said, 'Is everything all right?'

'The walls didn't crack, if that's what you mean. It sounds like doom, though, doesn't it? It sounds even worse when I've got to leave and the air lock fills up again. Be prepared for that.'

But Demerest was suddenly weary. Let's get on with it, he thought. I don't want to drag it out. He said, 'Do we go through now?'

'We go through.'

The opening in the 'scaphe wall was round and small; even smaller than the one through which they had originally entered. Javan went through it sinuously, muttering that it always made him feel like a cork in a bottle.

Demerest had not smiled since he entered the 'scaphe. Nor did he really smile now, but a corner of his mouth quirked as he thought that a skinny Moon-man would have no trouble.

He went through also, feeling Javan's hands firmly at his waist, helping him through.

Javan said, 'It's dark in here. No point in introducing an additional weakness by wiring for lighting. But that's why flashlights were invented.'

Demerest found himself on a perforated walk, its stainless metallic surface gleaming dully. And through the perforations he could make out the wavering surface of water.

He said, 'The chamber hasn't been emptied.'

'You can't do any better, Mr Demerest. If you're going to use steam to empty it, you're left with that steam, and to get the pressures necessary to do the emptying that steam must be compressed to about one-third the density of liquid water. When it condenses, the chamber remains one-third full of water – but it's water at just one-atmosphere pressure . . . Come on, Mr Demerest.'

John Bergen's face wasn't entirely unknown to Demerest. Recognition was immediate. Bergen, as head of Ocean-Deep for nearly a decade now, was a familiar face on the TV screens of Earth – just as the leaders of Luna City had become familiar.

Demerest had seen the head of Ocean-Deep both flat and in three dimensions, in black-and-white and in color. Seeing him in life added little.

Like Javan, Bergen was short and thickset; opposite in structure to the traditional (already traditional?) Lunar pattern of physiology. He was fairer than Javan by a good deal and his face was noticeably asymmetrical, with his somewhat thick nose leaning just a little to the right.

He was not handsome. No Moon-man would think he was, but then Bergen smiled and there was a sunniness about it as he held out his large hand.

Demerest placed his own thin one within, steeling himself for a hard grip, but it did not come. Bergen took the hand and let it go, then said, 'I'm glad you're here. We don't have much in the way of luxury, nothing that will make our hospitality stand out, we can't even declare a holiday in your honor – but the spirit is there. Welcome!'

'Thank you,' said Demerest softly. He remained unsmiling now, too. He was facing the enemy and he knew it. Surely Bergen must know it also and, since he did, that smile of his was hypocrisy.

And at that moment a clang like metal against metal sounded deafeningly and the chamber shuddered. Demerest leaped back and staggered against the wall.

Bergen did not budge. He said quietly, 'That was the bathyscaphe unhitching and the waterclap of the air lock filling. Javan ought to have warned you.'

Demerest panted and tried to make his racing heart slow. He said, 'Javan did warn me. I was caught by surprise anyway.'

Bergen said, 'Well, it won't happen again for a while. We don't often have visitors, you know. We're not equipped for it and so we fight off all kinds of big wheels who think a trip down here would be good for their careers. Politicians of all kinds, chiefly. Your own case is different of course.'

Is it? thought Demerest. It had been hard enough to get permission to make the trip down. His superiors back at Luna City had not approved in the first place and had scouted the idea that a diplomatic interchange would be of any use. ('Diplomatic interchange' was what they had called it.) And when he had overborne them, there had been Ocean-Deep's own reluctance to receive him.

It had been sheer persistence alone that had made his present visit possible. In what way then was Demerest's case different?

Bergen said, 'I suppose you have your junketing problems on Luna City, too?'

'Very little,' said Demerest. 'Your average politician isn't as anxious to travel a half-million-mile round trip as he is to travel a ten-mile one.'

'I can see that,' agreed Bergen, 'and it's more expensive out to the Moon, of course . . . In a way, this is the first meeting of inner and outer space. No Ocean-man has ever gone to the Moon as far *as* I know and you're the first Moon-man to visit a sub-sea station of any kind. No Moon-man has even been to one of the settlements on the continental shelf.'

'It's a historic meeting, then,' said Demerest, and tried to keep the sarcasm out of his voice.

If any leaked through, Bergen showed no sign. He rolled up his sleeves as though to emphasize his attitude of informality (or the fact that they were very busy, so that there would be little time for visitors?) and said, 'Do you want coffee? I assume you've eaten. Would you like to rest before I show you around? Do you want to wash up, for that matter, as they say euphemistically?'

For a moment, curiosity stirred in Demerest; yet not entirely aimless curiosity. Everything involving the interface of Ocean-Deep with the outside world could be of importance. He said, 'How are sanitary facilities handled here?'

'It's cycled mostly; as it is on the Moon, I imagine. We can eject if we want to or have to. Man has a bad record of fouling the environment, but as the only deep-sea station, what we eject does no perceptible damage. Adds organic matter.' He laughed.

Demerest filed that away, too. Matter was ejected; there were therefore ejection tubes. Their workings might be of interest and he, as a safety engineer, had a right to be interested.

'No,' he said, 'I don't need anything at the moment. If you're busy—'

'That's all, right. We're always busy, but I'm the least busy, if you see what I mean. Suppose I show you around. We've got over fifty units here, each as big as this one, some bigger—'

Demerest looked about. Again, as in the 'scaphe, there were angles everywhere, but beyond the furnishings and equipment there were signs of the inevitable spherical outer wall. Fifty of them!

'Built up,' went on Bergen, 'over a generation of effort. The unit we're standing in is actually the oldest and there's been some talk of demolishing and replacing it. Some of the men say we're ready for second-generation units, but I'm not sure. It would be expensive – everything's expensive down here – and getting money out of the Planetary Project Council is always a depressing experience.'

Demerest felt his nostrils flare involuntarily and a spasm of anger shot through him. It was a thrust, surely. Luna City's miserable record with the PPC must be well known to Bergen.

But Bergen went on, unnoticing. 'I'm a traditionalist, too – just a little bit. This is the first deep-sea unit ever constructed. The first two people to remain overnight on the floor of an ocean trench slept here with nothing else beyond this bare sphere except for a miserable portable fusion unit to work the escape hatch. I mean the air lock, but we called it the escape hatch to begin with – and just enough controls for the purpose. Reguera and Tremont, those were the men. They never made a second trip to the bottom, either; stayed Topside forever after. Well, well, they served their purpose and both are dead now. And here we are with fifty people and with six months as the usual tour of duty. I've spent only two weeks Topside in the last year and a half.'

He motioned vigorously to Demerest to follow him, slid open a door which moved evenly into a recess, and took him into the next unit. Demerest paused to examine the opening. There were no seams that he could notice between the adjacent units.

Bergen noted the other's pause and said, 'When we add on our units, they're welded under pressure into the equivalent of a single piece of metal and then reinforced. We can't take chances, as I'm sure you understand, since I have been given to understand that you're the head safe—'

Demerest cut him off. 'Yes,' he said. 'We on the Moon admire your safety record.'

Bergen shrugged. 'We've been lucky. Our sympathy, by the way, on the rotten break you fellows had. I mean that fatal—'

Demerest cut him off again. 'Yes.'

Bergen, the Moon-man decided, was either a naturally voluble man or else was eager to drown him in words and get rid of him.

'The units,' said Bergen, 'are arranged in a highly branched chain – three-dimensional actually. We have a map we can show you, if you're interested. Most of the end units represent living-sleeping quarters. For privacy, you know. The working units tend to be corridors as well, which is one of the embarrassments of having to live down here.

'This is our library; part of it, anyway. Not big, but it's got our records, too, on carefully indexed and computed microfilm, so that for its kind it's not only the biggest in the world, but the best and the only. And we have a special computer designed to handle the references to meet our needs exactly. It collects, selects, coordinates, weighs, then gives us the gist.

'We have another library, too, book films and even some printed volumes. But that's for amusement.'

A voice broke in on Bergen's cheerful flow. 'John? May I interrupt?'

Demerest started; the voice had come from behind him. Bergen said, 'Annette! I was going to get you. This is Stephen Demerest of Luna City. Mr Demerest, may I introduce my wife, Annette?'

Demerest had turned. He said stiffly, a little mechanically, 'I'm pleased to meet you, Mrs Bergen.' But he was staring at her waist-line.

Annette Bergen seemed in her early thirties. Her brown hair was combed simply and she wore no makeup. Attractive, not beautiful, Demerest noted vaguely. But his eyes kept returning to that waistline.

She shrugged a little. 'Yes, I'm pregnant, Mr Demerest. I'm due in about two months.'

'Pardon me,' Demerest muttered. 'So rude of me . . . I didn't—'

He faded off and felt as though the blow had been a physical one. He hadn't expected women, though he didn't know why. He *knew* there would have to be women in Ocean-Deep. And the ferry pilot had said Bergen's wife was with him.

He stammered as he spoke. 'How many women are there in Ocean-Deep, Mr Bergen?'

'Nine at the moment,' said Bergen. 'All wives. We look forward to a time when we can have the normal ratio of one to one, but we still need workers and researchers primarily, and unless women have important qualifications of *some* sort—'

'They all have important qualifications of *some* sort, dear,' said Mrs Bergen. 'You could keep the men for longer duty if—'

'My wife,' said Bergen, laughing, 'is a convinced feminist but is not above using sex as an excuse to enforce equality. I keep telling her that that is the feminine way of doing it and not the feminist way, and she keeps saying – Well, that's why she's pregnant. You think it's love, sex mania, yearning for motherhood? Nothing of the sort. She's going to have a baby down here to make a philosophical point.'

Annette said coolly, 'Why not? Either this is going to be home for humanity or it isn't going to be. If it *is*, then we're going to have babies here, that's all. I want a baby born in Ocean-Deep. There are babies born in Luna City, aren't there, Mr Demerest?'

Demerest took a deep breath. 'I was born in Luna City, Mrs Bergen.'

'And well she knew it,' muttered Bergen.

'And you are in your late twenties, I think?' she said.

'I am twenty-nine,' said Demerest.

'And well she knew that, too,' said Bergen with a short laugh. 'You can bet she looked up all possible data on you when she heard you were coming.'

'That is quite beside the point,' said Annette. 'The point is that for twenty-nine years at least children have been born in Luna City and no children have been born in Ocean-Deep.'

'Luna City, my dear,' said Bergen, 'is longer-established. It is over half a century old; we are not yet twenty.'

'Twenty years is quite enough. It takes a baby nine months.'

Demerest interposed, 'Are there any children in Ocean-Deep?'

'No,' said Bergen. 'No. Someday, though.'

'In two months, anyway,' said Annette Bergen positively.

The tension grew inside Demerest and when they returned to the unit in which he had first met Bergen, he was glad to sit down and accept a cup of coffee.

'We'll eat soon,' said Bergen matter-of-factly. 'I hope you don't mind sitting here meanwhile. As the prime unit, it isn't used for much except, of course, for the reception of vessels, an item I don't expect will interrupt us for a while. We can talk, if you wish.'

'I *do* wish,' said Demerest.

'I hope I'm welcome to join in,' said Annette.

Demerest looked at her doubtfully, but Bergen said to him, 'You'll have to agree. She's fascinated by you and by Moon-men generally. She thinks they're – uh – *you're* a new breed, and I think that when she's quite through being a Deep-woman she wants to be **a** Moon-woman.'

'I just want to get a word in edgewise, John, and when I get that in, I'd like to hear what Mr Demerest has to say. What do you think of us, Mr Demerest?'

Demerest said cautiously, 'I've asked to come here, Mrs Bergen, because I'm a safety engineer. Ocean-Deep has an enviable safety record—'

'Not one fatality in almost twenty years,' said Bergen cheerfully. 'Only one death by accident in the C-shelf settlements and none in transit by either sub or 'scaphe. I wish I could say, though, that this was the result of wisdom and care on our part. We do our best, of course, but the breaks have been with us—'

'John,' said Annette, 'I really wish you'd let Mr Demerest speak.'

'As a safety engineer,' said Demerest, 'I can't afford to believe in luck and breaks. We cannot stop Moon-quakes or large meteorites out at Luna City, but we are designed to minimize the effects even of those. There are no excuses or there should be none for human failure. We have not avoided that on Luna City; our record recently has been' – his voice dropped – 'bad. While humans are imperfect, as we all know, machinery should be designed to take that imperfection into account. We lost twenty men and women—'

'I know. Still, Luna City has a population of nearly one thousand, doesn't it? Your survival isn't in danger.'

'The people on Luna City number nine hundred and seventy-two, including myself, but our survival *is* in danger. We depend on Earth for essentials. That need not always be so; it wouldn't be so right now if the Planetary Project Council could resist the temptation toward pygmy economies—'

'There, at least, Mr Demerest,' said Bergen, 'we see eye to eye. We are not self-supporting either, and we could be. What's more, we can't grow much beyond our present level unless nuclear 'scaphes are built. As long as we keep that buoyancy principle, we are limited. Transportation between Deep and Top is slow; slow for men; slower still for materiel and supplies. I've been pushing, Mr Demerest, for—'

'Yes, and you'll be getting it now, Mr Bergen, won't you?'

'I hope so, but what makes you so sure?'

'Mr Bergen, let's not play around. You know very well that Earth is committed to spending a fixed amount of money on expansion projects – on programs designed to expand the human habitat – and that it is not a terribly large amount. Earth's population is not going to lavish resources in an effort to expand either outer space or inner space if it thinks this will cut into the comfort and convenience of Earth's prime habitat, the land surface of the planet.'

Annette broke in. 'You make it sound callous of Earthmen, Mr Demerest, and that's unfair. It's only human, isn't it, to want to be secure? Earth is overpopulated and it is only slowly reversing the havoc inflicted on the planet by the Mad Twentieth. Surely man's original home must come first, ahead of either Luna City or Ocean-Deep. Heavens, Ocean-Deep is almost *home* to me, but I can't want to see it flourish at the expense of Earth's land.'

'It's not an either-or, Mrs Bergen,' said Demerest earnestly. 'If the ocean and outer space are firmly, honestly, and intelligently exploited, it can only redound to Earth's benefit. A small investment will be lost but a large one will redeem itself with profit.'

Bergen held up his hand. 'Yes, I know. You don't have to argue with me on that point. You'd be trying to convert the converted. Come, let's eat. I tell you what. We'll eat here. If you'll stay with us overnight, or several days for that matter – you're quite welcome – there will be ample time to meet everybody. Perhaps you'd rather take it easy for a while, though.'

'Much rather,' said Demerest. 'Actually, I want to stay here . . . I would like to ask, by the way, why I met so few people when we went through the units.'

'No mystery,' said Bergen genially. 'At any given time, some fifteen of our men are asleep and perhaps fifteen more are watching films or playing chess or, if their wives are with them—'

'Yes, John,' said Annette.

' – And it's customary not to disturb them. The quarters are constricted and what privacy a man can have is cherished. A few are out at sea; three right now, I think. That leaves a dozen or so at work in here and you met them.'

'I'll get lunch,' said Annette, rising.

She smiled and stepped through the door, which closed automatically behind her.

Bergen looked after her. 'That's a concession. She's playing woman for your sake. Ordinarily, it would be just as likely for me to get the lunch. The choice is not defined by sex but by the striking of random lightning.'

Demerest said, 'The doors between units, it seems to me, are of dangerously limited strength.'

'Are they?'

'If an accident happened, and one unit was punctured—'

'No meteorites down here,' said Bergen, smiling.

'Oh yes, wrong word. If there were a leak of any sort, for any reason, then could a unit or a group of units be sealed off against the full pressure of the ocean?'

'You mean, in the way that Luna City can have its component units automatically sealed off in case of meteorite puncture in order to limit damage to a single unit.'

'Yes,' said Demerest with a faint bitterness. 'As did *not* happen recently.'

'In theory, we could do that, but the chances of accident are much less down here. As I said, there are no meteorites and, what's more, there are no currents to speak of. Even an earthquake centered immediately below us would not be damaging since we make no fixed or solid contact with the ground beneath and are cushioned by the ocean itself against the shocks. So we can afford to gamble on no massive influx.'

'Yet if one happened?'

'Then we could be helpless. You see, it is not so easy to seal off component units here. On the Moon, there is a pressure differential of just one atmosphere; one atmosphere inside and the zero atmosphere of vacuum outside. A thin seal is enough. Here at Ocean-Deep the pressure differential is roughly a thousand atmospheres. To secure absolute safety against that differential would take a great deal of money and you know what you said about getting money out of PPC. So we gamble and so far we've been lucky.'

'And we haven't,' said Demerest.

Bergen looked uncomfortable, but Annette distracted both by coming in with lunch at this moment.

She said, 'I hope, Mr Demerest, that you're prepared for Spartan fare. All our food in Ocean-Deep is prepackaged and requires only heating. We specialize in blandness and non-surprise here, and the non-surprise of the day is a bland chicken à la king, with carrots, boiled potatoes, a piece of something that looks like a brownie for dessert, and, of course, all the coffee you can drink.'

Demerest rose to take his tray and tried to smile. 'It sounds very like Moon fare, Mrs Bergen, and I was brought up on that. We grow our own micro-organismic food. It is patriotic to eat that but not particularly enjoyable. We hope to keep improving it, though.'

'I'm sure you *will* improve it.'

Demerest said, as he ate with a slow and methodical chewing, 'I hate to ride my specialty, but how secure are you against mishaps in your air-lock entry?'

'It *is* the weakest point of Ocean-Deep,' said Bergen. He had finished eating, well ahead of the other two, and was half through with his first cup of coffee. 'But there's got to be an interface, right? The entry is as automatic as we can make it and as fail-safe. Number one: there has to be contact at every point about the outer lock before the fusion generator begins to heat the water within the lock.

'What's more, the contact has to be metallic and of a metal with just the magnetic permeability we use on our 'scaphes. Presumably a rock or some mythical deep-sea monster might drop down and make contact at just the right places; but if so, nothing happens.

'Then, too, the outer door doesn't open until the steam has pushed the water out and then condensed; in other words, not till both pressure and temperature have dropped below a certain point. At the moment the outer door begins to open, a relatively slight increase in internal pressure, as by water entry, will close it again.'

Demerest said, 'But then, once men have passed through the lock, the inner door closes behind them and sea water must be allowed into the lock again. Can you do that gradually against the full pressure of the ocean outside?'

'Not very.' Bergen smiled. 'It doesn't pay to fight the ocean too hard. You have to roll with the punch. We slow it down to about one-tenth free entry but even so it comes in like a rifle shot – louder, a thunderclap, or waterclap, if you prefer. The inner door can hold it, though, and it is not subjected to the strain very often. Well, wait, you heard the waterclap when we first met, when Javan's 'scaphe took off again. Remember?'

'I remember,' said Demerest. 'But here is something I don't understand. You keep the lock filled with ocean at high pressure at all times to keep the outer door without strain. But that keeps the inner door at full strain. Somewhere there has to be strain.'

'Yes, indeed. But if the outer door, with a thousand-atmosphere differential on its two sides, breaks down, the full ocean in all its millions of cubic miles tries to enter and that would be the end of all. If the inner door is the one under strain and it gives, then it will be messy indeed, but the only water that enters Ocean-Deep will be the very limited quantity in the lock and its pressure will drop at once. We will have plenty of time for repair, for the outer door will certainly hold a long time.'

'But if both go simultaneously—'

'Then we are through.' Bergen shrugged. 'I need not tell you that neither absolute certainty nor absolute safety exists. You have to live with some risk and the chance of double and simultaneous failure is so microscopically small that it can be lived with easily.'

'If all your mechanical contrivances fail—'

'They fail safe,' said Bergen stubbornly.

Demerest nodded. He finished the last of his chicken. Mrs Bergen was already beginning to clean up. 'You'll pardon my questions, Mr Bergen, I hope.'

'You're welcome to ask. I wasn't informed, actually, as to the precise nature of your mission here. "Fact finding" is a weasel phrase. However, I assume there is keen distress on the Moon over the recent disaster and as safety engineer you rightly feel the responsibility of correcting whatever shortcomings exist and would be interested in learning, if possible, from the system used in Ocean-Deep.'

'Exactly. But, see here, if all your automatic contrivances fail safe for some reason, for any reason, you would be alive, but all your escape-hatch mechanisms would be sealed permanently shut. You would be trapped inside Ocean-Deep and would exchange a slow death for a fast one.'

'It's not likely to happen but we'd *hope* we could make repairs before our air supply gave out. Besides we *do* have a manual backup system.'

'Oh?'

'Certainly. When Ocean-Deep was first established and this was the only unit – the one we're sitting in now – manual controls were all we had. *That* was unsafe, if you like. There they are, right behind you – covered with friable plastic.'

'In emergency, break glass,' muttered Demerest, inspecting the covered setup.

'Pardon me?'

'Just a phrase commonly used in ancient fire-fighting systems . . . Well, do the manuals still work, or has the system been covered with your friable plastic for twenty years to the point where it has all decayed into uselessness with no one noticing?'

'Not at all. It's periodically checked, as all our equipment is. That's not my job personally, but I know it is done. If any electrical or electronic circuit is out of its normal working condition, lights flash, signals sound, everything happens but a nuclear blast . . . You know, Mr Demerest, we are as curious about Luna City as you are about Ocean-Deep. I presume you would be willing to invite one of our young men—'

'How about a young woman?' interposed Annette at once.

'I am sure you mean yourself, dear,' said Bergen, 'to which I can only answer that you are determined to have a baby here and to keep it here for a period of time after birth, and that effectively eliminates you from consideration.'

Demerest said stiffly, 'We hope you will send men to Luna City. We are anxious to have you understand our problems.'

'Yes, a mutual exchange of problems and of weeping on each other's shoulders might be of great comfort to all. For instance, you have one advantage on Luna City that I wish we could have. With low gravity and a low pressure differential, you can make your caverns take on any irregular and angular fashion that appeals to your aesthetic sense or is required for convenience. Down here we're restricted to the sphere, at least for the foreseeable future, and our designers develop a hatred for the spherical that surpasses belief. Actually it isn't funny. It breaks them down. They eventually resign rather than continue to work spherically.'

Bergen shook his head and leaned his chair back against a microfilm cabinet. 'You know,' he continued, 'when William Beebe built the first deep-sea chamber in history in the 1930s it was just a gondola suspended from a mother ship by a half-mile cable, with no buoyancy chambers and no engines, and if the cable broke, good night, only it never did . . . Anyway, what was I saying? Oh, when Beebe built his first deep-sea chamber, he was going to make it cylindrical; you know, so a man would fit in it comfortably. After all, a man is essentially a tall, skinny cylinder. However, a friend of his argued him out of that and into a sphere on the very sensible grounds that a sphere would resist pressure more efficiently than any other possible shape. You know who that friend was?'

'No, I'm afraid I don't.'

'The man who was President of the United States at the time of Beebe's descents – Franklin D. Roosevelt. All these spheres you see down here are the great-grandchildren of Roosevelt's suggestion.'

Demerest considered that briefly but made no comment. He returned to the earlier topic. 'We would particularly like someone from Ocean-Deep,' he said, 'to visit Luna City because it might lead to a great enough understanding of the need, on Ocean-Deep's part, for a course of action that might involve considerable selfsacrifice.'

'Oh?' Bergen's chair came down flat-leggedly on all fours. 'How's that?'

'Ocean-Deep is a marvelous achievement; I wish to detract nothing from that. I can see where it will become greater still, a wonder of the world. *Still—*'

'Still?'

'Still the oceans are only a part of the Earth; a major part, but only a part. The deep sea is only part of the ocean. It is inner space indeed; it works inward, narrowing constantly to a point.'

'I think,' broke in Annette, looking rather grim, 'that you're about to make a comparison with Luna City.'

'Indeed I am,' said Demerest. 'Luna City represents outer space, widening to infinity. There is nowhere to go down here in the long run; everywhere to go out there.'

'We don't judge by size and volume alone, Mr Demerest,' said Bergen. 'The ocean is only a small part of Earth, true, but for that very reason it is intimately connected with over five billion human beings. Ocean-Deep is experimental but the settlements on the continental shelf already deserve the name of cities. Ocean-Deep offers mankind the chance of exploiting the whole planet—'

'Of polluting the whole planet,' broke in Demerest excitedly. 'Of raping it, of ending it. The concentration of human effort to Earth itself is unhealthy and even fatal if it isn't balanced by a turning outward to the frontier.'

'There is nothing at the frontier,' said Annette, snapping out the words. 'The Moon is dead, all the other worlds out there are dead. If there are live worlds among the stars, light-years away, they can't be reached. This ocean is *living*.'

'The Moon is living, too, Mrs Bergen, and if Ocean-Deep allows it, the Moon will become an independent world. We Moon-men will then see to it that other worlds are reached and made alive and, if mankind but has patience, we will reach the stars. We! We! It is only we Moon-men, used to space, used to a world in a cavern, used to an engineered environment, who could endure life in a spaceship that may have to travel centuries to reach the stars.'

'Wait, wait, Demerest,' said Bergen, holding up his hand. 'Back up! What do you mean, if Ocean-Deep allows it? What have we to do with it?'

'You're competing with us, Mr Bergen. The Planetary Project

Commission will swing your way, give you more, give us less, because in the short term, as your wife says, the ocean is alive and the Moon, except for a thousand men, is not; because you are a half-dozen miles away and we a quarter of a million; because you can be reached in an hour and we only in three days. And because you have an ideal safety record and we have had – misfortunes.'

'The last, surely, is trivial. Accidents can happen any time, anywhere.'

'But the trivial can be used,' said Demerest angrily. 'It can be made to manipulate emotions. To people who don't see the purpose and the importance of space exploration, the death of Moon-men in accidents is proof enough that the Moon is dangerous, that its colonization is a useless fantasy. Why not? It's their excuse for saving money and they can then salve their consciences by investing part of it in Ocean-Deep instead. That's why I said the accident on the Moon had threatened the survival of Luna City even though it killed only twenty people out of nearly a thousand.'

'I don't accept your argument. There has been enough money for both for a score of years.'

'Not enough money. That's exactly it. Not enough investment to make the Moon self-supporting in all these years, and then they use that lack of self-support against us. Not enough investment to make Ocean-Deep self-supporting either . . . But now they can give you enough if they cut us out altogether.'

'Do you think that will happen?'

'I'm almost sure it will, unless Ocean-Deep shows a statesmanlike concern for man's future.'

'How?'

'By refusing to accept additional funds. By not competing with Luna City. By putting the good of the whole race ahead of self-interest.'

'Surely you don't expect us to dismantle—'

'You won't have to. Don't you see? Join us in explaining that Luna City is essential, that space exploration is the hope of mankind; that you will wait, retrench, if necessary.'

Bergen looked at his wife and raised his eyebrows. She shook her head angrily. Bergen said, 'You have a rather romantic view of the PPC, I think. Even if I made noble, self-sacrificing speeches, who's to say they would listen? There's a great deal more involved in the matter of Ocean-Deep than my opinion and my statements. There are economic considerations and public feeling. Why don't you relax, Mr Demerest? Luna City won't come to an end. You'll receive funds. I'm sure of it. I tell you, I'm sure of it. Now let's break this up—'

'No, I've got to convince you one way or another that I'm serious. If necessary, Ocean-Deep must come to a halt unless the PPC can supply ample funds for both.'

Bergen said, 'Is this some sort of official mission, Mr Demerest? Are you speaking for Luna City officially, or just for yourself?'

'Just for myself, but maybe that's enough, Mr Bergen.'

'I don't think it is. I'm sorry, but this is turning out to be unpleasant. I suggest that, after all, you had better return Topside on the first available 'scaphe.'

'Not yet! Not yet!' Demerest looked about wildly, then rose unsteadily and put his back against the wall. He was a little too tall for the room and he became conscious of life receding. One more step and he would have gone too far to back out.

He had told them back on the Moon that there would be no use talking, no use negotiating. It was dog-eat-dog for the available funds and Luna City's destiny must not be aborted; not for Ocean-Deep; not for Earth; no, not for all of Earth, since mankind and the Universe came even before the Earth. Man must outgrow his womb and—

Demerest could hear his own ragged breathing and the inner turmoil of his whirling thoughts. The other two were looking at him with what seemed concern. Annette rose and said, 'Are you ill, Mr Demerest?'

'I am *not* ill. Sit down. I'm a safety engineer and I want to teach you about safety. Sit *down*, Mrs Bergen.'

'Sit down, Annette,' said Bergen. 'I'll take care of him.' He rose and took a step forward.

But Demerest said, 'No. Don't you move either. I have something right here. You're too naive concerning human dangers, Mr Bergen. You guard against the sea and against mechanical failure and you don't search your human visitors, do you? I have a weapon, Bergen.'

Now that it was out and he had taken the final step, from which there was no returning, for he was now dead whatever he did, he was quite calm.

Annette said, 'Oh, John,' and grasped her husband's arm. 'He's—'

Bergen stepped in front of her. 'A weapon? Is that what that thing is? Now slowly, Demerest, slowly. There's nothing to get hot over. If you want to talk, we will talk. What is that?'

'Nothing dramatic. A portable laser beam.'

'But what do you want to do with it?'

'Destroy Ocean-Deep.'

'But you can't, Demerest. You know you can't. There's only so much energy you can pack into your fist and any laser you can hold can't pump enough heat to penetrate the walls.'

'I know that. This packs more energy than you think. It's Moonmade and there are some advantages to manufacturing the energy unit in a vacuum. But you're right. Even so, it's designed only for small jobs and requires frequent recharging. So I don't intend to try to cut through a foot-plus of alloy steel . . . But it will do the job indirectly. For one thing, it will keep you two quiet. There's enough energy in my fist to kill two people.'

'You wouldn't kill us,' said Bergen evenly. 'You have no reason.'

'If by that,' said Demerest, 'you imply that I am an unreasoning being to be somehow made to understand my madness, forget it. I have every reason to kill you and I *will* kill you. By laser beam if I have to, though I would rather not.'

'What good will killing us do you? Make me understand. Is it that I have refused to sacrifice Ocean-Deep funds? I couldn't do anything else. I'm not really the one to make the decision. And if you kill me, that won't help you force the decision in your direction, will it? In fact, quite the contrary. If a Moon-man is a murderer, how will that reflect on Luna City? Consider human emotions on Earth.'

There was just an edge of shrillness in Annette's voice as she joined in. 'Don't you see there will be people who will say that Solar radiation on the Moon has dangerous effects? That the genetic engineering which has reorganized your bones and muscles has affected mental stability? Consider the word "lunatic", Mr Demerest. Men once believed the Moon brought madness.'

'I am not mad, Mrs Bergen.'

'It doesn't matter,' said Bergen, following his wife's lead smoothly. 'Men will say that you were; that all Moon-men are; and Luna City will be closed down and the Moon itself closed to all further exploration, perhaps forever. Is that what you want?'

'That might happen if they thought I killed you, but they won't. It will be an accident.' With his left elbow, Demerest broke the plastic that covered the manual controls.

'I know units of this sort,' he said. 'I know exactly how it works. Logically, breaking that plastic should set up a warning flash – after all, it might be broken by accident – and then someone would be here to investigate or, better yet, the controls should lock until deliberately released to make sure the break was not merely accidental.'

He paused, then said, 'But I'm sure no one will come; that no warning has taken place. Your manual system is not fail-safe because in your heart you were sure it would never be used.'

'What do you plan to do?' said Bergen.

He was tense and Demerest watched his knees carefully, and said, 'If you try to jump toward me, I'll shoot at once, and then keep right on with what I'm doing.'

'I think maybe you're giving me nothing to lose.'

'You'll lose time. Let me go right on without interference and you'll have some minutes to keep on talking. You may even be able to talk me out of it. There's my proposal. Don't interfere with me and I will give you your chance to argue.'

'But what do you plan to do?'

'This,' said Demerest. He did not have to look. His left hand snaked out and closed a contact. 'The fusion unit will now pump heat into the air lock and the steam will empty it. It will take a few minutes. When it's done, I'm sure one of those little red-glass buttons will light.'

'Are you going to—'

Demerest said, 'Why do you ask? You know that I must be intending, having gone this far, to flood Ocean-Deep?'

'But why? Damn it, why?'

'Because it will be marked down as an accident. Because your safety record will be spoiled. Because it will be a complete catastrophe and will wipe you out. And PPC will then turn from you, and the glamor of Ocean-Deep will be gone. *We* will get the funds; *we* will continue. If I could bring that to pass in some other way, I would, but the needs of Luna City are the needs of mankind and those are paramount.'

'You will die, too,' Annette managed to say.

'Of course. Once I am forced to do something like this, would I *want* to live? I'm not a murderer.'

'But you will be. If you flood this unit, you will flood all of Ocean-Deep and kill everyone in it – and doom those who are out in their subs to slower death. Fifty men and women – an unborn child—'

'That is not my fault,' said Demerest, in clear pain. 'I did not expect to find a pregnant woman here, but now that I have, I can't stop because of that.'

'But you must stop,' said Bergen. 'Your plan won't work unless what happens can be shown to be an accident. They'll find you with a beam emitter in your hand and with the manual controls clearly tampered with. Do you think they won't deduce the truth from that?'

Demerest was feeling very tired. 'Mr Bergen, you sound desperate. Listen— When the outer door opens, water under a thousand atmospheres of pressure will enter. It will be a massive battering ram that will destroy and mangle everything in its path. The walls of the Ocean-Deep units will remain but everything inside will be twisted beyond recognition. Human beings will be mangled into shredded tissue and splintered bone and death will be instantaneous and unfelt. Even if I were to burn you to death with the laser there would be nothing left to show it had been done, so I won't hesitate, you see. This manual unit will be smashed anyway; anything I can do will be erased by the water.'

'But the beam emitter, the laser gun. Even damaged, it will be recognizable,' said Annette.

'We use such things on the Moon, Mrs Bergen. It is a common tool; it is the optical analogue of a jackknife. I could kill you with a jackknife, you know, but one would not deduce that a man carrying a jackknife, or even holding one with the blade open, was necessarily planning murder. He might be whittling. Besides, a Moon-made laser is not a projectile gun. It doesn't have to withstand an internal explosion. It is made of thin metal, mechanically weak. After it is smashed by the waterclap I doubt that it will make much sense as an object.'

Demerest did not have to think to make these statements. He had worked them out within himself through months of self-debate back on the Moon.

'In fact,' he went on, 'how will the investigators ever know what happened in here? They will send 'scaphes down to inspect what is left of Ocean-Deep, but how can they get inside without first pumping the water out? They will, in effect, have to build a new Ocean-Deep and that would take – how long? Perhaps, given public reluctance to waste money, they might never do it at all and content themselves with dropping a laurel wreath on the dead walls of the dead Ocean-Deep.'

Bergen said, 'The men on Luna City will know what you have done. Surely one of them will have a conscience. The truth will be known.'

'One truth,' said Demerest, 'is that I am not a fool. No one on Luna City knows what I planned to do or will suspect what I have done. They sent me down here to negotiate cooperation on the matter of financial grants. I was to argue and nothing more. There's not even a laser-beam emitter missing up there. I put this one together myself out of scrapped parts... And it works. I've tested it.'

Annette said slowly, 'You haven't thought it through. Do you know what you're doing?'

'I've thought it through. I know what I'm doing. And I know also that you are both conscious of the lit signal. I'm aware of it. The air lock is empty and time's up, I'm afraid.'

Rapidly, holding his beam emitter tensely high, he closed another contact. A circular part of the unit wall cracked into a thin crescent and rolled smoothly away.

Out of the corner of his eye, Demerest saw the gaping darkness, but he did not look. A dankly salt vapor issued from it; a queer odor of dead steam. He even imagined he could hear the flopping sound of the gathered water at the bottom of the lock.

Demerest said, 'In a rational manual unit, the outer door ought to be frozen shut now. With the inner door open, nothing ought to make the outer door open. I suspect, though, that the manuals were put together too quickly at first for that precaution to have been taken, and it was replaced too quickly for that precaution to have been added. And if I need further evidence of that, you wouldn't be sitting there so tensely if you knew the outer door wouldn't open. I need touch one more contact and the waterclap will come. We will feel nothing.'

Annette said, 'Don't push it just yet. I have one more thing to say. You said we would have time to persuade you.'

'While the water was being pushed out.'

'Just let me say this. A minute. A *minute*. I said you didn't know what you were doing. You don't. You're destroying the space program, the *space* program. There's more to space than *space*.' Her voice had grown shrill.

Demerest frowned. 'What are you talking about? Make sense, or I'll end it all. I'm tired. I'm frightened. I want it over.'

Annette said, 'You're not in the inner councils of the PPC. Neither is my husband. But I am. Do you think because I am a woman that

I'm secondary here? I'm not. You, Mr Demerest, have your eyes fixed on Luna City only. My husband has his fixed on Ocean-Deep. Neither of you know *anything*.

'Where do you expect to go, Mr Demerest, if you had all the money you wanted? Mars? The asteroids? The satellites of the gas giants? These are all small worlds; all dry surfaces under a blank sky. It may be generations before we are ready to try for the stars and till then we'd have only pygmy real estate. Is that your ambition?

'My husband's ambition is no better. He dreams of pushing man's habitat over the ocean floor, a surface not much larger in the last analysis than the surface of the Moon and the other pygmy worlds. We of the PPC, on the other hand, want more than either of you, and if you push that button, Mr Demerest, the greatest dream mankind has ever had will come to nothing.'

Demerest found himself interested despite himself, but he said, 'You're just babbling.' It was possible, he knew, that somehow they had warned others in Ocean-Deep, that any moment someone would come to interrupt, someone would try to shoot him down. He was, however, staring at the only opening, and he had only to close one contact, without even looking, in a second's movement.

Annette said, 'I'm not babbling. You know it took more than rocket ships to colonize the Moon. To make a successful colony possible, men had to be altered genetically and adjusted to low gravity. You are a product of such genetic engineering.'

'Well?'

'And might not genetic engineering also help adjust men to greater gravitational pull? What is the largest planet of the Solar System, Mr Demerest?'

'Jupi—'

'Yes, Jupiter. Eleven times the diameter of the Earth; forty times the diameter of the Moon. A surface a hundred and twenty times that of the Earth in area; sixteen hundred times that of the Moon. Conditions so different from anything we can encounter anywhere on the worlds the size of Earth or less that any scientist of any persuasion would give half his life for a chance to observe at close range.'

'But Jupiter is an impossible target.'

'Indeed?' said Annette, and even managed a faint smile. 'As impossible as flying? Why is it impossible? Genetic engineering could design men with stronger and denser bones, stronger and more compact muscles. The same principles that enclose Luna City against the vacuum and Ocean-Deep against the sea can also enclose the future Jupiter-Deep against its ammoniated surroundings.'

'The gravitational field—'

'Can be negotiated by nuclear-powered ships that are now on the drawing board. You don't know that but I do.'

'We're not even sure about the depth of the atmosphere. The pressures—'

'The pressures! The *pressures*! Mr Demerest, look about you. Why do you suppose Ocean-Deep was *really* built? To exploit the ocean? The settlements on the continental shelf are doing that quite adequately. To gain knowledge of the deep-sea bottom? We could do that by 'scaphe easily and we could then have spared the hundred billion dollars invested in Ocean-Deep so far.

'Don't you see, Mr Demerest, that Ocean-Deep must mean something more than that? The purpose of Ocean-Deep is to devise the ultimate vessels and mechanisms that will suffice to explore and colonize *Jupiter*. Look about you and see the beginnings of a Jovian environment; the closest approach we can come to it on Earth. It is only a faint image of mighty Jupiter, but it's a beginning.

'Destroy this, Mr Demerest, and you destroy any hope for Jupiter. On the other hand, let us live and we will, together, penetrate and settle the brightest jewel of the Solar System. And long before we can reach the limits of Jupiter, we will be ready for the stars, for the Earth-type planets circling them, *and* the Jupiter-type planets, too. Luna City won't be abandoned because *both* are necessary for this ultimate aim.'

For the moment, Demerest had altogether forgotten about that last button. He said, 'Nobody on Luna City has heard of this.'

'*You* haven't. There are those on Luna City who know. If you had told them of your plan of destruction, they would have stopped you. Naturally, we can't make this common knowledge and only a few people anywhere can know. The public supports only with difficulty the planetary projects now in progress. If the PPC is parsimonious it is because public opinion limits its generosity. What do you suppose public opinion would say if they thought we were aiming toward Jupiter? What a super-boondoggle that would be in their eyes. But we continue and what money we can save and make use of we place in the various facets of Project Big World.'

'Project Big World?'

'Yes,' said Annette. 'You know now and I have committed a serious security breach. But it doesn't matter, does it? Since we're all dead and since the project is, too.'

'Wait now, Mrs Bergen.'

'If you change your mind now, don't think you can ever talk about Project Big World. That would end the project just as effectively as destruction here would. And it would end both your career and mine. It might end Luna City and Ocean-Deep, too – so now that you know, maybe it makes no difference anyway. You might just as well push that button.'

'I said wait—' Demerest's brow was furrowed and his eyes burned with anguish. 'I don't know—'

Bergen gathered for the sudden jump as Demerest's tense alertness wavered into uncertain introspection, but Annette grasped her husband's sleeve.

A timeless interval that might have been ten seconds long followed and then Demerest held out his laser. 'Take it,' he said. 'I'll consider myself under arrest.'

'You can't be arrested,' said Annette, 'without the whole story coming out.' She took the laser and gave it to Bergen. 'It will be enough that you return to Luna City and keep silent. Till then we will keep you under guard.'

Bergen was at the manual controls. The inner door slid shut and after that there was the thunderous waterclap of the water returning into the lock.

Husband and wife were alone again. They had not dared say a word until Demerest was safely put to sleep under the watchful eyes of two men detailed for the purpose. The unexpected waterclap had roused everybody and a sharply bowdlerized account of the incident had been given out.

The manual controls were now locked off and Bergen said, 'From this point on, the manuals will have to be adjusted to fail-safe. And visitors will have to be searched.'

'Oh, John,' said Annette. 'I think people are insane. There we were, facing death for us and for Ocean-Deep; just the end of everything. And I kept thinking – I must keep calm; I mustn't have a miscarriage.'

'You kept calm all right. You were magnificent. I mean, Project Big World! I never conceived of such a thing, but *by-by-Jove*, it's an attractive thought. It's wonderful.'

'I'm sorry I had to say all that, John. It was all a fake, of course. I made it up. Demerest wanted me to make something up really. He wasn't a killer or destroyer; he was, according to his own overheated lights, a patriot, and I suppose he was telling himself he must destroy in order to save – a common enough view among the smallminded. But he *said* he would give us time to talk him out of it and I think he was praying we would manage to do so. He wanted us to think of something that would give him the excuse to save in order to save, and I gave it to him. I'm sorry I had to fool you, John.'

'You didn't fool me.'

'I didn't?'

'How could you? I knew you weren't a member of PPC.'

'What made you so sure of that? Because I'm a woman?'

'Not at all. Because *I'm* a member, Annette, and *that's* confidential. And, if you don't mind, I will begin a move to initiate exactly what you suggested – Project Big World.'

'Well!' Annette considered that and, slowly, smiled. 'Well! That's not bad. Women do have their uses.'

'Something,' said Bergen, smiling also, 'I have never denied.'

2430 AD

Between midnight and dawn, when sleep will not come and all the old wounds begin to ache, I often have a nightmare vision of a future world in which there are billions of people, all numbered and registered, with not a gleam of genius anywhere, not an original mind, a rich personality, on the whole packed globe.

— J. B. Priestley

'He'll talk to us,' said Alvarez when the other stepped out the door.

'Good,' said Bunting. 'Social pressure is bound to get to him eventually. An odd character. How he escaped genetic adjustment I'll never know. – But *you* do the talking. He irritates me past tact.'

Together they swung down the corridor along the Executive Trail, which was, as always, sparsely occupied. They might have taken the Moving Strips, but there were only two miles to go and Alvarez enjoyed walking, so Bunting didn't insist.

Alvarez was tall and rather thin, with the kind of athletic figure one would expect of a person who cherished the muscular activities; who routinely used the stairs and rampways, for instance, almost to the edge of being considered an unsettling character himself.

Bunting, softer and rounder, avoided even the sunlamps, and was quite pale.

Bunting said dolefully, 'I hope the two of us will be enough.'

'I should think so. We want to keep it in our sector, if we can.'

'Yes! You know, I keep thinking – why does it have to be *our* sector? Fifty million square miles of seven-hundred-level living space, and it has to be in our apartment bloc.'

'Rather a distinction, in a grisly kind of way,' said Alvarez. Bunting snorted.

'And a little to our credit,' Alvarez added softly, 'if we settle the matter. We reach peak. We reach end. We reach goal. All mankind. And *we* do it.'

Bunting brightened. He said, 'You think they'll look at it that way?'

'Let's see to it that they do.'

Their footsteps were muted against the plastic-knit crushed rock underfoot. They passed crosscorridors and saw the endless crowds on the Moving Strips in the middle distance. There was a fugitive whiff of plankton in its varieties. Once, almost by instinct, they could tell that up above, far above, was one of the giant conduits leading in from the sea. And by symmetry they knew there would be another conduit, just as large, far below, leading out to sea.

Their destination was a dwelling room set well back from the corridor, but one that seemed different from the thousands they had passed. There was about it an intangible and disconcerting note of space, for on either side, for hundreds of feet, the wall was blank. And there was something in the air. 'Smell it?' muttered Bunting.

'I've smelled it before,' said Alvarez. 'Inhuman.'

'Literally!' said Bunting. 'He won't expect us to look at them, will he?'

'If he does, it's easy enough to refuse.'

They signaled, then waited in silence while the hum of infinite life sounded all around them in utterly disregarded manner, for it was always there.

The door opened. Cranwitz was waiting. He looked sullen. He

wore the same clothes they all did; light, simple, gray. On him, though, they seemed rumpled. *He* seemed rumpled, his hair too long, his eyes bloodshot and shifting uneasily.

'May we enter?' asked Alvarez with cold courtesy.

Cranwitz stood to one side.

The odor was stronger inside. Cranwitz closed the door behind them and they sat down. Cranwitz remained standing and said nothing.

Alvarez said, 'I must ask you, in my capacity as Sector Representative, with Bunting here as Vice-Representative, whether you are now ready to comply with social necessity.'

Cranwitz seemed to be thinking. When he finally spoke his deep voice was choked and he had to clear his throat. 'I don't want to,' he said. 'I don't have to. There is a contract with the government of long-standing. My family has always had the right—'

'We know all this and there's no question of force involved,' said Bunting irritably. 'We're asking you to accede voluntarily.'

Alvarez touched the other's knee lightly. 'You understand the situation is not what it was in your father's time; or even, really, what it was last year?'

Cranwitz's long jaw quivered slightly. 'I don't see that. The birth rate has dropped this year by the amount computerized, and everything else has changed correspondingly. That goes on from year to year. Why should this year be different?'

His voice somehow did not carry conviction. Alvarez was sure he *did* know why this year was different, and he said softly, 'This year we've reached the goal. The birth rate now exactly matches the death rate; the population level is now exactly steady; construction is now confined to replacement entirely; and the sea farms are in a steady state. Only you stand between all mankind and perfection.'

'Because of a few mice?'

'Because of a few mice. And other creatures. Guinea pigs. Rabbits. Some kinds of birds and lizards. I haven't taken a census—'

'But they're the only ones left in all the world. What harm do they do?'

'What good?' demanded Bunting.

Cranwitz said, 'The good of being there to look at. There was once a time when—'

Alvarez had heard that before. He said, with as much sympathy as he could pump into his voice (and, to his surprise, with a certain amount of real sympathy, too), 'I know. There was once a time! Centuries ago! There were vast numbers of life forms like those you care for. And millions of years before that there were dinosaurs. But we have microfilms of *everything*. No man need go ignorant of them.'

'How can you compare microfilms with the real thing?' asked Cranwitz.

Bunting's lips quirked. 'The microfilms don't smell.'

'The zoo was much larger once,' said Cranwitz. 'Year by year we've had to get rid of so many. All the large animals. All the carnivores. The trees. There's nothing left but small plants, tiny creatures. Let them be.'

Alvarez said, 'What is there to do with them? No one wants to see them. Mankind is against you.'

'Social pressure—'

'We couldn't persuade people against real resistance. People don't want to see these life distortions. They're sickening; they really are. What's there to do with them?' Alvarez's voice was insinuating.

Cranwitz sat down now. A certain feverishness heightened the color in his cheeks. 'I've been thinking. Someday we'll reach out. Mankind will colonize other worlds. He'll want animals. He'll want other species in these new, empty worlds. He'll start a new ecology of variety. He'll . . .'

His words faded under the hostile stare of the other two. Bunting said, 'What other worlds are we going to colonize?'

'We reached the moon in 1969,' said Cranwitz.

'Sure, and we established a colony, and we abandoned it. There's no world in all the solar system capable of supporting human life without prohibitive engineering.'

Cranwitz said, 'There are worlds circling other stars. Earthlike worlds by the hundreds of millions. There must be.'

Alvarez shook his head. 'Out of reach. We have finally exploited Earth and filled it with the human species. We have made our choice, and it is Earth. There is no margin for the kind of effort needed to build a starship capable of crossing light-years of space. – Have you been immersing yourself in twentieth-century history?'

'It was the last century of the open world,' said Cranwitz.

'So it was,' said Alvarez dryly. 'I hope you haven't over-romanticized it. I've studied its madness, too. The world was empty then, only a few billions, and they thought it was crowded – and with good reason. They spent more than half their substance on war and preparations of war, ran their economy without forethought, wasted and poisoned at will, let pure chance govern the genetic pool, and tolerated the deviants-from-norm of all descriptions. Of course, they dreaded what they called the population explosion, and dreamed of reaching other worlds as a kind of escape. So would we under those conditions.

'I needn't tell you the combination of events and of scientific advances that changed everything, but just let me remind you briefly in case you are trying to forget. There was the establishment of a world government, the development of fusion power, and the growth of the art of genetic engineering. With planetary peace, plentiful energy, and a placid humanity men could multiply peacefully, and science kept up with the multiplication.

'It was known in advance exactly how many men the Earth could support. So many calories of sunlight reached the Earth, and, using that, only so many tons of carbon dioxide could be fixed by green plants each year, and only so many tons of animal life could be supported by those plants. The Earth could support two trillion tons of animal life—'

Cranwitz finally broke in, 'And why shouldn't all two trillion tons be human?'

'Exactly.'

'Even if it meant killing off all other animal life?'

'That's the way of evolution,' said Bunting angrily. 'The fit survive.'

Alvarez touched the other's knee again. 'Bunting is right, Cranwitz,' he said gently. 'The teleosts replaced the placoderms, who had replaced the trilobites. The reptiles replaced the amphibians and were in turn replaced by the mammals. Now, at last, evolution has reached its peak. Earth bears its mighty population of fifteen trillion human beings—'

'But how?' demanded Cranwitz. 'They live in one vast building over all the face of the dry land, with no plants and no animals beside, except what I have right here. And all the uninhabited ocean has become a plankton soup; no life but plankton. We harvest it endlessly to feed our people; and as endlessly we restore organic matter to feed the plankton.'

'We live very well,' said Alvarez. 'There is no war; there is no crime. Our births are regulated; our deaths are peaceful. Our infants are genetically adjusted and on Earth there are now twenty billion tons of normal brain; the largest conceivable quantity of the most complex conceivable matter in the universe.'

'And all that weight of brain doing *what*?'

Bunting heaved an audible sigh of exasperation but Alvarez, still calm, said, 'My good friend, you confuse the journey with the destination. Perhaps it comes from living with your animals. When the Earth was in process of development, it was necessary for life to experiment and take chances. It was even worthwhile to be wasteful. The Earth was empty then. It had infinite room and evolution had to experiment with ten million species or more – till it found *the* species.

'Even after mankind came, it had to learn the way. While it was learning, it had to take chances, attempt the impossible, be foolish or mad. – But mankind has come home, now. Men have filled the planet and need only to enjoy perfection.'

Alvarez paused to let that sink in, then said, 'We *want* it, Cranwitz. The whole world wants perfection. It is in our generation that perfection has been reached, and we *want* the distinction of having reached it. Your animals are in the way.'

Cranwitz shook his head stubbornly. 'They take up so little room; consume so little energy. If all were wiped out, you might have room for what? For twenty-five more human beings? Twenty-five in fifteen trillion?'

Bunting said, 'Twenty-five human beings represent another seventy-five pounds of human brain. With what measure can you evaluate seventy-five pounds of human brain?'

'But you already have billions of tons of it.'

'I know,' said Alvarez, 'but the difference between perfection and not-quite-perfection is that between life and not-quite-life. We are so close now. All Earth is prepared to celebrate this year of 2430 AD This is the year when the computer tells us that the planet is full at last; the goal is achieved; all the striving of evolution crowned. Shall we fall short by twenty-five – even out of fifteen trillion. It is such a tiny, tiny flaw, but it is a flaw.

'Think, Cranwitz! Earth has been waiting for five billion years to be fulfilled. Must we wait longer? We cannot and will not force you, but if you yield voluntarily you will be a hero to everyone.'

Bunting said, 'Yes. In all future time men will say that Cranwitz acted and with that one single act perfection was reached.'

And Cranwitz said, imitating the other's tone of voice, 'And men will say that Alvarez and Bunting persuaded him to do so.'

'If we succeed!' said Alvarez with no audible annoyance. 'But tell me, Cranwitz, can you hold out against the enlightened will of fifteen trillion people forever? Whatever your motives – and I recognize that in your own way you are an idealist – can you withhold that last bit of perfection from so many?'

Cranwitz looked down in silence and Alvarez's hand waved gently in Bunting's direction and Bunting said not a word. The silence remained unbroken while slow minutes crept by.

Then Cranwitz whispered, 'Can I have one more day with my animals?'

'And then?'

'And then – I won't stand between mankind and perfection.'

And Alvarez said, 'I'll let the world know. You will be honored.' And he and Bunting left.

Over the vast continental buildings some five trillion human beings placidly slept; some two trillion human beings placidly ate; half a trillion carefully made love. Other trillions talked without heat, or tended the computers quietly, or ran the vehicles, or studied the machinery, or organized the microfilm libraries, or amused their fellows. Trillions went to sleep; trillions woke up; and the routine never varied.

The machinery worked, tested itself, repaired itself. The plankton soup of the planetary ocean basked under the sun and the cells divided, and divided, and divided, while dredges endlessly scooped them up and dried them and by the millions of tons transferred them to conveyors and conduits that brought them to every corner of the endless buildings.

And in every corner of the buildings human wastes were gathered and irradiated and dried, and human corpses were ground and treated and dried and endlessly the residue was brought back to the ocean. And for hours, while all this was going on, as it had gone on for decades, and might be doomed to go on for millennia, Cranwitz fed his little creatures a last time, stroked his guinea pig, lifted a tortoise to gaze into its uncomprehending eye, felt a blade of living grass between his fingers.

He counted them over, all of them – the last living things on Earth that were neither humans nor food for humans – and then he seared the soil in which the plants grew and killed them. He flooded the cages and rooms in which the animals moved with appropriate vapors, and they moved no more and soon they lived no more.

The last of them was gone and now between mankind and perfection there was only Cranwitz, whose thoughts still rebelliously departed from the norm. But for Cranwitz there were also the vapors, and he didn't want to live.

And, after that, there was really perfection, for over all the Earth, through all its fifteen trillion inhabitants and over all its twenty billion tons of human brain, there was (with Cranwitz gone) not one unsettling thought, not one unusual idea, to disturb the universal placidity that meant that the exquisite nothingness of uniformity had at last been achieved.

Thiotimoline to the Stars

'Same speech, I suppose,' said Ensign Peet wearily.

'Why not?' said Lieutenant Prohorov, closing his eyes and carefully sitting down on the small of his back. 'He's given it for fifteen years, once to each graduating class of the Astronautic Academy.'

'Word for word, I'll bet,' said Peet, who had heard it the year before for the first time.

'As far as I can tell. – What a pompous bore! Oh, for a pin that would puncture pretension.'

But the class was filing in now, uniformed and expectant, marching forward, breaking into rows with precision, each man and woman moving to his or her assigned seat to the rhythm of a subdued drumbeat, and then all sitting down to one loud boom.

At that moment Admiral Vernon entered and walked stiffly to the podium.

'Graduating class of '22, welcome! Your school days are over. Your education will now begin.

'You have learned all there is to know about the classic theory of space flight. You have been filled to overflowing with astrophysics and celestial relativistic mechanics. But you have not been told about thiotimoline.

'That's for a very good reason. Telling you about it in class will do you no good. You will have to learn to *fly* with thiotimoline. It is thiotimoline and that alone that will take you to the stars. With all your book learning, you may still never learn to handle thiotimoline. If so, there will yet be many posts you can fill in the astronautic way of life. Being a pilot will not, however, be one of them.

'I will start you off on this, your graduation day, with the only lecture you will get on the subject. After this, your dealings with thiotimoline will be in flight and we will find out quickly whether you have any talent for it at all.'

The admiral paused, and seemed to be looking from face to face as though he was trying to assay each man's talent to begin with.

Then he barked:

'Thiotimoline! First mentioned in 1948, according to legend, by Azimuth or, possibly, Asymptote, who may, very likely, never have existed. There is no record of the original article supposed to have been written by him; merely vague references to it, none earlier than the twenty-first century.

'Serious study began with Almirante, who either discovered thiotimoline, or rediscovered it, if the Azimuth Asymptote tale is accepted. Almirante worked out the theory of hypersteric hindrance and showed that the molecule of thiotimoline is so distorted that one bond is forced into extension through the temporal dimension into the past; and another into the future.

'Because of the future-extension, thiotimoline can interact with an event that has not yet taken place. It can, for instance, to use the classic example, dissolve in water approximately one second before the water is added.

'Thiotimoline is, of course, a very simple compound, comparatively. It has, indeed, the simplest molecule capable of displaying endochronic properties – that is, the past-future extension. While this makes possible certain unique devices, the true applications of endochronicity had to await the development of more complicated molecules; polymers that combined endochronicity with firm structure.

'Pellagrini was the first to form endochronic resins and plastics, and, twenty years later, Cudahy demonstrated the technique for binding endochronic plastics to metal. It became possible to make large objects endochronic – entire spaceships, for instance.

'Now let us consider what happens when a large structure is endochronic. I will describe it qualitatively only; it is all that is necessary. The theoreticians have it all worked out mathematically, but I have never known a physics-johnny yet who could pilot a starship. Let them handle the theory, then, and you handle the ship.

'The small thiotimoline molecule is extraordinarily sensitive to the probabilistic states of the future. If you are certain you are going to add the water, it will dissolve before the water is added. If there is even the slightest doubt in your mind as to whether you will add the water, the thiotimoline will not dissolve until you actually add it.

'The larger the molecule possessing endochronicity, the less sensitive it is to the presence of doubt. It will dissolve, swell, change its electrical properties, or in some way interact with water, even if you are almost certain you may not add the water. But then what if you don't, in actual fact, add the water? The answer is simple. The endochronic structure will move into the future in search of water; not finding it, it will continue to move into the future.

'The effect is very much that of the donkey following the carrot fixed to a stick and held two feet in front of the donkey's nose; except that the endochronic structure is not as smart as the donkey, and never gets tired.

'If an entire ship is endochronic – that is, if endochronic groupings are fixed to the hull at frequent intervals – it is easy to set up a device that will deliver water to key spots in the structure, and yet so arrange that device that although it is always apparently on the point of delivering the water, it never actually does.

'In that case, the endochronic groupings move forward in time, carrying all the ship with it and all the objects on board the ship, including its personnel.

'Of course, there are no absolutes. The ship is moving forward in time relative to the universe; and this is precisely the same as saying that the universe is moving backward in time relative to the ship. The rate at which the ship is moving forward, or the universe is moving backward, in time, can be adjusted with great delicacy by the necessary modification of the device for adding water. The proper way of doing this can be taught, after a fashion; but it can be applied perfectly only by inborn talent. That is what we will find out about you all; whether you have that talent.'

Again he paused and appraised them. Then he went on, amid perfect silence:

'But what good is it all? Let's consider starflights and review some of the things you have learned in school.

'Stars are incredibly far apart and to travel from one to another, considering the light-speed limit on velocity, takes years; centuries; millennia. One way of doing it is to set up a huge ship with a closed ecology; a tiny, self-contained universe. A group of people will set out and the tenth generation thereafter reaches a distant star. No one man makes the journey, and even if the ship eventually returns home, many centuries may have passed.

'To take the original crew to the stars in their own lifetime, freezing techniques may keep them in suspended animation for virtually all the trip. But freezing is a very uncertain procedure, and even if the crew survives and returns home, they will find that many centuries have passed on Earth.

'To take the original crew to the stars in their own lifetime, without freezing them, it is only necessary to accelerate to near-light velocities. Subjective time slows, and it will seem to the crew that it will have taken them only months to make the trip. But time travels at the normal rate for the rest of the universe, and when the crew returns they will find that although they, themselves, have aged and experienced no more than two months of time, perhaps, the Earth itself will have experienced many centuries.

'In every case, star travel involves enormous duration of time on Earth, even if not to the crew. One must return to Earth, if one returns at all, far into the Earth's future, and this means interstellar travel is not psychologically practical.

'But— *But*, graduates—'

He peered piercingly at them and said in a low, tense voice, '*If* we use an endochronic ship, we can match the time-dilatation effect exactly with the endochronic effect. While the ship travels through space at enormous velocity, and experiences a large slowdown in rate of experienced time, the endochronic effect is moving the universe back in time with respect to the ship. Properly handled, when the ship returns to Earth, with the crew having experienced, say, only two months of duration, the entire universe will have likewise experienced only two months' duration. At last, interstellar travel became practical.

'But only if very delicately handled.

'If the endochronic effect lags a little behind the time-dilatation effect, the ship will return after two months to find an Earth four months older. This is not much, perhaps; it can be lived with, you might think; but not so. The crew members are out of phase. They feel everything about them to have aged two months with respect to themselves. Worse yet, the general population feels that the crew members are two months younger than they ought to be. It creates hard feelings and discomforts.

'Similarly, if the endochronic effect races a little ahead of the time-dilatation effect, the ship may return after two months to find an Earth that has not experienced any time duration at all. The ship returns, just as it is rising into the sky. The hard feelings and discomforts will still exist.

'No, graduates, no interstellar flight will be considered successful in this star fleet unless the duration to the crew and the duration to Earth match minute for minute. A sixty-second deviation is a sloppy job that will gain you no merit. A hundred-twenty-second deviation will not be tolerated.

'I know, graduates, very well what questions are going through your minds. They went through mine when I graduated. Do we not in the endochronic ship have the equivalent of a time machine? Can we not, by proper adjustment of our endochronic device, deliberately travel a century into the future, make our observations, then travel a century into the past to return to our starting point? Or vice versa, can we not travel a century into the past and then back into the future to the starting point? Or a thousand years, or a billion? Could we not witness the Earth being born, life evolving, the sun dying?

'Graduates, the mathematical-johnnies tell us that this sort of thing creates paradoxes and requires too much energy to be practical. But *I* tell you the hell with paradoxes. We can't do it for a very simple reason. The endochronic properties are unstable. Molecules that are puckered into the time dimension are sensitive indeed. Relatively small effects will cause them to undergo chemical changes that will allow unpuckering. Even if there are no effects at all, random vibrations will produce the changes that will unpucker them.

'In short, an endochronic ship will slowly go isochronic and become ordinary matter without temporal extension. Modem technology has reduced the rate of unpuckering enormously and may reduce it further still, but nothing we do, theory tells us, will ever create a truly stable endochronic molecule.

'This means that your starship has only a limited life as a star ship. It must get back to Earth while its endochronicity still holds, and that endochronicity must be restored before the next trip.

'Now, then, what happens if you return out-of-time? If you are not very nearly in your own time, you will have no assurance that the state of the technology will be such as to enable you to re-endochronicize your ship. You may be lucky if you are in the future; you will certainly be unlucky in the past. If, through carelessness on your part, or simply through lack of talent, you come back a substantial distance into the past, you will be certain to be stuck there because there will be no way of treating your ship in such a fashion as to bring it back into what will then be your future.

'And I want you to understand, graduates,' here he slapped one hand against the other, as though to emphasize his words, 'there is no time in the past where a civilized astronautic officer would care to spend his life. You might, for instance, be stranded in sixth-century France or, worse still, twentieth-century America.

'Refrain, then, from any temptation to experiment with time.

'Let us now pass on to one more point which may not have been more than hinted at in your formal school days, but which is something you will be experiencing.

'You may wonder how it is that a relatively few endochronic atomic bonds placed here and there among matter which is overwhelmingly isochronic can drag all with it. Why should one endochronic bond, racing toward water, drag with it a quadrillion atoms with isochronic bonds? We feel this should not happen, because of our lifelong experience with inertia.

'There is, however, no inertia in the movement toward past or future. If one part of an object moves toward the past or future, the rest of the object does so as well, and at precisely the same speed. There is no mass-factor at all. That is why it is as easy for the entire universe to move backward in time as for this single ship to move forward – and at the same rate.

'But there is even more to it than that. The time-dilatation effect is the result of your acceleration with respect to the universe generally. You learned that in grade school, when you took up elementary relativistic physics. It is part of the inertial effect of acceleration.

'But by using the endochronic effect, we wipe out the time-dilatation effect. If we wipe out the time-dilatation effect, then we are, so to speak, wiping out that which produces it. In short, when the endochronic effect exactly balances the time-dilatation effect, the inertial effect of acceleration is canceled out.

'You cannot cancel out one inertial effect without canceling them all. Inertia is therefore wiped out altogether and you can accelerate at any rate without feeling it. Once the endochronic effect is well-adjusted, you can accelerate from rest relative to Earth, to 186,000 miles per second relative to Earth in anywhere from a few hours to a few minutes. The more talented and skillful you are at handling the endochronic effect, the more rapidly you can accelerate.

'You are experiencing that now, gentlemen. It seems to you that you are sitting in an auditorium on the surface of the planet Earth, and I'm sure that none of you has had any reason or occasion to doubt the truth of that impression. But it's wrong just the same.

'You are in an auditorium, I admit, but it is not on the surface of the planet, Earth; not anymore. You – I – all of us – are in a large starship, which took off the moment I began this speech and which accelerated at an enormous rate. We reached the outskirts of the solar system while I've been talking, and we are now returning.

'At no time have any of you felt any acceleration, either through change in speed, change in direction of travel, or both, and therefore you have all assumed that you have remained at rest with respect to the surface of the Earth.

'Not at all, graduates. You have been out in space all the time I was talking, and have passed, according to calculations, within two million miles of the planet Saturn.'

He seemed grimly pleased at the distinct stir in the audience.

'You needn't worry, graduates. Since we experience no inertial effects, we experience no gravitational effects either (the two are essentially the same), so that our course has not been affected by Saturn. We will be back on Earth's surface any moment now. As a special treat we will be coming down in the United Nations Port in Lincoln, Nebraska, and you will all be free to enjoy the pleasures of the metropolis for the weekend.

'Incidentally, the mere fact that we have experienced no inertial effects at all shows how well the endochronic effect matched the time-dilatation. Had there been any mismatch, even a small one, you would have felt the effects of acceleration – another reason for making no effort to experiment with time.

'Remember, graduates, a sixty-second mismatch is sloppy and a hundred-twenty-second mismatch is intolerable. We are about to land now; Lieutenant Prohorov, will you take over in the conning tower and oversee the actual landing?'

Prohorov said briskly, 'Yes, sir,' and went up the ladder in the rear of the assembly hall, where he had been sitting.

Admiral Vernon smiled. 'You will all keep your seats. We are exactly on course. My ships are always exactly on course.'

But then Prohorov descended again and came running up the aisle to the admiral. He reached him and spoke in a whisper. 'Admiral, if this is Lincoln, Nebraska, something is wrong. All I can see are Indians; hordes of Indians. Indians in Nebraska, *now*, Admiral?'

Admiral Vernon turned pale and made a rattling sound in his throat. He crumpled and collapsed, while the graduating class rose to its feet uncertainly. Ensign Peet had followed Prohorov onto the platform and had caught his words and now stood there thunderstruck.

Prohorov raised his arms. 'All's well, ladies and gentlemen. Take it easy. The admiral has just had a momentary attack of vertigo. It happens on landing, sometimes, to older men.'

Peet whispered harshly, 'But we're stuck in the past, Prohorov.'

Prohorov raised bis eyebrows. 'Of course not. You didn't feel any inertial effects, did you? We can't even be an hour off. If the admiral had any brains to go with his uniform, he would have realized it, too. He had just *said* it, for God's sake.'

'Then why did you say there was something wrong? Why did you say there are Indians out there?'

'Because there was and there are. When Admiral Sap comes to, he won't be able to do a thing to me. We didn't land in Lincoln, Nebraska, so there was something wrong all right. And as for the Indians – well, if I read the traffic signs correctly, we've come down on the outskirts of Calcutta.'

The Winnowing

Five years had passed since the steadily thickening wall of secrecy had been clamped down about the work of Dr Aaron Rodman.

'For your own protection—' they had warned him.

'In the hands of the wrong people—' they had explained.

In the right hands, of course (his own, for instance, Dr Rodman thought rather despairingly), the discovery was clearly the greatest boon to human health since Pasteur's working out of the germ theory, and the greatest key to the understanding of the mechanism of life, ever.

Yet after his talk at the New York Academy of Medicine soon after his fiftieth birthday, and on the first day of the Twenty-first Century (there had been a certain fitness to that), the silence had been imposed, and he could talk no more, except to certain officials. He certainly could not publish.

The government supported him, however. He had all the money he needed, and the computers were his to do with as he wished. His work advanced rapidly and government men came to him to be instructed, to be made to understand.

'Dr Rodman,' they would ask, 'how can a virus be spread from cell to cell within an organism and yet not be infectious from one organism to the next?'

It wearied Rodman to have to say over and over that he did not have all the answers. It wearied him to have to use the term 'virus.' He said, 'It's not a virus because it isn't a nucleic acid molecule. It is something else altogether – a lipoprotein.'

It was better when his questioners were not themselves medical men. He could then try to explain in generalities instead of forever bogging down on the fine points. He would say, 'Every living cell, and every small structure within the cell, is surrounded by a membrane. The workings of each cell depend on what molecules can pass through the membrane in either direction and at what rates. A slight change in the membrane will alter the nature of the flow enormously, and with that, the nature of the cell chemistry and the nature of its activity.

'All disease may rest on alterations in membrane activity. All mutations may be carried through by way of such alterations. Any technique that controls the membranes controls life. Hormones control the body by their effect on membranes and my lipoprotein is an artificial hormone rather than a virus. The LP incorporates itself into the membrane and in the process induces the manufacture of more molecules like itself – and that's the part I don't understand myself.

'But the fine structures of the membranes are not quite identical everywhere. They are, in fact, different in all living things – not quite the same in any two organisms. An LP will affect no two individual organisms alike. What will open the cells of one organism to glucose and relieve the effects of diabetes, will close the cells of another organism to lysine and kill it.'

That was what seemed to interest them most; that it was a poison. 'A selective poison,' Rodman would say. 'You couldn't tell, in advance, without the closest computer-aided studies of the membrane biochemistry of a particular individual, what a particular LP would do to him.'

With time, the noose grew tighter about himself, inhibiting his freedom, yet leaving him comfortable – in a world in which freedom and comfort alike were vanishing everywhere, and the jaws of hell were opening before a despairing humanity.

It was 2005 and Earth's population was six billion. But for the famines it would have been seven billion. A billion human beings had starved in the past generation, and more would yet starve.

Peter Affare, chairman of the World Food Organization, came frequently to Rodman's laboratories for chess and conversation. It was he, he said, who had first grasped the significance of Rodman's talk at the Academy, and that had helped make him chairman. Rodman thought the significance was easy to grasp, but said nothing about that.

Affare was ten years younger than Rodman, and the red was darkening out of his hair. He smiled frequently although the subject of the conversation rarely gave cause for smiling, since any chairman of an organization dealing with world food was bound to talk about world famine.

Affare said, 'If the food supply were evenly distributed among all the world's inhabitants, all would starve to death.'

'If it were evenly distributed,' said Rodman, 'the example of justice in the world might lead at last to a sane world policy. As it is, there is world despair and fury over the selfish fortune of a few, and all behave irrationally in revenge.'

'You do not volunteer to give up your own oversupply of food,' said Affare.

'I am human and selfish, and my own action would mean little. I should not be asked to volunteer. I should be given no choice in the matter.'

'You are a romantic,' said Affare. 'Do you fail to see that the Earth is a lifeboat? If the food store is divided equally among all, then all will die. If some are cast out of the lifeboat, the remainder will survive. The question is not whether some will die, for some *must* die; the question is whether some will live.'

'Are you advocating triage – the sacrifice of some for the rest – officially?'

'We can't. The people in the lifeboat are armed. Several regions threaten openly to use nuclear weapons if more food is not forthcoming.'

Rodman said sardonically, 'You mean the answer to "You die that I may live" is "If I die, you die." ... An impasse.'

'Not quite,' said Affare. 'There are places on Earth where the people cannot be saved. They have overweighted their land hopelessly with hordes of starving humanity. Suppose they are sent food, and suppose the food kills them so that the land requires no further shipments.'

Rodman felt the first twinge of realization. 'Kills them how?' he asked.

'The average structural properties of the cellular membranes of a particular population can be worked out. An LP, particularly designed to take advantage of those properties, could be incorporated into the food supply, which would then be fatal,' said Affare.

'Unthinkable,' said Rodman, astounded.

'Think again. There would be no pain. The membranes would slowly close off and the affected person would fall asleep and not wake up – an infinitely better death than that of starvation which is otherwise inevitable – or nuclear annihilation. Nor would it be for everyone, for any population varies in its membranal properties. At worst, seventy per cent will die. The winnowing out will be done precisely where overpopulation and hopelessness are worst and enough will be left to preserve each nation, each ethnic group, each culture.'

'To deliberately kill billions—'

'We would not be killing. We would merely supply the opportunity for people to die. Which particular individuals would die would depend on the particular biochemistry of those individuals. It would be the finger of God.'

'And when the world discovers what has been done?'

'That will be after our time,' said Affare, 'and by then, a flourishing world with limited population will thank us for our heroic action in choosing the death of some to avoid the death of all.'

Dr Rodman felt himself flushing, and found he had difficulty speaking. 'The Earth,' he said, 'is a large and very complex lifeboat. We still do not know what can or can't be done with a proper distribution of resources and it is notorious that to this very day we have not really made an effort to distribute them. In many places on Earth, food is wasted daily, and it is that knowledge that drives hungry men mad.'

'I agree with you,' said Affare coolly, 'but we cannot have the world as we want it to be. We must deal with it as it is.'

'Then deal with me as I am. You will want me to supply the necessary LP molecules – and I will not do so. I will not lift a finger in that direction.'

'Then,' said Affare, 'you will be a greater mass murderer than you are accusing me of being. And I think you will change your mind when you have thought it through.'

He was visited nearly daily, by one official or another, all of them well fed. Rodman was becoming very sensitive to the way in which all those who discussed the need for killing the hungry were themselves well fed.

The National Secretary of Agriculture said to him, insinuatingly, on one of these occasions, 'Would you not favor killing a herd of cattle infected with hoof-and-mouth disease or with anthrax in order to avoid the spread of infection to healthy herds?'

'Human beings are not cattle,' said Rodman, 'and famine is not contagious.'

'But it is,' said the Secretary. 'That is precisely the point. If we don't winnow the overcrowded masses of humanity, their famine will spread to as yet unaffected areas. You must not refuse to help us.'

'How can you make me? Torture?'

'We wouldn't harm a hair on your body. Your skill in this matter is too precious to us. Food stamps can be withdrawn, however.'

'Starvation would harm me, surely.'

'Not you. But if we are prepared to kill several billion people for the sake of the human race, then surely we are ready for the much less difficult task of withdrawing food stamps from your daughter, her husband, and her baby.'

Rodman was silent, and the Secretary said, 'We'll give you time to think. We don't want to take action against your family, but we will if we have to. Take a week to think about it. Next Thursday the entire committee will be on hand. You will then be committed to our project and there must be no further delay.'

Security was redoubled and Rodman was openly and completely a prisoner. A week later, all fifteen members of the World Food Council, together with the National Secretary of Agriculture and a few members of the National Legislature, arrived at his laboratory. They sat about the long table in the conference room of the lavish research building that had been built out of public funds.

For hours they talked and planned, incorporating those answers which Rodman gave to specific questions. No one asked Rodman if he would cooperate; there seemed no thought that he could do anything else.

Finally Rodman said, 'Your project cannot, in any case, work. Shortly after a shipment of grain arrives in some particular region of the world, people will die by the hundreds of millions. Do you suppose those who survive will not make the connection and that you will not risk the desperate retaliation of nuclear bombs?'

Affare, who sat directly opposite Rodman, across the short axis of the table, said, 'We are aware of that possibility. Do you think we have spent years determining a course of action and have not considered the possible reaction of those regions chosen for winnowing?'

'Do you expect them to be thankful?' asked Rodman bitterly.

'They will not know they are being singled out. Not all shipments of grain will be LP-infected. No one place will be concentrated on. We will see to it that locally grown grain supplies are infected here and there. In addition, not everyone will die and only a few will die at once. Some who eat much of the grain will not die at all, and some who eat only a small amount will die quickly – depending on their membranes. It will seem like a plague, like the Black Death returned.'

Rodman said, 'Have you thought of the effect of the Black Death returned? Have you thought of the panic?'

'It will do them good,' growled the Secretary from one end of the table. 'It might teach them a lesson.'

'We will announce the discovery of an antitoxin,' said Affare, shrugging. 'There will be wholesale inoculations in regions we know will not be affected. Dr Rodman, the world is desperately ill, and must have a desperate remedy. Mankind is on the brink of a horrible death, so please do not quarrel with the only course that can save it.'

'That's the point. *Is* it the only course or are you just taking an easy way out that will not ask any sacrifices of you – merely of billions of others?'

Rodman broke off as a food trolley was brought in. He muttered, 'I have arranged for some refreshments. May we have a few moments of truce while we eat?'

He reached for a sandwich and then, after a while, said between sips of coffee, 'We eat well, at least, as we discuss the greatest mass murder in history.'

Affare looked critically at his own half-eaten sandwich. 'This is not eating *well*. Egg salad on white bread of indifferent freshness is not eating well, and I would change whatever coffee shop supplied this, if I were you.' He sighed. 'Well, in a world of famine, one should not waste food,' and he finished the sandwich.

Rodman watched the others and then reached for the last remaining sandwich on the tray. 'I thought,' he said, 'that perhaps some of you might suffer a loss of appetite in view of the subject matter of discussion, but I see none of you did. Each one of you has eaten.'

'As did you,' said Affare impatiently. 'You are still eating.'

'Yes, I am,' said Rodman, chewing slowly. 'And I apologize for the lack of freshness in the bread. I made the sandwiches myself last night and they are fifteen hours old.'

'You made them yourself?' said Affare.

'I had to, since I could in no other way be certain of introducing the proper LP.'

'What are you talking about?'

'Gentlemen, you tell me it is necessary to kill some to save others. Perhaps you are right. You have convinced me. But in order to know exactly what it is we are doing we should perhaps experience it ourselves. I have engaged in a little triage on my own, and the sandwiches you have all just eaten are an experiment in that direction.'

Some of the officials were rising to their feet. 'We're poisoned?' gasped the Secretary.

Rodman said, 'Not very effectively. Unfortunately, I don't know your biochemistries thoroughly, so I can't guarantee the seventy per cent death rate you would like.'

They were staring at him in frozen horror, and Dr Rodman's eyelids drooped. 'Still, it's likely that two or three of you will die within the next week or so, and you need only wait to see who it will be. There's no cure or antidote, but don't worry. It's a quite painless death, and it will be the finger of God, as one of you told me. It's a good lesson, as another of you said. For those of you who survive, there may be new views on triage.'

Affare said, 'This is a bluff. You've eaten the sandwiches yourself.'

Rodman said, 'I know. I matched the LP to my own biochemistry, so I will go fast.' His eyes closed. 'You'll have to carry on without me – those of you who survive.'

Birth of a Notion

That the first inventor of a workable time machine was a science fiction enthusiast is by no means a coincidence. It was inevitable. Why else should an otherwise sane physicist even dare track down the various out-of-the-way theories that seemed to point toward maneuverability in time in the very teeth of General Relativity?

It took energy, of course. Everything takes energy. But Simeon Weill was prepared to pay the price. Anything (well, almost anything) to make his hidden science-fictional dream come true.

The trouble was that there was no way of controlling either the direction or distance through which one was chronologically thrust. It was all the result of random temporal collisions of the harnessed tachyons. Weill could make mice and even rabbits disappear – but future or past, he couldn't say. One mouse reappeared, so he must have traveled but a short way into the past – and it seemed quite unharmed. The others? Who could tell?

He devised an automatic release for the machine. Theoretically, it would reverse the push (whatever the push might be) and bring back the object (from whichever direction and whatever distance it had gone). It didn't always work, but five rabbits were brought back unharmed.

If he could only make the release foolproof, Weill would have tried it himself. He was *dying* to try it – which was not the proper reaction of a theoretical physicist, but was the absolutely predictable emotion of a crazed s.f. fan who was particularly fond of the spaceo-perish productions of some decades before the present year of 1976.

It was inevitable, then, that the accident should happen. On no account would he have stepped between the tempodes with conscious determination. He knew the chances were about two in five he would not return. On the other hand, he was *dying* to try it, so he tripped over his own big feet and went staggering between those tempodes as a result of total accident . . . But are there really accidents?

He might have been hurled into the past or into the future. As it happened, he was hurled into the past.

He might have been hurled uncounted thousands of years into the past or one and a half days. As it happened, he was hurled fifty-one years into the past to a time when the Teapot Dome Scandal was burning brightly but the nation was keeping Cool with Coolidge and knew that nobody in the world could lick Jack Dempsey.

But there was something that his theories didn't tell Weill. He knew what could happen to the particles themselves, but there was no way of predicting what would happen to the relationships between the various particles. And where are relationships more complex than in the brain?

So what happened was that as Weill moved backward through time, his mind unreeled. Not all the way, fortunately, since Weill had not yet been conceived in the year before America's Sesquicentennial, and a brain with less than no development would have been a distinct handicap.

It unreeled haltingly, and partially, and clumsily, and when Weill found himself on a park bench not far from his 1976 home in lower Manhattan, where he experimented in dubious symbiosis with New York University, he found himself in the year 1925 with an abysmally aching head and no very clear idea as to what anything was all about.

He found himself staring at a man of about forty, hair slicked down, cheekbones prominent, beaky nose, who was sharing the same bench with him.

The man looked concerned. He said, 'Where did you come from? You were not here a moment ago.' He had a distinct Teutonic accent.

Weill wasn't sure. He couldn't remember. But one phrase seemed to stick through the chaos within his skull even though he wasn't sure what it meant.

'Time machine,' he gasped.

The other man stiffened. He said, 'Do you read pseudo-scientific romances?'

'What?' said Weill.

'Have you read H. G. Wells's *The Time Machine*?'

The repetition of the phrase seemed to soothe Weill a bit. The pain in his head lessened. The name Wells seemed familiar, or was that his own name? No, his own name was Weill.

'Wells?' he said. 'I am Weill.'

The other man thrust out a hand. 'I am Hugo Gernsback. I write pseudo-scientific romances at times, but of course, it is not right to say "pseudo". That makes it seem there is something fake about it. That is not so. It should be properly written and then it will be scientific fiction. I like to shorten that' – his dark eyes gleamed – 'to scientifiction.'

'Yes,' said Weill, trying desperately to collect shattered memories and unwound experiences and getting only moods and impressions. 'Scientifiction. Better than pseudo. Still not quite—'

'If done *well*. Have you read my "Ralph 124C41+"?'

'Hugo Gernsback,' said Weill, frowning, 'Famous—'

'In a small way,' said the other, nodding his head. 'I have been publishing magazines on radio and on electrical inventions for years. Have you read "Science and Invention"?'

Weill caught the word 'invention' and somehow that left him on the edge of understanding what he had meant by 'time machine.' He grew eager and said, 'Yes, yes.'

'And what do you think of the scientifiction that I add in each issue?'

Scientifiction again. The word had a soothing effect on him and yet it was not quite right. Something more— Not quite—

He said it, 'Something more. Not quite—'

'Not quite enough? Yes, I've been thinking that. Last year I sent out circulars asking for subscriptions to a magazine to contain nothing but scientifiction. I would call it *Scientifiction*. The results were very disappointing. How would you explain that?'

Weill didn't hear him. He was still concentrating on the word 'scientifiction,' which didn't seem quite right, but he couldn't understand why it didn't.

He said, 'The name is not right.'

'Not right for a magazine? Maybe that's so. I have not thought of a good name; something to catch the eye, to get across just what the reader will get, and what he will want. That is it. If I could get a good name I would start the magazine and not worry about circulars. I would not ask anything. I would simply put it on every newsstand in the United States next spring; that is all.'

Weill stared at him blankly.

The man said, 'Of course, the stories I want should teach science even as they amuse and excite the reader. They should open to him the vast scope of the future. Airplanes will cross the Atlantic non-stop.'

'Airplanes?' Weill caught a fugitive vision of a large metal whale, rising on its own exhaust. A moment, and it was gone. He said, 'Large ones, carrying hundreds of people faster than sound.'

'Of course. Why not? Staying in touch at all times by radio.'

'Satellites.'

'What?' It was the other man's turn to look puzzled.

'Radio waves bounce off an artificial satellite in space.'

The other man nodded vigorously. 'I predicted the use of radio waves to detect at a distance in "Ralph 124C41+". Space mirrors? I've predicted that. And television, of course. And energy from the atom.'

Weill was galvanized. Images flashed before his mind's eye in no suitable order. 'Atom,' he said, 'Yes. Nuclear bombs.'

'Radium,' said the other man complacently.

'Plutonium,' said Weill.

'What?'

'Plutonium. And nuclear fusion. Imitating the Sun. Nylon and plastics. Pesticides to kill the insects. Computers to kill the problems.'

'Computers? You mean robots?'

'Pocket computers,' said Weill enthusiastically. 'Little things. Hold them in your hand and work out problems. Little radios. Hold them in your hand, too. Cameras take photographs and develop them right in the box. Holographs. Three-dimensional pictures.'

The other man said, 'Do you write scientifiction?'

Weill didn't listen. He kept trying to trap the images. They were growing clearer. 'Skyscrapers,' he said. 'Aluminum and glass. Highways. Color television. Man on the Moon. Probes to Jupiter.'

'Man on the Moon,' said the other man. 'Jules Verne. Do you read Jules Verne?'

Weill shook his head. It was quite clear now. The mind was healing a bit. 'Stepping down onto the Moon's surface on television. Everyone watching. And pictures of Mars. No canals on Mars.'

'No canals on Mars?' said the other man, astonished. 'They have been seen.'

'No canals,' said Weill firmly. 'Volcanoes. The biggest. Canyons the biggest. Transistors, lasers, tachyons. Trap the tachyons. Make them push against time. Move through time. Move through time. A-ma—'

Weill's voice was fading and his outlines trembled. It so happened that the other man looked away at this moment, staring into the blue sky, and muttering, 'Tachyons? What is he saying?'

He was thinking that if a stranger he met casually in the park was so interested in scientifiction, it might be a good sign that it was time for the magazine. And then he remembered he had no name and dismissed the notion regretfully.

He looked back in time to hear Weill's last words, 'Tachyonic time travel-an-amazing-stor-y—' And he was gone, snapping back to his own time.

Hugo Gernsback stared in horror at the place where the man had been. He hadn't seen him come and now he really hadn't seen him go. His mind rejected the actual disappearance. How strange a man – his clothes were oddly cut, come to think of it, and his words were wild and whirling.

The stranger himself said it – an amazing story. His last words.

And then Gernsback muttered the phrase under his breath, 'Amazing story . . . *Amazing Stories*?'

A smile tugged at the corners of his mouth.

Copyright information

The Prime of Life © 1966 by Mercury Press, Inc.
Mother Earth © 1949 by Street & Smith Publications, Inc.
Darwinian Pool Room © 1950 by World Editions.
Shah Guido G. © 1951 by Stadium Publishing Corporation.
Button, Button © 1952 by Better Publications, Inc.
Everest © 1953 by Palmer Publications, Inc.
The Pause © 1954 by Farrar, Straus & Young.
Let's Not © 1954 by the Trustees of Boston University.
Youth © 1955 by Isaac Asimov.
Sucker Bait © 1954 by Conde Nast Publications, Inc.
What's in a Name? © 1956 by King-Size Publications, Inc.
The Dust of Death © 1956 by Fantasy House, Inc.
Blank! © 1957 by Royal Publications, Inc.
Silly Asses © 1957 by Columbia Publications, Inc.
Buy Jupiter © 1958 by Mercury Press, Inc.
Author! Author! © Isaac Asimov 1964.
The Proper Study © 1968 by the Boy Scouts of America.
Waterclap © 1970 by Universal Publishing and Distributing Corporation.
2430 AD © 1970 by International Business Machines Corporation.
Thiotimoline to the Stars © 1973 by Random House, Inc.
The Winnowing © 1976 by the Conde Nast Publications, Inc.
Birth of a Notion © 1976 by Ultimate Publishing Co., Inc.

UNLOCK THE SECRETS OF ROBOTICS AND ARTIFICIAL INTELLIGENCE WITH ISAAC ASIMOV'S GROUNDBREAKING STORIES.

ROBOT STORIES AND NOVELS

I, Robot

The Rest of the Robots

The Complete Robot

The Caves of Steel

The Naked Sun

The Robots of Dawn

Robots and Empire

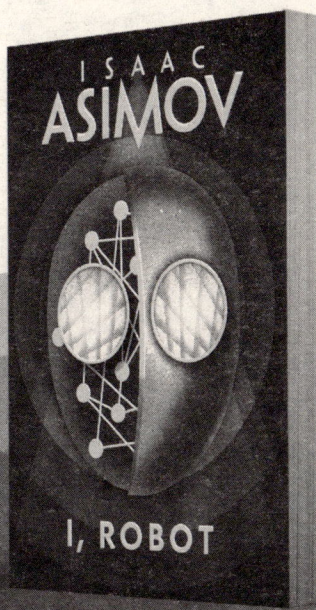

VENTURE INTO THE COSMOS WITH ISAAC ASIMOV'S EPIC TALES.

THE GALACTIC EMPIRE NOVELS

The Currents of Space

The Stars, Like Dust

Pebble in the Sky

The End of Eternity

HARPER Voyager

EMBARK ON A JOURNEY THROUGH ISAAC ASIMOV'S UNIVERSE AND DIVE INTO THE SAGA THAT DEFINES SCIENCE FICTION STORYTELLING.

THE FOUNDATION SAGA

Prelude to Foundation
Forward the Foundation
Foundation
Foundation and Empire
Second Foundation
Foundation's Edge
Foundation and Earth

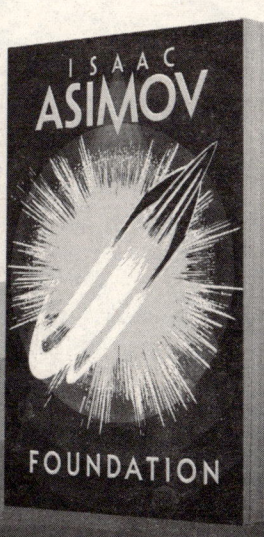

STEP INTO WORLDS OF WONDER WITH ISAAC ASIMOV'S CAPTIVATING SHORT STORY COLLECTIONS.

SHORT STORY COLLECTIONS

The Complete Stories:
Living Space: And Other Stories
Nightfall: And Other Stories
The Martian Way: And Other Stories
The Bicentennial Man: And Other Stories
Ring Around the Sun: And Other Stories
Mother Earth: And Other Stories
Gold: The Final Science Fiction Collection
Magic: The Final Fantasy Collection

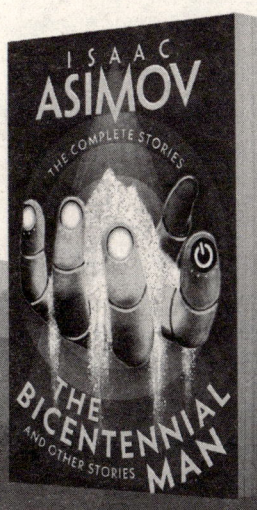